A STUDY OF GEORGE ORWELL

The Man and His Works

By
CHRISTOPHER HOLLIS

Foreword by JOHN RODDEN, PHD

Racehorse Publishing

First published in 1956 by Henry Regnery Company, Chicago

First Racehorse Publishing Edition 2017

Foreword © 2017 John Rodden

Racehorse Publishing books may be purchased in bulk at special discounts for sales promotion, corporate gifts, fund-raising, or educational purposes. Special editions can also be created to specifications. For details, contact the Special Sales Department, Skyhorse Publishing, 307 West 36th Street, 11th Floor, New York, NY 10018 or info@skyhorsepublishing.com.

Racehorse Publishing™ is a pending trademark of Skyhorse Publishing, Inc.®, a Delaware corporation.

Visit our website at www.skyhorsepublishing.com.

10 9 8 7 6 5 4 3 2 1

Library of Congress Cataloging-in-Publication Data is available on file.

Cover design by Brian Peterson
Cover photograph: AP Images

Print ISBN: 978-1-63158-223-3
Ebook ISBN: 978-1-63158-224-0

Printed in the United States of America

Contents

Foreword		v
Introduction		xiv
I.	Crossgates	1
II.	Eton	11
III.	Burma	26
IV.	*Down and Out in Paris and London*	41
V.	*A Clergyman's Daughter*	57
VI.	*Keep the Aspidistra Flying*	69
VII.	*The Road to Wigan Pier*	77
VIII.	*Homage to Catalonia*	92
IX.	*Coming Up for Air*	108
X.	Dickens	119
XI.	England and War	124
XII.	*Animal Farm*	139
XIII.	Swift and Burnham	154
XIV.	Nationalism	168
XV.	Kipling, Wells, Yeats and Kostler	182
XVI.	*1984*	188
XVII.	Gandhi and Lear	202
	Index	209

Acknowledgments

My thanks are due to my friends, Mr. Laurence Brander, Mr. Malcolm Muggeridge, Mr. Anthony Powell, Mr. Noel Blakiston, Mr. Frederick Warburg, Sir Richard Rees, Mr. John Christie, Mr. John Lehmann and Mr. A. S. F. Gow who have helped me either by reading my manuscript or by advice on various points—also to Mr. McWatters, the Master in College at Eton, and to Mr. Forman and Mr. Russell, Captain of the School and Keeper of College Wall, who put the various relevant College archives at my disposal. Naturally none of these has any sort of responsibility for any of the judgments of this book.

I am indebted to the B.B.C. and to the proprietors of the *London Magazine* for permission to reprint portions of essays which first appeared with them.

M. C. H.

Foreword

Reconsiderations, Revaluations

When I first read Christopher Hollis's *A Study of George Orwell: The Man and His Works* around 1980, not long after Hollis's death, I regarded it as a well-written, provocative, and serious examination of an author who had already become a political icon and leading figure in twentieth-century English literature. Nonetheless, I expressed strong reservations about Hollis's "shadow-boxing" style of jumping into the ring with Orwell and counter-punching his way through round after round of argument on practically every single issue that separated the two men, with unceasing blows directed against Orwell's deviations from Hollis's orthodox Catholicism and political Conservatism. One Catholic historian later wrote that I was "indignant" about Hollis's approach to Orwell. Yet it was much more so that I, as a fellow Catholic layman who shared Hollis's admiration for Orwell, felt rather chagrined by Hollis's aggressive, no-holds-barred proselytism—as if Hollis were obsessed with converting his old schoolmate acquaintance posthumously into a pious churchman. Or, at minimum, into what I termed a "religious fellow-traveler."

Rereading Hollis's *Study* decades later—and it is indeed a close "study" by a masterful polemicist that scrutinizes his debating opponent's positions, weighs the evidence thoughtfully, and counts up the ayes and noes of the "case" carefully—I am much more impressed by its frank and forthright style of presentation. Especially in the current political climate of criminal disinformation campaigns, false news, endless spin control, and utter disrespect for and blatant distortion of an adversary's statements, I would now emphasize much more that Hollis pays Orwell the deep respect of appraising his positions with full seriousness. And that decision—to which Christopher Hollis brings literary clarity, political candor, and even moral courage—warrants our respect.

Let me also note that this "study" is not a biography. Rather, it is a critical assessment and biographical portrait, as the subtitle—"The Man and His Works"—reflects. Hollis's *Study* appeared just six years after Orwell's death when Orwell's reputation was just beginning to skyrocket. The book played a major role in defining Orwell as a man of "common decency," the signature phrase of his *oeuvre*.

In hindsight, Hollis's *Study of George Orwell* represents the most substantial, lively, and thorough analysis of Orwell's life and work in the first two post–World War II decades, the best—if highly controversial—book on Orwell (1903–50) among the first five book-length assessments of him. Until George Woodcock's *The Crystal Spirit* (1966), written by an anarchist thinker-activist and man of letters who befriended Orwell during the last decade of his life, Hollis's *Study* remained the most influential book on Orwell. Today it still stands as a classic of the 1950s, the most comprehensive eyewitness account of Eric Blair (a.k.a. George Orwell) during the Eton and Burma years. In a trim 200 pages, Hollis (1902–77) combined intellectual biography and personal reminiscence of Blair in an engrossing, combative engagement with the man and his works.

The Man

Born just eighteen months before Eric Blair in December 1902, Hollis was one of four sons of an Anglican bishop. He attended Eton on a scholarship. Another scholarship took him to Balliol College at Oxford University where he carved out a distinguished career, including president of the Oxford Union Society. In 1924, he converted to Catholicism and soon became a well-known figure in Catholic intellectual circles. After graduation, Hollis travelled with the Oxford debating team on an international tour that included Australia and New Zealand, providing him the opportunity to stop off and visit Blair in Burma for a week in 1925. During the next decade,

Hollis taught at Stonyhurst in Lancashire, a Jesuit secondary school, and then spent five years teaching and doing economic research at the University of Notre Dame, returning to serve the British war effort when the war broke out in 1939. During World War II, he joined the Royal Air Force as an intelligence officer.

Elected as a Conservative Member of Parliament for Devizes in Wiltshire in 1945—against the liberal-left political tide that swept the Labour Party to power over Winston Churchill and the Conservatives that July—Hollis gained reelection twice before retiring undefeated in 1955. Chairman of the educational publishing house Hollis & Carter and a member of *The Tablet*'s board of directors for three decades (and frequent contributor to the pages of Britain's foremost Catholic magazine), Hollis was one of England's prominent postwar Catholic laymen.

Hollis's *Study of George Orwell*, published just after Hollis left Parliament, is probably his best-known work. It gained an enthusiastic reception in English Catholic circles, within which it exerted a significant shaping influence on the Catholic intelligentsia. Hollis's detailed report of Blair's schooldays at Eton was received as authoritative, even more so than had been classmate Cyril Connolly's vignette in *Enemies of Promise* in the 1930s. Except for Connolly, "No one knows more of [Orwell's] early years than I," said Hollis, noting that only he among Orwell's memoirists had met Blair in Burma and had read Orwell's work in the order it had appeared, without the distortions of Orwell's later fame. Until Peter Stansky and William Abrahams's *The Unknown Orwell* (1972), their book-length biography of the Blair years, Hollis's personal account of Blair's Eton and Burma periods was generally accepted as the final word. In fact, it reads today as a miniature version and rich foretaste of that book—the "Unknown Orwell," as it were, before *The Unknown Orwell*.

Both the elective affinities and sharp contrasts between Hollis, the Conservative Catholic apologist, and Blair-Orwell, the adamant atheist and heterodox democratic Socialist (he always upper-cased the noun), are notable. As near-contemporaries, Hollis entered Eton College—the famed public school—in 1914; Blair arrived two years later. Sharing a similar social and economic background—the rising middle classes of late Victorian and early Edwardian England—both Blair and Hollis came from families of modest means and were "scholarship boys" at prep school. Blair's father worked in the Indian Civil Service; Hollis's father was vice-principal of the Wells Theological College and later Bishop of Taunton.

Although both Hollis and Blair underwent the prevailing preparatory school rigors of the English upper classes, they responded in utterly different ways. Blair's horrific experience at St. Cyprian's, which he recalled with still-lingering outrage in his posthumously published essay "Such, Such Were the Joys," scarred him for life. Hollis attended the more fashionable Summer Fields school where he enjoyed the benefactions of his headmaster, Dr. Williams, who guided him to Eton. Both young Etonians read and esteemed G.K. Chesterton, who defended Christian and Catholic orthodoxy aggressively and formally converted to Catholicism in 1922 (and influenced Hollis's own conversion two years later); Blair-Orwell prized the literary gifts of "G.K.C." and his patriotism, while lamenting (and lambasting) his religious views.

Hollis's biographical chapters on Blair at Eton and in Burma in 1925 are the most authoritative in the book. Hollis's views on Orwell at Eton are opinionated and disputable—and much disputed. He argues that Orwell's "grievances"—that he was a poor boy among the rich, that he was unpopular and branded "ugly"—were nonsense. Rather, Blair was "a natural solitary" who enjoyed the fact that Eton allowed him to pursue his own interests and read whatever he wished—and otherwise largely left him alone. Even though Hollis seldom crossed paths with Blair at Eton and knew him only slightly there, his *Study* does not hesitate to draw conclusions about Blair. Hollis notes, for example, that in contrast to his lengthy critique of his prep school and despite his complaints about English public schools, Orwell wrote virtually nothing about his time at Eton. Here again, Hollis believes the reason lies in the simple fact that Blair "was little interfered with" at Eton. As to Orwell's later evaluation of his Eton years, notes Hollis, when Orwell and his wife Eileen adopted a little boy, they made sure to enroll him there.

Hollis also contests the widespread assumption that Blair applied to enter the civil service because his mediocre academic record prevented him from attending Oxford or Cambridge. Hollis believes that Orwell rejected Oxbridge in an act of defiance. Hollis also contends that economic issues did not have anything to do with Orwell's decision because Blair could have (like Hollis) probably won a university scholarship. Blair missed much by spending five important years of his youth in the Indian Imperial Police in Burma instead of at Oxford or Cambridge among his intellectual peers, Hollis asserts, adding that despite passages in his writings criticizing Oxford and Cambridge, Blair-Orwell came to regret and resent his exclusion from those circles. Such speculations are difficult to confirm or refute. But a recently unearthed letter to Jacintha Buddicom, Blair's childhood friend (and adolescent sweetheart), suggests that Blair may have decided to join the Indian Civil Service after she rejected his proposal of marriage.

So Hollis went up to Oxford while Blair followed in his father's footsteps and joined the Indian Civil Service as a policeman in Burma. During their two meetings in Burma in 1925, Hollis describes Blair as behaving like the stereotypical sahib and imperialist, exhibiting "no trace of liberal opinions" such as he had paraded at Eton. "At pains to be the imperial policemen," Hollis thought, loneliness had embittered Blair, who explained to Hollis that "theories of no punishment and not beating were all very well at public schools but they did not work with the Burmese." Blair voiced a special hatred for the Burmese priests—not for religious reasons, but rather "because of their sniggering insolence."

Hollis writes that he maintained this view of Blair until he read Orwell's superb autobiographical short story, "Shooting an Elephant," years later and discovered how much Blair had hated his role in policing the natives. Is it possible that Blair was pulling Hollis's leg and merely play-acting the cartoonish sahib? Orwell's first biographer, Bernard Crick, argues that Blair-Orwell considered Hollis "a glib and priggish liberal, Oxford Union to boot; so he probably gave him the 'realist' line" with satiric tongue in cheek.

After Eric Blair started to establish himself in London as a writer and adopted the pen name "George Orwell" in 1933, the two men reconnected. They met occasionally during the last twenty years of Orwell's life, and Hollis

visited Orwell in the hospital just a few weeks before Orwell's death from
tuberculosis in January 1950. Acquaintances rather than confidants, they
shared, in Hollis's phrase, "years of continuing friendly argument."

Or perhaps not so friendly, at least to Orwell's mind. When Orwell was
having difficulties securing a publisher for *Animal Farm* in 1944 because of
its political implications—i.e., its satire of wartime ally Russia, its indictment
of the Bolshevik Revolution, and its scorn for Joseph Stalin—Orwell's literary agent Leonard Moore wanted to approach Hollis's firm, Hollis & Carter.
Orwell's reaction in a letter to Moore (23 March 1944) discloses the ideological gulf that separated these two cordially contentious Old Etonians and
suggests Orwell's ambivalent relationship with Hollis. Orwell told Moore "on
no account" to offer the book to Hollis because his firm was pro-Catholic
and has "published some of the most poisonous stuff since he set up business.
It would do me permanent harm to be published" by him.

Frenemies at fisticuffs? Or was the relationship much warmer on Hollis's
side? Perhaps. Perhaps. Their considerable differences of opinion and diver-
gent religious, social, and political convictions notwithstanding, however,
they did agree on one burning question of the day: the travesty of capital punishment. Blair spoke out against this "unspeakable" crime as early as
1931 in his short story, "A Hanging," while Hollis played a prominent role
that led eventually to the abolition of capital punishment (not a popular
campaign to head in his party in the 1940s and '50s) soon after his exit as a
Conservative MP.

The Works

A recurrent theme of Hollis's *Study of George Orwell* is that, despite his
atheism, Orwell possessed a religious sensibility, even a spiritual hunger, a
yearning for the kind of meaning that Hollis himself had sought when he
became a Catholic. What makes Hollis's account of Blair-Orwell fair-minded
and yet incendiary and controversial is that, despite his own deep Catholic
belief, he looks beyond Orwell's anti-Catholicism and finds what he calls "a
naturally Christian soul" whose thought rested on a subconscious Christian
foundation.

Left-wing critics have charged Hollis with attempting to "press-gang" Orwell for "the papists." Hollis's portrait of Orwell as some kind of crypto-
Christian has also outraged other readers. Kingsley Amis observed that Hollis
"cannot resist drawing Orwell in his own image." Indeed, the book at times
reads like a dual biography as Hollis carries on an argument with Orwell
about religious and political issues, explaining away his atheism and trans-
lating their opposing ideological outlooks into agreement. Whatever the ex-
cesses of his enthusiastic apologetics and defense of the Church, however,
Hollis is always direct and pulls no punches. His influence in the shaping of
Orwell's posthumous reputation—the social-ethical canonization of Orwell
as a secular "St. George"—is also undeniable. Proceeding from Orwell's view
that religious belief was without foundation and thus no longer credible in
the contemporary, scientific world, yet its collapse left what Orwell called "a
gap to be filled," Hollis noted that Orwell vaguely acknowledged (though
never explicitly admitted) that no earthly faith—whether democratic Socialism or any other "ism" or ideology—could ever fill it. Orwell indicated his
own lifelong struggle with this yawning "gap" inside him, contended Hollis,
when he granted that one of "the major problems of our time is the decay of
the belief in personal immortality."

A Study of George Orwell: The Man and His Works amounts to a running,
spirited commentary on Orwell's writings, including his fiction, documen-
taries and reportage, and essays and journalism. Hollis's analysis is sharp and
shows an appreciation of the complexity of Orwell's thought even while
Hollis searches relentlessly for the religious dimension in his literary oeuvre.
Casting Orwell in his own image, Hollis claims that Orwell resembled the
kind of old-fashioned cultural conservative for whom tradition, decency, patriotism, and love of nature were important. Hollis believes Orwell shared
his own views opposing nationalists, jingoists, and other Conservatives who
championed colonialism and Empire, that is, he despaired of modern "Conservatives because they despaired of Conservatism."

Hollis also has a good critical eye. He was the first to point out the autobiographical attributes of Orwell's fictional anti-heroes, especially John Flory
in Burmese Days and Gordon Comstock in Keep the Aspidistra Flying, describing the latter as Orwell with all the fun left out. Like Blair-Orwell, the two

protagonists are public school boys thrown into an atmosphere for which they are unprepared.

Hollis's verdict on Orwell's nonfiction reportage is mixed. Although it gained Orwell literary prominence for the first time in the mid-1930s, Hollis does not have a high opinion of *The Road to Wigan Pier*, which addressed the terrible conditions of the miners in the north of England during the worst years of the depression. Hollis found unimpressive Orwell's denunciation of soulless industrialism, his call for social justice, and even his biting derision of the failures of socialism because Orwell conceives these issues exclusively in sociopolitical terms, failing to grasp them more deeply as questions only "soluble within a religious framework." Furthermore, given the nature of the modern state, Hollis argues, the destruction of existing class distinctions would lead not to equality but to a more ruthless ruling class.

Even though they stood firmly in opposite political camps on the Spanish Civil War, with Hollis and most English Catholics supporting the fascists under General Franco and Orwell on the Republican side as a militiaman fighting to defend the Loyalist government, Hollis generously praises *Homage to Catalonia* as Orwell's most attractive book. Hollis also concedes that Franco's defeat would have been a blow to Hitler's prestige and might have changed the course of history. What particularly impressed and gratified Hollis was Orwell's realization that the Spanish war witnessed the concept of objective truth being lost in the ceaseless steam of lies spread by the both sides in the struggle. Catalonia turned Orwell into an implacable foe of Stalinism and of the English leftists who parroted its line, and the political outlook expressed in *Animal Farm* and *Nineteen Eighty-Four* is traceable to Orwell's experiences in Spain.

Orwell's journalism during World War II is of particular interest to Hollis because of their shared patriotism and sense of "Englishness." Hollis applauds Orwell's severe criticism of the British pacifists who opposed the war effort, most especially the naïve, sentimental pacifist who imagines good will always triumph. Orwell's critique included religious pacifists like Gandhi, a man whom both he and Hollis otherwise admired for his moral courage. Gandhi's argument that the Jews should have committed collective suicide as a way of arousing the world against the Nazis was flawed, Orwell and Hollis concurred, because Gandhi's pacifism could only succeed in liberal societies like Britain, not in Hitler's totalitarian Germany.

Hollis lauded Orwell's last two indictments of totalitarianism, the fable *Animal Farm* and the dystopian *Nineteen Eighty-Four*. As a stellar work of art—literary genius united with a good cause—*Animal Farm* combined Lord Acton's bromide that "power corrupts" with James Burnham's claim that revolutions lead not to classless societies but instead to new ruling classes.

Orwell's final, towering masterwork, *Nineteen Eighty-Four,* was more problematic for Hollis, ultimately too bleak and negative. The tyrannical superstate of Oceania emerged not from the degeneration of Communism but rather as the inevitable outcome of a trend toward totalitarianism after a half-century of war, argued Hollis, insisting yet again that Orwell's atheism undermined his emotional and spiritual awareness: Orwell saw but could not endorse that the answer to the pessimism and despair of *Nineteen Eighty-Four* entailed the acceptance of religious belief and the corollary that this life is a preparation for the next. Orwell could not, therefore, resolve a dilemma that he recognized as the paramount challenge for the modern age: how to "restore the religious attitude while accepting death as final."

Introduction

GEORGE ORWELL expressed a wish that no biography of him should be written and it is proper that such a wish be respected. The public may have the right to intrude up to a point into the lives of those who serve it in public posts, to insist on knowing of a man who has altered and immediately dominated his times what were the private influences that made him as he was. But there is no greater vulgarian than the gossip writer who thinks of every private secret as a marketable article. The burden of justification rests upon anyone who discovers and reveals secrets contrary to an expressed wish, and a writer in particular is entitled to say to the public, 'I have sought to influence you by my writings. Judge them, if you will, but what I was—apart from my writings—is my own business.' There are secrets of the heart which every man has a right to keep to himself and which decent men, as a rule, prefer to keep to themselves. It is no compliment to the world to pay it

> The evil and the insolent courtesy
> Of offering it my baseness as a gift.

On the other hand we can assess more profitably even the writer who traffics in the most objective of ideas if we know a little of the background from which he came. Orwell with his sometimes carefully absurd definition of the most precise detail of social origin of himself or of his characters—with his meticulous claim that he belonged to 'the lower-upper-middle class'—was the first to recognize this. 'I do not think anyone can assess a writer's motives without knowing something of his early development,' he wrote, and we find in one or another of his books a fairly full autobiography of a considerable proportion of his life. I should not think it right to probe further into private secrets that he has himself seen fit to reveal, nor do I see how I could expect to succeed even if I tried to do so. My main concern, as it has been the concern of Mr. Brander, Mr. Atkins and others who have written on Orwell before me, is to criticize his writings and his ideas. Mr. Brander's and Mr. Atkins' are admirable books from which I have learnt much, but they only came to know Orwell towards the end of his life and during the war. Orwell and I, on the other hand, had curiously similar origins. We went under the same sort of circumstances to the same sort of private school. We were in College together at Eton, and this similarity of origin gives me perhaps an advantage in judging his accounts of his early years and development over those who learnt of them only from the printed page. Of those who now make a habit of writing, there is, I fancy, no one except Mr. Cyril Connolly who knows from experience more of those early years of Orwell than I.

During the rest of his life, as will be seen from this book, while I make no claim to have enjoyed his intimacy—how many did?—yet by chance we flitted into one another's lives. After we had left school I remade his acquaintance in Burma in 1925. Then after an interval he got in touch with me again in 1932—the story, not in itself of great interest, will be told in its place—and from time to time with intervals for wars in Spain and Europe, we saw one another until my last visit to him in hospital a few weeks before his death.

All this is only important in that it meant that the years were years of a continuing friendly argument. I can claim up to a point to have known off and on, but continuously, what he was saying and thinking, and this does perhaps put me into a position somewhat different from that of the majority of critics who judge of him only from his writings and who probably—since the sales on publication of the earlier books were so meagre—read the earlier books only after the success of the later and already in the knowledge of the success to which Orwell was destined—a success which he himself did not at all foresee at the time of the earlier writing.

If as a result of all this I had been an obedient convert to every doctrine that Orwell championed, such a book would have been an essay in tedium. If I had rejected and quarrelled with every one of his doctrines, it would have been again as tedious. I should not think it justifiable to write such a book as this save about a man whom I deeply respect—about one to whom I thought it worth while to pay the final tribute of respect which is to explain the reason of difference where one differs. But we had, with a somewhat curious exactness, I fancy, enough in common and enough in difference to make argument between us stimulating. It is my hope that this same degree of difference and similarity may give an interest to this book.

Crossgates

ERIC BLAIR, as George Orwell was really called, was born in 1903 at Motihari in Bengal. His father was a minor official in the Customs and Excise. He had two sisters, one five years older and one five years younger than he, but they seem to have played little or no part in his early life. He was sent back to England at a very early age, for, as he tells us, he hardly ever saw his father before he was eight, when his father returned to England on retirement. He remembered him then only 'as a gruff-voiced elderly man, for ever saying "Don't"'. Of those early years he wrote, 'Looking back on my childhood, after the infant years were over, I do not believe I ever felt love for any mature person except my mother, and even her I did not trust, in the sense that shyness made me conceal most of my real feelings from her.'

We have not, then, enough evidence to say whether his elders were to blame for driving him in upon himself or whether he was a natural solitary, defending himself against the world by impenetrable barriers, and his elders wise not to attempt to break those barriers down. Whichever way it was, it is clear that in those early years his nature was taking on itself the pattern by which it was to be marked through life. The Orwellian man, whether we take Orwell's fragments of autobiography or the main characters in any of his novels, is always a solitary—a member of a society which is uncongenial to him—standing out alone in front of it, as Orwell stood in *Shooting an Elephant*—refusing obstinately and often unreasonably to make compromises with it as Gordon Comstock refuses in *Keep the Aspidistra Flying*, and finding his true life in a private life to which others could not penetrate but which they might, and all too frequently did, destroy. This pattern had already taken form in these young years. He was lonely. He could not give himself even to his mother whom he loved. He had, he wrote, 'the lonely child's habit of making up stories and holding conversations with imaginary persons', and, as a result, 'from a very early age, perhaps the age of five or six, I knew that, when I grew up, I should be a writer'.

There is, I fancy, little that is unusual in that. Certainly during those early years I always lived a second, imaginary life—was a grown-up, a county cricketer, a successful politician, a professional footballer, married and begat children in my mind, looked up in Bradshaw the railway journeys that such an important person would have to make —and the experience of such a second life is, I fancy, most common, if not universal. The question is whether it can survive the busy-ness of school life. When I went to my preparatory school, I discovered that there were so many real people around me that my mind no longer had the leisure to live its second life. For a time I deliberately dropped the second life during term time and took it up again in the holidays. After a while I dropped it altogether. Orwell remained solitary through all his schooldays and indeed in a large measure throughout all his life.

> I was very young [he writes in *The Road to Wigan Pier*], not much more than six, when I first became aware of class-distinctions. Before that age my chief heroes had generally been working-class people because they always seemed to do such interesting things, such as being fishermen and blacksmiths and bricklayers. I remember the farm hands on a farm in Cornwall who used to let me ride on the drill when they were sowing turnips and would sometimes catch the ewes and milk them to give me a drink and the workmen building the new house next door, who let me play with the mortar and from whom I first learnt the word 'b——'; and the plumber up the road with whose children I used to go out birdnesting. But it was not long before I was forbidden to play with the plumber's children; they were 'common' and I was told to keep away from them.

At the age of eight, in 1911, Orwell went to a preparatory school on the south coast, where he remained until he passed on with a scholarship to Eton in the Lent of 1917. That school under the name of Crossgates he describes in an essay called *Such, Such were the Joys*, which has never been published in England but which was published in America by Messrs. Harcourt, Brace and Company. A large part of the essay is a familiar catalogue of the faults which we should expect to find imputed to a preparatory school of those last pre-war years by one who did not like it. The boys were freely caned. The food was bad. Snobbery and purse-pride were rampant among boys and masters. There was bullying. An unpleasant incident of sexual immorality was handled by the authorities with ineptitude. The teaching, indifferent to true education, was concerned only with cramming as many boys as possible into scholarships at public schools.

How far the accusations which Orwell levels against Crossgates and against Mr. and Mrs. Simpson—Sim and Bingo—the Headmaster and the Headmaster's wife—are true, it is impossible to say. The only other witness who, so far as I am aware, has put on paper his reminiscences of Crossgates at this period was Mr. Cyril Connolly in *Enemies of Promise*, where it appears under the name of St. Wulfric's. Mr. Connolly was at the school with Orwell, though slightly his junior. From Mr. Connolly's pages, written before *Such, Such were the Joys*, we should get the impression that the school did, indeed, suffer from the faults from which most fashionable private schools suffered at that time, and that Mr. and Mrs. Simpson were indeed snobs, though not snobs of so outstanding a beastliness as we should guess from Orwell. Indeed, where Orwell speaks of Mrs. Simpson as detestably indifferent to any intellectual distinction or to any values except the values of snobbery, Mr. Connolly tells the story how he revisited the school after leaving Eton and before going up to Oxford and how Mrs. Simpson, with some simplicity of mind, told him that 'a Balliol scholar has the ball at his feet'.

Yet in truth Mr. Connolly and Orwell so differed from one another in nature that the account of the one does little either to confirm or refute that of the other. To Mr. Connolly at St. Wulfric's, only less than a few years afterwards at Eton, the important relations were the relations with other boys. These are analysed and dissected with a minuteness which the critic might condemn as sentimental. The masters, at St. Wulfric's and at Eton, are secondary figures. Orwell, on the other hand, gives no indication whether he liked or disliked the boys who appear fitfully in his essay—save only one, Johnny Hall, who used to bully him and whom he presumably disliked. Even Hall is only brought in to illustrate an anecdote. Orwell's sole concern with the other boys is to record the details of their fate and to argue whether it was just or unjust. His interest is in the Headmaster and his wife, the peculiar nature of his relationship with them and the moral problem which that relationship posed.

Thus again both Mr. Connolly and Orwell objected to being caned when they were at school. Mr. Connolly's objection to the cane both at St. Wulfric's and, still more, later at Eton was the not uncommon objection that it hurt. The beatings, he tells us, were 'torture'. He gives us a picture which I cannot but think somewhat overdrawn of 'a monster rushing towards us with a cane, his face upside down and distorted'. But Orwell's objection to corporal punishment had nothing to do with its painfulness. Indeed he is careful to point out of his first beating that it did not hurt at all and, when, because he boasted of this, he was dragged back and beaten a second time with a riding crop till he cried and till the crop was broken over him, even then he insists that it did not actually hurt and that he cried, not out of pain, but out of remorse. There was a trait in Orwell's character which drove him on to accept unpleasant experiences in order to prove to himself that he 'could take it'. Nor did he deny that corporal punishment was within its limits effective of its purpose—that his work improved after a beating. He objected to corporal punishment because it was, he said, 'obscene'. Like Macaulay's Puritan with bear-baiting, he objected to it, not because it gave pain to the boy, but because it gave pleasure to the master—a very reasonable objection but not at all the point that especially troubled Mr. Connolly's more fragile bottom.

The peculiarity of Orwell's position at Crossgates was that he was of much poorer parents than the majority of the other boys, that he was taken cheap by the Headmaster and that this imposed upon him, as he thought at the time, an obligation of gratitude towards the Headmaster and his wife. But their behaviour to him was so detestable— particularly in the continual reminder to him of his dependence—that he could feel no gratitude. The richer boys were odious in their purse-pride and their boasts of servants and motor-cars and Scottish holidays. Later, as he pretended, Orwell came to see that Mr. Simpson had taken him cheap, not at all out of goodness of heart, but simply in order that he might give the school an advertisement by winning a scholarship.

Now of the secret of Mr. Simpson's motives I have, as I say, no means of judging. But my own experience of preparatory school life was both so strikingly similar to and so strikingly different from that of Orwell that it is worth while setting the two side by side. I, too, was at a fashionable preparatory school. I, too, was of poor parents and only able to go to the school because of the charity of the Headmaster. Doubtless my Headmaster, Dr. Williams of Summer Fields, when he took me, hoped that I would win a scholarship for the school, but it is only fair to him to remember that he took me at the age of nine, just as Mr. Simpson took Orwell at the age of eight. At that age it is still highly uncertain whether boys will turn out to be of scholarship calibre or not. It is therefore only reasonable and charitable to think that there must have been some other motive than a mere desire for advertisement in the conduct of the two Headmasters.

Yet it is certainly true, if Orwell's facts are correct, that Mr. Simpson made it much harder to remember these motives than did Dr. Williams. I was not enormously happy at my preparatory school. That stage in life is a stage of which I cannot recollect ever to have heard anybody confess that he enjoyed it inordinately. Summer Fields was a stern school. There, as at Crossgates, the cane was freely in play. Dr. Williams was in many ways a frightening and unbending man. Yet the major accusations which Orwell brings against Mr. Simpson would have been incredible if brought against Dr. Williams by his bitterest enemy. So far from throwing up his charity to me at a moment of rebuke or punishment, he never referred to it, directly or indirectly, all the time that I was at Summer Fields or ever afterwards until his death. Indeed it was only through an incautious remark of my mother a year or two after I had gone to Summer Fields that I learnt that Dr. Williams was the anonymous benefactor who was saving my father from school fees that he would never have been able to pay. As far as I am aware, Dr. Williams never knew that I had been told the secret.

Summer Fields was, as I have said, a fashionable school, and I do not think that Dr. Williams was above rejoicing if he attracted to his school the son of a famous or wealthy parent. But that the son of a wealthy parent, once he had arrived there, would have been less likely to be punished than would have been the son of a poor parent, as, Orwell tells us, was the rule at Crossgates, would have been un-thinkable to the world of Summer Fields. Dr. Williams had his critics but I never heard of any critic to accuse him of this fault.

So, too, the snobbery of the boys, though real, was not nearly as gross as that which was alleged by Orwell to have reigned at Cross-gates. My father was at the time the vicar of a Leeds slum parish with an income of a little over £400 a year and four children to educate. I had come on from Leeds Grammar School to Summer Fields when Dr. Williams made the transfer possible. I spoke, when I first arrived at Summer Fields, with a broad accent and my manners were uncouth. I was told so once or twice but very soon found little difficulty in adapting myself to the new life and being, I fancy, as popular as I had any business to be. 'A shabby genteel family', writes Orwell, 'is in much the same position as a family of poor whites living in a street where everyone else is a negro.' It is an extreme exaggeration. It is true that I can remember at Summer Fields lying about my father's income—telling another boy on a walk an absurd story about the shooting at home. It is true that of course I never confessed that I had been at a Grammar School and still had an elder brother there. Boys who would not have been shocked at the notion that my father was poorer than theirs would certainly have been shocked at the notion of anyone going to a Grammar School. It is true also that I imagined that I was unique in being the son of a father who did not pay the fees, whereas now it is clear to me that there were a number who, for one reason or another, did not pay. Poverty in fact was a slight embarrassment to me. It did not impose upon me this feeling of outcast from my fellows which Orwell alleges that he learnt to feel at Crossgates. The truth was that at Summer Fields, even more than in later years at Eton, we were too ignorant of the meaning or value of money for parents' incomes to bulk large in our talk. It was of far less importance to have rich parents than to be good at cricket and it was apparent that athletic ability did not depend on parents' incomes. That, I think, both is and always has been the general truth about schoolboys. The problem of such a play as the *Guinea Pig* seems to my experience absurdly exaggerated. If things really were different at Crossgates, the fault must have been entirely with Mr. and Mrs. Simpson and their unbelievably uncouth and caddish habit, as Orwell alleges, of reminding boys to their faces and in public of the riches or poverty of their parents.

As for work, Summer Fields was certainly a school that valued scholarships. It was thought a bad year if Summer Fields boys did not gain more public-school scholarships than any other preparatory school. At Summer Fields, as at Crossgates, we competed for the Harrow History Prize—a somewhat absurd prize awarded for the greatest number of correct one-word answers to historical conundra. At Summer Fields, as at Crossgates, we used *memoriae technica* to learn the names of the Battles of the Wars of the Roses. Where Orwell was taught the names by the sentences, 'A black negress was my aunt; there's her house behind the barn', I was taught them by 'All boys not wakeful must attempt to bottle these battles'. Crossgates, it will be seen, threw in two battles beginning with 'h' that Summer Fields did not recognize. I think that it would be fair criticism of Summer Fields that there was too much cramming for scholarships, that the scholarship boys received both the blows and the attention and that those not destined for scholarships were somewhat neglected. But,

when Orwell goes on from that to complain that the terror of the
scholarship examination hung over him like a cloud for two years
before he tried it, he describes an experience that is wholly unfamiliar.
It was at least as important to me as it was to him that I should win a
scholarship. Had I not done so, my father could not possibly have
afforded the fees at a public school and I should presumably have had
to go back to Leeds Grammar School. Leeds Grammar School was
an excellent school and I should in fact have fared as well there as
anywhere else. But, as I saw things at the age of twelve, to return to
the Grammar School would have been a fate worse than death. I was
by no means an exceptionally brilliant boy. The Eton Scholarship
which I eventually won was, like Orwell's, a humble one. Yet the odd
thing was that it never occurred to me that there was any doubt at
all that I would get a scholarship. The reasons for that are, I fancy,
two. First, Dr. Williams, though no scholar, was an excellent coach.
From years of experience he could gauge exactly who would win a
scholarship. He knew almost to a certainty, after I had been at his
school for a year or so, that I should get a scholarship, although only
a low one, and therefore did not need to nag at me. Secondly, at Eton
and, I think, at all other schools one had two chances at the scholarship—one at twelve and one at thirteen. Dr. Williams sent us in for
'a preliminary canter' at the age of twelve, and therefore those of us
who were fortunate were able to sit for, and win, our scholarships at
an examination where our fate was not irrevocably at stake. Perhaps,
if I had sat and failed at twelve, I might have approached the examination at thirteen with greater anxiety. Orwell—for some reason that
is not clear—was not allowed by Mr. Simpson to sit until he was
thirteen.

Judging therefore by probabilities and by my own parallel experience, I form the conclusion that Crossgates was indeed a school full
of defects, but I also form the conclusion that Orwell was lonely
there, not primarily because of the unkindness of boys or masters, not
for obscure economic reasons the importance of which he always
exaggerated, but because he was a natural solitary. 'X', writes Mr.
Fyvell—it is thus that he calls the Headmaster's wife—'deepened the
dualism in Orwell's character. While he rebelled against her censure,
somewhere her voice, upholding the right sort of views, remained. . . .
Did he not, as it were, "act out" this part fifteen years later, when he
spent a year living with Paris slum dwellers and casual tramps as one
of them? Or did he not at least have to go through this experience of

being a social outcast in order to get it out of his system?' There seems to be altogether too much of Jung in such a view and it ascribed to Mrs. Simpson a wholly excessive importance in his life. What he was acting out in Paris, in so far as he was acting out anything, was surely not Crossgates but Burma.

'Tall, pale, with his flaccid cheeks, large spatulate fingers and supercilious voice, he was one of those boys who seem born old,' records Mr. Connolly of Orwell at this stage. Or again: 'You know, Connolly,' said Orwell to him, 'there's only one remedy for all diseases!' 'I felt the usual guilty tremor when sex was mentioned,' comments Mr. Connolly, 'and hazarded, "You mean, going to the lavatory?" "No, I mean death," said Orwell.' And Orwell made at this time— in the early years of the 1914 war—a remark which appears to me from my memories remarkable from one private schoolboy to another. He said, 'Of course, you realize, Connolly, that, whoever wins this war, we shall emerge a second-rate nation.' When he said this he doubtless said it because he had read it somewhere, but to anyone who remembers the manner in which the war was presented to schoolboys it remains an extraordinary remark. The war was at its beginning presented to schoolboys entirely as a gigantic football match. 'And there are loud cheers whenever anything German goes to the bottom,' I remember Dr. Williams writing to me to tell me of the news of Summer Fields during my first half at Eton. I remember the astonishment of a whole division at Eton when a master let drop the casual remark, 'Of course there will be gigantic problems to solve when the war is over.' We had understood that to win the war was a gigantic problem. But how could there still be a problem when the war was over? When the war was over, what need would there be to do anything except eat unending sock-suppers?

Orwell's remark, whatever its origin, shows indeed how different he was from other boys. He was different, but he was almost wholly at fault in his diagnosis of the reasons for his difference. For instance he was continually complaining of his 'ugliness'—or at least about the fact that all his schoolfellows thought him ugly. 'Until after I had left school for good,' he writes in Such, Such were the Joys, 'I continued to believe that I was preternaturally ugly. It was what my schoolfellows told me and I had no other authority to refer to.' 'I was somewhat lonely,' he writes of his schooldays in 'Why I write'—this was true—'and I soon developed disagreeable mannerisms which made me unpopular throughout my schooldays'—this was completely untrue.

It was not in the least my memory of him as a schoolboy either that he was ugly, that anybody thought him ugly or that he was unpopular, and I received only the other day a striking confirmation that my memory was just. I happened to give a talk on Orwell on the wireless, and it was listened to by a friend of mine who had been an Oppidan at Eton at the time that Orwell and I were in College. This friend had never connected the Orwell whom he read in later life with the Blair whom he had known at school. 'Oh, yes,' he said to me, 'Blair. I remember him well. A tall, good-looking chap, wasn't he?'

Yet this essay is mainly valuable because of its philosophic reflections. Orwell records how it never occurred to him at the time to have any feeling of injustice at the punishments that were heaped upon him. When, on coming out of the Headmaster's study after a beating with a smile on his face, he was overheard to say that it had not hurt, he was sent back to receive a second beating. This seemed to him perfectly reasonable. The gods were jealous gods. The sin that they punished was the sin of hubris, and anyone who was so foolish as to boast that he had outwitted them, had only himself to thank if retribution overtook him.

This seems to me quite true to life. In my own case—and, I fancy, most commonly—this sense of hubris survived until well after preparatory school days. Punishment was something that fell from time to time. Its coming was as capricious as that of the rain. It was as idle to complain of it. I remember in my second year at Eton, when I was thirteen, a member of the Sixth Form summoned down all the boys who lived along a certain gallery known as Lower Passage—about twenty of them I suppose that there were. It had been noticed that a Minimax fire extinguisher had been bashed in. Who had done it? No one was prepared to own up. 'Very well,' said the Sixth Former. 'All Lower Passage—all the twenty—will be beaten.' It was obviously a monstrous decision. To the best of my belief and memory all the twenty were honestly innocent and honestly ignorant of the culprit. There was no reason why the culprit should have been a resident of Lower Passage at all. He might have been a boy who lived elsewhere. He might well have been one of the servants, dragging luggage about. As we were going down to this beating together, a fellow victim said to me—not unreasonably—'Isn't he a beast?' The remark, I remember, utterly surprised me. It was the first time that it had ever occurred that it was possible to criticize the capriciousness of punishment and that such methods of discipline were not unalterable.

Orwell draws out these reflections simply in the first place to demonstrate his own immaturity. His experience at Crossgates at the time seemed to teach him that he both was wicked and could not help being wicked. He owed a debt of gratitude to Mr. and Mrs. Simpson. He ought, he thought, to have felt gratitude, but he did not feel it—and that was the end of that.

Whether or not Mr. and Mrs. Simpson had by their behaviour forfeited whatever right they had to gratitude is as it may be. That is a matter of the facts. But the fundamental problem is a much more difficult one than Orwell saw at the time that he wrote *Such, Such were the Joys*—a problem which, he thought at the time of writing, could be disposed of by ridicule, but which remained ever after to bother him as indeed it has bothered every thinker since the time of St. Paul, or indeed even of Job. The fact is, whether we like it or not, whether Orwell liked it or not, that people are born with defects of character or of physique—one of one sort and another of another. He who believes in freedom believes that there are further defects for which a person is responsible—sins where he has chosen evil when he might have chosen good—and it may perhaps be that human authority is justified in punishing sins and is not justified in punishing defects. But, whether defects are or are not punished by human edict, the difficulty still remains. A humane society may perhaps stop Mr. Simpson from beating Orwell, but Mr. Simpson's folly is not the real point at issue. The real point at issue is that people are sent into this world, saddled with these defects for which they are not responsible —that a little boy, wetting his bed, against his will, does nevertheless feel shame for his action—that Flory in *Burmese Days* is ashamed of his birthmark though he could not help it. Sympathetic treatment may perhaps lessen his embarrassment, but it will not remove it. We may say that it is unfair or that it is ridiculous. We may defy a God who can ordain such things. But none of these gestures avail anything to alter the fact that that is what happens—that the lots of men are in this sense profoundly unequal. As Orwell was to write afterwards in *Animal Farm*, 'All animals are equal, but some animals are more equal than others.' It is the summary of the whole dilemma of life.

II

Eton

PEOPLE vary greatly from one another in the vividness of their recall of their schooldays, nor can any just generalization be made what sort of people recall most vividly. There is, it is true, the bore who lives in his schooldays because he has never grown out of them and never come to the mentality of an adult. But such a description would be by no means just of all those to whom those early days are vivid. Nor, though it may be a general truth that the mind retains that which it has most enjoyed, is it universally true that those remember their schooldays best who enjoyed them most. The retentive mind of Sir Charles Oman held to the last, as he showed in his *Memories of Victorian Oxford*, every detail of the ill treatment which he had received at Winchester half a century before, and Bismarck in his retirement lay awake, hating the schoolmaster of his youth. From time to time I meet again over the arches of the years one who was at school with me. Sometimes I find, as Mr. Connolly has shown the world in *Enemies of Promise* to be the case with him, that every detail of Eton life is vivid to the mind. With others—by no means necessarily the stupid or unobservant—I am almost embarrassed to see how completely the picture and arrangement of the life there have passed from them and how they have forgotten the part that they themselves played in incidents that are still utterly familiar to me.

Mr. Connolly was certainly not one who found nothing to complain of in his Eton life, and a superficial critic might say that he was certainly not one who remembered it because it was pleasant. In the latter judgment the critic would, I think, be wrong. Although Mr. Connolly's story is in large part the story of a battle, it was a battle which, as he himself would confess, he greatly enjoyed. The life of personal relationships meant much to him. He wrote, 'Were I to deduce anything from my feelings on leaving Eton, it might be called The Theory of Permanent Adolescence. It is the theory that experiences undergone by boys at the great public schools are so intense as to dominate their lives and to arrest their development.'

To Orwell personal relations of that sort meant little, and therefore it was natural perhaps that his attitude towards it should be polemical, that, excellent as his humour was in general, there should be throughout the whole of *Such, Such were the Joys* no hint that there was ever any joke in the life of Crossgates. To a strong solitary such as Orwell there was little that school could do to him save not interfere with him. It was therefore perhaps natural that to him—a rare case—his preparatory school remained more vividly in his mind than his public school. It remained more vividly in his mind because he was interfered with more. He wrote little about College at Eton because he was little interfered with there. But it does not follow from that that Eton had little influence on him.

It was at Eton that my own path and that of Orwell first crossed. I was of the Election of 1914, Orwell that of 1916. But, as I have said, I was a twelve-year-old of my Election and he a thirteen-year-old of his. So there was not much difference between us in age. But in the curious hierarchy of College they were not years of age which counted at all. All was reckoned by the years of Election. The bottom Election —that of those still in their first year—was the Election of the fags. Those immediately above them gave themselves great airs, called themselves the Senior Election, and would not speak to the Junior Election at all or spoke to them only with great condescension. They were continually on the alert for any sign of the fags 'giving themselves airs'.

It is, I think, a universal experience of school that in his first year a boy soon gets to know by name almost everybody in his school or house. His seniors are more prominent than he and there is every cause to discover who they are. In fact he had better know—for many reasons. But, as he goes up the school, he comes to know fewer and fewer by name. It is only for some special reason that he has occasion to know by name boys junior to himself. As a result, when we of our Election attained to the seniority of a third year we soon indeed formed some confident general judgments about 'the scruffiness' of the new fags, but we were very content to pride ourselves considerably on not knowing one from another. So some weeks went by before I knew that there was in the new Election, recently arrived as a late reinforcement to it, a Blair, K. S.—or at least before I knew which of the fags Blair, K. S., might be.

And the first thing that I got to know about him and the way I got to know about him was this.

There was in my Election a boy—today a distinguished peer. We will call him Johnson—Johnson major. In the ordinary way we would have had no means of knowing what were the topics of conversation in the underworld of the fags, but it so happened that Johnson major had a younger brother who was then a member of the fags' Election —who is today a scholar of world renown. There was not the rigid ban on conversation of brother with brother which ruled among the generality of the unrelated. One day Johnson minor reported to Johnson major that there was a boy in his Election of the name of Blair, who had taken a most violent dislike to the elder brother, and, lacking wax and wishing to give effective expression to his dislike, Blair had made out of soap an image of his hated enemy. He had extracted all the pins out of his returned washing and stuck them at odd angles into this soapen image. I do not remember that we ever saw the image. It was reported to us that it was not a very recognizable likeness but that, in order that there might be no misunderstanding on the part of either boy or demon, Blair had labelled it 'Johnson major' and stuck it upon the bracket below the mirror in his cubicle or 'stall' as it was called.

We made some inquiries what was the reason for this so great hatred, for Johnson major was not conscious that he even knew Blair by sight. Blair, it transpired, did not pretend that Johnson had ever done him any harm, but said that he detested him because he was so 'noisy', as indeed he was. Clearly it was a case of

> I do not like thee, Doctor Fell,
> The reason why I cannot tell

—and this was more or less admitted.

It was on Friday that Johnson minor told this tale to his elder brother.

Now the régime in College in those days was a régime of fairly rough justice. The Colleger had to expect to be beaten a number of times during his first two years. It was thought to be good for him, and, even if he did not commit an offence, some offence would probably be fathered on him quite without malice and for the good of his bottom and general entertainment. But, after these two years of novitiate, unless a boy had won for himself a reputation for being 'pretty awful', it was possible with a little trouble to avoid punishment. Perhaps a blow would descend once in a while—just to remind even those in Upper Division that they were not yet exempt—but apart from such a mischance those in their third year or beyond could usually escape.

Now it so happened that by what was, I dare say, little more than happy accident Johnson major had during his first two years been more fortunate than most and had won for himself something of a reputation of being magically protected by the gods against such indignities. But on the next Monday he was suddenly and unexpectedly summoned before Sixth Form. He had, it seems, come in late for lunch that day and, when asked if he had got leave from a member of Sixth Form—as was the obligation—had replied that he could not find anybody to give him leave. It appeared—so the Sixth Formers alleged —that there were several Sixth Formers about. He was told that he could easily have found somebody to give him leave if he had taken a little trouble, that this was casual behaviour, that there was a great deal too much of such casual behaviour and that it was time that something was done to stop it. Before he knew where he was he was being beaten.

That was on Monday. On Tuesday there was a field day, from which we had to return by train. Johnson was the senior boy in his carriage. During the journey a boy in that carriage, with great folly, threw a bottle out of the window as the train was passing through Reading (West). The matter was reported. There was a great row. The culprit was discovered. He was summoned before Sixth Form on the Wednesday and, not surprisingly, punished, but while he was about it, the Sixth Former who was the head of the College contingent of the Corps thought to ask also who was the senior boy in the carriage. It was Johnson major of course and he—a little harshly perhaps—was beaten into the bargain. The news was carried back to the fags. Blair accepted it with a smile of wry triumph, but that evening just before lights out—so Johnson minor told us—the soapen image slipped into a basin full of hot water and was dissolved. Blair did not re-erect it on its bracket. It was a symbol, we comforted the damaged elder brother, that the jealous gods were no longer athirst and that the curse had been expiated. And so indeed it proved, for he had no more troubles in his immediate future.

This tale convinced me that Blair must be 'an odd fellow' and that it would be amusing to get to know him and find out what were his ideas. It was always at school my hobby to defy as far as might be possible the bans of convention and to talk to amusing people wherever I might find them. I did not, needless to say, believe in Blair's magic, but even a bogus magician was better than no magician at all. So the next time that we passed each other in the passage I said to him 'Hullo, Blair'—which was an outrageous thing to say to a fag. He replied 'Hullo' and smiled a little feebly.

There are limits to daring, and for the moment I could think of no more to say. So after stopping and staring at one another we both passed on without a further word. It was our first conversation, and it left on me the impression that here was a boy of a peculiar humour—a saturnine perhaps and not wholly benevolent humour but above all a humorist. So he certainly was. It is as such that I primarily remember him—as a boy saying and doing funny things. It is well to set this against his own picture of himself at Crossgates and at Eton in which humour plays no part.

Mr. Noel Blakiston, who was a few years Orwell's junior in College, has told me of his first meeting with him. Mr. Blakiston was fielding in a cricket match. Orwell came up to him with a paper and pencil in his hand.

'I'm collecting the religions of the new boys,' said Orwell. 'Are you Cyrenaic, Sceptic, Epicurean, Cynic, Neoplatonist, Confucian or Zoroastrian?'

'I'm a Christian,' said Blakiston.

'Oh,' said Orwell, 'we haven't had that before.'

My other early memory of him is at Chamber Singing. In their first Michaelmas half, a few weeks after its beginning, all new boys in College had one by one to stand upon a table in their dormitory which was known as Chamber and each to sing a song. Orwell sang—not very well—'Riding down from Bangor', about which he was some thirty years later to write one of his *Tribune* essays. At the time that he wrote the essay he had no copy of the song at hand and had, he said, to quote from memory—the memory no doubt of Chamber Singing.

For my next memory I move on some three years. I was then a junior member of Sixth Form. A fellow Sixth Former conceived, rightly or wrongly, that he had been cheeked by the members of Orwell's Election in a complicated dispute over the borrowing of some tennis balls, and the whole Election was summoned before Sixth Form and told that they were all to be beaten. There was a tremendous argument whether they had insulted him or not, and in that argument Orwell stood out as the spokesman for his Election—first, maintaining that there had been no insult and then, with melodramatic gesture, that at least there could be no point in beating the whole Election. It would suffice if there was a scapegoat and for that he offered himself. The argument was to no purpose, and the whole Election was in fact beaten. The incident only remains in my mind because I noticed that Orwell's trousers were more shiny than those of his fellows—and that was certainly the only suggestion that ever came to my mind during his schooldays that he was perhaps poorer than the rest of us.

It certainly was not true that he was unpopular with his fellow Collegers. It certainly was not true that he was insignificant among them or what I might call superficially solitary. As for work, he may not have worked as hard as he could. Indeed it is true that, in an order, based upon marks obtained in Trials, or the term examination, he sank to the bottom of his Election, but these marks were given predominantly for proficiency in Latin and Greek, in which he was not especially interested, and he was in competition against the most expert mark-grubbers in England. He was a science specialist. Mr. A. S. F. Gow, now Fellow of Trinity College, Cambridge, was his tutor when first he went to Eton. When he became a science specialist, he was attached for a time to Mr. Christie, of Glyndbourne, but that was, it seems, little more than a formal connection, and he soon went back to Mr. Gow.

Orwell maintained that, as an Etonian, he was an anarchical prig, an idler and despised by the other boys for his poverty. Let me deal with these claims.

As for anarchy, it is certainly true. 'We all thought of ourselves', he wrote, 'as the enlightened creatures of a new age, casting off the orthodoxy that had been forced upon us.' 'I was against all authority. I had read and re-read the entire published works of Shaw, Wells and Galsworthy, at that time still regarded as 'dangerously advanced' writers, and I loosely described myself as a Socialist.' Mr. Connolly confirms this. He speaks of Orwell as 'immersed in the *Way of All Flesh* and the atheistic arguments of *Androcles and the Lion*' at the age of fifteen. He was, I remember, known as 'the Election atheist'.

But the operative words in these extracts are 'We all'. Orwell records how in a division of sixteen, fifteen nominated Lenin as one of the ten greatest men of the age. The period was the period of Woodrow Wilson and of reaction against tradition and discipline, the period of the years after the armistice of 1918. What Monsignor Knox —then by no means Monsignor—speaking of an earlier crisis, called in his leaving entry, in College Annals, 'a healthy wind of antinomianism'

was then blowing over almost all schools in England. Certainly it
blew like a gale at Eton and particularly in College. Anarchical
opinions by no means made Orwell isolated. They made him a notable
leader. They put him in the fashion. As Mr. Brander truly says, the
anecdote about Lenin proves that Orwell was by no means peculiar in his opinions. He was only peculiar in that he was solitary and
that he did not, as Mr. Connolly truly says, throw himself into
the conflicts of College politics by which so many of the rest of us
were absorbed. Perhaps there was in his rebellion against authority a
kind of obstinate and puritan sincerity which contrasted a little
with the more light-hearted ragging in which at any rate the greater
number of the escapades of the rest of us were conceived. 'Well,
Blair,' said the Master in College, 'things can't go on like this. Either
you or I will have to go.' 'I'm afraid it'll have to be you, sir,' answered
Orwell. It may be—I do not know—that some of the masters felt that
he was a serious danger, where the rest of us were merely silly nuis-
ances. I fully accepted the whole grammar of anarchy about no discipline and no punishments and was always delighted to find pretended
abuses and tyrannies to denounce. But there was a custom at Eton by
which boys touched their caps to a master when they passed him. It
seemed, and seems to me, a very harmless courtesy and, questioning
all else, I had never thought to question that custom, but I remember
discovering to my surprise that Orwell resented passionately the
indignity of this servile action that was demanded of him.

Orwell tells how the boys ragged the peace celebrations in School
Yard in 1919. As he records it, 'We were to march into School Yard,
carrying torches and singing jingo songs of the type of *Rule Britannia*.
The boys—to their honour, I think—guyed the whole proceeding.'
The reason why we guyed the proceedings was that they were
organized by the O.T.C., and the O.T.C. in those post-war years was
a very unpopular institution. Mr. Fyvell cannot believe that Orwell's
account of the deriding of the O.T.C. and the mocking of the flag
was not exaggerated and even confesses to the strange belief that
Orwell himself 'rather enjoyed serving in the O.T.C.', which is certainly not true, whatever Orwell may afterwards have pretended.
Both then, as later in the Home Guard, it was one of his curious whims
to pretend that he was an efficient soldier, but it was completely untrue. He was appallingly untidy and, rebel as he was, not even he
would have dared to carry eccentricity so far as to have enjoyed the
O.T.C. in the early 1920s. But Orwell's account of the peace

celebrations is not at all exaggerated. Antinomianism that would not
have been tolerated at any other school in England was, and I hope
still is, tolerated at Eton. But the rag was to most of us, I think, a
straightforward rag. There was not the element of principle in our
protest which Orwell imports.

It may seem both from this narrative and from Mr. Connolly's
Enemies of Promise that life at Eton was a very vapulatory business.
And so indeed in general it was. But it so happened that shortly after
the incident of the tennis balls those of us who held after the new ways
came into power in Sixth Form and as a result, for better or for worse,
beatings became extremely rare. It is true that at the end of Orwell's
time there, after we had left, there was a certain reaction, as one result
of which Orwell, according to Mr. Connolly, was, at eighteen, beaten
by a boy of substantially his own age, for being late for prayers. But
on the whole, far from suffering brutality at Eton, he had an easier
time than the average public schoolboy. Nor indeed did he ever deny
this. If it is true that his interests even during his schooldays were not
bounded by the world of Eton, Eton, I think, deserves some credit
for this. The general freedom of Eton life combined fortuitously with
the special freedom which the régime of College allowed him. There
was a kind of insolent carelessness about what was taught at Eton,
arising from a confidence that the pupils would not attend to it very
much anyway, that could not be found, I imagine, anywhere else. I
remember in 1920 having to write an essay for Mr. Aldous Huxley,
then one of the masters, to explain how there could never again be
any dictators in the modern world. A good many of the things
that were taught there were palpably untrue, but they were very
well taught. Indeed this was substantially Orwell's own verdict. He
wrote in an article in the *Observer*, 'For Ever Eton', on August 1,
1948:

> Whatever may happen to the great public schools when our
> educational system is reorganized, it is almost impossible that Eton
> should survive in anything like its present form, because the training
> it offers was originally intended for a landowning aristocracy and
> had become an anachronism long before 1939. The top hats and tail
> coats, the pack of beagles, the many-coloured blazers, the desks still
> notched with the names of Prime Ministers had charm and function
> so long as they represented the kind of elegance that everyone looked
> up to. In a shabby and democratic country they are merely rather a

nuisance, like Napoleon's baggage wagons, full of chefs and hair-dressers, blocking up the roads in the disaster of Sedan.

But he added:

> It has one great virtue . . . and that is a tolerant and civilized atmo-sphere which gives each boy a fair chance of developing his indi-viduality. The reason is perhaps that, being a very rich school, it can afford a large staff, which means that the masters are not over-worked; and also that Eton partly escaped the reform of the public schools set on foot by Dr. Arnold and retained certain characteristics belonging to the eighteenth century and even to the Middle Ages. At any rate, whatever its future history, some of its traditions deserve to be remembered.

And indeed, like most other Etonians, he owed many of his oppor-tunities in later life to his old schoolfellows—in his case, to Mr. Connolly and Sir Richard Rees.

In his essay *Inside the Whale*, Orwell takes Mr. Connolly to task, with some ridicule, for suggesting in the passage already quoted that an Eton career is likely to be a permanent formative influence in the life of an intellectual—'five years', as he put it, 'in a lukewarm bath of snobbery'. But I think that Mr. Connolly was right and Orwell wrong. The great mark of most iconoclasts is their lack of self-confi-dence. Attacking society, they yet need somewhere where they can feel the security of support, and thus it follows that, criticizing the evils of society at large, they allow themselves a blind spot to the evils of the particular organization to which they belong. If you wish for the self-confidence not to need this support of an organization I think that it helps a great deal to have been an Old Etonian. Orwell was so wholly unique a character that if, knowing nothing of him, I had been shown his work and asked to guess whence he had sprung, I should not perhaps have known how to answer, but if I had been told—which would not have seemed to me an improbability—that he was a public schoolboy, I should certainly have guessed that he was an Eton Colleger, for I think that at Eton that peculiar excess of individualism is more kindly treated than elsewhere. An Old Etonian is far more likely to 'dare to be a Daniel' than is a Nonconformist. Class privilege has seldom been effectively attacked except by a writer who has to some extent benefited from it, as Orwell, whatever he may have pretended, naturally did.

I would not say that he was a typical Old Etonian, but then it is the especial mark of Eton that it is peculiarly easy for an Old Etonian not to be a typical Old Etonian. His private school may, for all that I know, have played its part in driving him to spiritual loneliness, and this loneliness certainly was sharpened and embittered by a life in Burma, in which none of his fellow Europeans were people at all sympathetic to him, but I think that Eton had a good deal to do with the unique courage with which he gave expression to that spiritual loneliness. Eton left him free to develop his own interests without constraint to a degree that he might not have found equalled at any other school in the world. 'I did not work', writes Orwell of his Eton life, 'and I don't feel that Eton has been much of a formative influence.' And Mr. Stephen Spender has passed on him what seems to me the curious verdict—'the least Etonian character who has ever come from Eton'. Mr. Brander, an acute observer who did not make his friendship until the Second World War, not himself an Old Etonian, writes much more penetratingly than Orwell himself or than Mr. Spender: 'To anyone who knew him it was obvious where he had been to school.'

If it be true, as Orwell tells us, that during all his early years he always assumed that all his enterprises would inevitably end in failure the sense came from an accident of his temperament—perhaps from his ill health. In fact his career was averagely successful. Of direct literary work during his schooldays he writes, 'Apart from school work, I wrote *vers d'occasion*, semi-comic poems which I could turn out at what now seems to me astonishing speed—at fourteen I wrote a whole rhyming play in imitation of Aristophanes in about a week—and helped to edit school magazines, both printed and in manuscript. These manuscripts were the most pitiful burlesque stuff that you could imagine, and I took far less trouble with them than I now would with the cheapest journalism.' These verses gained, I remember, a reputation for wit among his schoolfellows and I should be surprised if they were not better than he pretended. But I cannot quote any of them at this distance of time. So there is no way of proving my point.

But as for his main grievance against Eton, that he was a poor boy among the rich, it was, I am sure, entirely a grievance of his own imagination. Eton is about as completely a classless society within itself as can be imagined. The Etonian of my day was childishly arrogant about anyone who was not at Eton—Marlburians, Hottentots, barrow-boys, Americans and what-have-you were all dismissed with sweeping gesture as beyond the pale. But his very arrogance meant that anyone who was at Eton was accepted. At Leeds Grammar School there certainly was much more awareness than there was at Eton whose parents were rich and whose were poor and which lived in the fashionable and which in the unfashionable parts of the town. The only vestige of what by any stretch could be called internal class-feeling in Etonian life was the contempt with which some years before Oppidans, who paid for their schooling, used to treat Collegers, who got it free. But, just at the time when Orwell and I were at Eton, this feeling of contempt had quite died down, and Collegers had far more than their fair share of members of Pop, or the Eton Society. 'Probably the greatest cruelty one can inflict on a child', wrote Orwell in *Keep the Aspidistra Flying*, 'is to send it to school among children richer than itself.' It is an absurd exaggeration. To one who sees things in proportion it is not by any means an unmixed evil to be brought up in sufficiency but in the company of somewhat richer children. By far the greater number of notable achievements of man, I should say, have come from those who have had such experience in youth, and to one who has common sense there is no better discipline in economy. By the side of the advantages the few incidental embarrassments are trivial.

Orwell complained of himself and of the rest of us that we were snobs. 'When I was fourteen,' he writes, 'I was an odious little snob, but no worse than other boys of my age and class.' We must use words carefully. It was of course true that, while we were still at Eton, we had not at all learnt how to be at ease with those who did not come from a public school. It was not that we claimed superiority. On the contrary, in our anarchical mood we indulged in a good deal of frothy egalitarian talk. It is true, of course, as Orwell says, that we wanted to have it both ways—that while we clamoured that the workers should have better opportunities, we never faced the corollary that this would in any way mean that we should have worse opportunities. In an illogical fashion we looked forward to an unprivileged society in which we still had all our privileges. But what is that but to say that we were still very young?

Orwell in *The Road to Wigan Pier* claims that class consciousness is a reality and that the hypocrite who denies it deceives himself. Everyone, he argues, on either side of the fence as a general rule does prefer to associate with those who were brought up to the same habits as himself, and, if we want to lessen class distinctions, we must be content to hasten slowly. Otherwise our well-meant folly will only succeed in accentuating them. This is sensible enough. We shall certainly never succeed in building the classless society so long as we are always talking about it. We can only begin to move towards it, when we can school ourselves to talk and think about more interesting and more important things.

Class consciousness in Orwell, as he claims, showed itself during his boyhood most clearly in his conviction that the lower classes smell. This conviction remained with him for years even after he left school, and indeed it is not quite clear, from the pages in *The Road to Wigan Pier*, whether he ever abandoned it. It is far from clear whether he thought even in maturity that this was a vulgar prejudice which snobbery had imposed upon him or whether he agreed with Mr. Somerset Maugham that they did smell but that, considering the circumstances of their life, it was neither unnatural nor reprehensible that they should. But if we are to pursue this peculiar topic—and, as Mr. Quinton argued in an interesting broadcast on 'Orwell's Sense of Smell', delivered on January 16, 1954, smell played so large a part in forming his opinions that we must pursue it if we are to judge Orwell at all— it is important to see his crudity in perspective. At the time when he was most insistent that the lower classes smelt—the time of his own schooldays—he also firmly believed that he smelt himself. As he writes of his schooldays in *Such, Such were the Joys*, 'I was weak. I was ugly. I was unpopular. I had a chronic cough. I smelt. This picture, I should add, was not altogether fanciful. I was an unattractive boy. Crossgates soon made me so, even if I had not been so before. But a child's belief in its own shortcomings is not much influenced by facts. I believed, for example, that I smelt, but this was based simply on general probability. It was notorious that disagreeable people smelt, and therefore presumably I did so, too.'

How keen was Orwell's sense of smell it is difficult to say. His whole point about the soldiers with whom he served in Burma and of whose smell he speaks in *The Road to Wigan Pier* is that he thought that they smelt and said that they smelt because that was what prejudice had taught him to expect. He never thought of smelling himself to see. When faced with the question whether they smelt, he did not ask whether he could smell them but whether they were the sort of people whom on ideological principle he would expect to smell. He had a great liking for shocking people, and he knew that in no way could they be more easily shocked than by a frank discussion who smelt and

who did not—or rather, to be pedantic and Johnsonian, who stank
and who did not. But surely to settle such matters by ideological
probability is not the mark of a smelling man. The smelling man smells
and when a man is for ever thinking about what he ought or ought
not to feel, it becomes very difficult to discover what he does feel.
No doubt, like the rest of us, Orwell did not think very much about
the working classes when he was a boy at Eton, but I do not think
that he had any deliberate prejudice which could justly be called snobbery, nor, even though he thought as an intellectual proposition that
they smelt, do I believe that he thought about it very much.

He was reasonably good at games. He was in the College Wall
Eleven and played against the Oppidans on St. Andrew's Day. He
played at goals, and the College Wall book in a number of places
commends his cool and skilful kicking, both on St. Andrew's Day
and throughout the season. 'Blair made some neat kicks.' 'Blair kept
his head and stopped the rush,' I read in the Wall book. In the Wall
game the common score, corresponding to a rugby try, is a shy.
When a shy is scored, the scoring side, as in rugby, attempts to convert it into a goal. A goal is scored at the Wall game by throwing the
ball at one end against a garden door, at the other end against a mark
on a tree. The throw is inordinately difficult and for years on end no
one ever scores a goal. But Orwell scored one in a match played on
October 29, 1921. He threw the ball to Robert Longden, afterwards
Headmaster of Wellington, who passed it on to the door. Mr. John
Lehmann, who was a new boy at the time, remembered it happening
and on looking the game up in the College Wall book, I was delighted
to discover—what I had, I confess, quite forgotten—that I was playing
in the match on the side opposite to Orwell.

Much in Orwell can be explained by the acute sense of sin by which
he was haunted. Sometimes, as in his criticisms of Mr. and Mrs. Simpson, this discomfort of sin made him attack those who had caused it.
He tried—and failed—to relieve himself of it by denouncing its alleged
irrationality. Elsewhere, where a genuine moral judgment led him to
acclaim the goodness of equality, he attacked those, such as the masters
of the totalitarian states, who preached equality but practised inequality.
He thought it necessary to punish himself for his privileges by voluntarily embracing the lot of the 'down and outs' in London and Paris
or of the Spanish revolutionaries, and in the same spirit he did not
care to talk much of his Eton life, not because it had not had influence
on him, but because he had enjoyed it and, since it was an inheritance

of privilege, he felt it wrong to have enjoyed it. He was willing to talk about Crossgates because he genuinely disliked Crossgates. When it came to the planning of the education of his adopted son, Orwell argued, as Mr. Fyvell tells us, that it would be a good thing if the public-school system should have come to an end before he had to go to school, but that, if there were still public schools, he should go to one.

In various places throughout his books there are scattered and incidental remarks about the public-school system—condemning it for its inegalitarianism—and various scattered and incidental remarks about classical education—which he disliked professedly because it diverted the mind of the pupil from the real problems of the day—which he disliked in truth perhaps because all his own interests were in the present and the future and he did not care greatly about the past, whether of Greece or Rome or of any other land or period. But the nearest that he comes to a systematic criticism of the place in society of the public school is in his study of the stories of the *Gem* and the *Magnet* in his essay on 'Boys' Weeklies'. He there notes two important truths—first, that England is the only country in which there is a large, continuing market for the school story—second, that such stories are invariably about expensive and exclusive public schools but are generally read by boys of humble origin who have never had any hope of going to such schools. The stories themselves are, if considered realistically, both fantastic and outdated and he submits their absurdities to a witty analysis. But the lesson that he draws from this analysis is that there is an enormous proportion of the unmoneyed youth of the country who are living 'fantasy' lives as pretended public schoolboys. For this reason the public schools receive an absurd and adventitious aid in their struggle for survival. There is not the unqualified hostility to them which one would expect on pure egalitarian principles. He analyses the financial ownership of these papers, and finds that they belong to the Amalgamated Press and suggests—I do not think quite seriously—that Lord Camrose deliberately flooded the market with this literature for reasons of Conservative propaganda. The truth is, I think, less subtle. 'What I have seen of our governing class', he more justly writes in *The Road to Wigan Pier*, 'does not convince me that they have that much intelligence.' Lord Camrose and his associates did not invent this strange English mentality any more than the producers of Hollywood taught the American public to worship wealth. But they astutely observed its existence and exploited it. Whether it should

be so or not, in fact the English is not an egalitarian nation. It is rare
to find among the English those who care greatly about equality, so
long as the grossest injustices are avoided. Where we do find an English
egalitarian we find him sometimes indeed among the unprivileged,
but more often among those who have themselves received privileges
and are made uncomfortable in the possession of them by a sense of
sin. Which makes for the greater general human happiness—equality
or a frankly unequal society with a comparatively easy ebb and flow
between class and class—what Pareto called 'the circulation of the
élites'—is a question with which Orwell was to spend the rest of his
life in wrestling and to which, like the rest of us, he never found the
certain answer.

III

Burma

THE great majority of Eton Collegers, when their school time ended, went on with a scholarship either to Oxford or Cambridge. Such would have been the natural next step for Orwell to take, but some master at Eton, neither, it seems, Mr. Christie nor Mr. Gow, instead gave him the advice, 'You've had enough of education. Take a job abroad and see something of the world.' So instead he went out straight from school to a job in the Indian Imperial Police in Burma.

There were perhaps cross purposes in the spirit in which this advice was given and taken. The master perhaps thought that the form which Orwell's intellectual development had taken was unhealthy alike for him and for his companions and therefore advised him to throw himself up against the realities, fancying that such experience might knock out of him the nonsense which would only grow rank in a University hot-house. Orwell, on the other hand, in an iconoclastic mood was ready to reject the Universities simply because it was the normal thing to go to them. The question of family poverty, however freely it may have been brought in, had really nothing to do with it. Eton at that date—as I myself learnt to my advantage—was generous in making up scholarship emoluments for needy boys to figures that made it possible for them to make use of their scholarships, and, if such a condition was necessary, there is no doubt that Orwell could have gone to Oxford or Cambridge without costing his father a penny.

The advice or misunderstanding was certainly unfortunate. In that strange and turbulent period immediately after the war the greater number of those undergraduates who have later won distinction in the literary or artistic world went down from Oxford without a degree. Those who took degrees took bad ones, and there can be little doubt that Orwell, more rebellious than the average, would have added his name to one or other of those distinguished lists. There can be as little doubt that he missed much through having to spend these important years in what was virtually solitude in Rangoon rather than in the company of intellectual equals who shared his interests. He came

26

to regret and to resent his exclusion. He makes Gordon Comstock say in anger in *Keep the Aspidistra Flying*, 'The Editor regrets! Why be so bloody mealy-mouthed about it? Why not say outright," We don't want your bloody poems. We only take poems from chaps we were at Cambridge with. You proletarians, keep your distance."'

It may of course be argued that his art was stimulated by the tang of uncongenial life and that there would have been less vigour in his writing if his paths had lain in more pleasant places. But to argue thus is to argue that Milton might have written less well if he had not gone blind. It is a possibility but not one on which Milton's oculist would have been justified in dwelling, and within the limits that a reasonable ethics allows the Eton master's advice was certainly bad advice.

Orwell had left school a year after me. I vaguely knew that he had gone 'out East' but did not know exactly where. I chanced to arrive in Rangoon in the summer of 1925 on my way back from Java. I had no notion that he was there but learnt it to my delight on the night of my arrival from a friend with whom he used to play squash. He came to dinner a few nights afterwards and a few nights after that I went back to dine with him.

We had a long talk and argument. In the side of him which he revealed to me at that time there was no trace of liberal opinions. He was at pains to be the imperial policeman, explaining that these theories of no punishment and no beating were all very well at public schools but that they did not work with the Burmese—in fact that

> Libbaty's a kind o' thing
> Thet don't agree with niggers.

He had an especial hatred, as he was afterwards to confess in *Shooting an Elephant*, for the Buddhist priests, against whom he thought violence especially desirable—and that not for any theological reason but because of their sniggering insolence.

There was, he argued, no physical repulsion between the European and the Burmese, as there was perhaps between the European and the African. 'One did not feel', as he was afterwards to write in *The Road to Wigan Pier*, 'towards the "natives" as one felt towards the "lower classes" at home. The essential point was that the "natives", at any rate the Burmese, were not felt to be physically repulsive. One looked down on them as "natives", but one was quite ready to be physically intimate with them; and this, I noticed, was the case even with white men who had the most vicious colour-prejudice.' Even Kipling's soldier on the road to Mandalay has no prejudice against a Burmese girl. But this readiness of the white man for physical intimacy without conceding any sort of social equality, which Orwell, at this time, took for granted, he came afterwards to feel as the crowning evil of imperialism.

If I had never heard or read of Orwell after that evening, I should certainly have dismissed him as an example of that common type which has a phase of liberal opinion at school, when life is as yet untouched by reality and responsibility, but relapses easily after into conventional reaction. But of course the first pages of *Shooting an Elephant* tell us—which is inherently probable—that at this time there was a struggle within him of two minds—the policeman who hated the rudeness and insubordination of the native and the new man who was coming to see imperialism as the evil thing—and I do not doubt that it was only the one side of himself that he happened to reveal, or chose to reveal, to me and that, arguing with me, he was in some sense arguing with his second self, and, arguing thus, as it were, against his sense of sin, he exposed, in the complexity of his character, his imperial creed in a manner more crude and brutal than truth demanded. For in fact he was, as those who were out in Burma bore witness, a good police officer, and, although one side of him hated the inequality of human relationship which imperialism imposed and saw the degradation which it brought to the characters both of rulers and of ruled, there was, as Mr. Malcolm Muggeridge has truly argued, also 'a Kiplingesque side to his character which made him romanticise the Raj and its mystique'.

It is also typical of him that at the same time, as I afterwards learnt, he insisted on befriending an Englishman who was greatly cold-shouldered by Rangoon society for having married an Indian lady, even though the marriage seemed to Orwell a folly.

Orwell returned from Burma in 1927. He returned nominally on leave, but, as he has told us in *The Road to Wigan Pier*, he felt in his bones that he would never go back, and he never did go back. He had come to hate the imperial system which, as a policeman, he had to serve. As he wrote in *Wigan Pier*, 'I hated the imperialism I was serving with a bitterness that I cannot make clear.'

His feelings about this imperial system we can deduce from his novel, *Burmese Days*, two essays, *Shooting an Elephant* and 'A Hanging', and a number of incidental autobiographical confessions in *The Road to Wigan Pier* and elsewhere.

Burmese Days, the first of his novels, was published in 1934, seven years that is to say after his return from Burma. 'I was conscious', he wrote, 'of an immense weight of guilt which I had got to expiate', and 'the landscapes of Burma, which, when I was among them, so appalled me as to assume the qualities of nightmare, afterwards stayed so hauntingly in my mind that I was obliged to write a novel about them to get rid of them'.

The scene of *Burmese Days* is set in the little up-country town of Kyauktada—a town inhabited by a few thousand Burmese, a handful of Indians, a few Eurasians and a tiny colony of Europeans, to be numbered in a single figure. Word has come down from the central government that it would be desirable for the Europeans to elect a native to their club, and the plot is concerned with the consequences which flow from that expressed wish. On the one hand there are the scenes in the club itself, where opinion is hostile to this surrender of what they think of as the white man's last privacy. This hostile opinion varies from that of the Deputy Commissioner who mildly wishes that such an issue had never been raised through a number of middle opinions down to that of Ellis, a man so violent in his hatred of any concession to the native that his condition is quite pathological. There is only one white man, Flory, the hero of the book, who is not opposed to the admission.

The other side to the story is the competition among the Indians for admission. The senior native, the natural candidate, is the service doctor, a Madrasi Brahmin, Dr. Veraswami. He is a man of probity, fanatically pro-British, carrying indeed his admiration for British ways and Western progress and his contempt for his own culture to ridiculous lengths. Whatever the incidental absurdities of his character, there can be no question about it that, if a native is to be elected, it should be he. But he has a bitter and very unscrupulous rival, U Po Kyin, a local Burmese magistrate, who has raised himself by means of unvaried villainy from the most obscure of origins to affluence and to the second position among the natives of the district. He is determined to raise himself still further from the second position to the first—in order to do this to ruin Dr. Veraswami, his only rival—to obtain election to the club and finally to be decorated by the governor. With this end in view he obtains the publication in the local native paper of villainous attacks on the Deputy Commissioner and then puts it about that Veraswami was responsible for those attacks. He has anonymous letters sent to all the European inhabitants accusing

Veraswami of every conceivable crime. He arranges the escape from the local gaol of a notorious criminal and then fastens the responsibility for the escape on to Veraswami. He even arranges a pathetic rebellion in a neighbouring village and then takes to himself the credit for its suppression. When two of the villagers after the rebellion kill Maxwell, the young Divisional Forest Officer, in revenge for his killing of one of their relatives in the fighting, U Po Kyin, though he has not arranged this further killing, yet does not conceal his delight, thinking that it will yet further strengthen his position.

There remains at last only one obstacle to his complete triumph. There is a friendship between the Englishman, Flory, and Dr. Veraswami, and although all the other Europeans greatly disapprove of this friendship, yet the prestige of a white man is such that it is not possible for an Oriental wholly to ruin another Oriental while a white man is known to be his friend. By veiled threats U Po Kyin attempts to persuade Flory to drop Dr. Veraswami, but, though Flory is cast in no heroic mould, yet he cannot quite be persuaded to do this. U Po Kyin therefore sees that for his success it is necessary that he drive Flory to final ruin.

Flory, a timber merchant of about thirty-five, is the central character of the book. He has been out in the East ever since he left a minor public school fifteen years before. He has never been home on leave. First he did not take his leave because of the war and then, when at last he had embarked on the boat, he was recalled by cable from Colombo because three of the firm's other employees had suddenly died. He no longer has any relatives left in England and no longer has any wish to go home. Intellectually he is greatly the superior of the other Europeans in the club. He reads new books whenever he can get hold of them from Rangoon. He has a deep love of flowers and birds, and the philistine monotony of the conversation at the club with its dreary repetition of complaints and denunciation of the native drives him almost to frenzy. For relief he takes himself to the company of Dr. Veraswami. He and his Indian friend converse together in inverted rôles, the Doctor always defending the British imperial system and Flory bitterly attacking it.

But in his loneliness he has developed other characteristics that are less admirable. Like all of the rest of the Europeans except the Deputy Commissioner, he drinks too much. He sometimes gets drunk at the club and sometimes alone at home. He has fallen into slovenly ways and, when he is in Kyauktada, lies at home until the evening and does not shave until dinner-time. Disfigured by a horrible birth-mark, he has never been able to marry and in any event in the European society at Kyauktada there is only one European woman—and she is married —Mrs. Lackersteen, the empty and snobbish wife of the manager of the timber firm. Continence is however beyond him and his life in the East has been a life of constant fornication—of which however he is as constantly ashamed. At the beginning of the story he is keeping a Burmese mistress from the village, Ma Hla May.

Then Mrs. Lackersteen's niece from England, Elizabeth, comes out to stay with them. Flory makes her acquaintance the day after her arrival, when he saves her from a bison. She satisfies the need for which his spirit was craving and, wholly empty-headed and philistine as she is, he yet falls madly in love with her. She has no curiosity whatsoever to learn anything of native life and is disgusted both when he takes her to a native play, or pwe, and when he takes her to the bazaar and to call on a Chinese friend, Li Yeik. On the other hand, a shooting expedition when she shoots for the first time and with success, and when Flory kills a leopard, is a great triumph and makes him, for all his deficiencies, appear as a hero in her eyes. She is about to accept him and is only prevented in the nick of time by an earthquake and her aunt, Mrs. Lackersteen.

Mrs. Lackersteen has just discovered from the perusal of the civil list that Verrall, the newly arrived military policeman, is an honourable. As soon as she knows that, it is clear to her that she must keep her niece away from Flory in order to preserve her for this higher prize. She therefore tells her niece that Flory is keeping a Burmese mistress. Mrs. Lackersteen had of course known this all along, as everyone in Kyauktada knew it, but had kept it from her niece so long as she had designs of palming her niece off on Flory. Now she tells her. It is a doubly foul blow, because, as it happens, Flory has just got rid of Ma Hla May, seeing that there was obviously no place for her and Elizabeth together. Ma Hla May, who has no affection at all for Flory nor had ever been faithful to him, yet has lost great prestige among the villagers as she had formed the habit of boasting among them that she was Bo-Kadaw, the white man's wife. She therefore attempts to fight back in a number of humiliating scenes of threats and entreaties and eventually resorts to somewhat ineffectual blackmail.

Elizabeth has no more intention of wasting herself on Flory so long as there is an honourable available than had her aunt the intention of allowing her so to waste herself. She is therefore only too glad to seize the excuse of the Burmese mistress to break with Flory. But jilting Flory is one thing; capturing Verrall is quite another. Verrall is a bore and a cad, quite indifferent to any requirements of manners and with no interest in anything except horse-riding and physical fitness.

He despised the entire non-military population of India, a few famous polo-players excepted. He despised the entire Army as well, except the cavalry. He despised all Indian regiments, infantry and cavalry alike. It was true that he himself belonged to a native regiment, but that was only for his own convenience. He took no interest in Indians, and his Urdu consisted mainly of swear-words, with all verbs in the third person singular. His Military Policemen he looked on as no better than coolies. . . . Up and down India, wherever he was stationed, he left behind him a trail of insulted people, neglected duties and unpaid bills. Yet the disgraces that ought to have fallen on him never did. He bore a charmed life, and it was not only the handle to his name that saved him. There was something in his eye before which duns, burra memsahibs and even colonels quailed. . . . Spending, or rather owing, fabulous sums on clothes, he yet lived almost as ascetically as a monk. He exercised himself ceaselessly and brutally, rationed his drink and his cigarettes, slept on a camp-bed (in silk pyjamas) and bathed in cold water in the bitterest winter. Horsemanship and physical fitness were the only gods he knew. The stamp of hooves on the maidan, the strong, poised feeling of his body, wedded centaur-like to the saddle, the polo-stick springy in his hand—these were his religion, the breath of his life.

Verrall will not go to the club. He will not reply to invitations. He will not pay the ordinary courtesy calls. The Lackersteens find it difficult to get to know him and only manage it in the end by swallowing all pride and brazenly going up and introducing themselves. Then Verrall notices something attractive in Elizabeth's figure and, while still continuing to treat all the male Europeans in Kyauktada with the utmost insolence, yet consents to come to the club in order to dance with Elizabeth, and goes out riding with her by day. Elizabeth and Mrs. Lackersteen are in high hope but Verrall is merely amusing himself so as to pass the time in what is to him an outlandish place of almost unbelievable boredom. He may or may not have seduced her during one of their rides. That is a question concerning which there is a good deal of speculation in Kyauktada society, but naturally he never had from the first the smallest intention of marrying her.

Meanwhile Flory has his finest hour. Colour feeling is tense in Kyauktada after Maxwell's murder. Some native schoolboys jeer in an ill-mannered fashion at Ellis and Ellis revenges himself by striking one of them with his stick over the eyes. As a result of the incompetence of a native doctor the boy goes blind. There is a fight in the streets, and then that evening the whole native population surrounds the club, demanding that Ellis be surrendered and threatening to destroy it if surrender is refused. The mob has neither clear plan nor discipline. Still the situation is ugly. Stones are flying about and there is panic within the club. The question is how to get to the police with instructions to them to rescue. On three sides the club is strongly surrounded by the besiegers. On the fourth is the river. It is Flory who suggests that it might be possible for someone to get to the river and then to swim down it to a point from which he can reach the police station. He volunteers to do this himself and does it. Then, having reached the police, he is careful to get them to fire indeed but to fire over the heads of the mob. Thus the riot is dispersed and at the same time dispersed with a minimum of bloodshed. Flory for all the differences of the past is accepted by the Europeans as their saviour and hero.

Shortly afterwards Verrall is recalled to his regiment. With a characteristic insolence he departs from Kyauktada by train, leaving behind him a number of debts and not bothering to say good-bye to Elizabeth. Having lost Verrall, Elizabeth is only too willing to fall back upon Flory, and her aunt is only too willing that she should do so, the more so, as Flory's prestige has by now been so greatly raised. It looks as if there is no reason why the story should not peter out in what could at any rate have been dressed up as a happy ending—a peaceful marriage between Elizabeth and Flory. But the last trick is with evil and U Po Kyin. Dr. Veraswami had fought bravely for the Europeans in the attack on the club. What between his own good name and Flory's prestige there was little doubt that Flory would propose him for the club and that he would be elected. To prevent this, U Po Kyin suborns Ma Hla May to break into the Anglican service next Sunday and there to demand money from Flory and to denounce him in face of the whole congregation, of which of course Elizabeth is a member. She does this. Flory is utterly humiliated. Elizabeth refuses at any price to have any more to do with him. In despair he goes home and shoots himself. Dr. Veraswami, with Flory's protection lost, is without resources. He is disgraced and U Po Kyin is elected to the club. U Po Kyin goes forward from strength to strength until his final decoration by the governor. The only qualification to the total triumph of evil over good is that U Po Kyin dies three days after his triumph from a fit. The pagodas by which he was to atone for his evil deeds are still unbuilt.

Burmese Days is certainly an indictment of the British rule in Burma, but it is important to see clearly just what it is that Orwell indicts. He did for a time, as he confesses in *The Road to Wigan Pier*, fall to the sentimentalists' temptation of thinking that those who wield power are always wrong and those who suffer it always right, but he never, even in his mood of greatest extravagance in this sentimentality, thought that that meant that every individual of a subject race was of angelic nature. On the contrary, if the British left Burma, then obviously Burma would fall under the rule of the most ruthless and wicked of the Burmese. There is nothing either in *Burmese Days* or elsewhere in Orwell's writings to suggest that he for one moment thought that Burma would be better governed when it was governed by U Po Kyin. But for all that imperialism was an evil and brought evil to the governors and to the governed. It brought evil to the governors because it condemned them to a life of lies and loneliness. It was a life of lies and loneliness because every European knew in his heart that the régime was an evil one, and yet none dared to say so to his neighbour. There was indeed a callousness about these Europeans —Westfield, boasting that somebody would be hanged for the murder of Maxwell and that it would be better to hang the wrong man than to hang nobody—Ellis, complaining that the police shot over the heads of the mob and not into it and saying that, even if they had shot into the mob and shot one of their own number, it would have been 'only a nigger' so it would not have greatly mattered. But there is no suggestion that there was more tyranny and injustice under the British rule than there would have been under Burmese self-government—if we look at U Po Kyin clearly, very much the reverse. But the great sin of the white man is his philistinism. These Europeans were men of no deep culture or curiosity in any event. But by deliberate policy they refused to take any interest in the native life around them and thus narrowed themselves intolerably and further than was necessary.

But in this novel there is no confrontation of the British Raj by

Burmese nationalists. There are no Burmese nationalists in the book. The rebels at Thongwa and the rioters at Kyauktada are represented as simple people, used by an unscrupulous intriguer for purposes that they did not in the least understand—quite incapable of any general ideas such as those of nationalism. The only two Orientals of whom there are full-length portraits—U Po Kyin and Dr. Veraswami—are both supporters of the British Raj—U Po Kyin because he thinks it invincible and because he thinks at the same time that he can use it for his own villainous purposes, Dr. Veraswami out of a romanticism that was almost infantile in its exaggeration. The Orientals of Flory's own household never had any ideas about nationalism one way or the other.

It is not very clear, then, why from the point of view of the Oriental it was desirable that the imperial system should come to an end, nor at that date, as *The Road to Wigan Pier* makes clear, had it ever occurred to Orwell that there was any possibility that it had as short a life before it as events were to prove. Nor had it at that time occurred to him that, if it came to an end, it was likely either immediately or after a short time to be succeeded, not by national freedom, but by a new foreign imperialism a great deal more ruthless and cruel than that of Britain.

Orwell, for all his criticism of the English, always remembered that they were his people, and for all his accusations against them of cruelty he always remembered that they had in them a strange and almost unique streak of kindliness. Years later in *England, Your England,* at the time of the Second World War, he was to proclaim this almost with sentimentality. Even now in *Burmese Days*, at his most bitter, he does not forget it in his character of Flory. In every one of Orwell's novels there is one character who stands out in solitude before the world, as Orwell himself was to stand out between the elephant and the Burmese mob, and who is indeed not a self-portrait of Orwell in all the details, but a portrait of Orwell as he imagined that he might have behaved in certain circumstances. There is clearly a certain similarity between Flory in this book, Gordon Comstock in *Keep the Aspidistra Flying*, and Orwell himself. They were alike in that they were all public-school boys thrown into a highly unpublic-school atmosphere. It would be false—and indeed villainously uncharitable—to suggest that Flory is in any way a self-portrait of Orwell—that Orwell did, or could be imagined to do all the things which Flory did, but we must remember that Flory was thirty-five at the time of

his suicide. Orwell left Burma for good when he was twenty-four.
Of Flory's life in Burma before he was twenty-four Orwell writes:

From Rangoon he had gone to a camp on the jungle, north of
Mandalay, extracting teak. The jungle life was not a bad one, in
spite of the discomfort, the loneliness and, what is almost the worst
thing in Burma, the filthy, monotonous food. He was very young
then, young enough for hero-worship, and he had friends among
the men in his firm. There was also shooting, fishing and perhaps
once in a year a hurried trip to Rangoon—pretext, a visit to the
dentist. Oh, the joy of those Rangoon trips! The rush to Smart and
Mookerdum's bookshop for the new novels out from England, the
dinner at Anderson's with beefsteaks and butter that had travelled
eight thousand miles on ice, the glorious drinking bout! He was too
young to realize what this life was preparing for him. He did not
see the years stretching out ahead, lonely, eventless, corrupting.

He acclimatized himself to Burma. His body grew attuned to the
strange rhythms of the tropical season. Every year from February
to May the sun glared in the sky like an angry god, then suddenly
the monsoon blew westward, first in sharp squalls, then in a heavy
ceaseless downpour that drenched everything until neither one's
clothes, one's bed nor even one's food ever seemed to be dry. It
was still hot with a stuffy vaporous heat. The lower jungle paths
turned into morasses, and the paddy fields were great wastes of
stagnant water with a stale, mousy smell. Books and boots were
mildewed. Naked Burmans in yard-wide hats of palm-leaf ploughed
the paddy fields, driving their buffaloes through the knee-deep
water. Later the women and children planted the green seedlings of
paddy, dabbing each plant into the mud with little three-pronged
forks. Through July and August there was hardly a pause in the rain.
Then one night, high overhead, one heard a squawking of invisible
birds. The snipe were flying southward from Central Asia. The
rains tailed off, ending in October. The fields dried up, the paddy
ripened, the Burmese children played hopscotch with gonyin seeds
and flew kites in the cool winds. It was the beginning of the short
winter when Upper Burma seemed haunted by the ghost of England. Wild flowers sprang into blossom everywhere, not quite the
same as the English ones but very like them—honeysuckle, in thick
bushes, field roses smelling of pear drops, even violets in dark places
of the forest. The sun circled low in the sky, and the nights and

early mornings were bitterly cold, with white mists that poured through the valleys like the steam of enormous kettles. One went shooting after duck and snipe. There were snipe in countless myriads, and wild geese in flocks that rose from the jeel with a roar like a goods train crossing an iron bridge. The ripening paddy, breast-high and yellow, looked like wheat. The Burmans went to their work with muffled heads and their arms clasped across their breasts, their faces yellow and pinched with the cold. In the morning one marched through misty, incongruous wildernesses, clearings of drenched, almost English grasses and naked trees where monkeys squatted in the upper branches, waiting for the sun. At night, coming back to camp through the cold lanes, one met herds of buffaloes which the boys were driving home, with their huge horns looking through the mist like crescents. One had three blankets on one's bed, and game pie instead of the eternal chicken. After dinner one sat on a log by the vast camp-fire, drinking beer and talking about shooting. The flames danced like red holly, casting a circle of light at the edge of which servants and coolies squatted, too shy to intrude on the white man and yet edging up to the fire like dogs. As one lay in bed one could hear the dew dripping from the trees like large but gentle rain. It was a good life while one was young and need not think about the future or the past.

It was after twenty-four—just the age at which Orwell came home —that Flory began to deteriorate. Flory was clearly to some extent Orwell as he imagined that he might have been if he had stayed in Burma.

Flory, even in deterioration, is by no means wholly bad. 'In all novels about the East,' Orwell has written, 'the scenery is the real subject-matter', and there is both pathos and beauty in Flory's repeated attempts to open the eyes of the philistine Elizabeth to the glories of flower and bird life. The shooting of the leopard is a piece of vivid and sensitive description, and Orwell surrenders without apology to that side of him in which, as Mr. Muggeridge truly says, he loved to 'romanticize the Raj and its mystique', when he makes Flory take command at the time of the attack on the club, make the plan, execute it, save the Europeans and save them without shedding the blood of the Orientals. Here was a man who for one splendid hour at any rate knew how *parcere subiectis et debellare superbos*. 'And so', as Mr. Trilling, bringing to bear the objective judgment of an intelligent foreigner, truly says, 'Orwell clung with a kind of wry, grim pride to the old ways of the last class that had ruled the old order.' It is the fashion of the left-wing intellectuals today to pretend that Orwell did not hate them—but it is not true. He loved the poor—but that is a very different story.

Yet it is the undoubted lesson of *Burmese Days* that the evil business ought not to be preserved simply to provide a theatre for the occasional fleeting acts of heroism. Orwell's indictment of the Imperial system stands clear. The question remains whether the indictment is a true one. No opinion is of much value save that of one who has had long experience of life in the East under that system, and I have not had that experience. I have little doubt that Orwell's accusation of philistinism is broadly just. It is extraordinary how few of the English who went out to the East acquired there any curiosity to understand how the Oriental mind works. But I have as little doubt that Mr. Brander, who speaks here with authority, is right in saying that the charge that no Englishman ever dared to speak his mind to another is greatly exaggerated. It was the natural consequence of Orwell's solitariness that he tended always greatly to exaggerate the difficulties of communication. Because he found it difficult to reveal himself to others, he thought that everybody found it difficult. He tells the story in *The Road to Wigan Pier* how he spent the night in the train in Burma with a man in the Educational Service. They got talking over bottled beer and each revealed to the other his conviction of the total rottenness of the system. 'In the haggard morning light when the train crawled into Mandalay', records Orwell, 'we parted as guiltily as any adulterous couple.' Mr. Brander dismisses this last sentence as absurd —and surely rightly. Conversations between Englishmen, criticizing the system radically with varying degrees of severity, were, he alleges, of every-day occurrence, and from my own very limited experience I should say that he was certainly right.

Before he wrote *Burmese Days*—some years after his return from Burma—Orwell also wrote his two essays—*Shooting an Elephant* and 'A Hanging'.

Shooting an Elephant begins by a description of his double mind during those closing years in Burma. On the one hand he was as infuriated as any other Englishman by the constant hostility of the Burmese. Burmese players tripped him up when he played football. The Burmese referee looked the other way. The Burmese crowd jeered and laughed. The insolence of the Buddhist priests was insuffer-

able, and he often 'thought that the greatest joy in the world would
be to drive a bayonet into a Buddhist priest's guts'. On the other
hand he had come to think that the Imperial system was evil for all
the reasons we have discussed.

From these generalizations he comes on to the particular story of
the elephant. One day in Moulmein a message came to him that an
elephant that had gone must, or mad, was ravaging the bazaar. He
went along, armed with a rifle. Arriving, he found that the elephant's
fit had passed and was convinced in his reason that there was no cause
at all to shoot it. On the other hand, the native crowd that had followed
him had clearly come out to see an elephant shot. He dared not disappoint them, and therefore, to his shame, shot the elephant—incidentally, making a considerable mess of the business. From this sorry
story he derived the lesson that in an imperial system the masters are
not really the masters. Their authority depends upon gesture and
prestige and therefore they do not dare to disappoint their subjects,
even when they know very well that what their subjects are demanding
is barbaric and foolish.

'A Hanging' appeared some time before *Burmese Days* in the
Adelphi in 1931. It is a gruesome and realistic account, most vividly
written in prose of perfect balance, of an execution which Orwell was
compelled to attend in his capacity of a police officer. In a way the
story has nothing particular to do with the imperial system, for, though
the hanging happened to take place in Burma, it might in all the
essentials of the story just as well have taken place anywhere else. We
are shown that a hanging is a horrible business—as everyone will admit
that it is—and we are bidden to draw the lesson from Orwell's
experience 'of the unspeakable wrongness of cutting a life short when
it is in full tide'. But the case is not really argued and, though I yield
to none in the vigour of my opposition to capital punishment, I do
not think that this essay is likely to advance the cause of its abolition.
For there is no hint what this man's crime had been, no discussion
whether he had been certainly guilty of it, no consideration of the
evidence whether capital punishment is an effective deterrent. If it can
first be shown that capital punishment is not an effective deterrent,
then it is reasonable to ask readers to be shocked by such stories as
this. But the unfortunate truth about murder—and hanging—stories
is that they shock but they also fascinate. If we can show that hanging
is silly, then there is hope that the reader will be more shocked than
fascinated, but, so long as people think that hanging is sensible, they

can invoke an ally of common sense against surrender to the shock and, thus disarmed, surrender instead to the fascination. The weapon of sentimentalism, which Orwell here so unashamedly uses, is not an effective weapon where perverted passions can be aroused. 'I thought then', writes Orwell in *The Road to Wigan Pier* '—I think now, for that matter—that the worst criminal who ever lived is morally superior to a hanging judge'. If by a 'hanging judge' he means 'a judge who delights in hanging' we need not quarrel with him. That indeed is a depth of wickedness beneath which it is hardly possible for a human being to sink, but, if he means by a 'hanging judge' a judge who happens to pass a capital sentence, when capital punishment is, rightly or wrongly, the law, then the sentimentality of Orwell's judgment is so extreme as to be quite unbalanced. What is certain is that you do not make capital punishment unpopular by public executions. Too many people like that sort of thing.

Yet his protest against the 'unspeakable wrongness' of capital punishment—his protest that it is wrong in itself, irrespective of its consequences—whether defensible or not, is interesting. For it is clearly a position that is only tenable on the basis of a theology. Since man is destined to die anyway, nothing could well be less self-evident than the proposition that the preservation of life for a few more years is of enormous importance. Among secularists those who maintain that capital punishment should be inflicted whenever it is to the general convenience have the better of the argument. Orwell's position is only tenable if man has a destiny beyond this world. Here was one of a number of his opinions which only made sense on the assumption of an implicit acceptance of a future life.

IV

Down and Out in Paris and London

ORWELL, as has been said, came back from Burma in 1927 and never returned there. Our ways had drifted apart and I did not know what had happened to him during those years. It was somewhere about Easter time in 1931 that he came back into my life. I received one day a letter from him, written from an address in Suffolk, from a little village which was, as he told me, on the River Orwell. He wrote to tell me of his news—that he had thrown up his job in Burma, that for the last four years he had been trying to live by his pen but up to the present had had 'nothing' published. I remember that he used the unqualified negative. It was, I found afterwards, a slight exaggeration. He speaks in *Down and Out in Paris and London* of receiving 200 francs for an article and remarks casually, 'I had sometimes earned money from newspaper articles'. He had published 'A Hanging', a chapter from *Down and Out*, called 'The Spike', and some poems of no very great merit in the *Adelphi*, but up till then his success had been negligible. In the letter he said nothing about his circumstances but he gave me no impression either that he was in want or, still less, that he was in any way condemning himself on principle to a life of poverty. I imagined him as possessing, like most English middle-class people, a small private income on which he was living quietly but without want. I remember showing his letter to a common friend and we both agreed that it looked all too much as if he was destined to the futile life of a small rentier, who lives out his days proclaiming that he is a writer without ever actually getting around to writing anything, and that it was a pity that so pleasant, able and sensible a companion should have proved too feckless or too proud to do an ordinary job of work.

His reason for reopening the acquaintance was that he had among his neighbours a Catholic lady who had a ward for whom she was anxious to provide a Catholic education and Orwell wanted my advice about the best Catholic schools.

In one of these letters he remarked in casual aside and in apology for interesting himself in a boy's Catholic education that he 'always read the *Universe* because he wanted to know what the other side was up to'. Orwell has told us in *Such, Such were the Joys* that up till the age of fourteen he accepted mechanically the Christian religion without having any sort of affection for it. Then his rejection of it took an unpleasantly aggressive form. He was told to love God but he says, 'I hated Him, just as I hated Jesus and the Hebrew patriarchs. If I had any sympathetic feelings towards any character in the Old Testament, it was towards such people as Cain, Jezebel, Haman, Agar, Sisera; in the New Testament my friends, if any, were Ananias, Caiaphas, Judas and Pontius Pilate.' This was obviously merely silly and schoolboy perversity to shock his fellows and annoy the masters. There are honourable reasons for rejecting the Christian revelation, but there are not even sensible reasons for making a hero of Ananias or Judas, and the grown-up Orwell, of course, made no pretence that there were. But his fight at that time was primarily against the school authorities and school traditions. To attack the religion of the school chapel might, it was hoped, annoy the school authorities.

Up to 1931 it had not, I think, occurred to Orwell that the Catholic Church, could be a serious factor in modern politics. His attitude, I fancy, at that time was that the teaching of the Catholic Church was clearly false but it was not a matter of much importance. Experience in Spain a few years later was of course to change that.

Why did he in his grown years think that the teaching of the Church, and indeed the teaching of Christianity, was clearly false? In a number of passages in different essays he shows himself fully conscious of the difficulty of finding a sound basis for ethics. Man should be decent and happiness is the end of Man. There are indeed a number of men who are not happy unless they are behaving decently. But there are unfortunately others whose happiness does not impose upon them any desire to behave decently. Sad experience was showing him, as the years went on, that the numbers of this second class were considerable and that there was all too much reason to believe that they would prove strong enough to destroy civilization. What sanction could one provide that would induce the bad to behave decently?

In several essays Orwell shows that he fully understands that religion provides an answer that in theory very neatly fills this gap. If you can believe that villainy, when it escapes punishment in this world, will nevertheless meet its deserts in the next and that virtue will be similarly rewarded, you have very satisfactorily provided a motive for good conduct. Nor, to refute religion's claims, was Orwell at all concerned, like a nineteenth-century rationalist or like his own hero, Samuel Butler, to play some detective game of the collation of gospel manuscripts in order to show that the New Testament story was false and that miracles did not happen. Of such games Orwell would, I think, have said that the evidence was so scanty and unreliable that an ingenious man could perfectly easily reach to his own satisfaction any conclusion which he wished to reach, and the result therefore would tell us nothing. He rejected religion on the argument of the *consensus universalis* turned inside out. The sanctions of religion, he argued, were of no use as a foundation for morality because almost nobody really believed them. A large number of people in the modern world, he argued, did not even profess to believe. Of those who professed, the great majority did not really believe. You had only to observe their conduct and you found that, whatever their professions, they always acted on an assumption that death was the end, that the values of this world were the only values and that he who escaped punishment in this world escaped it for good. It was, as he said in his review of T. S. Eliot's *Four Quartets*, idle to waste time in scholastic logic-chopping about religion because the modern man just could not believe—and there was an end of it. Religion to him was not so much false as valueless. But its collapse left a gap to be filled. 'The major problem of our time', he wrote in 'Looking Back on the Spanish War', 'is the decay of the belief in personal immortality.'

How far is he correct in his assertion of this decay? The appeal to men's observable conduct is up to a point fair. It can indeed be powerfully asserted against all of us believers that the consequences of mortal sin are so appalling that it is incredible, if we really believe what we profess, that we should ever commit sin. And yet we do commit it. But of course we can with Bishop Blougram just as powerfully turn that argument the other way round. If it is illogical to assert a certainty of belief it is much more illogical to assert the certainty of unbelief.

> All we've gained is, that belief,
> As unbelief before, shakes us by fits,
> Confounds us like its predecessor. Where's
> The gain? How can we guard our unbelief?
> Make it bear fruit to us?—the problem here.
> Just when we are safest there's a sunset-touch,
> A fancy from a flower-bell, some one's death,
> A chorus-ending from Euripides—
> And that's enough for fifty hopes and fears

As old and new at once as Nature's self,
To rap and knock and enter in our soul,
Take hands and dance there, a fantastic ring,
Round the ancient idol on his base again—
The grand Perhaps! We look on helplessly.
There the old misgivings, crooked questions are—
This good God—what He could do, if He would,
Would if He could—then must have done long since . . .
All we have gained then by our unbelief
Is a life of doubt diversified by faith
For one of faith diversified by doubt.
We called the chess-board white—we call it black.

For this assertion of a certainty of unbelief Orwell can be fairly criticized.

Throughout this correspondence of 1931 Orwell continued to sign himself to me 'Eric Blair'. I should have been astonished had it been otherwise. I first heard of him as George Orwell when he published his first book, *Down and Out in Paris and London*, in 1933, but he had, I think, used it as a *nom de plume* for a few obscure articles before that. It was the name by which he generally called himself for the rest of his life, although up at any rate until the end of the war he sometimes used 'Eric Blair' in his private affairs and he never changed his name by deed-poll. The reasons that he gave for changing his name are oddly unconvincing. He complained that Blair was a Scots name and that he disliked Scotland because of its association with the deer-forests about which his rich schoolfellows used to boast at his private school. Gordon Comstock in *Keep the Aspidistra Flying* has elements of a self-portrait, and of the name Gordon Comstock he writes:

> Gordon Comstock was a pretty bloody name, but then Gordon came of a pretty bloody family. The 'Gordon' part of it was Scotch, of course. The prevalence of such names nowadays is merely a part of the Scotchification of England that has been going on these last fifty years. 'Gordon', 'Colin', 'Malcolm', 'Donald'—these are the gifts of Scotland to the world, along with golf, whisky, porridge and the works of Barrie and Stevenson.

But he did not dislike Scotland sufficiently to stop him from going to live there at the end of his life. We most of us develop a certain boredom with the names that we have borne through life, but this boredom does not as a general rule drive us without reason to the

eccentricity of choosing a new name. We reflect that the new name
will soon become as boring as the old. He liked the little River Orwell
by which at the time he was living, and, if he was to choose a new
name, it was perhaps as natural to choose that as another. As for why he
chose 'George', I have no sure explanation. Mr. Brander says that it
was 'a Christian name that naturally goes with Orwell', but this is a
judgment to which I can attach no meaning. There was at this time
of his life at any rate, as *The Road to Wigan Pier* shows, something of
the 'muck mystic' in him in his hatred of industrialism, and I think
that he chose a name that by its Greek etymology linked him with
the land.

But why did he want to choose at all?

The Road to Wigan Pier, I think, again gives the answer. After his
return from Burma he was doing much more than reorientate his
political views. He was passing through a spiritual crisis. 'I had got to
expiate', he writes, ' . . . I wanted to submerge myself, to get right
down among the oppressed, to be one of them and on their side
against the tyrants. And chiefly because I had to think out everything
in solitude, I had carried my hatred of oppression to extraordinary
lengths. At that time failure seemed to me the only virtue. Every suspicion of self-advancement, even to "succeed" in life to the extent of
making a few hundreds a year, seemed to me spiritually ugly, a species
of bullying.' He soon reacted from the extravagances of this faith, but
it was powerful with him for a time, and its power made it seem
necessary to him to break utterly with his past, to blot out all that had
been—like Nicodemus, to be born again.

I have not attempted to follow in detail the pattern of Orwell's
adventures between 1927 and 1933, when he published his first book,
Down and Out in Paris and London. 'I had several years of fairly severe
poverty', is all that he tells us, 'during which I was, amongst other
things, a dish-washer, a private tutor and a teacher in cheap private
schools.' He lived for a year and a half in Paris. The experiences of
Down and Out in Paris and London were substantially autobiographical.
'Nearly all the incidents described there actually happened', he tells
us, 'though they have been arranged.' The story, if we reckon it up,
is a story of two months in Paris followed by one in London, and the
months are summer months. They followed on eighteen months spent
at the Hôtel des Trois Moineaux. That is to say, if he returned from
Burma in 1927, these adventures cannot have happened before 1929.
He was, so *The Road to Wigan Pier* tells us, seeing unemployment in

England for the first time at first hand in 1928. So his eighteen months cannot have been spent quite continuously in Paris. Yet we know from his essay on 'How the Poor Die' that he was in Paris in February of 1929—in a hospital and in such straitened circumstances that he had to go to a non-fee-paying public ward. Nor can his London tramp experiences have happened after 1929 because Bozo, the London pavement artist, speaks of Churchill as being still Chancellor of the Exchequer—which he ceased to be in the autumn of 1929. Therefore these experiences happened in the summer of 1929, but, since he speaks in a footnote of having returned later to the 'spike' at Ide Hill, Orwell was on the tramp again after that date.

A more important question is the parallel question to that of why he changed his name. Why was he down and out at all? He gives no explanation in the book, and every indication is that his condition was quite unnecessary in every normal economic sense. He merely tells us the unvarnished fact that his money was running out and that therefore he had to start looking for a job. 'Hitherto I had not thought about the future, but now I realized that I must do something at once. I decided to start looking for a job', he writes. Such zany fecklessness was quite contrary to his nature, nor, even supposing that all the luck was against him, was he without friends to whom he could turn. Mr. Fyvell in his article in the *World Review* has told us how Orwell told him that he 'had little money, few social connections and no special trade; it was a time of unemployment; a respectable job would have been difficult'. But it would quite certainly have been by no means impossible. Whatever he may have told Mr. Fyvell, he had in fact friends, and among them one would certainly have found him a job of some sort. But the fact was that in his letters he never asked for one. He deliberately kept from us his need of a job—and that, quite certainly, because he did not want one, because he wanted to go 'down and out', independent and unobliged to anyone.

His pride did not prevent him from turning to a friend nor his hatred of discipline from taking a job in the end. He does take jobs in the end—a *plongeur*'s job in Paris, the guardianship of an idiot in England. He does in the end borrow from his friend, B., when he can stand the Paris job no longer. Why did he not turn to B. in the first place? When, returning to England, he finds that the job that B. offered him is not immediately available, he knows that he will borrow again from B. in the end but does not like to do so immediately. 'Sooner or later I should have to go to B. for some more money, but it seemed hardly decent to do so yet.' Why not? Why, if he was to go sooner or later, should he not go sooner as B. knew very well that he had no resources until the job was available? B. pops in and out of the story in a bewildering fashion. Sometimes Orwell can borrow from him; sometimes, although B. expresses his willingness to lend, he cannot.

There is no explanation within the terms of *Down and Out in Paris and London*. But in *Down and Out* Orwell was concerned to write a book of straightforward reminiscences, free of psychological complications. 'It is a fairly trivial story', he writes, 'and I can only hope that it has been interesting as a travel diary is interesting.' He did not want to trouble the reader with spiritual metaphysics. But the sentences quoted from *The Road to Wigan Pier* provide the key. This was a period of profound spiritual crisis for Orwell. He went down and out not through necessity but because he deliberately chose to go down and out—to identify himself with the oppressed. Having had the experience, he found that it was not as spiritually valuable as he had imagined. 'Once I had been among them and accepted by them, I should have touched bottom and—this is what I felt—I was aware even then that it was irrational—part of my guilt would drop from me', he writes. '. . . Down there in the squalid and, as a matter of fact, horribly boring sub-world of the tramp I had a feeling of release, of adventure, which seems absurd when I look back but which was sufficiently vivid at the time.'

'You discover the boredom which is inseparable from poverty', he writes again. A passing experience of such poverty is valuable but not a permanent condition. 'It is a kind of duty', to quote from *The Road to Wigan Pier*, 'to see and smell such places now and again, especially smell them, lest you forget that they exist; though perhaps it is better not to stay there too long.'

Down and Out in Paris and London begins with Orwell in a slummy little hotel, the Hôtel des Trois Moineaux, in the Rue du Coq d'Or in Paris. He has lived there for eighteen months and has suddenly discovered—there is nothing for it but to take the tale as it is told to us—that his money is running out, that he cannot afford to live on the very unremunerative English lessons which he gives and that therefore he must look for a job. Before his job-hunting has got under way, an Italian fellow guest has stolen from him all his money and made away with it. He has only forty-seven francs left in the world, with the franc at twopence. He is truly down and out. He takes what he can to the pawnshop and ekes out things for a few days of starvation. Then he remembers Boris. Boris was a White Russian, an ex-captain of the Second Siberian Rifles who had promised him that he would always have a job if Orwell ever found himself in need. He makes his way round to Boris' lodgings, only to find, alas, that Boris is in even worse plight than himself. He is living in the room of a Jew, who owes him a debt and who is paying it off at the rate of two francs a day, and is both jobless and starving. Boris is a creature of fatuous optimism who is always certain that things will soon turn out all right. He will get a job as a waiter and will then worm Orwell into the same hotel. But in the meanwhile they tramp the streets together. They have nothing left to pawn. For two and a half days they have nothing at all to eat. Boris tries to get Orwell a job writing some articles for a Communist newspaper, but the so-called Communists turn out to be frauds who take some money off them and then decamp. At last after three weeks Boris does succeed in getting a job as a waiter in the Hotel X. He makes it his first business to tell Orwell the good news. 'After ten or twelve hours' work, and with his game leg, his first thought had been to walk three kilometres to my hotel and tell me the good news', Orwell writes. For a few days Boris keeps Orwell with food that he is able to smuggle out of the hotel. Then he succeeds in getting him a job there as a *plongeur*.

For a fortnight they both work in the hotel, one of the biggest and best in Paris, and we are given a vivid picture of the chaos and fury of life in the kitchens of a big hotel, of the quarrels and insults of the Italian waiters, the fraudulence of the door-keeper, the dirty habits of the cook, the soft and quiet deference in the dining-room on the one side of the baize-door and the raging and blaspheming madness on the other side. Then after a fortnight a new Russian restaurant, the Auberge de Jehan Cottard, where Boris and Orwell had been promised employment, is at last ready, and they transfer to it. Boris is again waiter and Orwell is again *plongeur*. But the Hotel X., with all its defects, was a prosperous and efficient hotel. This restaurant is an incompetent fraud. The hours are longer, the conditions of work worse, the chaos more appalling. Orwell sticks to it as best he can for a fortnight, and then writes in despair to his friend B. in England. B. tells him that he has got him a job as keeper to a tame imbecile and sends him £5 for his fare home. He at once gives notice to the Auberge de Jehan Cottard, lounges about for a couple of days, saying farewell to his friends, and then returns to England.

Arriving there, he finds that the job will not be ready for him for another three weeks. Though he knows that he will borrow money from B. again in the end, somewhat incomprehensibly he does not feel able to borrow it at once. Even more incomprehensibly B., though he knows his plight and though afterwards he is going to show himself perfectly ready to provide money, yet lets him go without asking him how he will manage.

The result is that he is left with nineteen shillings and sixpence to fend for himself for at least three weeks. He exchanges his suit for tramp's clothing and goes to a common lodging house. Before long he is reduced to a single halfpenny. Then he makes friends with an Irishman, called Paddy, and they set out together on the tramp from 'spike' to 'spike'. He spends the three weeks in company with Paddy and with a strange pavement artist, called Bozo, who hates God and loves astronomy.

This bare summary does but little justice to the book. It is a book of most brilliant and lively descriptions, and the main mark of it, as Mr. Brander most truly points out, is the contrast between the high spirits with which he meets calamity in France and the low spirits with which he meets it in England. In France there is no attempt to belittle the appalling suffering of poverty, and the baize-door in the Hotel X. separates two nations—the comfortable and the insecure, the swindled and the swindlers.

It is an instructive sight to see the waiter going into a hotel dining-room. As he passes the door a sudden change comes over him. The set of his shoulders alters; all the dirt and hurry and irritation have dropped off in an instant. He glides over the carpet, with a solemn priest-like air. I remember our assistant *maître d'hotel*, a fiery Italian, pausing at the dining-room door to address an apprentice who had broken a bottle of wine, shaking his fist above his head he yelled (luckily the door was more or less soundproof): '*Tu me fais*—Do you call yourself a waiter, you young bastard? You a waiter! You're not fit to scrub floors in the brothel your mother came from. *Maquereau!*'

Words failing him, he turned to the door and as he opened it he delivered a final insult in the same manner as Squire Western in *Tom Jones*. Then he entered the dining-room and sailed across it dish in hand, graceful as a swan. Ten seconds later he was bowing reverently to a customer. And you could not help thinking, as you saw him bow and smile with that benign smile of the trained waiter, that the customer was put to shame by having such an aristocrat to serve him.

But Orwell tells the story of the hotel's swindles, of the meretricious service and pretentious, dirty adulterated food with high-spirited lack of pity. For all his self-identification with the oppressed, for all his vow at the end of this book never again to 'enjoy a meal at a smart restaurant', Orwell knew good food and wine when he saw them, and despised those who did not know them. He despised the rich not so much because they lived well as because, while they had the money to live well, they lived expensively but barbarously. The clientèle of the Hotel X. were mostly rich, uncouth Americans and Orwell has no pity for the impositions that were practised upon them.

They would stuff themselves with disgusting American 'cereals' and eat marmalade at tea, and drink vermouth after dinner, and order a *poulet à la reine* at a hundred francs and then souse it in Worcester sauce. One customer from Pittsburg dined every night in his bedroom on grape-nuts, scrambled eggs and cocoa. Perhaps it hardly matters whether such people are swindled or not.

The most memorable pages in the Paris part of the book are not those which tell of Orwell's work but of his all too scanty leisure—of the drinking on Saturday nights at the bistro at the foot of the Hôtel des Trois Moineaux.

The brick-floored room, fifteen feet square, was packed with twenty people, and the dim air with smoke. The noise was deafening, for everyone was either talking at the top of his voice or singing. Sometimes it was just a confused din of voices; sometimes everyone would burst out together in the same song—the 'Marseillaise', or the 'Internationale', or 'Madelon', or 'les Fraises et les Framboises'. Azaya, a great clumping peasant girl who worked fourteen hours a day in a glass factory, sang a song about, '*Il a perdu ses pantalons, tout en dansant le Charleston*'. Her friend, Marinette, a thin, dark Corsican girl of obstinate virtue, tied her knees together and danced the *danse de ventre*. The old Rougiers wandered in and out, cadging drinks and trying to tell a long, involved story about someone who had once cheated them over a bedstead. R., cadaverous and silent, sat in his corner quietly boozing. Charlie, drunk, half danced, half staggered to and fro with a glass of sham absinthe balanced in one fat hand, pinching the women's breasts and declaiming poetry. People played darts and dice for drinks. Manuel, a Spaniard, dragged the girls to the bar and shook the dice-box against their bellies for luck. Madame F. stood at the bar rapidly pouring chopines of wine through the pewter funnel, with a wet dishcloth always handy, because every man in the room tried to make love to her. Two children, bastards of big Louis the bricklayer, sat in a corner sharing a glass of sirop. Everyone was very happy, overwhelmingly certain that the world was a good place and we a notable set of people.

And there was Charlie with his extraordinary stories of love, and Furex, who was a Communist when he was sober but became violently patriotic and nationalist when he was drunk.

In contrast the English pages are sombre reading. The whole atmosphere is overcast by the weight of a lonely and humourless charity —by the Salvation Army and earnest Methodists giving cups of tea in exchange for hymn-singing, by the efforts of poor bewildered men to outwit a senseless and inhuman bumbledom, by the system that keeps the man without resources continuously on purposeless peripatetic and the cruelty that segregates the sexes. He meets no vivid character in all his English experiences save only Bozo, the pavement artist, and Bozo had lived much of his life in France and greatly preferred France to England. There is all the difference in the world between poverty on wine and poverty on tea, and Orwell himself ever afterwards trained his moustache to make him look as much like a French *ouvrier* as possible.

Brilliant descriptive writer as he was, Orwell was never content with mere description. He liked also to raise questions—questions that contained within themselves a very fundamental criticism of things as they are. Thus, what need is there for *plongeurs* at all? he asks. Why are there tramps? He was so fond of clear-cut answers, so contemptuous of grey evasions that he sometimes pretended that the answers were clearer than they were. Thus, on *plongeurs*, he notes, very truly, that a large part of the work done in expensive hotels and restaurants is simply unnecessary. The patrons are made to pay for things and workers are made to work for things that can hardly give pleasure to anybody. So they are, and one might well ask, Who wants all this useless and insignificant decoration to pillars in the lounge or dining-room? Would not the workers have been better employed on work elsewhere and would not every guest have been the happier if such meaningless, pompous adornment had simply not been there? Who wants an absurd commissionaire dressed up as a bogus Cossack to push round revolving doors that one could much more easily push round for oneself? Who wants an orchestra to make a noise as one eats—a noise which those who want it cannot properly hear above the hubbub but is just sufficient to make all conversation a nervous strain? Would we not all gladly pay a little extra on our bills for the orchestra not to play?

Orwell deploys arguments of this sort with characteristic force, but of course the only comment on them in this context is that they have no bearing on *plongeurs*. Whatever else the guest may not want in a hotel, he does want clean plates. Orwell may well have been right— I expect that he was—in saying that Parisian restaurants in 1929, owing to the meanness of proprietors, were very old-fashioned and inadequate in their scullery-equipment, that by racks and more space and so on the work of the *plongeur* could have been made much easier. But this, though doubtless true, is not in the least startling. The argument that there need not be *plongeurs* at all, though not true, is startling. Orwell always liked to use startling arguments.

So, too, with beggars. Why should beggars be despised? Why should begging be an offence? It is idle hypocrisy, he argues, to pretend that we despise beggars because of the way in which they make their income. Nobody cares in the least how anybody makes his income. The only reason why we despise beggars is because they only make a small income. This is perhaps a half-truth, but it is certainly not more than a half-truth. The argument against beggars is that production is necessary for the well-being of society and that beggars consume without producing. Admittedly such an argument could hardly carry its full force at such a time as that in which Orwell wrote when there were several millions of unemployed, but he puts the argument forward as a general argument and it is as a general argument that it must be treated. Now it is indeed true that there are others besides beggars who consume without producing, but it is not true that those who take it upon themselves to pass moral judgments on the way in which their fellow citizens make their living do not care in the least how these others get their money. Those who defend a system in which some people live on unearned and inherited wealth defend it on arguments. They argue that without a possibility of inheritance there would not be a sufficient motive for saving. They argue that it is to the advantage of society that there should be a small number of its members freed from the anxiety of earning a living, that the greater part of the cultural achievement of mankind has come from members of this class, that, if here and there a man of independent income uses his independence to live a life of wholly useless luxury, that is doubtless in itself an evil, but that on balance this system justifies itself. The arguments may be good or bad, but at least it is only fair to recognize that they are arguments—that Orwell is unjust in pretending that no one has ever faced the question.

Or, again, it is doubtless true that of those who earn livings some earn them by wholly dubious means—by rendering services to society that society would be better without—by taking advantage of their fellows' necessity. But it is simply not true that 'nobody minds' such activities. Those who tolerated them—tolerated harsh employers, scrim-shanking workmen, peddlers of meretricious entertainment—did so because they thought on balance that it did more good than harm to allow these evils to work themselves out—that on balance it would do more harm than good to have the State interfering in every detail of life. They never pretended that every activity that was not interfered with by legislation was in itself good. Again, as I say, they may have been right or wrong. They may have drawn the line at the right place or not, but where Orwell is manifestly unfair is in his suggestion that nobody ever considered the problem.

But he is on much stronger ground when he asks why begging should be illegal. Certainly, if society is to be free at all, it is only right for the law to interfere with the action of a citizen when there is an overwhelming case for doing so. It is hard to see that the inconvenience which the passer-by suffers from the importunity of beggars constitutes such an overwhelming case and, as so often happens in such instances, the beggar who puts himself technically in the right by selling matches or boot-laces easily makes such laws ridiculous.

In the same way Orwell is again on strong ground when he asks, Why should there be tramps? The reasons most commonly advanced for the existence of tramps—that some people like tramping, that the tramps tramp to avoid work—are evidently ridiculous, and Orwell's suggestion that allotments should be attached to the casual ward and that the tramp should stay at the casual ward for a reasonable time and not move on until there is work for him is a suggestion worth consideration.

There is much that Orwell has to teach us in *Down and Out in Paris and London*, and he is able to teach us much because he has learnt much. Whatever the reservations that should be made—and that he himself, to do him justice, freely makes—about the spiritual difference between one who embraced that life voluntarily, temporarily and with the prospect of escape and those who are condemned to it irretrievably and by necessity, yet clearly Orwell emerged from it with an understanding of it that is not possessed by many writers. He had had experience and he had profited from experience, and, when he lectures us on the wickedness of harsh moral judgments on such people, based on superficial knowledge, he is reading a lecture which he has a right to read and we a duty to accept. But we must face it that in this life he had acquired not only experience but also pride. From now onwards —from his next work, *The Road to Wigan Pier*, on for the rest of his life—there was always a strong note of contempt for 'intellectuals' and sheltered people to whom 'nothing had happened'. The contrast with himself was clear. There was more than a touch of mock modesty in the penultimate paragraph in *Down and Out in Paris and London*. 'I should like to know', he writes, 'people like Mario and Paddy and Bill the moocher, not from casual encounters but intimately; I should like to understand what really goes on in the souls of *plongeurs* and tramps and Embankment sleepers. At present I do not feel that I have seen more than the fringe of poverty.' The 'fringe' was more than other writers had touched.

He was proud of what he had endured. He had reason to be proud, for he had shown at the least great courage, and, in so far as his contempt was reserved for those literary people who have passed straight from an ancient University to the chatter of cocktail-parties about royalty rates, or to pedantic sociologists who spend their lives in swopping statistics about how to rearrange the poor whom they have never met, it was abundantly justified. But there are experiences and experiences and if Orwell was richer in some experiences than his fellow writers, there were others in which he was poorer, and he was more conscious of his riches than of his poverty. Sometimes he would solemnly lecture his more sheltered companions on habits or phrases which he from his greater experience alleged that he knew to be prevalent among the poor—such as for instance that they never used the word 'bloody'—which it was hard for even the most sheltered to take quite seriously.

Orwell was what the jargon calls an extrovert. To him experience meant unusual events which happened to him in the external world.

The obstinate questionings of the soul within he either dismissed impatiently as unanswerable or in a plain, blunt, Johnsonian fashion, striking the stone with his stick, 'refuted Berkeley thus'. Like a philistine before a picture, he almost boasted that he did not know much about morals but that he knew what he liked, and he dismissed with impatience the sophist who asked him why he liked it and by what right he liked it. In a world so confused by the psychologists' explanations of all moral choices there was something robust and admirable in such bluff, hearty good sense. Yet there are the secret places of the soul. When every allowance has been made for fools and charlatans and cocktail-parties, there are rare beings who genuinely try to wrestle with the 'mystery of things' and who cannot, even if they will, be put off from asking the ultimate questions, simply because those questions cannot be easily answered. Of such beings Orwell had an insufficient understanding.

There was another defect in his experience on a more mundane plane. Whatever the handicaps of being educated as a poor boy among richer, such an education was an admirable inoculation against the danger of the worship of what Professor Gilbert Murray has made Aeschylus call 'the man of mere success'. He was much better protected against that danger than he would have been if he had 'come up the hard way'. His lack of a tradition of command did not prevent him from behaving with responsibility as a police officer in Burma nor of admiring the quality of responsibility in others. But he had no understanding of the feelings of those who desire large responsibilities. I am the last to idealize such men, to deny 'God's scorn for all men governing', to belittle the corrupting dangers of power. Yet Orwell condemned their motives as too crudely evil. Dangerous as are the temptations of power, yet some one must brave the dangers and wield it if society is to go on. It is because he never set himself to the task of understanding such men—like them or not—that, while Orwell shows us so clearly what is wrong with the tendencies of modern society, it is almost impossible to discover what he would have us do to curb those tendencies.

Interesting book as it is, the most interesting pages in *Down and Out in Paris and London* are certainly the pages that are not there. It must be read side by side with *The Road to Wigan Pier*. Among his companions in Paris and London Orwell found much virtue. He learnt many lessons, but clearly there was not one of them that could have even begun to understand what he was talking about if he had tried to explain to them the motives that had led him to their life. How could he have expected them to do so? and how could he have expected that he would do them any good by identifying himself with their lot, except in so far as the identification was merely temporary in order that he might gain experience? The trouble about identifying oneself with the oppressed is that there is nothing less like the oppressed than he who voluntarily identifies himself with them. In all the world there is no gap so large as that between those who are driven to poverty by necessity and those who voluntarily embrace it. The truly poor can much more easily understand the rich than they can understand those who voluntarily embrace poverty. For to them taking riches when you can get them makes sense.

It is hard to say for certain if Orwell did expect anything more than a little experience from his adventures, but it appears from *The Road to Wigan Pier* that he did. If so, what was it—what spiritual vision or satisfaction—that he did expect? The truth surely is once more that all this language—'expiation from guilt', 'self-identification with the oppressed'—only makes sense within a religious framework and that Orwell demanded a particular religious experience, while at the same time violently denying the reality of all religious experience. There is always this contradiction lying behind his denunciations of 'crankiness' and his appeals to a sometimes too facile 'common sense'.

V

A Clergyman's Daughter

Down and Out in Paris and London appeared in 1933. Orwell's next book to be published was *Burmese Days* in 1934, but his next book after that clearly showed that his Parisian and London experiences had compelled him to ask himself the questions, Is there spiritual value in the acceptance of poverty? and how can there be such a value except within a religious framework? His very avoidance of these insistent questions in *Down and Out in Paris and London* for fear that they would spoil the reminiscent and anecdotal character of his writing compelled him the more insistently to face them once he had got this first book off his mind.

In these years, he tells us, 'I was, amongst other things, a dish-washer, a private tutor and a teacher in cheap private schools.' We have seen him as a dishwasher in *Down and Out in Paris and London* and the closing pages of that book leaves him as a private tutor to a lunatic. That job did not last long. Later 'for a year or more I was also a part time assistant in a London book-shop'. It was a sprawling great shop on a corner near Hampstead Heath. He had rented an upper room from the bookseller for twelve and sixpence a week, and, when he found it difficult to pay, the bookseller allowed him to work off his rent by attending to the shop in the afternoons. He was there, according to Mr. Hopkinson, for about eighteen months between 1932 and 1934. He was also 'by now doing a certain amount of casual journalism— in particular contributing to the *Adelphi*, then edited by Sir Richard Rees, an Etonian contemporary who befriended him'.

The work in the bookshop was 'interesting in itself', he wrote, 'but had the disadvantage of compelling me to live in London which I detest'. However, he used the experience of these years to provide himself with the background for his two London novels, *A Clergyman's Daughter* and *Keep the Aspidistra Flying*, which were his next two works, the one appearing in 1935 and the other in 1936. In *A Clergyman's Daughter* he made use of his experience in a private school and in *Keep the Aspidistra Flying* of his experience in the bookshop.

He tackled first the more obstinate of his two fundamental questions —the questions of the claims of religion and of the nature and place of faith. To say that he tackled the question is not to say that he answered it satisfactorily. He certainly did not answer it to his own satisfaction, for he soon came greatly to dislike *A Clergyman's Daughter.* He always afterwards refused to allow that book to be republished and bought up and destroyed all the copies on which he could lay his hands, so that it is today a book very difficult to come by. Nevertheless, if we are seeking to follow out the development of his mind it is important to see where he stood at this moment.

The form of the novel, apart from its substance, is open to grave criticism. It falls into five phases. The first phase describes a day in the life of Dorothy Hare, daughter, housekeeper and for all practical purposes unpaid curate and manager of the parish to her selfish and incompetent widower father, the Reverend Charles Hare, Rector of St. Athelstan's, Knype Hill, Suffolk. At the end of the day, for no very clear reason—but doubtless aphasia comes like that—she loses her memory and runs away. She comes-to ten days later in the New Kent Road in London. She has no notion, nor are we ever told, how she got there nor does she remember who she is. She knows nothing of herself except that she has lost her memory. She gets picked up by a gang who are on their way to the hop-picking in Kent and joins up with them. The second phase tells of her life among the hop-pickers, which goes on until her companion, Nobby, is arrested for theft. Then the memory of her identity comes back to her. She discovers from a newspaper that the world has been ringing with the story of her disappearance and that the evil-minded gossip in Knype Hill, Mrs. Semprill, has spread abroad the rumour that she has escaped with an easy-living neighbour, a Mr. Warburton. Dorothy at once writes off to her father to explain the truth and asks him to send her £2 so that she can come home. Her father had at first been very angry at her desertion and had believed the tales that had been spread about her, though he had pretended not to. Yet, selfish as he is, he is not quite so hard-hearted as to ignore Dorothy's appeal altogether. But he is dilatory and incompetent. Instead of writing to her direct he sends off £10 to a baronet cousin of his, asking the cousin to get in touch with Dorothy and find her a job. As a result of this conduct on the part of her father —conduct which does not read very plausibly—Dorothy receives no answer at the Kentish post office to the letter which she has sent to her father. So, thinking herself deserted, she goes off penniless to

London, hoping to pick up there some menial job for herself. She meets with no success, and the third phase of the book is concerned with the weird description of a night spent by a company of down-and-outs, of whom Dorothy is one, in Trafalgar Square. To keep out the bitter cold they wrap themselves together like cocoons in newspapers.

Shortly after that Dorothy is arrested for begging and on her emergence from the cells is approached by her baronet cousin's butler who has succeeded in tracing her. He takes her to her cousin's house. Her cousin is willing to do his duty in getting her a job but is at first somewhat at a loss to know what job would be available for a young lady with no qualifications whatever. His cynical solicitor solves that ·problem without hesitation by recommending teaching, and the fourth phase describes Dorothy's life for two terms as mistress at Mrs. Creevy's appalling and crookedly conducted private school. From that she is at one and the same time dismissed and rescued. Mrs. Semprill has gone too far in her scandal-mongering. The local bank-manager has sued her and won a verdict against her. She has had to leave the neighbourhood. She is wholly discredited and by consequence Dorothy received fully back into the favour of Knype Hill. Mr. Warburton comes to tell her the good news. She returns to her father, refusing Mr. Warburton's offer of marriage in the train on the way, and the fifth and final phase of the book shows her taking up again exactly the same life in all externals as she was living at its beginning.

With most of the aspects of life about which Orwell wrote, he was very much better acquainted than I and I accept him as my master on their details, but it does so happen that I know a good deal more about Anglican rectories than he did, and I cannot find the portrait of the Reverend Charles Hare or of St. Athelstan's Church life at all convincing. It is not incredible that a rector should be selfish or that he should be incompetent. He might well be in debt, but it is hard to believe that any clergyman could be so naïvely self-deceiving in his selfishness. Even if he had no natural capacity to see the contradiction between his practice and his principles, some one in these days would have at some time forcibly pointed out to him that contrast, so that at the least he would not have been able to carry it off with that absurd self-confidence which Orwell imagines. Nor did Orwell know very clearly how Anglican parish-life is organized nor what is the degree of responsibility of a rector for the upkeep of the fabric of his church. Churchwardens and parish-councils are mysteries beyond him. Nor, to move on to another plane, is it very probable that the rector's daughter, a rector's daughter who combined Dorothy's simple-minded piety with her morbid horror of all sexual acts, would have continued to visit Mr. Warburton in the evenings after he had attempted to seduce her—not even though she was deceived by his pretence that there would be another guest present.

Yet, beyond that, it is a criticism of this first phase that it occupies nearly a third of the book—ninety-three pages out of 317—and that in it nothing happens. One day is much the same as any other day in Dorothy's life. She is not conscious of being under any strain that is likely to lead to a breakdown at its end. Nothing happens that is even unusual except Mr. Warburton's kissing of her and, repugnant as that was, it was not his first attempt at seduction. If Orwell wished to give us a picture of the strain and futility of a life against which her sub-conscious was reacting, he should have concentrated his picture much more tightly.

The second phase begins with Dorothy's awakening in the New Kent Road. She is conscious, but she has not as yet any memory of her past or her identity. She is picked up by Nobby and his gang and taken down to the hop-picking. These pages contain some attractive anecdotes, illustrative of the kindness of poor hop-pickers to one another, but they are in reality an interesting documentary of the life of hop-pickers rather than a part of the story. There is no development of the character either of Dorothy or of her associates. Dorothy, when she has lost her memory, has lost with it all the habits of her past life. She, who in Knype Hill had been a girl of severely strict conduct, takes at once to the escapades of her new associates and joins Nobby without hesitation in his expeditions of robbery. Whether people, when they lose their memories, lose at the same time their past moral prejudices and take their characters from their new company is for the psychologist or the doctor to tell us. But, if so, it greatly detracts from the value of victims of aphasia as heroines of novels. For art requires a certain respect for the unities. A wholly discrete character may be medically possible, but she is artistically unsatisfactory.

Suddenly after Nobby's arrest the memory of her past comes back to Dorothy and, as soon as she remembers her past, she loathes her present and is anxious to get back to Knype Hill. Her father's apparent refusal to receive her, which she deduces from not getting any answer to her letters, leaves her with no alternative but to go up to London without resources and seek for work. Her search is unsuccessful because she is obviously a lady and no employer is willing to engage as a servant a lady without resources, luggage or reference, arguing, as they quite sensibly do, that such a person can only be in such a situation because of having done something disreputable. She is therefore quite soon driven down and out, and the third phase of the book consists substantially of the strange story of the down-and-outs spending their night on the benches in Trafalgar Square, being moved on from time to time by a policeman. The scene is written in dramatic form, and the change in form heightens the unreality of the scene. For it is written as if Trafalgar Square was dominated by this company. But at the beginning of the scene it is only ten o'clock, and at ten o'clock Trafalgar Square is still filled with the comings and goings of ordinary people. Such scenes as Orwell depicts may be going on on its benches, but at least they do not so dominate the life of the Square that they impose themselves on the ordinary passer-by. The conversation of this bizarre troop is incoherent. The most outstanding member of it is an unpleasant, unfrocked clergyman, Mr. Talboys, the late Rector of Little Fawley-cum-Dewsbury. He conducts an inconsequent, blasphemous running conversation, illuminated with Latin and ecclesiastical tags. It is hardly to be believed that the genuine down-and-outs would have tolerated such a wholly unintelligible monologue. At one point he approaches the blasphemy of a Black Mass, starting to recite the Lord's Prayer backwards, and a stage direction (if that be the phrase) tells us,

As he reaches the first word of the prayer he tears the consecrated bread across. The blood runs out of it. There is a rolling sound, as of thunder, and the landscape changes. Dorothy's feet are very cold. Monstrous winged shapes of Demons and Archdemons are dimly visible, moving to and fro. Something, beak or claw, closes upon Dorothy's shoulder.

It is impossible from the confused context to get clear what Mr. Talboys is supposed to have said or done, or whether Dorothy is supposed to have dreamed this scene. 'Had she dreamed the things he said or had he really said them?' she was herself afterwards to ask and get no answer.

In any event the experience seems to make no permanent impression on Dorothy. When she refers to Mr. Talboys afterwards, she refers to him—justly enough—as 'that dreadful unfrocked clergyman', and diabolism she dismisses without qualification as 'silly'. It has no bearing one way or the other on the question of her faith with which the book is primarily concerned. Again the main criticism of this grotesque scene is that, eery and impressive as it in some ways is, valuable, it may be, as a kind of fantastic documentary on the life of the down-and-outs, it is as a part of this story an irrelevant interlude. Dorothy is but a minor member of this company. Her contributions to its conversation are confined to a few platitudinous complaints about the cold and the other characters, colourful as some of them are, disappear henceforth from the book.

After a number of other experiences of the same sort, not recorded in detail, Dorothy is arrested for begging and, on leaving the court, is taken back by the butler to Sir Thomas Prawnishly's house. Sir Thomas is a comic stage baronet.

'Look here, Blyth, dammit,' said Sir Thomas Prawnishly—Blyth was the butler's name—'I suppose you've seen all this damn stuff in the newspapers, hey? This rector's daughter stuff? About this damned niece of mine.'

Orwell complains in *The Road to Wigan Pier* that the conversation of the English upper classes is so impoverished that there is no way of putting them into a book except by guying them. 'When a novelist has to put a definitely upper class person—a duke or a baronet or what-not—into one of his stories, he guys him more or less instinctively,' he writes. I do not know that that is true. There are baronets and baronets, and Orwell had met plenty who did not talk in the least like Sir Thomas Prawnishly. Sir Richard Rees was a baronet and he did not talk at all like that. But the truth was that plenty of other people had written about baronets and Orwell did not much care for writing about those of whom others had written. Usual experiences were to him the experiences of people like Mr. Cyril Connolly and the Comstocks to whom 'nothing ever happened', and therefore, having to write about Sir Thomas Prawnishly, he preferred to guy him—which was fair enough, even though he might, one feels, have introduced a little more subtlety into the guying.

But it is a comic stroke of genius to make the solicitor, when asked what jobs are open to a totally unqualified girl, give his unhesitating advice for teaching, and thus present Orwell with his opportunity for his gorgeously comic picture of life at Mrs. Creevy's disgusting school, with which the fourth phase of the book is filled. Orwell had had some experience of teaching and cheap private schools, and he felt strongly that their uninspected freedom was a scandal. No one can doubt the scandal of the worst of these schools, and Orwell makes the most of his opportunity of exposing them. The formula upon which Mrs. Creevy runs her school is a perfectly simple one. It is a money-making concern—and it is nothing else. She makes no pretence to any interest in education. She is simply selling a fraudulent commodity to some very stupid parents.

'After all the fees *are* what matter aren't they?' [she says to Dorothy] . . . 'As for all this stuff about "developing the children's minds" as you call it, it's neither here nor there. It's the fees I'm after, not developing the children's minds. After all, it's no more than common sense. It's not to be supposed as anyone'd go to all the trouble of keeping school and having the house turned upside down by a pack of brats, if it wasn't that there's a bit of money to be made out of it. The fees come first, and everything else comes afterwards.'

Or again:

'I don't want you to go thinking that all the girls are to be treated alike. They aren't—not by a long way, they aren't. Different girls —different treatment—that's my system. Now do you see this on the first pages?'
'Yes,' said Dorothy again.
'Well, the parents of that lot are what I call the *good* payers. You know what I mean by that? They're the ones that pay on the nail and no jibbing at any extra half a guinea or so every now and again. You're not to smack any of that lot, on *any* account. This lot over here are the *medium* payers. Their parents do pay up sooner or later, but you don't get the money out of them without you worry them for it night and day. You can smack that lot if they get saucy, but don't go and leave a mark their parents can see. If you'll take my advice the best thing with children is to twist their ears. Have you ever tried that?'
'No,' said Dorothy.
'Well, I find it better than anything. It doesn't leave a mark and the children can't bear it. Now these three over here are the *bad* payers. Their parents are two terms behind already, and I'm thinking of a solicitor's letter. I don't care *what* you do to that lot—well, short of a police court case, naturally.'

It is Crossgates and a bit more. For, as Orwell says in incidental comment, all private schools are money-making and evil. But those for the rich have at least to train their pupils for the public-school examinations, which keeps them up to some sort of mark. Schools such as Mrs. Creevy's have no standards at all; Dorothy discovers that the girls have learnt absolutely nothing. Their whole time is given to handwriting and arithmetic—the only two subjects which the parents can appreciate. Dorothy tries to introduce some ray of interest into their education, but soon gets into trouble with the parents for reading *Macbeth* with them. The parents get to hear of the passage in which Macduff is described as not born of woman and denounce it as indecent. Mrs. Creevy of course supports the parents and Dorothy, if she is to keep her job, has to return to the old curriculum of pothooks and arithmetic.

In spite of that she is sacked at the end of the second term because Mrs. Creevy has done a nefarious deal with another schoolmistress who has stolen a few pupils from a rival school and transferred them to Mrs. Creevy. Dorothy thinks that she will have to return to London and poverty, but fortunately she is saved from that by the arrival of Mr. Warburton, a suspiciously convenient *deus ex machina*, with the news that owing to Mrs. Semprill's disgrace it is now possible for Dorothy to return to Knype Hill. She does so, is received back by her father and the fifth phase shows her living exactly the same life in all externals as that of the beginning of the book.

So much for the framework of the novel, but the study, as is half implied by the title, is a study of faith and the loss of faith. In the first pages before her loss of memory Dorothy is a believing, practising and scrupulous Christian, a frequent communicant, her whole life wrapped up in the Church. Her loss of memory, as we have said, carried with it a loss of moral standards and she took without question to the thieving habits of the hop-pickers. It carried with it also a loss of faith. The one was as unnoticed as the other. She merely dropped in her new life the practice of saying her prayers. It was not until after a fortnight that she even noticed that she had given up this practice. With her recovery of memory she recovered, it seems, normal moral scruples. There is no suggestion of any attempted theft either when she is down and out in London, at her cousin, the baronet's, or at Mrs. Creevy's. On the other hand she does not recover her faith. It has left her completely and irrevocably. Orwell could have written, as well as any other, a study of the loss of faith for intellectual reasons —the mounting doubts, the obstinate questionings, leading up to a final decision of rejection. But that was not what he chose to write. He chose a character, whose faith and whose unfaith were in turn both of them entirely without base in reason, and for that the device of the loss of memory is convenient. Thus it is possible to show her before the loss believing—she did not know why—and after the loss as disbelieving—she did not know why.

But the complication of her character is that owing to her upbringing when she has lost her faith she has still the need of faith. Mrs. Creevy, for business reasons, compels her to go to the Anglican Church, and, though she no longer believes a word that she hears there, she is nevertheless glad to go.

She looked forward to her Sunday mornings as blessed interludes of peace; and that not only because Sunday morning meant a respite from Mrs. Creevy's prying eye and nagging voice. In another and deeper sense the atmosphere of the church was soothing and reassuring to her. For she perceived that in all that happens in church, however absurd and cowardly its supposed purpose may be, there is something—it is hard to define, but something—of decency, of spiritual comeliness, that is not easily found in the world outside. It seemed to her, even though you no longer believe, it is better to go to church than not; better to follow in the ancient ways than to drift in rootless freedom. She knew very well that she would never again be able to utter a prayer and mean it; but she knew also that for the rest of her life she must continue with the observances to which she had been bred. Just this much remained to her of the faith that had once, like the bones in a living frame, held all her life together.

But it was one thing to attend church once a week as an unknown member of the congregation. It was quite another to take up again the mantle of the rector's daughter. Could she do that, return to the full religious life, knowing that it was all a lie? Orwell saw very clearly, and Dorothy is made to see equally clearly, that the demands of Christianity are absolute. Christianity promises a future life. That is what it is about. There can be no half-way house. Either its promises are true or they are false. Devotion to any of the humanitarian causes cannot of its nature be substitute for or alternative to Christian faith. It is something quite different, for no humanitarian gospel can tell us anything about a future life.

In every detail of your life [she reflects], if no ultimate purpose redeemed it, there was a quality of greyness, of desolation, that could never be described, but which you could feel like a physical pang at your heart. . . . There was, she saw clearly, no possible substitute for faith; no pagan acceptance of life as sufficient to itself, no pantheistic cheer-up stuff, no pseudo-religion of 'progress', with visions of glittering Utopias and ant-heaps of steel and concrete. It is all or nothing. Either life on earth is a preparation for something greater and more lasting, or it is meaningless, dark and dreadful.

Meanwhile she went on cutting out brown paper in order to make Julius Caesar's breastplate for the pageant, while at the same time she was softening the glue on the oilstove.

The smell of the glue was the answer to prayer. She did not know this. She did not reflect consciously that the solution of her difficulty lay in accepting the fact that there was no solution; that, if one gets on with the job that lies to hand, the ultimate purpose of the job fades into insignificance; that faith and no faith are very much the same provided that one is doing what is customary, useful and acceptable.

In fact, to quote the lines which he put on his title-page,

> The trivial round, the common task
> Will furnish all we need to ask.

But is this sense? Doubtless it is possible to argue with St. Augustine that 'all things go out into mystery'—and that there is a general consent of the vast majority of mankind that there is a God, whatever His precise nature, and that there is a future life, whatever its precise arrangements, that somehow or other, we know not how, forces from beyond this world act upon this world, and that, since persons of unquestioned integrity and ability hold differing views about details of these ultimate mysteries, it is clear that we have no certain knowledge upon them. Therefore it is wisest for each person to live according to the code and customs to which he has been brought up, to show tolerance to others and not to put himself too much to the asking of questions to which in the nature of things there can be no certain answer. Certainly this is the true philosophy of a considerable proportion of all the practisers and adherents of every religion and it is not in itself a dishonourable or unintelligible philosophy. But it is only reasonable if one is able to retain at least a half faith—a belief that there is a purpose in life and a future existence where after some manner the crooked things will be made straight. It was precisely this future existence which Orwell was prepared most dogmatically to deny— and to deny also that the majority of those who professed really believe it. Dorothy, too, it seems, had lost not half her faith but all her faith, and, without even the half-faith in a purpose in things, it is hard to believe that for the rest of her life she could be satisfied to give her whole time to an ecclesiastical system of which there was nothing to be said except that it was 'customary' and 'acceptable' and of which, if it was not in any part of degree true, it must be very doubtful if it was 'useful'. One could imagine her satisfied with some life that was concerned with the relief of material suffering or poverty, even though she could not give a clear account why suffering or poverty should be relieved. One could imagine that she, like many others, would find no great discomfort in attending a religious service every now and again, when occasion called for her to do so, even though she saw no sense in it. But it is hardly to be believed that she would find a solution in a life wholly dedicated to a religion which was wholly false.

But the truth is that this was the dilemma not only of Dorothy but of Orwell himself. He was incapable of accepting a purely materialistic conception of man's purpose in life. Not only was the concept of honour real to him, but man's honour was his most important possession—far more important than his material standards—and yet Orwell could never find any clear answer which he could accept to the question whence that sense of honour came. To him at the first step in the argument, as to St. Augustine at the last, all things went out into mystery.

The only other noteworthy trait in Dorothy's character is that she has a deep repugnance to the sexual act or to any suggestion of the sexual act. It is this repugnance, allied of course at that time to religious principles, which causes her to reject the advances of Mr. Warburton at the beginning of the book and which had caused her, we are told, to reject other men's advances before. Her repugnance went beyond religious principle, for it was a repugnance to marriage as much as to any irregular relationship, and it survived her loss of faith, for she finds that, owing to it, she must reject the offer of marriage which Mr. Warburton makes to her in the train on her way back from London to Knype Hill. She reaffirms the necessity for herself of celibacy. It is of course notorious that, just as there are some people who are inordinate in their desire for sexual life, so there are others to whom it is morbidly repugnant. But desire and aversion of this kind have little relation to religious principles or the lack of them. It is possible to find people who have the strictest religious views and yet have the greatest difficulty in resisting temptation to incontinence, and on the opposite side some who are free-thinking in their scepticism and quite unwilling to be dogmatic in any acceptance of a code of condemnation are yet most fastidious in their own conduct through a mere dislike for such activities. If Orwell cared to create an example of such a person, to underline fastidiousness' independence of religious principle by showing it as surviving the loss of faith, there was no reason why he should not do so. But it is a little hard to see what purpose these episodes have in this story or how they help forward an understanding of Dorothy's character or her spiritual problems.

VI

Keep the Aspidistra Flying

Keep the Aspidistra Flying—a book quaintly banned in Australia—is mainly concerned with the spiritual problem of poverty, and is in measure an answer to *Down and Out in Paris and London*—an exposure of the falsity of the notion that there can be any permanent value in accepting a condition of utter destitution.

George Comstock is a young man who belongs to a dreary family to whose members 'nothing ever happened'. He has been to a minor public school where he has had a rebellious and unsuccessful career. Life, in his family's eyes, is simply a matter of getting a job and holding it. An uncle gets him a job first in a red lead factory and then afterwards in an advertising agency, called the New Albion. He has some talent for writing advertisements, the manager is kind to him and there is no reason why he should not have a successful career, as such success is reckoned, in the advertising firm. But he loathes advertising. His ambition is to be a poet. He hates what he thinks of as the worship of 'the money-god', to which it seems to him that all modern commerce and indeed all modern life is dedicated. Therefore, to the dismay alike of his employer and of his relations, he throws up his job and goes out on the streets with no plan or prospect before him. After a period of destitution and sleeping on the Embankment a friend gets him a job at two pounds a week serving in a bookshop. There he finds that, so far from being freed by poverty to give himself to creative writing, on the contrary poverty has destroyed all creative power within him. So far from being freed from the tyranny of a job he has merely exchanged a well-paid job for an ill-paid job, and poverty, instead of liberating him and giving him self-respect, has bred in him an intolerable pride and touchiness which causes him to resent all kindness as patronage and to see insult in every action or gesture of a friend.

Then unexpectedly he receives a cheque for fifty dollars—then about £10—from an American paper to whom he has sent a poem. He celebrates it by taking his girl and his one man friend out to dinner, but insists on wasting the money in senseless extravagance, gets hopelessly drunk, picks up a prostitute, assaults a policeman and finishes up the night in a cell and with not a penny in his pocket. The scenes both of his drunkenness and of his subsequent raid on Piccadilly are, it is true, lively scenes. 'The lights down in hell will look just like that', he says of Piccadilly, but their liveliness are lonely contrasts to a generally stagnant book.

He is fined in the courts and of course sacked from his job. After some difficulty and humiliation he gets a new job with a worse and more sordid bookseller at a lower wage—thirty-five shillings a week this time. Now he really is down and out.

Before, he had fought against the money-code, and yet he had clung to his wretched remnant of decency. But now it was precisely from decency that he wanted to escape. He wanted to go down, deep down, into some world where decency no longer mattered; to cut the strings of self-respect, to submerge himself—to sink, as Rosemary had said. It was all bound up in his mind with the thought of being underground. He liked to think about the lost people, the underground people, tramps, beggars, criminals, prostitutes. It is a good world that they inhabit, down there in their frouzy kips and spikes. He liked to think that beneath the world of money there is that great sluttish underworld where failure and success have no meaning; a sort of kingdom of ghosts where all are equal. That was where he wished to be, down in the ghost-kingdom, below ambition. It comforted him somehow to think of the smoke-dim slums of South London, sprawling on and on, a huge graceless wilderness, where you could lose yourself for ever.

What rescues him from this degradation is the confession of his girl, Rosemary, that she is with child by him. Rosemary does not insist that he marry her. She professes, if he should prefer it, to be quite ready to submit to an operation of abortion. It is by this suggestion that he is shocked into the feeling that to allow life to be thus destroyed would be a horrid sin. He insists that they must marry, that the child must be saved, that he must take the normal husband's responsibility for maintaining wife and child. He agrees to go back to the job at the New Albion, which is still open to him. He is even anxious for a church wedding and only consents to a registry office on Rosemary's insistence. The book ends with Gordon doing well at his advertising and with the couple installed, together with an aspidistra, in a respectable little flat near Paddington Station.

Keep the Aspidistra Flying is not one of Orwell's best books. It is not really a novel. It is an argument—or indeed hardly even an argument, but rather an assertion of the proposition that you cannot achieve spiritual peace by mere defiance and hatred of the world. To such an assertion the obvious comment is that no one in his senses ever imagined that you could. 'The Mental Homes of England—how choc-à-bloc, they stand,' writes Gordon Comstock, but there are times when he almost qualifies to strain yet further their accommodation. Orwell, it is true, had a few years before imagined that perhaps you could achieve spiritual peace by defiance of the world, but he had found himself wrong, and in any event Orwell had brought to the underworld of Paris high spirits, a sense of comedy and a capacity for affection that were very wholly lacking in Gordon Comstock. Spiritual poverty may be a noble thing, but poverty is a bride whom only one possessed of a certain charity of character can aspire to wed. Gordon Comstock, a bitter fool, most wholly lacked this charity. Comstock is Orwell with all the fun left out. He is an impossibly perverse, difficult, self-centred, unlovable man. It may be that Orwell could accuse himself sometimes of having been perverse and difficult at this, as indeed at other times of his life, but I am sure that at no time did he greet the unseen with so flat and humourless a cheer as does Gordon Comstock.

The symbolism of the aspidistra is well enough, but there are too many aspidistrae in this book popping up all over the place until we get entirely tired of them. The duty of the novelist is to show us the nature of his characters through their actions—not merely to inform us that they were of such a nature. This is the first rule of novel-writing but it is a rule that Orwell here neglects. Gordon Comstock, driven into the New Albion advertising firm, finds that it and all advertising is a swindle. 'Most of the employees were the hard-boiled Americanized, go-getting type—the type to whom nothing in the world is sacred except money. They had their cynical code worked out. The public are swine; advertising is the rattling of a stick inside a swill-bucket. And yet beneath their cynicism there was the final naïveté, worship of the money-god.' It may be so. That is a point of view that some people hold about advertising. It is a tenable point of view. The champion of advertising could indeed find something to say on the other side—could make a case for it that advertising performs a social service in informing the public what goods are available to it, but there certainly are advertising firms which pursue nothing but money in its crudest form, and, if Orwell wishes to create such a firm for the purpose of his fiction, he is entitled to do so. But the trouble is that he does not create it. To tell the truth, I do not think that he, any more than Dickens of whom he makes the same complaint, really knew very clearly from the inside how advertising firms or any other firms worked. So he merely informs us that the firm was a swindle and its employees swine. We are given indeed not a picture but a flash-back of the working of the firm. Gordon Comstock has already left it by the time that the novel opens, but all that we are told of life in the firm shows Gordon Comstock indeed in revolt against his environment, but shows the other members of the firm, engaged in no nefarious rackets but, in so far as they appear, as it were, on the stage, behaving in a crude but decent fashion. When they discover by chance that Gordon writes poetry, they do not persecute him for his odd talent. Their laughter was, we are told, 'not unkindly'. Mr. Erskine, his boss, expects him to use this talent for what at any rate in a boss's eyes would be his own advantage—that is to say, to make more money. Erskine is sorry to lose him when he gives notice, keeps the job open for him, takes him back, allows him scope for his talent within the limits that the firm's work makes possible. Warner, his new boss, was 'a live wire but quite a likeable man'. He, too, is in no way unfriendly.

Orwell himself had worked in a bookshop and found the work 'interesting'. Gordon Comstock found it much more disagreeable than Orwell. He did not so much dislike the work in itself as he disliked the incidental duty of having to flatter and to be polite to the customers. Obviously it must often be tiresome to have to talk to foolish people with whom there is no chance that one will ever achieve intimacy. But we all have to do that for a good deal of our lives, and only a very disagreeable person would have minded it as much as Comstock. But of course he had taken the job with no intention of liking it, but simply in order to give him an opportunity to write his poetry. It is true that he found that poetry could not be produced out of the poverty and squalid conditions of such a life, but it was absurd to have a grievance against a form of life which he had deliberately and unnecessarily embraced. The true moral surely is not that money demands all our service but that it demands a part of our service, that the world does not owe us a living and that, if we would pursue a private vocation, we must be prepared first to earn a living, perhaps in ways that are not wholly congenial, and then in what would otherwise be leisure time to pursue our further vocation. There is nothing s o very unreasonable in that. In his second bookshop in Lambeth Gordon has sunk too low for there to be any need for courtesy to customers, but that is no solution to his problem for he has also sunk too low for there to be any inspiration to poetry.

It was not only the customers of the shop whom he treated with a boorish discourtesy. Were it not that a bad social conscience compelled him to dedicate his life to helping lame dogs over stiles, it is hard to believe that Ravelston would have stuck to him, and we require a liberal dose of faith in the unpredictability of woman to believe that Rosemary would have stuck to him or would have returned to him in his Lambeth lodgings in the way that she did. He sponged shamelessly on his poor sister, Julia—the sponging being the more shameless because of his self-deception by which he was always persuading himself that he would repay her.

As in all Orwell's novels, there is really only one character—one character who stands out in loneliness before the crowd as Orwell himself stood before the Burmese in *Shooting an Elephant*. That there is, with all the differences of temperament that we have noted, nevertheless an element of self-portrait in Comstock as in all Orwell's central characters is evident enough. Comstock has been to a public school—though a much less distinguished public school than Eton—and has then in protest against the 'money god' deliberately submerged himself. He has suffered, as Orwell had at any rate persuaded himself that he had suffered, all the agonies of being a poor boy at a school where the other boys were rich. He serves in a bookshop as Orwell had served. He tries to write without much success, even as Orwell up to that date had not had much success with his writings. There is doubtless a hint of Orwell's friend, Sir Richard Rees, in Ravelston, the rich, kind-hearted bad-conscienced young Socialist editor who sometimes gets Comstock's poems published—though it would be as unfair to Sir Richard Rees to suggest that Ravelston is a full portrait of him as it would be to Orwell to suggest the same of Comstock. In the end Comstock revolts against revolt and the futile refusal to accept life as it is—the absurd attempt to submerge—even as Orwell had revolted. And yet in the end *Keep the Aspidistra Flying* is a dreary book about a dreary man. He is a man indeed who redeems himself at the last, but the book tells us of him when he was dreary and not when he was redeemed.

Keep the Aspidistra Flying is important as Orwell's definitive rejection of the ambition to de-class himself. But it is more interesting for his first attack on the philosophy of contraception—an attack which was to play an ever-increasing part in his thought and which of course set him in direct opposition to so much of so-called progressive thought. It plays a reiterated part in this book. First, it is a central feature of his indictment of the dreary Comstock family that, above all other failings, they never reproduced themselves. Gordon's grandfather's twelve children were betweeen them only able to produce him two grandchildren. 'Really vital people', writes Orwell, 'whether they have money or whether they haven't multiply almost as automatically as animals.' In the poem in defiance of the 'money god' which Comstock writes and which Orwell quotes, the final enormity of the 'money god' is that he inspires such terror in his cringing slaves, the modern man and woman, that they wreck their married lives by indulging in unnatural practices through servile fear of the cost of parenthood. The 'money god', says Comstock,

> lays the sleek, estranging shield
> Between the lover and his bride.

All this comes to a head when on a day out in the Thames Valley Rosemary at last agrees to give herself to him—a surrender which she had hitherto refused—and then, when the moment comes, withdraws the consent with horror at the discovery that Comstock has been so 'careless' as not to bring any contraceptive device with him.

The lesson which Orwell seeks to teach is thus by no means the lesson of traditional morality. There is no suggestion at all that intercourse outside matrimony is in itself wrong, but what is wrong— what inevitably must spoil and make foul all passion—is a too great prudence in love-making. For that he blames both contraceptive devices and an arrangement of life which almost compels people to use them. He praises in contrast the working-class boy who fornicates without forethought and then deals responsibly with the situation that arises. Life in passion is not worth living unless it is lived recklessly.

As a kind of foil to Gordon Comstock we are given the cheerfully immoral, uncomplicated, empty, philistine animal Flaxman, who shared his lodging at Mrs. Wisbeach's, to whom the physical pleasures of life are merely pleasures to be embraced greedily and without question and limit whenever opportunity offers. Gordon in contrast is as complicated *à rebours* as Dorothy Hare of *A Clergyman's Daughter*. For all his praise of the recklessness of the lower-classes his own attitude towards sex is far from simple or reckless. He resents it when Rosemary refuses to give herself to him and thinks her refusal an insult to his poverty. He is furious at her demand for a contraceptive device, but then afterwards, when she shows herself willing to relent on this point, he sulkily will not take advantage of her offer. Desire and repression go hand in hand and the consummation is to him alike 'past reason hunted' and 'past reason hated'. When at length it does take place it is in Gordon's Lambeth bedroom and certainly in no spirit of recklessness or enthusiasm on Gordon's part. Rosemary has gone to visit him in his degradation and he deeply resents it.

'You did quite right to leave me. You'd much better not have come back. You know we can't ever get married.'
'I don't care. That isn't how one behaves to people one loves. I don't care whether you marry me or not. I love you.'
'This isn't wise,' he said.
'I don't care. I wish I'd done it years ago.'
'We'd much better not.'
'Yes.'
'No.'
'Yes!'

After all she was too much for him. He had wanted her so long, and he could not stop to weigh the consequences. So it was done at last, without much pleasure, on Mother Meakin's dingy bed. Presently Rosemary got up and rearranged her clothes. The room, though stuffy, was dreadfully cold.

It was the baby begotten in such unromantic circumstances which was the cause of Gordon Comstock's return to sanity. As a general rule it is of course an error to ascribe to novelists views that are put into the mouths of their characters, but Orwell is not in this respect quite as other novelists. He leaves little doubt in his novels which of the expressed views are his own, and quite certainly he did hold strongly the views about birth control which he puts into the mouth of Gordon Comstock and he certainly did think that Comstock had redeemed himself by his final acceptance of responsibility. Comstock was right to clamour for reckless love-making when he was in love and right to accept, in defiance of his previous social theories, the discipline of marriage before the challenge of new life. However he would have answered some of the common incidental difficulties of the problem, he thought that it was a craven thing to avoid parenthood for merely financial reasons, and a craven thing to refuse the incidental responsibilities which parenthood imposes. *Keep the Aspidistra Flying* is the beginning of the story of Orwell's revolt against revolt.

VII

The Road to Wigan Pier

ORWELL'S next book was *The Road to Wigan Pier*, which appeared in 1937. It has not been commonly spoken of with much favour, and Mr. Hopkinson dismisses it without qualification as 'his worst book'. But Mr. Hopkinson's criticism is not to my mind wholly fair nor indeed his analysis of it wholly accurate. The last thing that Orwell calls for in this book is what Mr. Hopkinson asserts—'an immediate resolution of all class differences'. On the contrary, his plea is exactly the opposite. It is that it is an insincere folly for members of the bourgeoisie to pretend that they have not got snobbish habits. 'Ultimately', Orwell writes, 'you have got to drop your snobbishness, but it is fatal to pretend to drop it before you are ready to do so.' The book is a frank declaration that Orwell is not ready to drop those habits himself. If you want the classless society, 'the only sensible procedure is to go slow and not force the pace'. In the same way, read in its context, Orwell's sentence 'if there is one man to whom I do feel inferior it is a coal-miner' is by no means the confession of an unpleasantly false humility which it appears when taken alone and as which Mr. Hopkinson makes it appear. Orwell was not concerned to argue that the coal-miner, like some Nordic Gunga Din, was 'a better man than I am'. On the contrary, it would be a just criticism of his book that, while he gives us interesting descriptions of going down a mine, of the habits by which unemployed miners collect fuel, of miners' budgets, of miners' houses, he gives us no character-sketch of a miner at all. He could not sketch the characters of those whom he respected. His character-sketching is reserved for Mr. and Mrs. Brooker, the unpleasant oddities of his boarding-house.

By 1936 Orwell's circumstances were a little easier and he was able to move out of London, which he detested, into Essex, where he kept a village store, from which the profit was about £1 a week, and a few hens. In 1936 he married Eileen O'Shaughnessy. It was, it seems, in 1936 that Orwell definitely declared himself a Socialist. In *Keep the Aspidistra Flying* Ravelston is a Socialist but Gordon Comstock, though he is virulently anti-capitalist, is unable to see in Socialism any remedy for the world's disease.

Mr. Victor Gollancz was at that time running the Left Book Club in partnership with Professor Laski and Mr. John Strachey. They commissioned Orwell to go up to the north of England and write for them a documentary work on conditions among the unemployed. Orwell accepted and threw up his store. *The Road to Wigan Pier* was the result. Orwell delivered the manuscript to Mr. Gollancz, and then set off to Spain to the Spanish War, then in its second year. Mr. Gollancz, as the somewhat embarrassed preface with which he introduces *The Road to Wigan Pier* makes clear enough, when he came to look at the manuscript found that he had bought more than he bargained for. He marked more than a hundred passages about which he would have liked to argue with Orwell, but Orwell was by then in Spain and beyond the reach of argument.

Mr. Gollancz's embarrassment is not, to tell the truth, surprising. The book starts off with an account of life in a very sordid Wigan boarding house, with a vivid description of a coal-miner's day and with statistics about prices of food and housing conditions, which, even if someone else could have transcribed them as competently as Orwell —and of course they have of their nature dated—yet were the sort of matter which readers of the Left Book Club would naturally expect. Mr. Gollancz is able to praise this first part unreservedly. But then Orwell goes off into a large wad of autobiography about his schooldays and his life in Burma. We have made a number of references to these autobiographical chapters. Mr. Gollancz's puzzle clearly was not so much whether they were good or bad but what they were doing in such a book at all, what sort of connection they had with the chapters that preceded them. Then, even more embarrassingly to Mr. Gollancz, Orwell plunges into a slashing and unqualified denunciation of the shortcomings of Socialists—shortcomings which were, on his showing, so largely responsible for the failure of Socialism and for the grave danger that Fascism would defeat it. He repudiates as false a great deal of what others had claimed to be essential to Socialism. In particular he pours ridicule on the type of academic Socialism which Mr. Gollancz's two fellow editors, Professor Laski and Mr. Strachey, were so assiduously preaching. In opposition to 'the sacred sisters', 'thesis, antithesis and synthesis', he calls for 'liberty and justice', but Mr. Gollancz is justified in saying that this programme is so vague that it is impossible to know what he wants. Finally there is the curious passage, to which we have already referred, when he insists that what most deeply divides the classes is the conviction of the middle classes that the lower classes smell.

The book is strangely disconnected—strangely disconnected and strangely self-contradictory in some of its judgments. For instance, in the early chapters, while Orwell may perhaps be defended against the charge of sentimentality in his pretended inferiority to miners, we can hardly defend him against the charge in such passages as the following.

> Curiously enough it is not the triumphs of modern engineering, nor the radio, nor the cinematograph, nor the five thousand novels which are published yearly, nor the crowds at Ascot and the Eton and Harrow match, but the memory of working-class interiors— especially as I sometimes saw them in my childhood before the war, when England was still prosperous—that reminds me that our age has not been altogether a bad one to live in.

Orwell was born in 1903. Therefore, when the war broke out he was eleven, and, as in the rest of the book he was to complain that he was not allowed to play with working-class children for fear that they would contaminate his accent, that he was sent to schools so filled with snobbish prejudice that he was hardly able to think of working people as fully human, that he knew nothing of the poor whatsoever until 1927, it is hard to think what these early memories can have been.

Yet, whatever the demerits of *The Road to Wigan Pier* as a book, it demands a detailed study if we are to follow the development of Orwell's mind. One can, as I say, well understand Mr. Gollancz's dismay when he came to see the manuscript for some of the denunciations of Socialists are most scathing. It was indeed Orwell's view— and there is a lot to be said for it—that a writer should never accept a party line. The practical politician might have to compromise and work through organizations to achieve his ends, but 'acceptance of any political discipline seems to be incompatible with literary integrity', thought Orwell. 'No one who feels deeply about English literature, or even prefers good English to bad, can accept the discipline of a political party', he wrote. Yet sometimes in this book he has gone out of his way not merely to assert independence but to say the most offensive thing about his fellow Socialists that he could think of.

Here is an example of his method of denigration. He is travelling on a bus through Letchworth. Two unpleasantly dressed, unpleasant-looking old men get on to the bus. 'Socialists,' says to him the man who is sitting by Orwell's side, though in fact he knows nothing whatsoever about them. Orwell, equally ignorant, agrees that it is more than likely and on such premises proceeds to read an enormous lecture on the harm done to Socialism by the fact that so many Socialists are cranks. It is amusing to see how Orwell deals with such a manner of argument when it is not his whim to concede its contention. A friend who thought that all Northerners were superior to all Southerners was driving him through a village in East Anglia:

He glared disapprovingly at the cottages and said, 'Of course most of the villages in Yorkshire are hideous; but the Yorkshiremen are splendid chaps. Down here it's just the other way about—beautiful villages and rotten people. All the people in those cottages there are worthless, absolutely worthless.' I could not help inquiring whether he happened to know anybody in that village. No, he did not know them; but because this was East Anglia, they were obviously worthless.

What is cheese in Letchworth is chalk in East Anglia if it suits his purpose.

But, whatever the faults of mood or manner, it is important to understand what are Orwell's complaints against the Socialists, for they are much more than complaints of mood. They are in substance four. First, people differ in their habits as the result of upbringing. Many of those differences are harmless and in any event no one is willing suddenly to abandon the habits of a lifetime. Socialists do their cause great harm by insistent and insincere demands that everyone should behave exactly alike. Secondly, all too many Socialists are cranks and tie up Socialism with absurd and unattractive causes which are in no way connected with it. Thirdly, Socialist planners often have no love for the working man; what they like is tidiness and order, and in the name of Socialism 'we, the clever ones' intend to impose this tidiness on 'them, the lower classes', whether they want it or not, 'by violence, if necessary'. Fourthly, not content with accepting the fact of industrialism—which every sane man must accept, whether he likes it or not—the Socialist is all too often blind to the dangers of industrialism and recommends Socialism on the ground that it will bring a more rapid and total industrialization.

Each of these criticisms, so far from being petulant and impatient complaints thrown out in youth to 'rag the master', were criticisms that were to remain in Orwell's mind and to shape his thinking for the rest of his life.

First, as to the reality of class distinctions. Orwell, petulantly wrote Mr. Gollancz in his preface, 'is a frightful snob still (he must forgive me for saying this) and a genuine hater of every form of snobbery'. It is true that he hated snobbery and true also that, far from thinking that they could be easily talked away, he greatly exaggerated class distinctions. The classless society was not to him, as to some Socialists, a thing to be easily established by a few simple legislative changes. It was rather the place at infinity at which parallel straight lines would meet, some distant Grael destined to be for ever pursued and for ever to elude us, the will-o'-the-wisp of all man's strivings. 'The thing that attracts ordinary men to Socialism and makes them risk their skins for it', he was to write in *Homage to Catalonia*, 'the "mystique" of Socialism is the idea of equality; to the vast majority of people Socialism means a classless society, or it means nothing at all.' But, as he was to write in his introduction to *British Pamphleteers* after the war, 'The vision of a world of free and equal human beings, living in a state of brotherhood—in one age it is called the Kingdom of Heaven, in another the classless society—never materializes, but the belief in it never seems to die out.'

It never materializes and Orwell came, as he thought, to see that in our age, at any rate, far from moving towards it, we were moving away from it. There was, as he thought, a fundamental insincerity in the English Socialism of the day. The socialist rhetoric was ready to denounce Imperialism and privilege. But, taking the world over, all Englishmen of whatever class were privileged people. Owing to Imperialism the English in general enjoyed a standard of living far above that of the average of mankind. Socialist orators might rant against Imperialism, but they had no intention of abandoning that standard of living and therefore no serious intention of abandoning the Imperialism on which it was built. For the moment, it is true, we have to some extent—contrary to Orwell's prophecy—succeeded in keeping our dividends in overseas territories, while abandoning our government. But it is likely enough that this will prove to be but a temporary phase and that in the end Orwell will prove right. Indeed, an unconsidered destruction of class distinctions, far from making for greater equality, might well make for greater inequality. For industrial society requires to run it a great concentration of power. Power itself is the great corrupting force. If all traditional inequalities were abolished, then there would be no force or spirit left in society to stand up against the soulless tyranny of those who were masters of the machine. The destruction of existing class distinctions would merely open the way to the establishment of new and more ruthless class distinctions.

It was from the same spirit that Orwell also disliked the 'cranks' who, as he alleged, so often attached themselves to the cause of Socialism. The very fact that he made this protest shows the profundity of the spiritual revolution which he had undergone, for, whatever else may be said of the mood in which he was anxious to submerge himself and to identify himself with the oppressed, no one could reasonably deny that it was 'cranky'. But he had turned violently against all that. *The Road to Wigan Pier* is a work of recantation. Of the 'cranks' whom he denounced some, such as vegetarians and teetotallers, he denounced because they seemed to him merely silly—because they brought to ridicule any cause with which they were associated—but he is careful also always in his list of 'cranks' to include his *bête noire* of birth-controllers, and it is on this that Mr. Gollancz especially fastens in his preface. Mr. Gollancz must, I fancy, have commissioned *The Road to Wigan Pier* before he had read *Keep the Aspidistra Flying* for there is no reasoned argument against birth-control in *The Road to Wigan Pier*. Indeed, though birth-controllers figure there two or three times in the litany of cranks, the only reference to size of families in that book is one from which a reader might have deduced that Orwell had some sympathy with family limitation. Of bad housing conditions in the northern industrial towns he writes, 'The determining factor is probably the number of children. The best kept interiors I saw were always childless houses or houses where there were only one or two children; with, say, six children in a three-roomed house it is quite impossible to keep anything decent.' Mr. Gollancz naturally enough takes up this point.

> This last [he writes] is really startling. In the first part of the book Mr. Orwell paints a most vivid picture of wretched rooms swarming with children and clearly becoming more and more unfit for human habitation the larger the family grows; but he apparently considers anyone who wishes to enlighten people as to how they can have a normal sexual life without increasing this misery as a crank! The

fact, of course, is that there is no more 'common-sensical' work than that which is being done at the present time by the birth control clinics up and down the country.

But Orwell's point of course was that a sexual life which was driven to the use of such devices was not 'a normal sexual life'. It was society's business to provide housing so that people could have reasonable families, not the families' business to restrict their numbers so that they could fit into the houses. The cap should be made to fit the head —not the head cut about to fit the cap.

His third point was a point that was to hold an even more continuing place in his mind—the fear that Socialism was being used not to establish liberty and justice and the classless society at all but merely for 'the clever ones' to carry out experiments at their amusement in the rearrangement of the poor. He had a great distaste for Bernard Shaw and the Webbs and all that they stood for, and it is notable that nationalization never played in this book any part in his conception of Socialism. In all his discussion of the problems of the miner there is no mention of nationalization one way or the other—no suggestion that it could play any part in the solution of the social problem. It is true that six years later, in 1943, in the middle of the war, he was to write much more explicitly in favour of nationalization in *England, Your England* but at the end of his life in 1949 I remember that, summing up the pros and cons of the two parties and expressing the hope that the Socialists would get back to power at the coming election, he put down on the debit side the amount of time that, as he argued, they had wasted on valueless schemes of nationalization.

It may fairly be asked how he would have had the mines and other industries organized, for clearly any would-be reformer must have some scheme in his mind. It really is not sufficient to say, as Orwell does say, 'It seemed to me then—it sometimes seems to me now—that economic injustice will stop the moment we want it to stop and no sooner, and if we genuinely want it to stop the method adopted hardly matters.' And it is a fair criticism of him to say that he was always strangely unconstructive on this vital point.

But, if he was not clear of the direction in which things ought to be moving, he from now onwards until the end of his life was quite clear of the direction in which they were moving, and clear that that was an evil direction. Whatever an ideal Socialism might mean or ought to mean, most of the things that were being done in the name of

Socialism were simply a rearrangement of the poor in the interest of 'the clever ones'. The language of the classless society might be on the lips of 'the clever ones' but new presbyter was old priest writ very large. Old governing classes were overthrown but their place was taken not by a classless society but by a new governing class, more ruthless usually than that which it supplanted, by the 'half gramophones, half gangsters' of the Russian system, as he called them. In place of the easy optimism alike of Conservatives and of the Utopians he saw things going literally from bad to worse, and he sometimes came to think that there was even something to be said for preserving old governing classes—not that they were good in themselves but that they were at least a certain bulwark against much greater evils that were to come. The lesson of the corrupting effect of power was to be the lesson of *Animal Farm*, and of *1984* and indeed of all his thinking for the rest of his life.

Why was it that society in our time thus moved, not from bad to better, but from bad to worse? Was it that there was an inherent insufficiency in human nature which caused it inevitably to bungle all that it undertook? If so, no high state of civilization would ever have been achieved, and Orwell, though he had no very deep sense of history, was yet never such a fool as to deny that a high state of civilization had been achieved. With all the blemishes with which society in every age had been marred, yet ours had been a splendid heritage which we were in danger of losing. Things were getting worse but they had been better—had on the whole been good. If so, considering that it was man that had made them and considering what man was, how had they been good? and why was it that our own age was especially evil and especially cursed?

We cannot understand the answer which Orwell gave to these questions unless we understand the pages in *The Road to Wigan Pier* in which he discusses the mistake which Socialists are making by their too enthusiastic acceptance of industrialism. Mr. Gollancz, I think, quite misses the importance of these pages. To Mr. Gollancz they are merely pages of idle and tiresome grumbling with no bearing on reality. 'Though it may be amusing to speculate', writes Mr. Gollancz, 'on whether or not a pre-industrial civilization might be a more attractive one in which to live, it is a matter of plain common sense that, whatever individuals may wish, industrialism will go on.' But Orwell was well aware of this. He was well aware that for better or worse we had industrialism and the only thing was to make it work. But that to his mind by no means disposed of the problem.

The problem was this.

A good society must be a society of freedom and equality. The simplest way to give freedom and equality was to have widely distributed property of roughly equal shares—so that everybody had something and nobody had much more than his neighbour. There is no reason why you should not apply this direct form of distribution to an agricultural society which has enough land to go round, and such a society is probably as good a society as we can hope to see. The satisfactions of a high material standard of living are mostly deceptive, and a society which still has the choice open to it is wise to deny itself those satisfactions in order to preserve the more important liberty and equality which can flourish in a state of simple sufficiency.

But we unfortunately have no longer the choice open to us. Our ancestors have seen to it that they have crowded on to this island a population far too large to be maintained in self-sufficiency. They have herded that population into towns. They have set them to work in factories and created an economy where they can only live by exchanging their manufactured goods for the food of other nations. Therefore industrialism and its continuance are inevitable. But under industrialism it is much more difficult to preserve the free and equal society which could have been preserved in an agricultural society. For industrialism can only work in large units. It requires collectivism, and the people are quite right in demanding that, if there is to be collectivism, then it should be socialist collectivism rather than some other sort. They are right in demanding it, but is there any likelihood that their demand will be accepted?

In order that large units may work considerable power of discipline over the many must be placed in the hands of the few. We can wrap that fact up in whatever metaphysical jargon may be convenient—talk of our masters as the people's representatives, say that we have elected them, say that they incarnate our will and all the rest of it. But such jargon does not alter the brute facts that power is concentrated in the hands of a few people, that power is a corrupting force and that those who exercise it tend to abuse it. In the simple distributist society there is no need for anybody to have much power, and the body of the people, each member possessed of his own property in the most direct sense, has means of resisting the abuse of it. In the industrial society, whatever the form of its organization, there are

opportunities of tyranny which it is hard to resist. It is idle to say that
the new inventions of industrialism make possible the creation of a
world of universal plenty and that a society, thus freed from the fear
of want, would be able to defy its masters. For that very reason its
masters will see to it that industrialism is not allowed to bring this
universal plenty which will threaten their power. Less and less did
Orwell think that it was mere stupidity which prevented industrialism
from giving to the world the plenty of which it was capable. More
and more did he think that the prevention of plenty was inevitable to
the system—that the masters of the state, perhaps not yet fully understanding what they did, nevertheless created and prolonged crisis
because their own power depended on the creation and the prolonga-
tion of crisis.

And even supposing that such problems were overcome, that in a
world of no deflation and total disarmament man, using buttons as
his slaves, was to succeed in satisfying all his material desires, in over-
coming all obstacles, what good would that do? Are not all the
qualities in man which we admire—courage, compassion, patience,
fortitude—qualities which only have a meaning in a world in which
there are obstacles to be overcome? And, if man is fundamentally a
moral being rather than a mere consumer, is such a material Utopia,
even if it were obtainable, desirable? Orwell never doubted that man
was fundamentally a moral being, that this world was fundamentally
a testing place. But for what were we being tested?

Other things being equal, a higher standard of living was doubtless
preferable to a lower standard, but other things, he thought, were not
equal. The characteristics of the 'future paradise' to which the voter
looked forward when the politicians of either party offered him a
higher standard of living, were, thought Orwell in an article, 'Pleasure
Spots', which he wrote in *Tribune* on January 11, 1946, that

(*a*) one is never alone;
(*b*) one never does anything for oneself;
(*c*) one is never within sight of wild vegetation or natural objects
of any kind;
(*d*) light and temperature are always artificially regulated;
(*e*) one is never out of the sound of music;

and on this he comments:

It is difficult not to feel that the unconscious aim in the most
typical modern pleasure resort is a return to the womb. . . . Merely

having the power to avoid work and live one's life from birth to death in electric light and to the sound of tinned music is not a reason for doing so . . . [if we recognised this] the instinctive horror which all sensitive people feel at the progressive mechanization of life would be seen not to be a mere sentimental archaism but to be fully justified. For man only stays human by preserving large patches of simplicity in his life, while the tendency of many modern inventions—in particular, the film, the radio and the aeroplane—is to weaken his consciousness, dull his curiosity and in general drive him nearer to the animals.

Of course efficiency is necessary, but a society which looks on efficiency as the supreme good is a society that is lost. In his review of Herbert Read's *Coat of Many Colours* in the *Poetry Quarterly* for Winter, 1945, he writes

How are freedom and organization to be reconciled? If one considers the probabilities one is driven to the conclusion that Anarchism implies a low standard of living. It need not imply a hungry or uncomfortable world but it rules out the kind of air-conditioned, chromium-plated, gadget-ridden existence which is now considered desirable and enlightened. The processes involved in making, say, an aeroplane are so complex as to be only possible in a planned, centralized society, with all the repressive apparatus that that implies. Unless there is some unpredictable change in human nature, liberty and efficiency must pull in opposite directions.

It is idle to rail against industrialism and new inventions. The inventions may be blessings or they may be curses, but to invent is in the nature of man. Curiosity is born in him and it is idle to preach sermons or to pass laws to forbid him to find out the secrets of nature. Industrialism is inevitable and the evils of it are also inevitable. Where then lies the remedy? The superficial, evading the issue, pretend that a remedy is to be found in education. Orwell has little faith in that. True, a socialist society will demand the abolition of privilege in education —'a certain uniformity of education'. But he thought it most doubtful that a truly egalitarian society would demand that everybody should have more education. It was much more likely to demand that everybody should have less—to say that 'the godly need no learning'.

Take the working-class attitude towards 'education' [he writes].

How different it is from ours, and how immensely sounder! Working people often have a vague reverence for learning in others, but where 'education' touches their own lives they see through it and reject it by a healthy instinct. The time was when I used to lament over quite imaginary pictures of lads of fourteen dragged protesting from their lessons and set to work at dismal jobs. It seemed to me dreadful that the doom of a 'job' should descend upon anyone at fourteen. Of course I know now that there is not one working-class boy in a thousand who does not pine for the day when he will leave school. He wants to be doing real work, not wasting his time on ridiculous rubbish like history and geography. To the working-class, the notion of staying at school till you are nearly grown-up seems merely contemptible and unmanly. The idea of a great big boy of eighteen who ought to be bringing home a pound a week to his parents, going to school in a ridiculous uniform and even being caned for not doing his lessons!

This is an exaggeration today, for today many are still bewitched by the obviously fallacious argument, 'In the past those who had education had better jobs. Therefore if we all have education we shall all have better jobs.' So today anyone who calls for a reduction in the school-leaving age is denounced as a reactionary. It is quite likely that in a few years' time, when the fallacy of the argument from the job has become self-evident, that then he will be hailed as a liberator. But, even if that should be so, whether it will be a good thing is another question.

Orwell is content to denounce the Socialists for their folly in allowing Socialism to appear as an unquestioning friend of bigger and better industrialism. But the only remedy that he suggests in this book to the dilemma that industrialism is both inevitable and an evil is the singularly half-hearted and unconvincing one that we accept the machine 'rather as one accepts a drug—that is, grudgingly and suspiciously'. Whatever good would that do?

The truth is once again that Orwell is posing questions that are only soluble within a religious framework and at the same time denying the possibility of such a framework. Religion in his view, as I have said already, had to be rejected not so much because it could be shown to be untrue as because it was incredible—because the modern man was simply unable to believe its assertions and it was therefore an idle waste of time to drag them into the debate. As he was to write some years later in his essay on Koestler, 'few thinking people now believe in life after death, and the number of those who do is probably diminishing'. But man had not always been made in this pattern. As he wrote in a nostalgic poem,

> A happy vicar I might have been
> Two hundred years ago,
> To preach upon eternal doom
> And watch my walnuts grow

but he was 'born, alas, in an evil time', and such simple, comforting faith was not possible to him. But what have 'now' and 'two hundred years ago' to do with it? What rational argument is there which makes survival either less probable or more probable today than it was then? There is clearly none. No one was less inclined than Orwell to allow that mere fashion was a respectable reason either for belief or unbelief, and it is possible that, faced with the bankruptcy of his secular philosophy, he might at this time have taken himself to a more serious examination of religion's claims had not the development of the world's affairs at this moment complicated his philosophizing.

It was his argument that, just as Socialists were the main objection to Socialism, so Christians were the main objection to Christianity. The first time in his life that he came across Catholics in any numbers was among the unemployed in Lancashire when he was collecting material for *The Road to Wigan Pier*. He liked them, but he came across them at a moment when he was filled with what he imagined to be his discovery that in all societies the ambitious few use and misrepresent their followers. That was, he thought, the way of the world. I do not know that, to begin with, he thought of it as especially the way of the Catholic world. But doubtless he would have been surprised if Catholicism had provided an exception to what he imagined to be a general rule.

On the contrary it appeared to him from his first sight to provide a very striking confirmation of it. The literary Catholics whom he read about were generally conservative, sneerers at democracy, upholders of privilege. They sought to put across the impression that the general Catholic mind was of that sort. Yet the Catholic workers and unemployed whom he found in Lancashire voted Socialist and hated the Tories. Any claim of the literary Catholics to speak for the whole Catholic body seemed to him then to be a characteristic and impudent fraud.

The challenge was in itself a coherent and intelligible one, to be answered on its merits, but he put it across in *The Road to Wigan Pier* in a way that showed that he was curiously unfamiliar with his material. As a part of his general campaign against academic pedants, he draws a parallel between Communists and Catholics. Just as, he argues, the Communist leader insists on his absurd jargon and orthodoxy, but his more sensible follower cares for none of these things but is anxious only for liberty and decency, so among the Catholics. The literary Catholics—'Ronald Knox, Arnold Lunn *et hoc genus*', as he calls them —draw out their detailed list of Catholic habits of belief and behaviour. The decent working men of Lancashire care nothing for all this. The point is in itself a clear one, whether true or false. It is Orwell's two examples which are so curious. The one is the literary Catholic's praise of beer, the other the Lancashire Catholic's addiction to reading the *Daily Worker*. Now it is true that for many years Chesterton and Belloc amused themselves with their jokes about beer and wine, and that many of their disciples took up their jokes. It was perfectly open to anyone to say that this 'Cathalcoholic' joke was a bad joke, tediously overdone, and many, Catholics and others, did say so. But the point is that, whether a good joke or a bad joke, it was a joke. Belloc and Chesterton never seriously imagined that it was a mortal sin for a Catholic to drink a cup of tea or cocoa. They were as well aware as Orwell that there were many Catholics who belonged to the Temperance Movement and many Catholic working men who enjoyed their cup of tea.

The desire to be at the same time a Catholic and a Communist is a desire of a very different nature. It is not the intolerance of the Church which forbids that; it is the necessity of logic. It is not possible to hold at the same time two views that are mutually contradictory, to believe in God and not to believe in Him—and experience was to prove that Orwell was singularly mistaken in thinking that the condemnation of Communism was to prove one of those metaphysical subtleties about which the simple Catholic working man, and the simple Socialist Catholic working man, was not going to bother his head. One could perhaps find examples of such subtleties, but Communism is most ill-chosen as one of them.

Neither the Catholic unemployed nor the Catholic literati were very important features in the shaping of English opinion in the 1930s, and Orwell might well have continued to leave Catholicism alone, as he had on the whole left it alone up till then. But it was while he was preparing *The Road to Wigan Pier* that the Spanish War broke out, and the Catholic Church, which had up till then been for him a quaint and unimportant survival, now showed itself for the first time as one of the great claimants to power—a force much stronger and therefore, as it appeared to him, much more evil than any of its Protestant rivals.

VIII

Homage to Catalonia

In the summer of 1936 the Spanish War broke out and in December of that year, leaving the manuscript of *The Road to Wigan Pier* behind him, Orwell set off for Barcelona. His original plan had been to serve there as a journalist, but, once arrived, he enlisted in the P.O.U.M., or Trotzkyite, militia, as it was not very accurately called, and was sent to the Aragonese front, where he was shot by a sniper through the throat and only by great luck escaped with his life. In July of 1937 he and his wife had to cross the frontier into France in order to escape arrest in the Communist reign of terror in Barcelona.

Before we turn to his political adventures, let us first see the importance of his Spanish experience in his religious development. In Spain, as we said at the end of the last chapter, Orwell for the first time came face to face with organized religion as a strong force. He disliked it intensely. It was always his contention everywhere that only a small number of those who professed the Christian faith really believed it, in the sense at least of believing in a future life, and Spain, as he thought, confirmed him in this contention, when he visited the cemetery at the little Aragonese village of Sietamo.

Once or twice I wandered out to the little walled graveyard that stood a mile or so from the village. The dead from the front were normally sent to Sietamo; these were the village dead. It was queerly different from an English graveyard. No reverence for the dead here! Everything overgrown with bushes and coarse grass, human bones littered everywhere. But the really surprising thing was the almost complete lack of religious inscription on the gravestones, though they all dated from before the revolution. Only once, I think, I saw the 'Pray for the soul of so-and-so' which is usual on Catholic graves. Most of the inscriptions were purely secular, with ludicrous poems about the virtues of the deceased. On perhaps one grave in four or five there was a small cross or a perfunctory reference to Heaven; this had usually been chipped off by some industrious atheist with a chisel.

It struck me that the people in this part of Spain must be genuinely without religious feeling—religious feeling, I mean, in the orthodox sense. It was curious that all the time I was in Spain I never once saw a person cross himself; yet you would think such a movement would become instinctive, revolution or no revolution.

Orwell repudiated as mendacious and dishonest the foreign propaganda which was anxious to represent the Republicans as mild constitutional liberals and therefore pretended that they were prepared to admit some degree of religious toleration.

Some of the foreign anti-fascist papers [he wrote] even descended to the pitiful lie of pretending that churches were only attacked when they were used as Fascist fortresses. Actually churches were pillaged everywhere and as a matter of course, because it was perfectly well understood that the Spanish Church was part of the capitalist racket. In six months in Spain I only saw two undamaged churches, and until about July 1937 no churches were allowed to reopen and hold services, except for one or two Protestant churches in Madrid.

That is to say, he did not pay to the Church's religious claims the compliment of taking them seriously one way or the other. He thought that the Church was a powerful force—but a powerful political force, which used its influence to maintain privilege, and, as he was against privilege, he was against the Church. 'To the Spanish people,' he thought, 'at any rate in Catalonia and Aragon, the Church was a racket pure and simple.' When its political power was broken after the Loyalist victory, no doubt religious toleration would be introduced again. 'Obviously the Spanish Church will come back;' he wrote, 'as the saying goes, night and the Jesuits always return.' Few as were the numbers of sincere believers, there was no reason why, such as they were, their practices should not be tolerated, so long as it had been made certain that the Church no longer had political power and power to interfere in things that really mattered.

That was his view. How far it was true was another matter. Of the literary and devotional record of Spanish Catholicism he knew nothing and did not pretend to know anything. All that he claimed was that the ordinary Spanish worker and peasant knew nothing of them either. Willingness to suffer death for your faith is not a proof of the truth of that faith, but it is a proof of its sincerity, and by that test the overwhelming majority of the Spanish religious, male and female, had

proved that they at least sincerely believed the faith which they professed. But it is also true that in many regions of Spain the proportion
of people in general that either practised or knew its religion was very
small. How much value we should attach to the evidence of the
Sietamo tombstones—how far the absence of decoration was due to
the mere poverty of the peasants there—what exactly he means by
'perfunctory references to Heaven'—I cannot say. Certainly this was
a region where notoriously Catholicism was, and is, at a low ebb, but
the more cynical the view that we take of Franco's character, the more
does the fact that he saw fit to play for Catholic support prove that
the Church had some religious influence throughout Spain at large.
Landowners, capitalists and army officers may, on the critics' view,
have supported the Church because the Church would defend them
in the possession of their privileges. But at least as many workers and
peasants fought at least as well on Franco's side as on the Republican
side. The more that you take the view that the Church, politically,
was the Church of the rich, the more certainly the conclusion follows
that, where the poor accepted it, they accepted it because they—to
some extent at any rate—believed it. They may have been mistaken in
their belief, but they must at any rate have been sincere.

Yet all that concerns us for the moment is that Orwell from his
special experience formed this view of Catholicism as an evil political
force. Whatever degree of justification mixed with his exaggeration,
or whatever degree of exaggeration mixed with his justification, he
formed that view from this, his first and only intimate contact with a
land of Catholic traditions, and the view remained with him for the
rest of his life.

Yet, if, as it undoubtedly does, power corrupts when it is allied with
religion, it also corrupts when it is not allied with religion. It was not
with religious experience that Orwell was primarily concerned in his
Spanish adventure, and it was the directly secular lessons on the corruption of power which more immediately filled his mind and survived to colour his work. His book *Homage to Catalonia* opens with
an odd, if attractive, piece of pure sentimentality. On his first arrival
at the guard-room at Barcelona he meets there an Italian volunteer to
whom he barely speaks at the time and whom he is never to see again.
All that passes between them is that the Italian shakes hands with him.
Orwell never learns his name but at once he conceives for him a deep
affection. 'I have seldom seen anyone—any man, I mean,' he writes,
'to whom I have taken such an immediate liking.' He sees in him—

justly or not—there is no saying—the symbol of the ordinary decent man who is willing to fight to preserve the world's decency against the beastliness of Fascist tyranny. That is how he saw the issue of the Spanish War at its beginning. Decent people everywhere are anxious to go on living decent lives, and a few sadistic brutes, drunk with their lust of power, are anxious to prevent them. Owing to the laziness and cowardice of the majority the brutes have been able to win a number of victories. Now at last in Spain a people has been found with courage to stand up against them, and it is important that the decent everywhere should rally round with their support to make certain that that resistance is successful. But of course, although right up to the end, right up to the time of his writing of his book and beyond, Orwell continued to hope for a Republican victory, the truth turned out to be by no means as simple as he had at first thought.

The greater part of the book is straightforward and extremely interesting autobiography. He went to Spain, financed by an advance from Secker and Warburg for the writing of his reminiscences. 'I had come to Spain with some notion of writing newspaper articles, but I had joined the militia almost immediately because at that time and in that atmosphere it seemed the only conceivable thing to do. At that time there were three militias, organized according to political parties —the International Brigade, which was Communist—the P.O.U.M. which was non-Communist Socialist, loosely described as "Trotzkyite", and the C.N.T. which was Anarchist.' Orwell had at that stage no great preference as between the political parties. If anything, the Communists seemed to him the most sensible, as they appeared the most prepared to get on with the war and leave political squabbles until victory had been won, but, since he had come to Spain armed with papers from the I.L.P. he was drafted into the P.O.U.M. militia with which the I.L.P. was associated. There were a few days of inconceivable chaos and ill equipment at Barcelona. Then the rabble of their company—for such it was—was sent to the front.

You cannot possibly conceive what a rabble we looked. We straggled along with far less cohesion than a flock of sheep; before we had gone two miles the rear of the column was out of sight. And quite half of the so-called men were children—but I mean literally children, of sixteen years old at the very most. Yet they were all happy and excited at the prospect of getting to the front at last. As we neared the lines the boys round the red flag in front

began to utter shouts of 'Visca P.O.U.M! Fascistas-maricones!'
and so forth—shouts which were meant to be war-like and menacing,
but which from those childish throats sounded as pathetic as the
cries of kittens. It seemed dreadful that the defenders of the Republic
should be this mob of ragged children carrying worn-out rifles
which they did not know how to use.

Arriving at the front, Orwell finds that practically nothing is happening in the way of fighting. 'This is not a war,' his friend, Kopp,
used to say, 'it is a comic opera with an occasional death.' The real
enemies are boredom, cold, dirt and the lice—not the Fascists in the
trenches opposite. There is just one incident to relieve the monotony.
Fifteen volunteers are called for for an attack on the enemy's trenches.
Orwell puts himself among those volunteers. He describes how he
makes his way out into the no-man's land between the trenches. His
leader signals to him. 'I ran across to him. It meant crossing the line
of spouting loopholes, and as I went I clapped my left hand to my
cheek; an idiotic gesture—as though one's hand could stop a bullet!—
but I had a horror of being hit in the face.' Then the attack is called
off. They try to make their way back to their own trenches but they
get lost in the mist. By good luck more than by good management
they stumble on them. It is found that two of their wounded are
missing. So Orwell with other volunteers goes back for them. But the
enemy hears them and they all have to bolt.

By this incident alone the monotony of one hundred and fifteen
days in the trenches is relieved. Then Orwell goes back to Barcelona
on leave to see his wife and to buy some boots and clothes and, if
possible, a pistol. He finds it a very different place from the Barcelona
which he had left four months before. Then he had been conscious
that for the first time in his life he was a member of an egalitarian
society—a society in which no one was better dressed, no one ate
better, slept better or had more money than his neighbour. He found
that atmosphere exhilarating, and this exhilarating atmosphere per-
sisted, in spite of all discomforts, at the front. At the front he had been
quite cut off from all news either of Barcelona or of the world beyond,
and it is a complete shock to him on his return to discover how things
have changed in his absence, to discover waiters in boiled shirts and
the normal differences between rich eating-places and poor eating-
places. But, worse than that, he finds that those who object to the
return of privilege—his own militia and that of the Anarchists—are

being suppressed by the Assault Guard as enemies of order, that street fighting is going on, and Orwell, far from enjoying leave, has to spend days of intolerable boredom, sitting on a roof-top and waiting to attack the Assault Guards in the Café Moka next door. In the end the attack is called off. There is an armistice—renewed fighting—then defeat of the Trotzkyites and the Anarchists who are compelled to give in not because of defeat in battle but because with all Barcelona's life at a standstill provisions run out. The Government takes the opportunity to bring troops from Valencia and to suppress Catalan autonomous rights.

Orwell returns to the front and soon afterwards is wounded. At five o'clock in the morning while talking to the sentries before changing guard, he is shot through the neck, the bullet missing his windpipe 'by about a millimetre'. He tells the story with characteristic detachment because 'the whole experience of being hit by a bullet is very interesting and I think it is worth describing in detail'. At first he thinks that his wound is a light one and his reflection is that his wife will be pleased as he will get back from the front. Then, hearing the bystanders say that he has been shot through the neck, he assumes that the wound is mortal and that he will be dead in a few minutes. He has a feeling of 'resentment at having to leave this world, which, when all is said and done, suits me so well', but no resentment at all at the man who has shot him. He reflects that, if that man should chance to be taken prisoner and to be brought before him, he would congratulate him on his marksmanship. Then his arm, which has at first been paralysed, begins to hurt—and he takes this as a good sign, for he knows that sensations do not become more acute when a man is dying.

It proves of course that the wound is not mortal, though with another fraction of an inch to the side it would have been, and for the time he cannot speak. Indeed, even when he regained his speech owing to the other vocal chord 'compensating' for that which was lost, there was for the rest of his life a cracked quality in his voice. There follows the account of the agony of his journey down to hospital. When he gets out of hospital he finds that a pogrom is in progress against all members of the P.O.U.M. He is in great danger; his wife's room at the hotel has been searched. His friend Kopp has been arrested and is in prison. His friend Smillie, grandson of Bob Smillie, has been arrested at the frontier in order to prevent him from returning to Britain to tell the truth and sent to die in a prison in Valencia. Orwell is only able to escape arrest himself by going 'on the run', by hiding and sleeping

about the town. There is nothing more that he and his wife can do in
Spain. They get papers out of the British Consul and, after one last
visit to the police officer to try to get Kopp's release from prison—a
visit which, though Orwell nowhere says anything of this, is of
enormous risk to himself, as it involves his confession that he belongs
to the proscribed P.O.U.M. militia—Orwell and his wife are able to
reach the French frontier. Fortunately, owing to Spanish inefficiency,
the frontier guards have not yet received the list of persons to be appre-
hended, on which their names would certainly have figured, and they
are able to pass into safety.

   Homage to Catalonia is, as Mr. Brander truly says, the most attractive
of Orwell's autobiographical writings and in some ways the most
attractive, if not the most important, of his books. It is not surprising
that, though *Animal Farm* and *1984* have made Orwell, the satirist of
Communism, one of the most widely known of modern English
writers, the Spanish public, as I recently discovered in Spain, have not
been allowed to know of the existence of *Homage to Catalonia*, from
which so much of the ammunition for these later books was derived.
It is the most attractive of his books because he is for the most part
writing about people whom he likes and admires. He is learning lessons
and revealing them, and the lesson that he is learning and revealing is
a lesson that man is more lovable—not, as so often in Orwell's work,
less lovable. It was the first time that he had ever been in a battle line,
and war, he found, had all the horrors and more than all the horrors
of which he had been told. Yet there was a comradeship in arms. Men
acquired a dignity and decency when they found themselves face to
face with death. 'The soldiers do the fighting,' he wrote, 'the journalists do the shouting and no true patriot ever gets near to a front-line
trench, except on the briefest propaganda tours.' But in the front-line
political hatreds are forgotten and Orwell found no difficulty in thinking and writing even of the enemy as a normal human being.

   Early one morning another man and I had gone out to snipe at
the Fascists in the trenches outside Huesca. Their line and ours here
lay three hundred yards apart, at which range our aged rifles would
not shoot accurately, but by sneaking out to a spot about a hundred
yards from the Fascist trench you might, if you were lucky, get a
shot at someone through a gap in the parapet. Unfortunately the
ground between was a flat beet field with no cover except a few
ditches, and it was necessary to go out while it was still dark and

return soon after dawn, before the light became too good. This time no Fascists appeared, and we stayed too long and were caught by the dawn. We were in a ditch, but behind us were two hundred yards of flat ground with hardly enough cover for a rabbit. We were still trying to nerve ourselves to make a dash for it when there was an uproar and a blowing of whistles in the Fascist trenches. Some of our aeroplanes were coming over. At this moment a man, presumably carrying a message to an officer, jumped out of the trench and ran along the top of the parapet in full view. He was half-dressed and was holding up his trousers with both hands as he ran. I refrained from shooting at him. It is true that I am a poor shot and unlikely to hit a running man at a hundred yards, and also that I was thinking chiefly of getting back to our trench while the Fascists had their attention fixed on the aeroplanes. Still I did not shoot partly because of that detail about the trousers. I had come here to shoot at 'Fascists'; but a man who is holding up his trousers isn't a 'Fascist', he is visibly a fellow-creature, similar to yourself, and you don't feel like shooting him.

'The whole experience', he wrote of the war at large, 'has left me with not less but more belief in human beings.'

In narrative he always called Franco's troops Fascists because that was the name by which he was accustomed to hear his comrades call them, but in analysis he argued that 'Fascist' was not the accurate term for them. ' Franco', he wrote ' was not strictly comparable with Hitler or Mussolini. His rising was a military mutiny backed up by the aristocracy and the Church, and in the main, especially at the beginning, it was an attempt not so much to impose Fascism as to restore feudalism.'

But of course there was another side to the story. As he explains at the beginning of the book, Orwell deliberately spoiled his unity by breaking in two the autobiographical narrative and inserting two chapters of analysis of the political situation. If war brought out the best in those who fought in it, it by no means brought out the best in those who attempted to manage it from behind, and it was in many ways by these evil political experiences that his mind was for the rest of his life to be most powerfully moved rather than by his good military experiences. He was often afterwards to write about political things and never, except *en passant*, about military things. Catalonia had always been a home of extreme social theories as well as the home of a strong separatist movement. It was therefore natural enough that the challenge of a strong, centralizing military Spanish Government should be more vigorously resisted in Catalonia than anywhere else in Spain. But political feeling between rival groups in Catalonia ran so high that, as has been said, in the first days of the uprising the only way to enlist troops was by allowing the political groups each to enlist its own militia. The army thus raised was, as Orwell bears full witness, a most inefficient army. It is true that he argues that its inefficiency was not wholly due to its lax discipline and that with better arms it would have improved in time. But, whatever the degree of inconvenience of these peculiar arrangements, it cannot be denied that they were an inconvenience and that there was a strong case to be made that, from the purely military point of view, it would be desirable to unify the Republican Forces. It was for this reason that Orwell during his first months in Spain, not as yet deeply interested in politics, inclined to sympathize with the Communists and was even trying to get himself transferred from P.O.U.M. to the International Brigade. It seemed to him that the Communists were saying the common-sense thing. 'Let us go ahead first and win the war. After we have won it, it will be time enough to bother about our political squabble.' In contrast the Trotz-kyites and Anarchists seemed to him windy ideologues who would jeopardize the whole Republican cause by perpetuating and deepening divisions.

But, when he returned to Barcelona on leave in April, 1937, he found that the Assault Guards were engaged upon an attack on his own P.O.U.M. militia and that he had no alternative but to stand by his own comrades. The street fighting, probably, he thinks, unplanned and unpremeditated, was used as an excuse by the Valencia Government to send in troops and suppress Catalan liberties, and afterwards, under Communist direction, the Government launched an overt perse-cution against any who had been associated with the P.O.U.M. and the Anarchists. Absurd accusations of treason and Fascism were brought against all such people. The foreign left-wing press was allowed to print no version except a totally mendacious Communist version of what had happened, and Orwell discovered to his sorrow that 'the left-wing press is every bit as spurious and dishonest as the right', and the *Daily Worker*, to which in *The Road to Wigan Pier* he had been accustomed to refer with some respect, he had now to pillory as the worst of all offenders. In this persecution many innocent were pitilessly and shamelessly imprisoned and done to death—notably among them his friend Smillie, who certainly died in prison, whether through execution or through illness is uncertain, and Kopp, who vanished in imprisonment and who must be presumed to have been shot or to have died. As Orwell wrote with restraint,

> Smillie's death is not a thing I can easily forgive. Here was this brave and gifted boy, who had thrown up his career at Glasgow University in order to come and fight against Fascism, and who, as I saw for myself, had done his job at the front with faultless courage and willingness; and all they could find to do with him was to fling him into jail and let him die like a neglected criminal.

But further it was his accusation that not only were the Communists plotting to seize power but that they were plotting to seize it not in order to make but in order to prevent a revolution—that the spontaneous will of the people had established egalitarianism at the first uprising but that the Communists, who for reasons of Russian convenience wished to please the French capitalists and to establish bourgeois democracy, had deliberately imposed inequality by force, and treacherous force at that.

We must try to decide as well as we can whether Orwell was correct in his facts and in his explanations and ascriptions of motives. In his facts he was in the main correct. Certainly as time went on class privileges, which had for a time been notably driven underground, did reassert themselves in Barcelona. Certainly the central Republican Government did abridge Catalan local liberties and certainly the Communists favoured both these processes. On the other hand it is possible to put forward some reputable arguments for their policy. It was at least arguable that the successful prosecution of the war required more discipline and a stronger central government—that at the war's first outbreak it was necessary to recognize independent militias and an autonomous Catalonia but that the war could never be won until some central direction was imposed. It was at least arguable that the proletarian forces were not strong enough to win by themselves and that it was necessary for victory to attract to the Republican side bourgeois elements. Orwell, it is true, contended to the contrary that by playing down the revolutionary policy the Communists destroyed all chance of raising revolt for the Republican cause behind Franco's lines or in Morocco. But was there any chance of such revolts anyway? Was an egalitarian programme really popular among the Spanish proletariat at large? It is very doubtful. The evidence seems to show that, as in other civil wars, there was a period of intense enthusiasm and intense violence at the beginning of the war, but that, after a short time and as the war settled down, the reaction to it of the majority of people on both sides was 'A plague on both your houses' and of boredom and an anxiety to get it done with. As Orwell himself reported, 'It was becoming more and more obvious that working-class control was a lost cause, and the common people, especially the town proletariat who have to fill the ranks in any war, civil or foreign, could not be blamed for a certain apathy. Nobody wanted to lose the war, but the majority were chiefly anxious for it to be over. You noticed this wherever you went. Everywhere you met with the same perfunctory remarks, "This war— terrible, isn't it? When is it going to end?"' It is always a difficulty with those who wish to describe a great struggle in terms of a class-war between the workers and the rich, as Orwell did with the Spanish War, that in fact, if the struggle is prolonged at all it is inevitable that there must be about as many workers on the one side as on the other. The workers who support the conservative cause may, if you care to argue so, be blind to their own true interest, but there they are. If it were not so, the struggle could not be kept going. It is therefore only possible to box the struggle into the appearance of a class-war by drawing somewhat far-fetched metaphysical distinctions between the 'real will' of the workers and what the workers actually want.

Again, Anarchists were on the whole unpopular and it was arguable that the Republican Government's best hope of victory lay in showing itself the stern guardians of order. Himself, as it were, based on Barcelona, Orwell, I think, took it always too much for granted that the Catalan attitude to the war was a normal Spanish attitude. He did not understand to what extent to other Spaniards, whatever their politics, a Catalan appears as an extravagant eccentric—how the Valencia government, dependent on Catalan support, felt itself like the seventeenth-century Parliamentarians in England, dependent on the support of the Scots, and how glad they were to be free of the embarrassing support of Catalan autonomists. Nor indeed did he understand how odd Catalans are, quite apart from politics and quite apart from Spanish prejudices. Towards the end of his time in Barcelona he visited Gaudi's cathedral. He writes:

> For the first time since I had been in Barcelona I went to have a look at the cathedral—a modern cathedral and one of the most hideous buildings in the world. It has four crenellated spires exactly

the shape of hock bottles. Unlike most of the churches of Barcelona it was not damaged during the revolution—it was spared because of its 'artistic value', people said. I think the Anarchists showed bad taste in not blowing it up.

No one who is not a Catalan can complain of Orwell for laughing at and disliking Gaudi's architecture. But Catalans adore it, whether they find it in houses or in churches. There is in the Catalan soul an extraordinary popular liking for artistic eccentricity that you do not find anywhere else in the world, and no one can understand anything about Catalonia who does not understand that. I remember driving up the valley of the Llobregat with Mr. Keith Patterson, the New Zealand artist, and he pointed out to me the tooth-like line of hills of Montserrat and said, 'That is where Gaudi got his inspiration.' I dare say that he was right. The sky-line looks very like a Gaudi cathedral. Orwell was later to write an essay of very vigorous and just reprobation of the nihilistic art of Salvador Dali, but he failed to note that most important thing about Dali, that he is a Catalan. The Catalan Anarchists may have shown bad taste in their refusal to blow up Gaudi's cathedral, but the right not to blow up Gaudi's cathedral was exactly what they were fighting for. In Catalonia anarchism is an artistic even more than it is a political creed. It transcends ideologies.

For a time Orwell was persuaded by the Government's failure to make any counter-attack in Aragon which might relieve the pressure on Bilbao into thinking that it was planning to do a deal with Franco. In the light of the Nazi-Soviet Pact two years later there is obviously no reason to think that the Communists would have had any moral reluctance to a deal with Franco. If such a deal was not made and was not ever even a serious possibility, it was because Franco would not countenance it. Why indeed should he countenance it since all the time, although Orwell's loyalty refused to admit it, all the probabilities were that the war would end, as it did end, in Franco's total victory?

Orwell, in his later essay on 'Looking Back on the Spanish War' alleges that he foresaw the inevitable defeat of the Republicans long before the war ended. There is no reason to doubt this. He wrote *Homage to Catalonia* while the war was still going on, and, as a supporter of the Republicans, he may well have thought it wrong to prophesy their defeat, even though he saw that it was inevitable. Whether it was right to encourage them to go on fighting when their defeat was inevitable is another question. In an international war it may be right to persist in a forlorn cause because you wish both to create and to demonstrate a mentality which will make your victorious enemy fight shy of trying to govern you when the war is over, but in a civil war once you recognize that your cause is forlorn you recognize the inevitability of your enemy's government. A bitterly divided nation is so great an evil that the responsibility is heavy of any foreigner who urges a losing side to continue a struggle which can have no result except to make national divisions yet deeper.

Orwell first went to Spain, knowing nothing of Spanish affairs in particular but anxious to play a part in what appeared to him to be the first active resistance to the challenge of bestial tyranny which was imposing itself on the world.

> There was [he wrote] the question of the international prestige of Fascism, which for a year or two past had been haunting me like a nightmare. Since 1930 the Fascists had won all the victories, it was time they got a beating, it hardly mattered from whom. If we could drive Franco and his foreign mercenaries into the sea it might make an immense improvement in the world situation even if Spain itself emerged with a stifling dictatorship and all its best men in jail.

> When the fighting broke out on 18 July [he wrote again] it is probable that every anti-Fascist in Europe felt a thrill of hope. For here at last, apparently, was democracy standing up to Fascism. For years past the so-called democratic countries had been surrendering to Fascism at every step. The Japanese had been allowed to do as they liked in Manchuria. Hitler had walked into power and had proceeded to massacre political opponents of all shades. Mussolini had bombed the Abyssinians while fifty-three nations (I think it was fifty-three) made pious noises off.

> I had accepted [he confessed] the *News Chronicle-New Statesman* version of the war as the defence of civilization against a maniacal outbreak by an army of Colonel Blimps in the pay of Hitler.

Of course Franco was by no means to prove the obedient puppet of Hitler which left-wing opinion prophesied. Nevertheless it must be reckoned in the balance of arguments that a defeat for Franco after Hitler had intervened in his favour would have been a blow to Hitler's prestige which might have changed the whole course of history.

In Barcelona itself Orwell found an apparently classless society—the society of his dreams—and fell in love with it.

I had dropped more or less by chance [he wrote] into the only community of any size in Western Europe where political conscious-ness and disbelief in capitalism were more normal than their op-posites. . . . Many of the normal motives of civilized life—snobbish-ness, money-grubbing, fear of the boss, etc.—had simply ceased to exist. The ordinary class divisions of society had disappeared to an extent that is almost unthinkable in the money-tainted air of England. . . . One had been in a community where hope was more normal than apathy and cynicism, and where the word 'comrade' stood for comradeship and not, as in most countries, for humbug. One had breathed the air of equality.

Then, returning to Barcelona, he found that this egalitarian society had perished. It may have been the Communists who in fact had destroyed it, but fundamentally it had perished because, as Orwell recognized elsewhere, it was the sort of society that could not of its nature survive. 'Degree', in the sense in which Shakespeare's Ulysses uses the word, is necessary for the continuance of social life. Orwell can be defended against the charge that in Catalonia or elsewhere he was ever a revolutionary in the sense that he advocated violence in order to establish a certain sort of society. He had nothing to do with the events that led up to the Civil War. He found the egalitarian society in existence and wished it to be preserved. But if it could not of its nature survive, what sense was there in advocating the continu-ance of the war for its preservation? 'Of course such a state of affairs could not last,' he confessed.

As for the newspaper talk about this being a 'war for democracy' it was plain eyewash. No one in his senses supposed that there was any hope of democracy, even as we understand it in England or France, in a country so divided and exhausted as Spain would be when the war was over. It would have to be a dictatorship, and it was clear that the chance of a working-class dictatorship had passed. That meant that the general movement would be in the direction of some sort of Fascism—Fascism, called no doubt, by some politer name and—because this was Spain—more human and less efficient than the German or Italian varieties.

If this was so, was he justified in urging the Republicans to go on fighting at a time when he himself had ceased to believe that they had any hope of victory? Was he justified in urging them to go on fighting for a classless society at a time when he had no belief at all that they would get a classless society even if they won?

However these things may be, on these questions of tactics the balance of advantage was not certain. The Communist case, like other cases, was tenable. What was to Orwell intolerable was not what the Communists advocated but the way in which they advocated it— their ceaseless stream of lies and libels, their unhesitating denunciation as traitors of brave men who were risking their lives, the praise of cads, the doing to death of Kopp and Smillie and thousands of others, the total falsification of history. As he wrote six years afterwards in 'Looking Back on the Spanish War',

> I saw great battles reported where there had been no fighting and complete silence where hundreds of brave men had been killed. I saw troops who had been fighting bravely denounced as cowards and traitors; and others who had never seen a shot fired hailed as the heroes of imaginary victories.

The shock of the discovery of such wickedness did not of course cause him in any way to turn over to Franco's side or to cease to think that a victory for the Republicans was wholly to be desired. But, as he was to feel for the rest of his life, the battle of the individual against the evil power of the party machines from whichever side the parties might come, was now more important than the secondary quarrel between left and right. The machines were determined on the destruction of truth as their first casualty.

> I have little direct evidence about the atrocities in the Spanish civil war [writes Orwell], I know that some were committed by the Republicans, and far more (they are still continuing) by the Fascists. But what impressed me then, and has impressed me ever since, is that atrocities are believed in or disbelieved in solely on grounds of political predilection. Everyone believes in the atrocities of the enemy and disbelieves in those of his own side, without ever bothering to examine the evidence.

Real and terrible as the danger is, Orwell, with his sweeping generalization, a little exaggerates his case, as is proved by the example which he gives. He maintains that every Franco propagandist believed that there was an enormous Russian army in Spain and no German or Italian troops and that with Franco's victory those lies will pass as facts into the history books. I never heard of any Franco propagandist

who believed that there was a Russian army or who did not believe
that there were German or Italian troops and certainly with Franco's
victory no version of history such as that has passed into the history
books. On the other hand Orwell could quote at any rate one solid
argument in favour of his thesis. His was, I fancy, the only book
published in English during the Spanish war which attempted to hold
a balance and was not wholly adulatory of either the one side or the
other. It was the best written and the worst selling of all English books
on the Spanish War. Of 1500 copies printed only 900 had been sold
by Orwell's death and it was not printed in America until 1952.

In the individual was to be found kindness and generosity and
decency, and once or twice in optimistic or in sentimental mood, as in
his patriotic essay in *The Lion and the Unicorn*, Orwell was to comfort
himself with the hope that good might triumph over evil and decency
prevail. 'I myself', he writes, in 'Looking Back on the Spanish War',
'believe, perhaps on insufficient grounds, that the common man will
win his fight sooner or later.' In his poem on the Italian soldier, he
writes,

> No bomb that ever burst
> Shatters the crystal spirit.

But why shouldn't it? And in darker moments it was his view that in
the modern world evil was stronger than good and that the great
party machines were going irresistibly forward to the destruction of
all nobility. What was to take its place? What was the new evil
that would come? To take the words of Yeats,

> And what rough beast, its hour come round at last,
> Slouches towards Bethlehem to be born?

IX

Coming Up for Air

ORWELL returned from Spain in the late summer of 1937 and the two years between his return and the outbreak of war he spent for the most part in a little cottage which he had taken for himself in Hertfordshire. 'I cannot honestly say that I have done anything except write books and raise vegetables in Hertfordshire;' he wrote in 1939, 'outside my work the thing I care most about is gardening, especially vegetable gardening.'

The only break of importance in this life was a trip to Morocco where he spent the winter of 1938. He had suffered from lung trouble ever since private-school days and after his Spanish wound he was never again to be really well. His ill health certainly had its effect on the tone of his later writings—particularly on *1984*—and we must allow for it in judging his opinions. The visit to Morocco was in search of health, but it does not appear to have done him any especial good. The only important literary result of it was his essay of 'Marrakesch', which appeared in *New Writing* in 1939. It is a disjointed little piece of writing of some 2500 words—first, a word or two about the poverty of the Jews and the poverty of a municipal official who begged from him some bread which he was feeding to a gazelle, then the note that the coloured agricultural worker is invisible in the fields on account of his skin and the suggestion that this invisibility causes us to tolerate conditions for him that we would never tolerate for the white worker who at least by his skin reminds us of his existence, then some reflections aroused by seeing a troop of Senegalese troops march by. How long, he wonders, can this swindle of imperialism, this bluff of white superiority, the pretence to the coloured races that they are getting something out of imperialism be made to last?

> He has been taught that the white race are his masters, and he still believes it. But there is one thought which every white man (and in this connection it doesn't matter twopence if he calls himself a socialist) thinks when he sees a black army marching past.

'How much longer can we go on kidding these people? How long before they turn their guns in the other direction?' It was curious really. Every white man there had this thought stowed somewhere or other in his mind. I had it, so had the other onlookers, so had the officers on their sweating chargers and the white N.C.O.'s marching in the ranks. It was the kind of secret which we all knew and were too clever to tell; only the Negroes didn't know it.

Certainly the accusation cannot be brought against Orwell that he failed to foresee the coming of catastrophe. 'I have known, since 1931,' he wrote in his *War Diary of 1940* 'that the future must be catastrophic. . . . Since 1934 I have known war between England and Germany was coming, and since 1936 I have known it with complete certainty. I could feel it in my belly.'

His major work during the two years up to the coming of the war was *Coming up for Air*, which was the first of his books to meet with any considerable success and which ran into several editions. *Coming up for Air* is the fictional autobiography of a cheerful, boozy, amoral seller of Life Insurance of the name of George Bowling. The book finds George Bowling, fat, forty-five, the father of two children, living with a dreary wife at 191, Ellesmere Road, West Bletchley. He is an echo of, but nicer than, Flaxman of *Keep the Aspidistra Flying*. West Bletchley is one of the shapeless, sprawling modern suburbs of London. It is a January day and it so happens that he does not have to go to work that day as he is taking the day off to pick up his false teeth. The first chapters are concerned with the adventures of that day—George's bath, the interruption by the children clamouring to go to the lavatory, reflections on the dreary monotony of Ellesmere Road, the train journey up to London with a bombing plane zooming overhead, the filthy, false food when he tries to eat a hamburger in a milk-bar, the London crowds 'with that inane fixed expression on their faces that people have in London streets'. In the street he falls into a mood of reminiscence of the life to which he was brought up in the little Oxfordshire village of Lower Binfield. His father had been a small seedsman, the prosperity of whose business was steadily declining before the competition of the great multiple store of Sarazins, and there was nothing glamorous about that boyhood just before and just after the Boer War. Yet, as he looks back on it, it seems to have been a good life. The sun seems to have been always shining, and he remembers his escapades with his fellow schoolboys, his first affair with a girl.

life in the shop, life as a grocer's assistant, church with two gigantic
choirmen bellowing the psalms at one another across the chancel, his
first, undisciplined adventures in reading and—above all—the real
passion of his life—fishing. The originals of these choirmen, even down
to their nicknames, Thunderguts and Rumbletummy, used to sing in
Eton College Chapel. Orwell transferred them to Lower Binfield and
changed their social status.

George Bowling was a boy of twenty-one when the war of 1914
came. He joined up, got a commission, was wounded in France and
spent the last year of the war in a useless, forgotten existence, guarding
non-existent stores on the coast of Cornwall. By the time that the war
ended both his mother and father were dead. He had therefore no
reason to return to Lower Binfield. His tough make-up gave him a
certain talent for selling things and he ran through a number of dim
salesman's jobs until a chance meeting with Sir Joseph Cheam put him
in the way of a job with the Flying Salamander Life Insurance Company, where he had remained ever since, selling policies and holding
his place in the 'five to ten quid a week' class. He knew that he would
never rise above that class nor fall below it.

In 1923 he was living in Ealing and at the tennis-club came across
and married Hilda Vincent. He married—after a fashion—above himself. He had no sort of claim to gentility but Hilda was the daughter
of a miserable, impoverished gentle family, which had held second-
rate jobs in India through the generations. Like the Comstocks in *Keep
the Aspidistra Flying*, they were a family to whom 'nothing ever happened'. The marriage had proved from the first a dismal business.
George Bowling had the cheerful proletarian attitude to money—
spend what comes to hand, have a good time and let the morrow look
after itself. Hilda was a victim of insane anxieties and a passion for
petty economies, always fearing the worst and the workhouse, which,
Orwell alleges, is the price which dim people who bother about
middle-class status have to pay for their snobbery. George conquered
his first impulses to strangle his wife, before those impulses had become
serious, and they jogged along somehow, George from time to time
taking rare opportunities for infidelity, Hilda spying on him with
odious, idiot jealousy.

When he comes home that evening, he finds that Hilda and two
lady friends of hers have decided to go to a lecture of the Left Book
Club, to which they belong without having the faintest notion what
it is all about, on the Menace of Fascism. He says that he will accom-

pany them. He listens to the anti-fascist's unattractive and ranting lecture and then, feeling in no mood as yet to go home, goes off to spend the rest of the evening with a retired classical public school-master of the name of Porteous.

It is two months after that that on a very lovely spring day, as he is driving his car on his rounds through the country, there occurs to him the idea the fulfilment of which is to occupy the rest of the book. He has tucked away a secret nest-egg of £17 which he has won on a horse and about which he has said nothing to Hilda—an echo of Flaxman who played the same trick on his wife. It suddenly occurs to him that he will go off for a week on his own to Little Binfield and revisit the haunts of his youth. He knows that, even if he were prepared to confess to the £17, it would be useless to reveal such a plan to Hilda. She would neither understand him nor believe him. She would take it for granted that he had gone off after a woman. It is therefore necessary to deceive Hilda and in order to do this he invents a tale about being called off on business for a week to Birmingham. He even gives her the name of the hotel in Birmingham at which he will be staying, and, thus fur-nished with his alibi, he sets off one hot June day for Little Binfield.

The inter-war industrial development of England has come to Little Binfield. A number of industries have been set up there, and finally, to crown all, with rearmament a bomb-factory has been established and there is a big military aerodrome at Walton nearby. Bowling finds that the whole place has been transformed out of all recognition. The little Oxfordshire village which he knew has been swallowed up in the ghastly modern gimcrack Hayes-Slough-Dagenham which has taken its place. Every landmark of his childhood has been ruthlessly de-stroyed. His old home is now an art-and-crafty tea shop. Binfield Hall is 'a loony bin'. The pond in which he had watched the great fish swimming has been filled in by a colony of nudist nature-lovers and turned into a dump for tin-cans. The old vicar and his first girl friend are the only two inhabitants of his day that he can discover. His girl has grown into a shapeless middle-aged hag, married to a seedy tobac-conist. Neither she nor the vicar recognizes George.

After George has spent at Little Binfield three of the days of his week during which he has found little to do but drink, he overhears one evening in the hotel the tail-end of the news on the wireless, which consists of an S.O.S. coming, as he imagines, from his wife, saying that she is seriously ill. He does not believe this for an instant and has no intention of taking any notice of it. But the next morning, with a little strain on our credulity, we are told that a bomber drops a bomb on the town. A shop is destroyed and three people killed. Both George and everybody else of course at first imagine that the war, whose imminence has been hanging over the whole story, has started and that Hitler, without declaring war, has made a surprise attack on the country. It turns out however that the bomb is a 'friendly' bomb, dropped by accident by one of our bombers.

This decides George that his attempt to recapture the past has been a folly and a failure. The lesson that he has learnt from the whole adventure is that 'it is all going to happen'. The horrors of war and the even greater horrors of the after-war are irrevocably coming. There is no escaping them. He gets into his car and drives off for home. Just before he gets there, he has one moment of panic that Hilda may really have been ill—may indeed even be dead. It turns out not to be so. But it turns out also that the S.O.S. was a ridiculous misunderstanding—another person of the same name. However she has discovered that the hotel at which he pretended that he was staying at Birmingham was demolished two years ago and that his story was all a lie. She will not even listen to any explanation. Clearly he had been off with a woman, and the story peters out on a quarrel of husband and wife and the prospect before George of endless weeks of nagging and suspicion.

It would be idle to call *Coming up for Air* a great novel, for it has not really the qualities of a novel one way or the other. There is no conflict of characters—no development of character any more than there was in *Keep the Aspidistra Flying* or *A Clergyman's Daughter*. It is rather a documentary seen through the eyes of George Bowling—a description of one particular type of English life at the time of the Boer War and of another particular type of English life just before the last war. There are doubtless elements of autobiography in George Bowling as there are elements of autobiography in all Orwell's central characters. But Bowling leads quite a different sort of life to any that Orwell ever led. He comes from a different class, goes to a day-school, not a boarding-school and, above all, he is of a different age—just ten years older—and his memories of an earlier time than any to which Orwell's mind can ever have gone back. It is in the description of a boy's fishing—a sport to which Orwell was addicted—that we come probably nearest to straight autobiography, and, if so, most excellent autobiography it is, for these are the most attractive and vivid pages in the book.

I *am* sentimental about my childhood—not my own particular childhood, but the civilization which I grew up in and which is now, I suppose, just about at its last kick. And fishing is somehow typical of that civilization. As soon as you think of fishing you think of things that don't belong to the modern world. The very idea of sitting all day under the willow tree beside a quiet pool—and being able to find a quiet pool to sit beside—belongs to the time before the war, before the radio, before aeroplanes, before Hitler.

Indeed the book is on the whole, in spite of one or two faults—the excessive detail of philistinism and destruction in Lower Binfield, the clumsy device of the accidental bomb—the most excellent reading and it is not surprising that it was one of Orwell's favourites among his own works. It is certainly one of the books which it is most important to analyse in order to judge his mind.

The superficial critic who likes to settle everything by convenient labels is likely to be puzzled by *Coming up for Air*. 'But I thought that Orwell was a progressive writer,' he will say, 'and this is a reactionary book. This is all about how things used to be better than they are now. I cannot understand.'

It is not very difficult to understand nor does the understanding reveal any contradiction in Orwell's mind. To such labels as 'reactionary' or 'progressive' he was always supremely indifferent. The indifference was one of his greatest virtues. He was concerned to analyse the reality of things.

Now it is perfectly true that George Bowling does think that times were better in his boyhood than in his middle age—and that though his actual circumstances of life were slightly better then than they had been in his father's day. Why did he think that?

To some extent the answer is that to anyone who finds his pleasure in physical things rather than in contemplation boyhood is a happier period of life than middle age. Those of us who are of that type, unless our boyhood happens to have been exceptionally unhappy, all look back to it with sorrow for that which is irrevocably lost. In boyhood all is before us. There is no sense that time is flying, and on the other hand, in so far as time does move forward, it moves forward to better things. With every year new athletic feats come within our capacity; new freedoms are permitted. In middle age it is just the other way about. All the great experiences of life have been tasted. There is little prospect of much new excitement. The sense of mortality has come. We know all too well that the years ahead, be they few or many, will soon race away. Athletic capacity which in youth was growing is now declining. With every year we play our games slightly worse and first one game and then another has to be abandoned. To the physical man, which George Bowling pre-eminently was, middle age is not a time of joy, and it is not surprising that he should look back with regret to his boyhood, as men of his type must always have looked back since the beginning of time.

Orwell of course is also quite right in telling us how middle age romanticizes its youth. Memory tends to preserve the pleasures and to obliterate the pains. George Bowling knows very well that it was not always summer and sunshine in his youth in Little Binfield but it is thus that he remembers it.

There is no one who has not at times indulged in the sentimental grumble that things are not what they were. Yet there was much more in Orwell's and Bowling's complaint than that. One reason why the times of Bowling's boyhood were better than those of his middle age was the very simple one that in his boyhood he lived with a sense of security and continuity. Things would go on. In 1938 he lived under the shadow of the bomber and the coming war. Beyond that, these calamities which threatened him were not accidents. They were the products of deeper causes. No one had less sympathy with the Conservative party of the years between the wars than Orwell. Yet he was, as we can learn from *The Road to Wigan Pier*, in many ways a profoundly conservative man. Indeed his main complaint against the Conservative party is that it had failed to conserve. Man, he thought, if he was to be happy, needed a stable environment. He needed the ownership of property in a simple straightforward way, to know, to see and to handle what was his own. For that reason Orwell was always very doubtful whether industrialism was not a gigantic mistake, or, if it could not be avoided, at any rate a gigantic misfortune. Whatever the indefensible relics of feudalism that it might try to defend, there was at any rate something to be said for the earlier Conservatism which was suspicious of capitalism as a disrupting and liberal business. For capitalism is of its nature the most revolutionary force that has ever appeared in society. It is its very boast and title-deed that it leaves nothing alone, that it destroys, that in the name of what it calls progress it rebuilds continents, it defaces countrysides, it changes every one of the habits of the people. A little of this progress and capitalism, so long as it was balanced and kept in check by a strong conservatism which insisted on the maintenance of traditions, might be tolerable. But, when the later Conservatism surrendered to its arch-enemy, to Joseph Chamberlain and the Federation of British Industries, and came to boast that it was a party of progress and capitalism, there was no force left in the country that could fight for decency. In the name of Conservatism the big combines and multiple stores grew up and robbed the small man of his traditional livelihood, as Sarazins was driving George Bowling's father out of business he knew not why. And what has been the consequence of this rootless, shifting 'progressive' life which the Conservatives have created—this life in which everyone is always on the move and no one belongs anywhere? in which there is no self-sufficiency? in which all rest has been destroyed? in which there is no nexus but the cash nexus? It is that no one can live unless he can sell something. 'What are the realities of modern life?' asks George Bowling. 'Well, the chief one is an everlasting frantic struggle to sell things.'

That feeling that you've got to be everlastingly fighting and hustling, that you'll never get anything unless you grab it from somebody else, that there's always somebody after your job, that next month or the month after they'll be reducing staff and it's you that'll get the bird—*that*, I swear, didn't exist in the old life before the war.

This was coming of course because of Hitler and 'the stream-lined men'. But why was there Hitler? and 'the stream-lined men'? and why was anybody prepared to listen to them? Because we had allowed a traditional way of life to perish—a way of life which, whatever its injustices, was at any rate traditional and could therefore give some satisfaction to the nature of man. For that reason the empty modern souls, unsatisfied and ignorant where satisfaction was to be found, fell easy victims to 'the stream-lined men'. So 'I only know that if there's anything you care a curse about, better say good-bye to it now, because everything you've ever known is going down, down, into the muck, with the machine-guns rattling all the time.'

There is a Conservatism which has failed. In his essay, 'Raffles and Miss Blandish', first published in *Horizon* in 1944 and reprinted in his *Critical Essays*, Orwell contrasts the criminal-hero of 1900, who 'belongs to a time when people had standards, though they happened to be foolish standards', and the criminal-hero of 1939, the hero of James Hadley Chase's *He won't Need It Now*, 'stamping in someone's face and then, having crushed the man's mouth, grinding his heel round and round in it'—the riot of sexual perversion in modern 'tough' fiction. He concludes, 'Comparing the schoolboy atmosphere of the one book with the cruelty and corruption of the other, one is driven to feel that snobbishness, like hypocrisy, is a check upon behaviour whose value from a social point of view has been underrated.' Again, in his essay in *Tribune* on 'Riding down from Bangor' he notes a similar decline in America from the simple virtuous society of *Helen's Babies*, *Little Women* and the nineteenth-century schoolhouse to the corruptions of modern plutocracy and gangsterism, which are known as progress, and in the 'Decline of the English Murder' he notes the growth of beastliness between pre-war and post-war murders in this country.

After the anti-fascist lecture George goes to consult with his old friend, the retired classical schoolmaster, Porteous. Though they are of such different backgrounds, George derives comfort out of his companionship with Porteous, who had no interest in any problems that have vexed the world since the days of Greece and Rome. But, face to face with reality, Porteous is, he finds, though charming, quite futile.

'Tell me, Porteous, what do you think of Hitler?'

'Hitler? This German person? My dear fellow! I don't think of him. A mere adventurer. These people come and go. Ephemeral, purely ephemeral.'

Porteous was unable to see that the inventions and weapons and communications of today had made of the modern tyrannies something wholly different from any of the tyrannies of other days. Living in the past and in his books, he was in fact dead. 'He's dead,' said Bowling to himself. 'He's a ghost. All people like that are dead. . . . They're decent, but their minds have stopped.'

Very different was the anti-fascist lecturer to whom Bowling had been listening immediately before his visit to Porteous—not that the lecturer himself amounted to anything but what he symbolized amounted to a great deal. It is interesting that Orwell, straight from his Spanish experience, should have made him an anti-fascist lecturer, that his wife and her idiotic friends should have been made to join the Left Book Club rather than the Primrose League. The conventional left-wing writer would have made him a fascist lecturer. He might on Orwell's view equally have been either. The ordinary distinction between left-wing and right-wing was irrelevant. What threatened us were 'the stream-lined men', the ruthless men, the men without tradition. Driven to violence by the insufficiency of their insane metaphysics, they could be found equally on the left and on the right and it was little more than chance where each particular one was to be found.

You know the line of talk. These chaps can churn it out by the hour. Just like a gramophone. Turn the handle, press the button and it starts. Democracy, Fascism, Democracy. But somehow it interested me to watch him. A rather mean little man, with a white face and a bald head, standing on a platform shooting out slogans. What's he doing? Quite deliberately, and quite openly, he's stirring up hatred. Doing his damnedest to make you hate certain foreigners called Fascists. It's a queer thing, I thought, to be known as 'Mr. So-and-So, the well-known anti-Fascist'. A queer trade, anti-Fascism. This fellow, I suppose, makes his living by writing books against Hitler. But what did he do before Hitler came along? And what'll he do if Hitler ever disappears? . . . The grating voice went on and on, and another thought struck me. He *means* it. Not faking at all— feels every word he's saying. He's trying to work up hatred in the audience, but that's nothing to the hatred he feels himself. Every slogan's gospel truth to him. If you cut him open all you'll find inside would be Democracy-Fascism-Democracy. Interesting to know a chap like that in private life. But does he have a private life? Or does he only go round from platform to platform, working up hatred? Perhaps even his dreams are slogans. . . .

It was a voice that sounded as if it could go on for a fortnight without stopping. It's a ghastly thing really to have a sort of human barrel-organ shooting propaganda at you by the hour. The same thing over and over again. Hate, hate, hate. Let's all get together and have a good hate. Over and over. It gives you the feeling that something has got inside your skull and is hammering down on your brain. But for a moment with my eyes shut, I managed to turn the tables on him, I got inside *his* skull. It was a peculiar sensation. For about a second I was inside him, you might almost say I was him. At any rate, I felt what he was feeling.

I saw the vision that he was seeing. And it wasn't at all the kind of vision that can be talked about. What he's *saying* is merely that Hitler's after us and we must all get together and have a good hate. Doesn't go into details. Leaves it all respectable. But what he's *seeing* is something quite different. It's a picture of himself smashing people's faces with a spanner. . . . Smash! Right in the middle! The bones cave in like an egg shell and what was a face a minute ago is just a great big blob of strawberry jam. . . . It isn't the war that matters, it's the after-war. The world we're going down into, the kind of hate-world, slogan-world. The coloured shirts, the barbed wire, the rubber truncheons. The secret cells where the electric light burns night and day and the detectives watch you while you sleep. And the processions and the posters with enormous faces and the crowds of a million people all cheering for the Leader till they deafen themselves into thinking that they really worship him, and all the time, underneath, they hate him so that they want to puke.

All that matters is to avoid these dehumanizing fanaticisms whether they come from one side or the other.

'Listen, son,' says George to the earnest young humanitarian Communist, 'you've got it all wrong. In 1914 *we* thought it was going to be a glorious business. Well, it wasn't. It was just a bloody mess. If it comes again you keep out of it. . . . You don't feel like a hero. All you know is that you've had no sleep for three days, you stink like a polecat, you're pissing in your bags with fright, and your hands are so cold you can't hold a rifle. But that doesn't matter a damn either. It's the things that happen afterwards.'

But his warnings made no impression. 'Might as well be standing at the door of a knocking shop handing out tracts', he comments wryly.

X

Dickens

ORWELL'S next published work was a long essay of sixty pages on Charles Dickens, to be found today included in his *Critical Essays*. Orwell was, as was to be expected from a precocious youth, followed by exile in Burma and adventures in the underworld of Paris and London, a man of wide but erratic reading. There were large gaps in his reading. He had an almost unnatural fondness for trash and gave perhaps too much of his time to the study of his hobby. For the past, as past he did not greatly care. On the other hand there were a few central authors—Shakespeare, Swift, Dickens—on whom he had established himself and to whom he returned again and again. Without an understanding of his interpretation of them it is not possible to understand his mind. To his views on Shakespeare and Swift we will come later. I should not myself quite agree with Mr. Atkins in putting the influence of Dickens first among the literary influences upon him. I should have thought that Swift's influence was much greater. The exuberance of character-creation which was Dickens's especial talent was one in which Orwell was somewhat specially deficient. However that may be, the influence of Dickens on him was great, and this is the relevant moment to consider it.

Orwell's prime principle of literary criticism was the very sensible principle of *securus iudicat orbis terrarum*. If an author has survived the generations and found his appeal in a wide variety of nations and conditions of people, then that author must have merit. For after all the purpose of writing is to be read and he has therefore achieved his purpose. He may of course also have grave faults. It is right to point out these faults, but the critic who can find no merit in him merely writes himself down as a deficient. This was a sensible principle.

On that test Dickens was only less free from question than other great writers in that he happened to have been born later than they. But he had established his position and indeed, however much he might be tempted with other great writers, Orwell was never at all tempted to challenge Dickens's position. He knew his Dickens thoroughly and from his boyhood always held him as a favourite. So the essay is a very stimulating essay, which every student either of Orwell or of Dickens should read. Orwell had a competence in what is sometimes called 'pure' literary criticism. He could analyse as acutely as another the tricks of the trade—show why a writer did what he did—and in this essay there are some very illuminating observations about Dickens's trick of padding out his anecdotes with irrelevant visual details. But it was in a writer's 'message' that he was mainly interested.

He challenges the common opinion that Dickens was, as the Marxian T. A. Jackson had claimed, a revolutionary writer or, as Chesterton had claimed, a champion of the poor. On the contrary Dickens was, as he argued, a bourgeois—very conscious of the gulf that did separate and ought to separate bourgeois from proletarian—ready indeed with general and vague sympathy with the 'virtuous' poor but ignorant of the true manner of their life and markedly harsh to any who had fallen from virtue into crime. The great mark of Dickensian society, he argues, is that nobody ever does any work in it. Dickens has none of the curiosity of other novelists to discover how institutions, businesses, legal systems or mechanical processes really work (Orwell, to be fair, had little such curiosity himself although he sometimes pretended that he had). He was only interested in people. Dickens is a townee who cared nothing for agriculture—interested in the consumption of food, not in its production. He was only interested in the picturesque, external oddity. His attitude towards the state was that of an anarchist, in the sense that his mentality was essentially that of an early-nineteenth-century radical who saw the state simply as the protector of a number of indefensible privileges, and to whom politics was little more than a battle to abolish those privileges.

Dickens's central characters are people who, like Mr. Pickwick, feel no responsibility to play any part in the life of society. 'What did he think the most desirable way to live?' asked Orwell of Dickens and answered:

A hundred thousand pounds, a quaint old house with plenty of ivy on it, a sweet womanly wife, a horde of children and no work. Everything is safe, soft, peaceful and, above all domestic. . . . The servants are comic and feudal, the children prattle around your feet, the old friends sit at your fireside, talking of past days, there is the endless succession of enormous meals, the cold punch and sherry negus, the feather beds and warming-pans, the Christmas parties with charades and blind man's buff; but nothing ever happens except the yearly childbirth.

That was at least one more thing than happened to the Comstock family. But it was certainly a negative programme, and, if Dickens approved of anarchy, he by no means approved of violent anarchy. He hated all violence and cruelty—whether it was the violence and cruelty of the schoolmaster—a Creakle or a Squeers—or of the mob, as in the *Tale of Two Cities* and *Barnaby Rudge*.

These observations seem to me without exception to be shrewd, true and important. It is only surprising, seeing how much people have written and talked about Dickens, that they should be at all original. It is clear, whether we take our evidence from *David Copperfield* or from his own autobiography, that the wound of Dickens's experience in the blacking factory never healed and the nightmare of the blacking factory was, as Orwell truly says, not that any boy should have been treated thus but that a middle-class boy should have been treated thus. Mealy Potatoes is left in the factory without another thought to his fate. As the story of Mr. Pickwick and Sam Weller shows, so far from objecting to the relationship of master and servant, Dickens romanticized it. The only proletarians who receive full-length portraits in his gallery are colourful eccentrics like Bill Sykes, Weller or Mrs. Gamp and he shows no curiosity how ordinary working men do their work. As little curiosity does he show as to how his bourgeois characters have made their incomes. 'What exactly went on in Gradgrind's factories? How did Podsnap make his money? How did Merdle work his swindles?' Orwell asks. Dickens never tells us what 'Doyle's invention' was. He never takes the trouble to work out in detail Uriah Heep's methods of misappropriation. The state is simply the Circumlocution Office—to be mocked at and abolished. So little is he interested in progress that, though living in the railway age, he prefers to cast his stories back into the age of the stage-coach. On the other hand, though convention imposed upon him a reticence in the use of his words, it is clear that he was far more acutely alive than were most Victorians to the strength of perverted instincts in inciting acts of violence. How else account for the character of Dennis in *Barnaby Rudge* or of Creakle in *David Copperfield*? How many Victorians would have reflected, as Dickens reflected of the Terror, that 'a species of fervour or intoxication, known, without doubt, to have led some persons to brave the guillotine unnecessarily and to die by it, was not mere boastfulness but

a wild infection of the wildly shaken public mind. In seasons of pesti-
lence some of us will have a secret attraction to the disease—a terrible
passing inclination to die of it'? His mind was far removed from that
of those simple souls who think that violent measures are easily an
effective deterrent.

But what conclusion does Orwell draw from all this?

He argues that, for all his denunciation of abuses, whether it be in
matters political, educational, legal or social Dickens has no remedy
to suggest other than that bad men should behave better. It never seems
to have occurred to him that there is something radically wrong with
the system. This is indeed true. Whether it is as certainly a defect in
Dickens as Orwell thought is another matter. It is surely at least most
arguable that, whatever policies may be required by the different
circumstances of today, in Dickens's time the system was, by and large,
working—that, numerous as were the surviving abuses of society, they
were one after the other being remedied within the system and that
it was a far wiser plan to work within the system rather than to smash
it up with no certainty that you would not get a worse in its place.
In his essay on 'Raffles and Miss Blandish' Orwell was to advance such
a defence for Walt Whitman's acceptance of nineteenth-century
America. Is it not as valid as a defence of Dickens's acceptance of
nineteenth-century England?

Dickens's message in the end, argues Orwell, comes to little more
than, 'If men would behave decently the world would be decent.'

> The ordinary people in the western countries [writes Orwell] have
> never entered mentally into the world of 'realism' and power-
> politics. They may do so before long, in which case Dickens will be
> as out of date as the cabhorse. But in his own age and ours he has
> been popular chiefly because he was able to express in a comic,
> simplified and therefore memorable form the native decency of the
> common man.

But then Orwell, as he himself confessed, came more and more to
wonder whether, platitudinous and unsatisfying as it might sound,
there was any more than that which could legitimately be said.
Dickens denounced the educational system of his day—but then sent
his own son to Eton. Orwell in exactly the same way was, so Mr.
Fyvell tells us, at the end of his life proposing to send his adopted son
to a good public school. It was easy enough to think of some ideal form
of society, theoretically better than that which exists, but the trans-

formation from the old society to the new could only be made by men, to whom power was entrusted, and power of its nature corrupts. It was not possible to entrust this power to men without running the risk that they would be corrupted by the exercise of it. More and more, as the years went on, Orwell came to feel that the original ideological programme of the revolution was irrelevant and that what was likely to emerge out of the revolution would be a tyranny that was worse than that which created it. What then was the remedy? Was not Dickens perhaps right in thinking that the remedy was to reform but to reform within the framework of the system—to try to make the best alike of the old and of the new?

XI

England and War

GEORGE BOWLING, supposedly speaking his piece in 1938, in two or three places foretells 1941 as the date of the war. As a matter of fact, *Coming up for Air* appeared in 1939 and only beat the war by a few months. If we were to accept George Bowling as Orwell's *alter ego*, we should expect Orwell to have been neutral towards the war, and as a matter of fact, at the very moment that the war broke out, he was engaged on a long essay, *Inside the Whale*, which to an extent defends the Bowling thesis on a higher intellectual plane. *Inside the Whale* is an appreciation of the American writer, Henry Miller, and in particular his two books, *Tropic of Cancer* and *Black Spring*. In a few pungent paragraphs Orwell criticizes the other writers of the inter-war years—Housman, the Joyce-Eliot school of the 1920s, the Auden-Spender school of the 1930s. The writers of the 1920s stood apart from life and expressed their disillusionment; those of the 1930s threw themselves with a frenzy into the politics of the Popular Front. 'Suddenly', he writes, 'we have got out of the twilight of the gods into a sort of Boy Scout atmosphere of bare knees and community singing. The typical literary man ceases to be a cultured expatriate with a leaning towards the Church and becomes an eager-minded schoolboy with a leaning towards Communism. If the keynote of the writers of the "twenties" is "tragic sense of life", the keynote of the new writers is "serious purpose".' Orwell attacks these schoolboy-Popular Front poets of the 1930s, as he thinks of them, on the ground that, cradled in English security, they have no notion of reality, no notion what 'the stream-lined', totalitarian world is really like. He makes play of the phrase 'necessary murder' in Mr. Auden's poem, 'Spain', and argues that no one would write like that if he had really seen a murder committed. He is impatient of the fatuous optimism which imagines that the disease of modern life is capable of remedy by some easy political action.

What is quite obviously happening, war or no war, is the break-up of laissez-faire capitalism and of the liberal-Christian culture.

Until recently the full implications of this were not foreseen, because it was generally imagined that socialism could preserve and even enlarge the atmosphere of liberalism. It is now beginning to be realised how false this idea was. Almost certainly we are moving into an age of totalitarian dictatorships—an age in which freedom of thought will be at first a deadly sin and later on a meaningless abstraction. The autonomous individual is going to be stamped out of existence.

In face of this threat Orwell in this essay expresses his preference over the attitude of the writers with a 'serious purpose' for Henry Miller who was content, to use his own phrase, to take refuge 'inside the whale', who accepted the inevitable collapse of civilization, but preferred to observe it without making any attempt to influence events.

Henry Miller himself, to tell the truth, is poor stuff, and it is a little bit of a mystery why Orwell made so much fuss about him. Orwell was in general an inveterate moralist, a stern opponent of the irresponsibility of the artist. A later essay was to deny inflexibly 'benefit of clergy' to Salvador Dali, and it is hard not to feel that he wrote as gently of Henry Miller as he did mainly because he had met him in Paris, and it is natural to write more gently of those whom we have seen in the flesh. The *Tropic of Cancer*, when all is said and done, is a pathetic business of James Joyce for Wisconsin sophomores. It may well be argued that some Victorian conventions were so rigid that they unhealthily perverted writers from discussing matters of importance that they should have been free to discuss—though there was not much on that plane which Browning does not discuss in one place or another, and what more could anybody reasonably wish to say about sadism after he had finished with Mr. Dennis in *Barnaby Rudge*? But it is a superficial and question-begging view which thinks it especially natural to fill your page with the crudest words for the sexual functions. The desire to be reticent about these functions is as natural as the desire to be outspoken. As Shakespeare knew, what is 'past reason hunted' is also 'past reason hated'. It is for that cause that *fais que voudras* is not a maxim that gets us very much further. The inhibitions are as natural as the impulses. It is a profound human instinct to have two standards of frankness in these matters—one for private conversation, one for public display—and anyone who tries to confound these two standards is merely an immature fool. Rabelais, if he did so in his day, is hardly a parallel with the modern Joycean, for Rabelais in his careless way barely knew whether he was writing for publication or not. Orwell complained of the critics who condemned the modern naturalists and who then turned back to praise Rabelais and 'hearty Rabelaisian humour'. Rabelais, he thought, was 'an exceptionally perverse, morbid writer, a case for psycho-analysis'. But, whether other people enjoy him or not, Rabelais did at least enjoy himself. The modern naturalists who, having claimed their freedom, then go on to use that freedom in order to proclaim their misery and the pointlessness of everything are less easy to understand. If nothing is worth while, why is writing worth while? The so-called naturalist begs the question in much the same way as the so-called rationalist. The whole question is, What is natural? and what is rational?

But to our present purpose it is Henry Miller's irresponsibility and Orwell's praise of it which is more important than Miller's literary standing. Why, if Orwell felt like that, did he not declare himself and remain a pacifist?

For the optimistic sentimental pacifist—the man who thinks that good is strong enough to conquer evil merely by displaying itself—he had always a contempt. Such a man, as he put it, merely handed the world over to Al Capone. His criticisms in the *Notebooks* both of official Christian bellicosity and common Christian pacifism are penetrating and sensible.

> Yesterday attended a more or less compulsory Home Guard church parade to take part in the national day of prayer. . . . Appalled by the jingoism and self-righteousness of the whole thing . . . I am not shocked by the Church condoning war, as many people profess to be—nearly always people who are not religious believers themselves, I notice. If you accept government, you accept war, and, if you accept war, you must in most cases desire one side or the other to win. I can never work up any disgust over bishops blessing the colours of regiments, etc. All that kind of thing is founded on a sentimental idea that fighting is incompatible with loving your enemies. Actually you can only love your enemies if you are willing to kill them in certain circumstances. But what is disgusting about services like these is the absence of any kind of self-criticism. Apparently God is expected to help us on the ground that we are *better* than the Germans. In the set prayer composed for the occasion God is asked 'to turn the hearts of our enemies, and to

help us to forgive them; to give them repentance for their misdoings and a readiness to make amends'. Nothing about our enemies forgiving us. It seems to me that the Christian attitude would be that we are no better than our enemies—we are all miserable sinners, but it so happens that it would be better if our cause prevailed and therefore that it is legitimate to pray for this.

Fair enough. But if the only issue left to us is which of rival Al Capones shall be our master, is it worth fighting about? I do not know what answer Orwell would have given if the war had opened with Hitler and Stalin belligerents on opposite sides. As he was still willing to work and hope for a Republican victory in Spain even after the Communists had shown their hands and as there was an element of the genuine traditionalism which he valued in Franco and no traditionalism at all in Hitler, it is probable that even then he would on the balance have declared against Hitler. But of course the Nazi-Soviet Pact saved him, as it saved so many people, from a difficult moral choice. So long as 'the stream-lined men' stood together there was just a chance that by defeating them, we might escape them—or at any rate our children might escape them—altogether. It was worth taking.

If you set passage against passage in his writings, it is not possible to extract from them a single coherent theory about pacifism. Sometimes he wrote as if war was not only in itself a great evil but also a futility because out of its conflict emerged, not the victory of the just cause, but a new and more evil tyranny. At others he called on the upholders of just causes to fight on even when all hope of victory was gone and denounced pacifists as merely insincere, their pacifism 'secretly inspired by an admiration for power and successful cruelty'. Not only did he exhort the Spanish Republicans to fight on. In his *Notebooks* he wrote on May 28, 1940, 'Horrible as it is I hope that the B.E.F. is cut to pieces sooner than capitulate.' The memory of an heroic resistance, immediately futile, would help to preserve the love of freedom for the future. But what use was that if our future masters of 1984 were going to destroy our memories? He never settled these contradictions. Rather, like Walt Whitman, he gloried in them.

There are two sorts of pacifist. There is the hedonistic pacifist and the religious pacifist. The hedonistic pacifist will not fight because it is too much trouble to fight. Suffering and death are such great evils that any sort of surrender is to be preferred to them. Not only will he refuse to resist but he will accept any demands, however outrageous to honour, that may be made upon him rather than submit himself to inconvenience. In such a pacifism there is nothing that is at all admirable, nor did Orwell at all admire it. But the position of the religious pacifist is quite different. It is merely the physical weapons of war that are forbidden to him. He claims no right to disinterest himself in what happens or to accept dishonour. In both the great Biblical texts in which pacifism appears to be recommended a positive duty to endure and testify and suffer is asserted as a necessary alternative to physical resistance. We must turn the other cheek—a gesture of defiance rather than of weakness. We are bidden indeed not to resist evil but at the same time to overcome evil with good—a very positive policy indeed, if only we can find a way to carry it through, and it seems to have been Orwell's opinion that, in the modern world at any rate, the second policy—the policy of religious pacifism—was perhaps the best policy, but that the argument was a theoretical one of no practical importance because the overwhelming majority of pacifists were not pacifists of that sort and the pacifism which they would practise would be no more than the base hedonistic pacifism of surrender.

He discussed the question in some detail in his essay on Gandhi—written shortly before he died. So many pacifist arguments assume that, if the aggressor is not resisted, he will at once be shamed out of his violence. There is clearly no reason for such an assumption. On the contrary, as Orwell writes with common sense in his essay on 'Lear, Tolstoy and the Fool', 'If you throw away your weapons, some less scrupulous person will pick them up. If you turn the other cheek, you will get a harder blow on it than you got on the first one. This does not always happen, but it is to be expected and you ought not to complain if it does happen.'

It is arguable that, if the Christian pacifists all showed a worthy witness, in the long run the men of violence would be shamed out of violence. But even so we must be prepared for it that in the meantime and before this conversion a lot of innocent people, whom we in principle will not raise a finger to help, will be done to death. 'In relation to the late war', he wrote, 'one question that every pacifist had a clear obligation to answer was, "What about the Jews? Are you prepared to see them exterminated? If not, how do you propose to save them without resorting to war?" I must say that I have never heard from any Western pacifist an honest answer to this question.' Orwell admired Gandhi because he frankly faced that question and frankly said that 'the German Jews ought to commit collective suicide, which would have aroused the world and the people of Germany to Hitler's violence'. After the war, Gandhi said that 'the Jews had been killed anyway and might as well have died significantly'.

A pacifism which does not understand that such harsh consequences are inherent in its logic is beneath contempt. But is even a pacifism which clear-headedly accepts such consequences to be embraced? All turns surely on whether it can give any sort of assurance of final success. It can indeed be argued that Gandhi's pacifism both got the British out of India and got them out of India—if not without blood-shed—at least without an Anglo-Indian war—and that was a tremen-dous achievement. So it was. But there is much force in Orwell's argument that Gandhi's pacifism was only effective because he was opposed to the semi-liberal British régime, which was not prepared to go to final lengths against him and which allowed him to show the world his example. Hitler would have just put him in a gas-chamber where he would have been 'vaporized' and never heard of again. How could his example have been effective without advertisement? If we submit to tyranny, we take a great risk that our passive resistance will be ineffective and that we shall only discover its ineffectiveness when it is too late to do anything about it. On the other hand it is equally true that, if we resist it in arms, war—even a victorious war—raises new issues so that we can have no certainty that the society that emerges out of the war will not be worse—morally as well as physi-cally—than the society that went into it. The only golden rule is, as Ibsen says, that there is no golden rule. Each particular problem must be faced on the balance of its demerits.

But the truth is that Orwell was not by temperament a neutral. He was always contemptuous of the false and futile logic which argued that, because there was right and wrong on both sides, therefore there was equal right and wrong on both sides—that, because you could only have half a loaf, you might just as well have no bread. And certainly there was no trace of pacifism in the little book, *The Lion and the Unicorn*, which he wrote, as he records, when bombers were overhead during the Battle of Britain and the succeeding months—wrote, that is, after Dunkirk, when Russia was still a hostile neutral and when, since the Greek War had not yet broken out, we were still without an ally on the Continent. The exact timing is important.

The Lion and the Unicorn consists of three essays—'England, Your England', 'Shopkeepers at War', and 'The English Revolution'.

'England, Your England' tells us what, in Orwell's opinion England is. The English are a race devoted above all to private, unofficial activities. They are an inartistic race, excelling only in literature—of all arts the one least easily communicable to foreigners. 'Without definite religious belief,' he thinks, 'they have retained a deep tinge of Christian feeling.' The 'realism' of some other nations they have wholly rejected. They are a gentle people. They have an ineradicable belief in 'the law'—that there is a point beyond which wickedness and irregularity cannot go. Though 'England is the most class-ridden country under the sun,' yet there is behind all their differences a deep unity of the English people—often a unity in error, but a unity also in face of peril, which makes treason, when the nation is in danger, a thing unknown. England has been throughout her history for better or for worse an aristocratic country but in the years before the war her governing class had decayed. It had decayed because with the growing concentration of industry and with the passing of power into the hands of the new 'managerial' class, the old governing class had no longer a function in society. Self-preservation compelled it to 'stupidity' because, if it had understood the nature of the modern world it would have understood that it itself had no reason for exist- ence. If they had been wholly corrupt, the governing class would have sold the country to Hitler, but they were not wholly corrupt but stupid, and therefore neither willing to be traitors nor intelligent enough to recognize their country's true foes; 'tossed to and fro between their incomes and their principles, it was impossible that men like Chamberlain should do anything but make the worst of both worlds'. Meanwhile the obverse of the 'blimps' were the left-wing intellectuals who by their constant sniggering at all patriotic emotion had made their contribution to a condition in which Hitler was en- couraged to attack us and in which our will to resist had come so desperately near to being undermined. The old division of the nation into two classes was rapidly coming to an end. The middle class, far from vanishing as Marx had predicted, was spreading itself out over the territory of the other two classes. The death of class privilege was inevitable. 'This war, unless we are defeated, will wipe out most of the existing privileges,' he wrote. 'The gentleness, the hypocrisy, the thoughtlessness, the reverence for law and the hatred of uniforms will remain, along with the suet puddings and the misty skies.' In fact there'll always be an England.

Whatever criticisms of detail one may make of this essay, its major note is unmistakable. The deepest of all Orwell's emotions was his overwhelming love of England—a love which he made no attempt to keep clear of the sentimental. He had this love at all times, and naturally, and wholly admirably, it came out most strongly in England's hour of greatest danger. He records in his *Notebooks* on October 19, 1940, 'the unspeakable depression of lighting the fires every morning with papers of a year ago, and getting glimpses of their optimistic headlines as they go up in smoke'. And so, if we can find verbal contradictions between what Orwell said about the war and neutrality at such a time and what he may have said before the war in, say, *Inside the Whale*, the explanation is again wholly simple and wholly honourable. Many of us, from our different points of view, were willing to sit around debating shades of policy and the rights and wrongs of war and peace before the war came. In the day of peril we forgot these debates and closed the ranks. Need we be ashamed? That is what we all did and Orwell, along with the rest. He wrote in the 'Limit to Pessimism' in the *New English Weekly* of April 25, 1940:

> It is all very well to be 'advanced' and 'enlightened', to snigger at Colonel Blimp and proclaim your emancipation from all traditional loyalties, but a time comes when the sand of the desert is sodden red and what have I done for thee, my England? As I was brought up in this tradition myself I can recognise it under strange disguises, and also sympathise with it, for even at its stupidest and most sentimental it is a comelier thing than the shallow self-righteousness of the left-wing intelligentsia.

Mr. Fyvell has described how at this time he made the acquaintance of Orwell out of which sprang a literary collaboration.

> It was at his small mews-flat near Baker Street in London, a rather poverty-stricken affair of one or two rather bare, austere rooms with second-hand furniture. I saw an extremely tall, thin man, looking more than his years, with gentle eyes and deep lines that hinted at suffering on his face. The word 'saint' was used by one of his friends and critics after his death and—well—perhaps he had a touch of that quality. Certainly there was nothing of the fierce pamphleteer in his personal manner. He was awkward, almost excessively mild. Both about him and his wife (who was also not in very good health and died under a minor operation in 1945) there was something strangely unphysical.

On his desk I recall I saw several letters which were obviously from the Income Tax authorities—unopened. He had left the letters lying there, Orwell said, because at the moment he simply had no money . . . When I succeeded him for a time as literary editor of *Tribune*, I discovered a whole drawer full of manuscripts most hopelessly unsuitable, which Orwell had nevertheless accepted. I asked him why he had done this. He agreed sadly that it was almost incredible how badly some people could write. But the bad writers—that was the trouble—did not know how wretched their work was. And, however fiercely he might polemicise against intellectuals in general, he had not the heart to tell any individual writer that his work was fit only for rejection.

In spite of his health Orwell joined the Home Guard. There he was soon made a sergeant. He was not, according to Mr. Warburg, who served under him as a corporal, either a tidy or a very efficient soldier. He was a keen and conscientious one. But, since he had a ready pen, he put that pen at the service of his country. *The Lion and the Unicorn* was a work of conscious war-time propaganda. We must not forget this if we find in it one or two arguments which appear from the point of view of absolute truth to be a little twisted, here and there perhaps too much enthusiasm and once in a while an obvious answer to an argument slurred over.

Wretched as was the policy, in Orwell's opinion, of the National Government in the eight years before the war, that policy, he recognizes, had the broad support of the nation. And this is clearly true. The Socialist alternative to it of disarmament and pulling snooks at Hitler was not a policy but an essay in lunacy. The accusation against our leaders in those years was not that they did not act differently, granted that public opinion was as it was, but that they did so little to rouse public opinion to the nation's peril. Though our business is not with passing verdicts on particular politicians of the past, Baldwin's responsibility on this charge is a heavy one and would seem almost to justify Orwell's description of him as 'simply a hole in the air'. Orwell's ingenious theory that the governing class in these years was, and was compelled to be, exceptionally stupid, is less certain. It suits his revolutionary purpose to put the blame on them. I should myself give an almost exactly opposite explanation. I have no particular love for governing classes or for any other people who wield power, but I should say that it was inevitable in the nature of things that the period should have been a period of retreat in British power. The 1914 war had impoverished us and enriched America. The industrialization of other nations had robbed us of the position of unique advantage which we held in the nineteenth century. The aeroplane had changed the strategic situation greatly to our disadvantage. I should have said that an aristocracy, untrammelled by any necessity to carry public opinion with it on the details of its policy, had we had such a form of government, would have been much more likely to grasp this change in circumstances and to adjust its policy to it than a democracy, consisting of voters who paid no attention to foreign affairs. 'Of course you realize, Connolly . . . that whoever wins this war we shall emerge a second-rate nation,' Orwell had said thirty years before at his private school. But Connolly had not realized it, and the average British voter had not realized it thirty years afterwards and perhaps has not even realized it yet, and it would be asking much of a democratic politician, with an opponent ever ready to trip him up, to expect him to explain it.

The main argument of 'Shopkeepers at War' was that the war and Hitler's victories had proved that private capitalism does not work. 'War, for all its evil, is at any rate an unanswerable test of strength, like a try-your-grip machine', Orwell wrote. Hitler had proved that a planned society, whether it was planning for evil or for good, was a more efficient machine for war than an unplanned society. To that argument, developed over some pages, there are at any rate two answers. Orwell wrote in the months immediately after the defeat of France and Dunkirk. What experience had really proved was not so much that a planned society was more efficient for war as that it was more efficient for a short war. As the war dragged on and unexpected and unforeseen problems presented themselves, it became far from certain whether, even on a test of mere efficiency, an utterly rigid planned society was the more efficient—whether, even if some of the manifestations of liberty were ridiculous and disedifying, a society that was less closely planned did not show itself in the long run and for a long war more flexible and therefore more efficient than a planned society. Secondly, it was proved that power corrupts not only morally but intellectually and that in the end, as with the attack on Russia, the masters of the planned society make gigantic mistakes which bring upon them their ruin.

Therefore, whatever the intrinsic desirability of an egalitarian society and the English Revolution which Orwell recommends in his third essay, that society must stand or fall on its own merits to a much greater extent than he allowed. The conclusion does not follow inevitably out of his argument to nearly the extent that he pretended. It may be true, as he claimed, that 'in all Lord Halifax's speeches there is not one concrete proposal for which a single inhabitant of Europe would risk the top joint of his little finger', but, when the inhabitants of Europe came to rise against Nazi tyranny, they did not rise in order to fight for Lord Halifax's speeches. They rose to get rid of Hitler. It was, by and large, sufficient as a war aim.

The only cause for which Orwell thought that the peoples of England and of Europe would rise was the cause of 'Socialism'. By Socialism he did not mean the British Labour party, as it then existed, which was, he thought, an anti-revolutionary body for which he had contempt. Still less did he mean 'the suffocating stupidity of left-wing propaganda', which had frightened away those who should have been its first supporters by its folly in being 'anti-British'. As he wrote in his verses in reply to the left-wing pacifist, who wrote under the name of Obadiah Hornbrooke:

> At times it's almost a more dangerous deed
> *Not* to object; I know, for I've been bitten.
> I wrote in nineteen-forty that at need
> I'd fight to keep the Nazis out of Britain;
> And Christ! how shocked the pinks were! Two years later
> I hadn't lived it down; one had the effrontery
> To write three pages calling me a 'traitor'.
> So black a crime it is to love one's country.

By Socialism he meant that 'the State, representing the whole nation, own everything, and everyone is a state employee'. Added to it, we must have 'approximate equality of incomes (it need only be approximate), political democracy and abolition of all hereditary privilege, especially in education'. He set out the sort of political programme that he had in mind—something of the sort of language that was to be soon afterwards talked by the Commonwealth party.

  I. Nationalization of land, mines, railways, banks and major industries.
  II. Limitation of incomes, on such a scale that the highest tax-free income in Britain does not exceed the lowest by more than ten to one.
  III. Reform of the educational system along democratic lines.

IV. Immediate Dominion status for India, with power to secede
when the war is over.

V. Formation of an Imperial General Council, in which the
coloured peoples are to be represented.

VI. Declaration of formal alliance with China, Abyssinia and all
other victims of the Fascist Powers.

Such ideas, he thought, if boldly proclaimed, must inevitably conquer in the end. They would conquer in the end even if England was
immediately vanquished in the war and occupied. For a nation which
has dedicated itself can, like Bunyan's Mansoul—it is my comparison,
not Orwell's—only be finally captured by the consent of its own
inhabitants. The idea could only be defeated if it was abandoned. Once
we had proclaimed our vision all that we should have to fear would
be its destruction by a premature peace negotiated by those who hated
it. 'We may see German troops marching down Whitehall,' he wrote,
'but another process, ultimately deadly to the German power-dream,
will have been started. . . . The final ruin of England could only be
accomplished by an English government acting under orders from
Berlin. . . . An army of unemployed, led by millionaires quoting the
Sermon on the Mount—that is our danger.'

Again, in criticizing these essays we must remind ourselves that they
are essays in war-time propaganda and make allowance for phrases
and for enthusiasms which we would not find in Orwell's writing
either before or after the war. Thus no one was a more noble hater
than he of 'tough' policies. Indeed it was their quality of gentleness
that he loved above all other qualities of the English. It was because of
that quality in them that he felt justified in surrendering himself without qualification to his patriotism and to the cause of their resistance.
I do not think that in any other work than this would he have written
of his revolution, 'Whether it happens with or without bloodshed is
largely an accident of time and place.' He knew that it was essential if
the whole vision was not to be destroyed and made foul that it should
happen without the English shedding of English blood. In no other
work would he have written of his revolutionary government, 'It
will not have the smallest scruple about attacking hostile neutrals.' In
our hour of most desperate peril few of us perhaps would have been
willing to give an utterly unqualified pledge that, whatever the
Germans might do, we would never under any circumstances attack a
neutral state, but there is none among us today, I think, who is not

profoundly proud and profoundly thankful that we were able to preserve to the end of the war our respect for the rights of neutrals. Then
again there is an almost comically false logic in his sentences, 'It is
customary among the more soft-boiled intellectuals of the left to
declare that, if we fight against the Nazis we shall "go Nazi" ourselves. They might almost equally well say that if we fight against
Negroes we shall turn black.' Obviously the 'soft-boiled intellectuals'
exaggerated, as is their habit. Obviously there were features of Nazism
which were essentially German and which were unlikely to find imitation in detail in another country whatever its circumstances. But as
obviously the comparison of a Nazi and a negro is a foolish comparison. As Orwell himself had learnt in Spain, there is a great deal of
truth in Roy Campbell's line, 'We become that which we fight.' We
were only able to defeat the Germans by adopting their methods and
their discipline to a much greater extent than we would have liked,
and the England that emerged from two wars against Germany is
indeed a very different country from Germany but it is an England
much more like to Germany than was the England of 1914. 18B and
Crichel Down are indeed small things in comparison with Buchenwald
and Auschwitz. Still we would rather that there had not been 18B and
Crichel Down. With all his talk about progress and the future and the
insignificance of religion there was no one, as *The Road to Wigan Pier*
and *Coming up for Air* most fully show, who was more conscious that
there was loss as well as gain when the old ways gave place to new and
who was more frightened of the new world of Slough and Dagenham,
whose 'children grow up with an intimate knowledge of magnetos
and in complete ignorance of the Bible'. At the end of *Animal Farm*,
it will be remembered, all the pigs become like men and the men like
pigs. 'The creatures outside looked from pig to man, and from man
to pig, and from pig to man again; but already it was impossible to
say which was which.' It is true that this transformation resulted immediately from a collaboration, but it was a collaboration that emerged
out of a conflict and that degenerated into a conflict again—a very
temporary essay in 'peaceful co-existence'.

Orwell put 'nationalization' at the head of his suggested political
programme. But it is not, I think, unfair to suggest that he did that
primarily to keep himself 'on side' with those who were likely to give
him political support. 'Nationalization' had played no part in his pre-
war writing, and of all the policies of the post-war Socialist government it was that which left him coldest. 'Equality' was what he cared

about—not 'state ownership'. It was far too big a gamble who 'the State' was going to be, for state ownership to be at all a safe bet. And even on equality, when he ceased to be a political pamphleteer and became a philosopher, he was far from certain where the balance of advantage and disadvantage lay. Four years later, and before the war had even ended, as we have already noted, he was to write in the conclusion of his essay on 'Raffles and Miss Blandish', 'one is driven to feel that snobbishness, like hypocrisy, is a check upon behaviour whose value from a social point of view has been underrated'.

A Socialist Government was elected in 1945 and each reader has his own opinion how far its achievement corresponded to the revolutionary purpose which Orwell demanded. Certainly he proved wrong, as indeed he frankly admitted in a London Letter in the *Partisan Review* in the winter of 1945, in thinking that such revolutionary measures were immediately necessary to win the war or to persuade people on the Continent to fight the war. Nor did his fear of 'an army of unemployed led by millionaires quoting the Sermon on the Mount' in order to make peace ever prove real. Indeed most people would today agree that the mistake made was not so much that of a readiness for a premature peace as the demand for unconditional surrender not only of Hitler but of Germany, which has made it impossible for us to make peace at all. But all such criticisms, as criticisms of Orwell's *The Lion and the Unicorn* are irrelevant. For *The Lion and the Unicorn* was written, as we must remember, when Russia was still Germany's ally. All 'the stream-lined men' were against us, and it was their union which gave moral content to our resistance. With Germany's attack on Russia the whole moral nature of the struggle changed to his mind. He commented on it in his *Notebooks* in a characteristic, if obviously *ben trovato*, anecdote. 'The story is going round', he wrote, 'that when the news of Hitler's invasion of Russia reached a New York café, where some Communists were talking, one of them who had gone out to the lavatory returned to find that "the party line" had changed in his absence.'

I think that on balance he would have thought it better for us to have been beaten with Russia on Germany's side than to have won with Russia on our side. For evil as an ally is far more dangerous than evil as an enemy. If it is your ally, you have to compromise with it in your soul, to speak well of it, to admit the enemy within the gates of Mansoul, and Orwell never doubted that Russian Communism was evil, never doubted the immense danger of the Anglo-Russian alliance and thought it most doubtful if the England which he loved, which had survived the enmity of Germany, would be able to survive the friendship of Russia.

In 1941 Orwell undertook temporary work with the B.B.C. in its Far Eastern service, where he served along with Mr. Brander. He worked hard there until February 1945, giving most of the talks to Malaya himself, although as it afterwards appeared, there was little reason to think that anyone except the Japanese monitors ever heard those talks. He worked in underground bricked-up buildings, in airless rooms lit by artificial light. It was, alas, I fear, the war-time B.B.C. which served him as a model for *1984*'s Ministry of Truth. Such a life cannot have been good for one who was suffering in his lung. In the last year of the war his wife collapsed after a minor operation and died. Her death, Orwell said, was probably due to the fact that she was underfed as she had consistently surrendered her rations to others. There is no doubt that Orwell had done the same.

After his wife's death and for the last months of the war he went abroad as a correspondent for the *Observer* to France, Germany and Austria.

XII

Animal Farm

WHATEVER the advantages or disadvantages of the German invasion of Russia, at least it saved Britain from the risk of immediate invasion and defeat, and thus such a man as Orwell, who was alarmed at the ultimate consequences of the Russian alliance, was able to live his life under a lesser strain in the last years of the war than in the first. He was able to give his mind once more to creative writing. Yet the problem what to write was not simple. The crying need to his mind was to arouse public opinion to the dangers of the Russian alliance. Yet the mood of the country at the time when Stalingrad was being defended was not such that it would tolerate a straightforward and bitter attack on Russia—the kind of attack which he had already launched in his essay in the composite volume, the *Betrayal of the Left*, which he had published in 1941, when of course public opinion in Britain was willing to tolerate it because Russia was still bound in hostility to us by the Nazi-Soviet Pact. Now direction could only be found out by indirection. The consequence, immediately and apparently inconvenient to Orwell as a writer, turned out in the event to be brilliantly fortunate. For it caused Orwell to make his point by the indirect, roundabout, whimsical road of an animal fairy-story and thus led him to experiment with a new form of writing of which he proved himself magnificently the master. Whereas his previous books had never had more than small and struggling sales, *Animal Farm* at once caught the public fancy in almost every country of the world—particularly in the United States—was translated into every one of the leading languages, established him as one of the best-selling authors of the day and incidentally gave him for the first time in life a tolerable income.

Fortune favoured him in the timing of the publication which it imposed upon him. *Animal Farm*, a short book of less than a hundred pages, was written between November 1943 and February 1944. It was, said Orwell, 'the only one of my books I really sweated over'. What would have been its fate had it immediately found a publisher and appeared in the winter of 1944, when Russia was still fighting and

Western statesmen were full of optimism about the possibility of just arrangements with her, it is hard to say. Influences and the climate of opinion might well have prevented it from gaining any but a small and eccentric market. Happily for Orwell four publishers in succession rejected it on the ground that it would be against public policy at such a time to put on the market a book attacking our Russian ally. As a result it only appeared through Messrs. Secker and Warburg in the early summer of 1945, in the month of the German surrender, when fighting had come to an end, and its first circulation exactly coincided with the beginnings of popular disillusionment with Russian policy, as people in the West saw to their dismay the ugly methods by which the Russians were establishing themselves in the East. By chance it exactly struck the public mood and was the first book to strike it.

The story of *Animal Farm* is so familiar that it hardly needs detailed recapitulation. An old boar, of the name of Major, on the brink of death summons to the barn all the animals on the farm of a broken-down drunkard, called Jones, and gives to them his farewell message —the result of his long meditation on life. It is that the enemy of all animals is Man. Man lives by exploiting his animals. The animals produce their food of one sort or another, but they are not allowed to draw for themselves any benefit from their increased production. Man seizes it all for his own need, allows to the animals only sufficient to keep them alive and able to work, cynically and ruthlessly exploits them in their lives and as cynically and ruthlessly destroys them as soon as their days of work are done. Let the animals rise up, expel the enemy Man and run the farm as a co-operative farm of animals in the animals' own interest.

Three days later Major dies, but he has left behind him his message of revolt. The animals are, it is true, not as yet clear how to carry into practice this gospel of revolt. They meet and sing together their new hymn 'Beasts of England'. An unpremeditated accident eventually brings on the revolt. On mid-summer eve Jones gets drunk in the neighbouring village of Wilmington. The hired men milk the cows and then go off for a day's rabbiting, leaving the animals unfed. In the afternoon, when the animals can stand their hunger no longer, one of the cows breaks in the door of the store-shed with her horn and all the animals rush in and start helping themselves from the bin. Jones wakes up from his drunken slumber. He and the men rush out with whips in their hands and start laying about them. Though there had been no plan of resistance, the animals turn on Jones and the men, attack them and, before they know where they are, have driven them helter-skelter from the farm.

Thus the animals established themselves with unexpected ease as the masters of the farm. It is Orwell's humour to show no great difficulty in the task in which they had expected their main difficulty—in the seizure of power—but enormous and finally fatal difficulty in the task which they had hardly expected to present a problem at all—in the exercise of power when seized. With the death of Major the leadership of the animals falls into the hands of the two leading pigs, Snowball and Napoleon—for Orwell throughout represents the pigs as far more intelligent than any of the other animals. Of these he explains with delicious mock solemnity that Napoleon was 'not much of a talker' but had 'a reputation for getting his own way'. Snowball was quicker, but 'was not considered to have the same depth of character'. There is a full and vivid portrait gallery of other animals of which the most notable are Boxer, the good, stupid, unsuspicious horse, of immense physical strength, to whose unquestioning mind the remedy for all problems was to work harder—Squealer, another pig, who was, as it were, the P.R.O. to Napoleon—Benjamin, the donkey, the only cynic among the animals, who knows that life has always been hard, believes that it always will be hard and is sceptical of all promises of improvement, and Moses, the raven, who does no work but continually tells to the other animals his tale of the Sugar Candy Mountains above the sky where 'it was Sunday seven days a week, clover was in season all the year round and lump-sugar and linseed oil grew on the hedges'.

In the early days of Animal Farm the animals have to prepare themselves for the inevitable counter-attack when Jones and his fellow men will attempt to recapture the farm. The rivalry between Snowball and Napoleon is becoming increasingly evident and they differ and quarrel on every point of policy, but in face of the threat of Man's attack they do not dare to let things come to an open breach. Then in October Jones attacks and, owing to the heroism and strategy of Snowball, he is driven off in rout at the Battle of the Cowshed.

After the defeat of Jones there is no longer any reason why Snowball and Napoleon should preserve even an appearance of amity. The fundamental difference between them is that Snowball thinks that the animals should 'send out more pigeons and stir up rebellion among the animals on other farms', while Napoleon thinks that 'what the animals must do was to produce firearms and train themselves to the use of them'. They also differ over Snowball's ambition to build a windmill to which Napoleon is opposed.

Napoleon bides his time. He has made himself the master of a litter of young puppies which he is secretly training up as his gendarmerie. Then when the day comes, he suddenly introduces these dogs, as they have by then become, into the assembly and lets them loose on Snowball, whom they chase from the farm. It is then that the pace of the degradation increases. More and more Napoleon and the pigs who are faithful to him seize for themselves almost all the food of the farm. The other animals are forced down to a standard of living lower than that which they had in Jones's time. They have to work harder. Whenever anything goes wrong on the farm, the fault is ascribed to Snowball, who is supposed to be lurking in a near-by farm and making nocturnal raids into Animal Farm. He was, the animals are told, in league with Jones from the first. Documents had proved it. The history of Animal Farm is unblushingly falsified. The animals are told, first, that Snowball's part in the Battle of the Cowshed was greatly exaggerated, then that he had in fact fought in it on Jones's side. The windmill is built, but the animals are now told that it was Napoleon who was in favour of it all along and Snowball who was against it. To all complaints that the animals may make at their hard lot the invariable and crushing reply is, 'Do you want Jones back?' They must put up with all hardships as the only alternative to this more awful fate.

In the original constitution the animals had sworn to have no dealings with Man, but the next summer Napoleon announces the new policy by which the Farm is to trade with neighbouring men in order to obtain certain essential materials of life. The trade is of course to be kept entirely in Napoleon's own hands. No other animals than he are to have any contact with the surrounding men. Then he moves into Jones's house and establishes it as his palace. He lives a life increasingly remote from the other animals by whom he is rarely seen. In the autumn a storm blows down the windmill, but of course it is explained that its destruction is not at all due to defects in building but to the sabotage of Snowball. The winter is a hard one and there is a situation bordering on rebellion—particularly among the hens who object to the seizure of their eggs for the purpose of trade with men. Napoleon deals with it in characteristically unhesitating and terrible fashion.

The four pigs waited, trembling, with guilt written on every line of their countenances. Napoleon now called upon them to confess their crimes. They were the same four pigs as had protested when Napoleon abolished the Sunday Meetings. Without any further prompting they confessed that they had been secretly in touch with Snowball ever since his expulsion, that they had collaborated with him in destroying the windmill and that they had entered into an agreement with him to hand over Animal Farm to Mr. Frederick. They added that Snowball had privately admitted to them that he had been Jones' secret agent for years past. When they had finished their confession, the dogs promptly tore their throats out, and in a terrible voice Napoleon demanded whether any other animal had anything to confess.

The three hens who had been the ringleaders in the attempted rebellion over the eggs now came forward and stated that Snowball had appeared to them in a dream and incited them to disobey Napoleon's orders. They, too, were slaughtered. Then a goose came forward and confessed to having secreted six ears of corn during the last year's harvest and eaten them in the night. Then a sheep confessed to having urinated in the drinking pool, urged to do this, so she said, by Snowball—and two other sheep confessed to having murdered an old ram, an especially devoted follower of Napoleon, by chasing him round and round a bonfire when he was suffering from a cough. They were all slain on the spot. And so the tale of confessions and executions went on, until there was a pile of corpses lying before Napoleon's feet and the air was heavy with the smell of blood, which had been unknown there since the expulsion of Jones.

After that the old song 'Beasts of England' is suppressed, and there is substituted for it Minimus's new song,

> Animal Farm, Animal Farm,
> Never through me shalt thou come to harm.

One after another the commandments on which Animal Farm was built are found to have been secretly altered. For 'No animal shall kill another animal', the animals now find the commandment to read, 'No animal shall kill another animal without cause.' 'No animal shall sleep in a bed' is now 'No animal shall sleep in a bed with sheets.' It had been Napoleon's plan to sell a load of timber to their neighbouring human farmer, Frederick, with the money for which he will buy machinery for the windmill. The timber is delivered and five-pound notes are paid to the animals in exchange. It is only when through their agent the animals attempt to use the five-pound notes for purchases that they find that Frederick has cheated them and that the notes are forgeries. Napoleon attempts to enlist the alliance of the animals' other neighbour, Pilkington, against Frederick, but Pilkington is unsympathetic. 'Serves you right,' he says. The humans determine on a second attack on Animal Farm. They come this time armed with guns. They destroy the windmill but are driven off in a second defeat.

It is a few days later that the pigs discover a case of whiskey in Jones's cellar, and it is, naturally enough, at the same time that the commandment 'No animal shall drink alcohol' is found now to read 'No animal shall drink alcohol to excess.'

All comes to a climax when the faithful Boxer one day falls down between the shafts and is no longer strong enough to work. Under the pretence that they are sending him to the vet to be cured, the pigs sell him to a knacker, tell the other animals that he has died at the vet's, in spite of having received every attention, and that his last words were 'Forward, Comrades!! Forward in the name of Rebellion! Long live Animal Farm! Long live Comrade Napoleon! Napoleon is always right!' With the money that they have received from Boxer's carcass the pigs buy a case of whiskey and hold a banquet in Jones's house.

The great mark of Animal Farm had been its hostility to everything that went on two legs. 'Four legs good, two legs bad' had been the continual bleat of the sheep and four legs had been the great mark of animalism, of animal solidarity. But now the pigs set themselves to learning how to walk on two legs. The motto of the Farm is changed into 'All animals are equal, but some animals are more equal than others', and one day the pigs emerge from Jones's house walking on two legs and with whips in their hands. They take out subscriptions to *John Bull*, *Tit-Bits* and the *Daily Mirror*. The obedient sheep, trained in secret by Squealer, change their bleat of 'Four legs good, two legs bad' into 'Four legs good, two legs better.'

After their second defeat in the Battle of the Windmill the neighbouring men had given up all hope of defeating and destroying the animals, nor indeed once the pigs had shown themselves as ready to impose discipline on their animals as was any human farmer, was there any longer any need, from their point of view, for them to do so. A policy of peaceful co-existence in every way suited them better. Parties of men used to come on visits to the farm and were taken round on conducted tours. At last there comes the night of the great banquet of alliance between the human Pilkington and Napoleon. The animals, looking in through the windows, see pigs and men sitting together and hear the exchange of congratulatory speeches. Mr. Pilkington 'believed that he was right in saying that the lower animals on Animal Farm did more work and received less food than any animals in the country. . . . If you have your lower animals to contend with, we have our lower classes.' As the celebrations proceed, the pigs, the animals notice, come to look more and more like men and the men more and more like pigs. 'The creatures outside looked from pig to man and from man to pig, and from pig to man again, but already it was impossible to say which was which.' But assimilation cannot bring harmony. They fall to playing cards, and the banquet breaks up into chaos as Mr. Pilkington and Napoleon each play the ace of spades simultaneously.

The interpretation of the fable is plain enough. Major, Napoleon, Snowball—Lenin, Stalin and Trotzky—Pilkington and Frederick, the two groups of non-Communist powers—the Marxian thesis, as expounded by Major, that society is divided into exploiters and exploited and that all the exploited need to do is to rise up, to expel the exploiters and seize the 'surplus value' which the exploiters have previously annexed to themselves—the Actonian thesis that power corrupts and the Burnhamian thesis that the leaders of the exploited, having used the rhetoric of equality to get rid of the old exploiters, establish in their place not a classless society but themselves as a new governing class—the greed and unprincipled opportunism of the non-Communist states, which are ready enough to overthrow the Communists by force so long as they imagine that their overthrow will be easy but begin to talk of peace when they find the task difficult and when they think that they can use the Communists to satisfy their greed—the dishonour among total thugs, as a result of which, though greed may make original ideology irrelevant, turning pigs into men and men into pigs, the thugs fall out among themselves, as the Nazis and the Communists fell out, not through difference of ideology but because in a society of utter baseness and insincerity there is no motive of confidence. The interpretation is so plain that no serious critic can dispute it. Those Russian critics who have professed to see in it merely a general satire on bureaucracy without any special reference to any particular country can hardly be taken seriously.

Yet even a total acceptance of Orwell's political opinions would not in itself make *Animal Farm* a great work of art. The world is full of animal fables in which this or that country is symbolized by this or that animal, and very tedious affairs the greater number of them are—and that, irrespective of whether we agree or disagree with their opinions. To be a great book, a book of animal fables requires literary greatness as well as a good cause. Such greatness *Animal Farm* surely possesses. As Orwell fairly claimed, *Animal Farm* 'was the first book in which I tried, with full consciousness of what I was doing, to fuse political purpose and artistic purpose into one whole'—and he succeeded.

The problems that are set by this peculiar form of art, which makes animals behave like human beings, are clear. The writer must throughout be successful in preserving a delicate and whimsical balance. As Johnson truly says in his criticism of Dryden's *Hind and the Panther*, there is an initial absurdity in making animals discuss complicated intellectual problems—the nature of the Church's authority in Dryden's case, the communist ideology in Orwell's. The absurdity can only be saved from ridicule if the author is able to couch his argument in very simple terms and to draw his illustrations from the facts of animal life. In this Orwell is as successful as he could be—a great deal more successful incidentally than Dryden, who in the excitement of the argument often forgets that it is animals who are supposed to be putting it forward. The practical difficulties of the conceit must either be ignored or apparently solved in some simple and striking—if possible, amusing —fashion. Since obviously they could not in reality be solved at all, the author merely makes himself ridiculous if he allows himself to get bogged down in tedious and detailed explanations which at the end of all cannot in the nature of things explain anything. Thus Orwell is quite right merely to ignore the difficulties of language, to assume that the animals can communicate with one another by speech—or to assume that the new ordinance which forbids any animal to take another animal's life could be applied with only the comparatively mild consequence of gradual increase in animal population. He is justified in telling us the stories of the two attacks by men for the recapture of the Farm but in refusing to spoil his story by allowing the men to take the full measures which obviously men would take if they found themselves in such an impossible situation. The means by which the animals rout the men are inevitably signally unconvincing if we are to consider them seriously at all. It would as obviously be ridiculous to delay for pages to describe how animals build windmills or how they write up commandments on a wall. It heightens the comedy to give a passing sentence of description to their hauling the stone up a hill so that it may be broken into manageable fractions when it falls over the precipice, or to Squealer, climbing a ladder to paint up his message.

The animal fable, if it is to succeed at all, ought clearly to carry with it a gay and light-hearted message. It must be full of comedy and laughter. The form is too far removed from reality to tolerate sustained bitterness. Both Chaucer and La Fontaine discovered this in their times, and the trouble with Orwell was that the lesson which he wished to teach was not ultimately a gay lesson. It was not the lesson that mankind had its foibles and its follies but that all would be well in the end. It was more nearly a lesson of despair—the lesson that anarchy was intolerable, that mankind could not be ruled without entrusting power somewhere or other and, to whomsoever power was entrusted, it was almost certain to be abused. For power was itself corrupting. But it was Orwell's twisted triumph that in the relief of the months immediately after the war mankind was probably not prepared to take such dark medicine if it had been offered to it undiluted. It accepted it because it came in this gay and coloured and fanciful form.

The film version gives to *Animal Farm* a happy ending. The animals all the world over, hearing how Napoleon has betrayed the animal cause, rise up against him at the end and in a second revolution expel him. After this second revolution, we are left to believe, a rule of freedom and equality is established and survives. But of course this ending makes nonsense of the whole thesis. It was the Orwellian thesis, right or wrong, that power inevitably corrupts and that revolutions therefore inevitably fail of their purpose. The new masters are necessarily corrupted by their new power. The second revolution would necessarily have failed of its purpose just as the first had failed. It would merely have set up a second vicious circle.

Animal Farm possesses two essential qualities of a successful animal fable. On the one hand the author of such a fable must have the Swift-like capacity of ascribing with solemn face to the animals idiotic but easily recognized human qualities, decking them out in aptly changed phraseology to suit the animal life—ascribe the quality and then pass quickly on before the reader has begun to find the point overlaboured. This Orwell has to perfection. Thus:

Snowball also busied himself with organizing the other animals into what he called Animal Committees. He was indefatigable at this. He formed the Egg Production Committee for the hens, the Clean Tails League for the cows, the Wild Comrades' Re-education Committee (the object of which was to tame the cats and rabbits), the Whiter Wool Movement for the sheep, and various others, besides instituting classes in reading and writing. On the whole these projects were a failure. The attempt to tame the wild creatures, for instance, broke down almost immediately. They continued to behave very much as before and, when treated with generosity, simply took advantage of it. The cat joined the Re-education Committee and was very active in it for some days. She was seen one day sitting on a roof talking to some sparrows who were just out of reach. She was telling them that all animals were now comrades and that any sparrow who chose could come and perch on her paw; but the sparrows kept their distance.

Or:

When the laws of Animal Farm were first formulated, the retiring age had been fixed for horses and pigs at twelve, for cows at fourteen, for dogs at nine, for sheep at seven and for hens and geese at five. Liberal old-age pensions had been agreed upon. As yet no animal had actually retired on a pension, but of late the subject had been discussed more and more. Now that the small field beyond the orchard had been set aside for barley, it was rumoured that a corner of the large pasture was to be fenced off and turned into a grazing-ground for superannuated animals. For a horse, it was said, the pension would be five pounds of corn a day and, in winter, fifteen pounds of hay, with a carrot or possibly an apple on public holidays.

But what is also essential—and this is often overlooked—is that the writer should have himself a genuine love of animals—should be able to create here and there, in the midst of all his absurdity, scenes of animal life, in themselves realistic and lovable. In that Chaucer, the first and greatest of Orwell's masters in this form of art, pre-eminently excelled. It was in that that Orwell himself excelled. He had always been himself a lover of animals, intimate with their ways. 'Most of the good memories of my childhood, and up to the age of about twenty,' he wrote in Such, Such were the Joys, 'are in some way connected with animals', and it was the work with animals which attracted him in maturer years to agricultural life. There is a real poetic quality, mixed whimsically in with absurdity, in his picture of the first meeting of the animals in the barn with which the book opens.

At one end of the big barn, on a sort of raised platform, Major was already ensconced on his bed of straw, under a lantern which hung from a beam. He was twelve years old and had lately grown rather stout, but he was still a majestic-looking pig, with a wise and benevolent appearance, in spite of the fact that his tushes had never been cut. Before long the other animals began to arrive and make themselves comfortable after their fashions. First came the three dogs, Bluebell, Jessie and Pincher, and then the pigs, who settled down in the straw immediately in front of the platform. The hens perched themselves on the window-sills, the pigeons fluttered up to the rafters, the sheep and cows lay down behind the pigs and began to chew the cud. The two cart-horses, Boxer and Clover, came in together, walking very slowly and settling down their vast hairy hoofs with great care lest there should be some small animal concealed in the straw. Clover was a stout motherly mare approaching middle life who had never quite got her figure back after her fourth foal. Boxer was an enormous beast, nearly eighteen hands high, and as strong as any two ordinary horses put together. A white stripe down his nose gave him a somewhat stupid appearance, and in fact he was not of first-rate intelligence, but he was universally respected for his steadiness of character and tremendous powers of work. After the horses came Muriel, the white goat, and Benjamin, the donkey. Benjamin was the oldest animal on the farm, and the worst tempered. He seldom talked and, when he did, it was usually to make some cynical remark—for instance, he would say that God had given him a tail to keep the flies off, but that he would sooner have had no tail and no flies. Alone among the animals of the farm he never laughed. If asked why, he would say that he saw nothing to laugh at. Nevertheless, without openly admitting it, he was devoted to Boxer; the two of them usually spent their Sundays together in the small paddock beyond the orchard, grazing side by side and never speaking.

The two horses had just lain down when a brood of ducklings, which had lost their mother, filed into the barn, cheeping feebly and wandering from side to side to find some place where they would not be trodden on. Clover made a sort of wall round them with her great foreleg, and the ducklings nestled down inside it and promptly fell asleep. At the last moment Mollie, the foolish, pretty white mare who drew Mr. Jones' trap, came mincing daintily chewing at a lump of sugar. She took a place near the front and began flirting with her white mane, hoping to draw attention to the red ribbons it was plaited with. Last of all came the cat, who looked round, as usual, for the warmest place and finally squeezed herself in between Boxer and Clover; there she purred contentedly throughout Major's speech without listening to a word of what he was saying.

As I say, there is no difficulty in interpreting the symbolism of the story. But it is not quite so certain what is the total moral that we are supposed to draw from it. Is it that there is some special evil and fraud in Communism which makes it inevitable that all communist movements will turn only into a new and worse tyranny? or is it rather that power is in itself, to whatever ideology it may nominally be allied, inevitably corrupting? that all promises of equality and liberty will prove inevitably to be deceptions? and that history does not, and cannot, consist of anything other than the overthrow of old tyrants in order that new tyrants may be put in their place? It is obvious that the second alternative was much more natural to Orwell's mind than the first and that Conservatives who hailed *Animal Farm* as an attack simply on Communism interpreted it too narrowly and too much to suit their own convenience. Orwell's whole record from Spanish days onwards shows his impartial hatred of all tyrannies and of all totalitarian claims, and as a matter of history, it was against what he thought of as a fascist tyranny that he first enlisted to fight. In *Animal Farm* itself we must not be diverted by the satire on the animals from noticing how utterly worthless are without exception the parts played by men, who represent the conservative principle. He complained of Mr. Rayner Heppenstall's radio version of it for 'casting a sop to those stinking Catholics'. There is no hint of a suggestion that Jones, a drunken brute, who was letting the farm down, did not deserve all that he got. The parts that he played both when he had the farm and after he lost it were alike discreditable. His men were no better. When Jones was away drunk they took advantage of his absence not to feed the animals. The two neighbouring farmers—Pilkington, 'an easy-going gentleman farmer who spent most of his time in fishing or hunting according to the season'— and Frederick, 'a tough, shrewd man, perpetually involved in lawsuits and with a name for driving hard bargains'—are equally worthless. Their sole motive is greed. They are willing to destroy the animals, if possible, and, if it is not possible, to make out of them what they can, and they are incapable of honouring their bargains. The lesson of *Animal Farm* is clearly not merely the corrupting effect of power when exercised by Communists, but the corrupting effect of power when exercised by anybody. As for the Communists being worse than other people—clearly, rightly or wrongly, Orwell did not think that Communists were worse than Fascists. By Fascists he really meant Nazis, for he never bothered much about Mussolini one way or the other and, although in Catalonia he called the followers of Franco Fascists, he specifically recognized that they were something different. But Fascists, if Fascists means Nazis, he thought to be worse than Communists. It was of no great moment what were the nominal creeds either of the one party or the other, for absolute power tends to corrupt absolutely, and the totalitarian is in practice, whatever he may profess, solely concerned with maintaining and extending his power. It is power politics and nothing but power politics.

But was there then no remedy and no hope? There was certainly no hope in anything like the modern circumstances of life that we should see anything of the nature of free and equal society. From time to time Orwell expresses a hope that we may be moving 'eventually' to such a consummation, but with no great confidence and for no very clear reason. 'Of course no honest person claims that happiness is *now* a normal condition among adult human beings', he writes, 'but perhaps it *could* be made normal, and it is upon this question that all serious political controversy really turns.' All the evidence is, he admits, that we are moving away from it. All that we can really say is that time has a certain mollifying influence and that, though all governments are tyrannies, old tyrannies are less ruthless than new. The rule of law is a great deal better than the rule of public opinion or of an arbitrary tyrant. 'In a society in which there is no law, and in theory no compulsion, the only arbiter of behaviour is public opinion. But public opinion, because of the tremendous urge to conformity in gregarious animals, is less tolerant than any system of law.' Therefore it might appear that the conclusion that ought to follow is that no régime would be very good but that the least bad would be a moderate conservative régime—a régime which preserved the traditional structure of society and at the same time preserved the liberal principles so that those parts of it that in the development of events showed signs of collapse might be at necessity modified—indeed something of the nature of what we in the West call free institutions. The clean choice of Socialist theory

between production for profit and production for social use, which
Orwell had himself to some extent offered in 'England, Your England',
belongs to the lecture room rather than to real life. In the real world
of the years after 1945, with the Socialists leaving so many industries
under private enterprise and the Conservatives leaving so many industries nationalized, nationalization was clearly a matter of the balance of
advantage and disadvantage in each particular case rather than of absolute good and evil. It was not a stark choice of one sort of society
against another sort. The policy which Orwell believed that Dickens
recommended to the nineteenth century should, it would seem on this
argument, be the sort of policy which he should recommend to
the twentieth century.

I should myself be prepared to argue that this was the conclusion
which Orwell ought to have drawn from his own writings in general
and from *Animal Farm* in particular. But it must be admitted that it
was not a conclusion which Orwell ever did explicitly draw. As a
reporter of fact Mr. Brander is substantially accurate when he writes,
'Orwell wrote very little about the Church in his criticism of society.
He classed it with Conservatism as no longer serious enough to be
considered.' Orwell's complaint was not so much against an ideal
philosophy of Conservatism, for which, when he found it, he had a
reasonable respect, as against those who called themselves Conservatives and had captured the Conservative machine. His complaint against
them was that they were at once too arrogant and too compromising.
They were too arrogant in so far as they tended to claim their privileges as something which they had deserved and to arrogate to themselves the airs of superior people. These very claims obscured the true
case for Conservatism which was that society had to be arranged, that
there was little reason to think that it would ever be arranged ideally
well, that it was fatally easy for men to fritter away all their energies
in agitation and scheming for its rearrangement and that therefore
there was always something to be said, within limits, for accepting
society broadly as it is and getting on with the business of living. It
may very well turn out that there would be more liberty that way
than down a more revolutionary, more ideally perfectionist, road—
and liberty was what really mattered. Even in his most revolutionary
moods—as in 'England, Your England'—he was, if we analyse his
argument, primarily concerned with the proclamation of a libertarian
and egalitarian purpose. Once the purpose was proclaimed he was
quite content in practice to let things move forward at a slow and con-

servative pace. Willing to impose drastic sufferings upon himself, he never, save in moments of special exaltation, imagined that it would be possible to impose such drastic sufferings on society at large and to preserve freedom.

But a more important complaint against the Conservatives was that they were too compromising. While the case for Conservatism was that it stood for traditional ways and ancient liberties against the menace of the new philosophies, the Conservatives in practice, he complained, had shown themselves always only too ready to do a deal with the new philosophies and 'the stream-lined men', as Pilkington did his deal with Napoleon, as soon as the 'stream-lined men' had shown themselves to be in the least tough and strong. They did a deal with the Fascists before the war and with the Communists in the Anglo-Russian alliance during the war. Orwell despaired of the Conservatives because the Conservatives despaired of Conservatism. They were without principle.

XIII

Swift and Burnham

In order fully to understand the political philosophy of *Animal Farm* it is necessary to consider as appendices to it both Orwell's 'Notes on Nationalism', which appeared in 1945 in *Polemic* and at about the same time as *Animal Farm*, and also three critical essays which he wrote in the years immediately after the war, 'Politics *v.* Literature', the 'Prevention of Literature' and 'Second Thoughts on James Burnham'. Through them we come to the essay on Koestler and his final book, *1984*.

Among writers who have employed the fantasy of making animals behave as men, it is Chaucer from whom Orwell learnt the excellent device of interspersing the conceit of his story with, here and there, a piece of genuine and exact observation of animal habits, thus giving to the whole its quaint touch of realism in unrealism, which is lacking in, say, Dryden. But it is very clearly Swift who is Orwell's main master in this form of literature, for it was Swift who first used it to attack and insult man, as we know him, by showing us either animals, such as the Houyhnhnms, or a quite different sort of Man—so different that he is not in the proper sense, Man—such as the Brobdingnagians or the Severambians—and showing them as altogether superior to Man. Swift of course also employs the device, as with the Lilliputians and the Laputans, of caricaturing Man and using the caricature to exaggerate his absurdities. Both of these devices Orwell most freely uses in *Animal Farm*. The animals behave as men behave and the opportunity is taken in the conduct of one sort of animal or another to caricature various human failings, and the men of the story on the other hand behave in no way better than the animals. So in the upshot if Man is not so much worse than the animals as the Yahoos were worse than the Houyhnhnms at least he is in no way better.

Orwell was attracted to this technique partly because of his genuine love of animals and his genuine contempt of Man, and partly because of a strange trait which for some physical reason he shared with Swift. It is obvious from the writings of both of them that they were both

154

inordinately fascinated by man's lavatory activities and the problem of his smell. There are references to these matters both in Swift and Orwell enormously more frequently than most writers find necessary. They cannot leave them alone. Such a writer as Mr. Aldous Huxley with his

> Streptocock-G to Banbury-T
> To see a fine bathroom and W.C.

is willing light-heartedly to touch on what may be called 'the lavatory motif' for satirical purposes when it suits his thesis—and so are many others. But Swift and Orwell, almost every time that they introduce a character, find themselves under compulsion to set him to the performance of his natural functions, whether such a diversion is to the advantage of the story or not.

Swift also was equally fascinated and repelled by sex. By repute impotent himself, he resented the fact that he could not be merely incurious about sex. It is in his eyes a virtue in the Houyhnhnms that they are quite cold-blooded and passionless in their solution of these problems. In the world of Sporunda and Severambia the lesson to be learnt is that the best plan is to solve the problems of sex by conquering desire and giving the mind to more reasonable matters but that those who were not capable of asceticism should brutishly indulge and attempt to find relief in satiety. The worst solutions were, through continual struggle against temptation, to allow yourself to be tormented by desire, or to attempt to conceal by romantic rhetoric the essentially animal nature of the activity. Copulation among the Houyhnhnms is recognized as 'one of the necessary actions of a reasonable being' but is unaccompanied by emotion. Among the Lilliputians 'men and women are joined together like other animals by the motives of concupiscence', but do not seek to disguise their motives in poetic rhetoric. The animals had a dignity in desire which was denied to Man. They at least by a paradox were not merely animal. Swift wrote:

> See where the deer trot after one another—
> Male, female, father, daughter, mother, son,
> Brother and sister, mingled all together.
> No discontent they know, but in delightful
> Wildness and freedom, pleasant springs, fresh herbage,
> Calm harbours, lusty health and innocence
> Enjoy their portion. If they see a man,
> How will they turn together all, and gaze

Upon the monster—
Once in a season, too, they taste of love.
Only the Beast of Reason is its slave
And in that folly drudges all the year.

Man to Swift is an animal and is only tolerable, if he is tolerable at all, when he frankly admits that he is such. Swift can with difficulty tolerate all the other disgusting vices of the Yahoos, but that they, the Beasts of Reason, should add to those vices the further vice of pride is altogether beyond bearing. 'When I behold a lump of deformity and diseases, both in the body and mind, smitten with pride, it immediately breaks all the measures of my patience; neither shall I ever be able to understand how such an animal and such a vice could tally together.' They are, as the King of Brobdingnag said of this same human race, 'the most pernicious race of little odious vermin that Nature ever suffered to crawl upon the surface of the earth.'

I would not suggest that Orwell utterly adopted Swift's strangely savage attitude towards the human race. That would be an exaggeration. But Swift did, as he confessed, appeal to at least a part of his nature. *The Clergyman's Daughter* shows the loathing of some women for the frankness of sex as clearly as does Maurice's Dutch lady in *Gulliver's Travels*. 'There is', as Orwell puts it, 'a sort of inner self' which at least intermittently stands aghast at the horror of existence.' This inner self was fed by Swift and, since Swift is also the best of all masters of style for those who shrink from rhetoric, it is not surprising that Orwell put himself to school there, that of his literary essays one of the most important should be the essay called 'Politics *v.* Literature' on *Gulliver's Travels* and that in that essay we should read:

> He is one of the writers I admire with least reserve, and *Gulliver's Travels* in particular is a book which it seems impossible for me to grow tired of. I read it first when I was eight—one day short of eight, to be exact, for I stole and furtively read the copy which was to be given next day on my eighth birthday—and I have certainly not read it less than half a dozen times since. Its fascination seems inexhaustible. If I had to make a list of six books which were to be preserved when all others were destroyed, I would certainly put *Gulliver's Travels* among them.

That obviously makes it all the more important to consider whether Orwell was right in his interpretation. Amid much that is acute, entertaining and certainly true Orwell's two most challenging contentions about Swift are that he was the enemy of science and that he was irreligious, at any rate to the extent that he had no belief in a future life.

As for the charge of opposition to science, the case is mainly based on the absurdities of the inhabitants of Laputa and of the members of the Academy of Lagado. This is all of course well understood to be a satire on the then recently founded Royal Society, and the point of Swift's satire is that science is a futility because the scientists never discover anything that is either true or important. All the scientific activities and antics which Swift satirizes are activities and antics such as those in which Dr. Strabismus of Utrecht might indulge. This, though doubtless not a fair criticism, was at any rate a possible criticism of science as it had progressed up to Swift's time. Nothing that had as yet been discovered had radically transformed the habits of life, and it was possible for Swift in his general railings against the fatuity of all human activities, to include, along with other activities deserving of ridicule, those of scientists. But today, whatever else we may say about scientists, at least we can no longer accuse them of not having invented anything. Today the question is rather whether we should not have been better if they had not invented, and it is curious that Orwell, while he notes how Swift foresaw and foretold with surprising accuracy the methods of the police state and the political trial in his description of 'the kingdom of Tribnia by the natives called Langdon', misses the fundamental question which Swift was perhaps the first to raise about the very nature of reality. The optimism with which the scientific movement was launched was based upon the postulate that the universe was at heart good, that, if we could discover more of its laws and co-operate with it more fully, we should be better off. In fact Belloc's satirical lines,

> When science has discovered something more
> We shall be happier than we were before,

are an exact statement of what the vast majority of mankind have believed from Swift's time right up to our own. Invention, we were told, has on balance done very much more good than harm. Even where the Industrial Revolution brought evils in its train, as in the slums of early nineteenth-century manufacturing towns, these were incidental. The greed and impatience of men were to blame—not science—and in any event these blemishes would in time be eliminated. The universe in itself was friendly and its laws were good. It was Swift almost alone who doubted this from the first and, even if we think that there was an element of insanity in his challenge, yet Orwell certainly misunderstands the picture through wholly missing the point. If Swift alike in Laputa and among the Houyhnhnms holds out, in what seems to Orwell and what must have seemed to others an odd fashion, incuriosity about the laws of nature as a virtue, it was because he was frightened of what was at the heart of things. In the account of Severambia in the final part of *Gulliver's Travels*, to which oddly enough Orwell makes no reference in his criticism—were the fifth and sixth parts omitted from his edition?—there is an account of the Talismanic Powers which the magicians of that country can exercise. They at least are no futilitarians; they are magicians who really can effect something.

When we had refreshed ourselves with supper and moderately drinking some of the delicious wine of the country, we were told that there was a sight worth beholding in the air. We all ran into the galleries of our apartments, where we were much surprised to see fiery dragons, griffons and flying serpents fighting in the air. The first sight of such a terrible appearance made us all run in again, but Sermodas calmed our spirits by telling us what we saw was by a talisman formed to divert us by order of the King. We then beheld their encounters with satisfaction.

When this sport was over we retired to rest, but my imagination kept me some time waking. I thought the Divine Being had wisely confined so excellent a knowledge with such a virtuous people; for, if such a noble art was ever known in our vicious parts of the world, it would certainly be made a wrong use of, not to preserve, but to destroy mankind.

There was, Swift thought, something evil at the heart of things and it was better for Man not to know too much. Man, wielding power, he thought, was generally evil. Power without grace was generally misused. If destruction and tyranny had up till his time been kept within any sort of bounds, that was solely due to man's fortunate ignorance. Those in power lacked the technical knowledge how to destroy utterly or to push their tyranny to lengths that were absolutely unendurable. Once let them discover how to destroy the world or how to destroy all freedom and it was idle to expect that they would not do so.

This is a fear which the latest scientific discoveries have made suddenly common but which in the modern world was until recently

almost unknown. St. Thomas Aquinas was content in humility to note
that events in this world happened in accordance with law 'for the
most part' and to deduce from that the existence of a Law-Giver. But
he never took it on himself to deny that there might be miracles—that
sometimes the Creator might act by His own mere motion and in
indifference to any law. But the general trend of the last centuries has
been to insist on the universality of law. It is, we were told, through
laws, and through laws alone, that God, if there be a God, acted upon
this world. The possibility of miracles must be eliminated. Indeed lawlessness was the attribute of Satan, and, if the modern world came to
disbelieve in Satan, it did so merely because it came to disbelieve in
the possibility of lawlessness.

> Soaring through wider zones that prick'd his scars
> With memory of the old revolt from Awe,
> He reach'd a middle height and, at the stars,
> Which are the brain of heaven, he look'd and sank.
> Around the ancient track march'd, rank on rank,
> The army of unalterable law,

writes George Meredith in *Lucifer in Starlight*.

Now as Monsignor Knox has powerfully argued in *God and the
Atom*, the modern physicists have stripped from us this false security
which the modern philosophers had offered to us and brought us back
again face to face with the problem with which Aquinas confronted
us. The rule of law, they tell us, is only valid within limits. At the last
resort and when the atom is split we come face to face with the Un-
caused. 'The moment at which a radium atom will explode is a
moment which we cannot predict; that is certain. But more; the best
opinion is that the moment at which a radium atom will explode is a
thing essentially unpredictable; if you had all the knowledge of men
and angels, you would not be able to predict it, because it seems to lie
at the discretion of chance. And, if that is so, a kind of anarchy seems
to reign in the very heart of nature.' And Man is most powerful, it
seems, not when he is creating but when he is destroying. We reshape
the world, not by making something but by splitting something.
Therefore if the universe still stands, it stands either by mere chance
or because of the mere motion of its Creator and for no other reason.
He is "the strength and stay, upholding all Creation', and there is
nothing else to uphold it. But will He continue to uphold it? Is He
powerful enough to uphold it? Is it His will to uphold it? Indeed does

He exist? Or has the universe stuck together up to the present by mere chance and is it as likely that tomorrow out of mere chance it will disintegrate? Can we have confidence in a law of averages, if we cannot have confidence that a particular event has a cause? Unbridled curiosity has led men to unleash forces which they cannot control and by a dreadful paradox man by mastering power has made himself powerless.

It is interesting to note the effects of this new science on modern popular literature. Thus Mr. Aldous Huxley, writing *Brave New World* before the war, is content to limit his complaint against the science of the future to the charge that it will make life very dull, but in *Apes and Essence* after the war he advances the theory that the world is in the control of Belial, that Man generally acts for his own destruction, that he has only failed to destroy the world up till now because he has not known how to do so but that, when he has once acquired through science the knowledge how to destroy it, he will certainly destroy it before long. So in Orwell himself there is no trace of this final fear in *Animal Farm*, and—what is odder far—even in *1984*, written as we shall see in a mood in which he had come, for the moment at any rate, to take a view of Man that was almost Swiftean, to write of him as a creature almost entirely without virtue, Orwell has not at all come to any theory of the forces of nature as forces in themselves making for destruction. The men of 1984 are wickeder than the men of today. A few inventions such as that of the telescreen have come in since our day which make more complete a Government's control of its subjects, but weapons of destruction are not obliterating. Indeed they are very much the same as the weapons of the last war, and life is able to go on beneath their menace, uncomfortable but not carrying danger of complete destruction. It is rather the paradox of *1984* that, though the changes in human nature, which it envisages, have not up to the present fully worked themselves out, in the discovery of the destructive forces in nature we have already moved further in the short interval between Orwell's publication of his book and today than Orwell foresaw that we would move between publication and 1984. The weapons of *1984* are still substantially conventional. In this respect *1984* is already behind the times.

We will return to *1984* in later pages. For the moment our concern is with Swift. Swift's suspicion of an evil force at the heart of things, of a Tree of the knowledge of Good and Evil which man ate at his peril, adds greater strength than Orwell himself was able to marshal

to Orwell's suspicion that Swift was not a believer in religion or a
future life. Orwell's argument is on the face of it one that at least
throws upon him a clear burden of proof. It is, in summary, 'Swift
was a highly intelligent man. He was a clergyman of the Church of
England and professed belief. He had a philosophy which required, as
Orwell says several times, a belief in a future life and supernatural
rewards and punishments to give it sense. Yet he did not believe.'

Why did Orwell think that he did not believe? Is it not simpler and
more probable to hold that he sincerely believed? I think that Orwell
was the creature of a particular generation in which educated people
thought less about a future life than people do since his day or than
they ever did before it. He had little sense of history. The atheism of
our generation was a reaction against the Wordsworthian romanticism
which sought to base belief in immortality on intimations of immortality, and he did not fully understand how a man of Swift's age, if he
believed, would have been likely to believe on quite other grounds—
nor on intimation but on the necessary arguments of reason. Therefore
I should not inherently accept Orwell as a good judge of who was a
believer in a future life. I think that both belief and that suspension of
judgment which comes from the recognition of mystery are much
more common, dogmatic unbelief much less common, than he
imagined.

Orwell is much impressed that Swift makes Brutus, Brutus Junius,
Socrates, Epaminondas, Cato and Sir Thomas More 'a sextumvirate
to which all the ages of the world cannot add a seventh' and remarks
that of his six wise men only one is a Christian. It is true that Swift has
a strange sentimentality about classical philosophers. Yet surely, if we
are drawing conclusions from his choice about Swift's religious beliefs,
it is equally remarkable that for his one representative from Christian
ages he chooses, not, as he well might have chosen, a nominal Christian
—some great philosopher or poet—but a saint and martyr, whose
whole life was dominated by the fullness of his Christian faith.

Yet there is enough particular evidence about Swift to give at least
colour to Orwell's case. *The Tale of a Tub* is certainly in many ways
a blasphemous book, speaking of sacred things in a tone that many
people will find painful. But blasphemy is not in itself an evidence of
unbelief. It is rather, if anything, an evidence of a fear that there may
be some truth in doctrines which the author does not wholly like. The
argument of *The Tale of a Tub*, as opposed to the tone of it, is an
argument which is perfectly compatible with literal acceptance of

Anglican formularies, as indeed Swift was careful to point out in his reply to criticisms in the preface of his later edition. *The Tale of a Tub* is the tale of a man who has three sons whom he leaves as his heirs—Peter, Martin and Jack. The story shows how first Peter (the Catholic Church) and then John (the Calvinist) take their father's will and pervert its meaning, but Martin who stands, perhaps a little oddly, for the Anglican rather than the Lutheran Church, is shown as holding to a *via media* which avoids the extremes of the other two brothers. It is true that Martin is sketched in much less detail than either Peter or Jack, and it is open to the disbelievers in Swift's sincerity to suggest that he confined his attack to Catholics and Nonconformists for obvious reasons of self-interest. However, there is nothing in *The Tale of a Tub* which would in itself justify such a suspicion. But, when we turn to *Gulliver's Travels* and to the account of the controversy there between the Big-Endians of Blefuscu and the Little-Endians of Lilliput, it becomes harder to believe in Swift's sincere Anglicanism. Blefuscu is France and the Big Endians are the Catholics. Lilliput is England and the Little Endians are the Anglicans. There is obviously no room for any interpretation except that the controversy between Catholics and Anglicans was a very ridiculous controversy, carried on by very ridiculous people, and, in the last analysis, about nothing.

Why then, it may be asked, on the other hand, did Swift write the *Argument to Prove that the Abolishing of Christianity will be Attended with some Inconveniences*? This pamphlet Orwell seeks to dismiss as 'Timothy Shy' 'having some clean fun with the Brains Trust, or Father Ronald Knox exposing the errors of Bertrand Russell'. I should myself say that to compare even Swift with Monsignor Knox was to pay him a high compliment. However that may be, there is certainly no reason at all to doubt that the *Argument* was a very sincere work—in, of course, the satirical sense in which it was obviously intended. The argument was that real Christianity had been 'for some time wholly laid aside by general consent as utterly inconsistent with our present schemes of wealth and power', but that nevertheless there would be a great inconvenience in abolishing 'nominal' Christianity—that is to say, to apply the teaching of Christ would have catastrophic consequences but there was a great deal to be said for preserving a traditional framework of life. There is no reason to think that Swift did not sincerely believe this—and no reason to think that it is not believed by a great many more people than make the habit of confessing it.

It is typical of Swift's irony at its most powerful to suggest that the fear that the abolition of Christianity would weaken the Church is an exaggerated fear. 'Nor do I think it wholly groundless, or my fears altogether imaginary, that the abolishing of Christianity may bring the Church into danger.' 'I conceive some scattered notions about a superior power to be of singular use for the common people, as furnishing excellent materials to keep children quiet when they grow peevish, and providing topics of amusement in a tedious winter night.' And 'I do very much apprehend that in six months' time after the act is passed for the extirpation of the Gospel, the Bank and East India stock will fall at least one per cent. And since this is fifty times more than ever the wisdom of our age thought fit to venture for the preservation of Christianity, there is no reason why we should be at so great a loss merely for the sake of destroying it.'

Swift clearly was enraged at the superficiality and folly of Christianity's popular critics. But his rage by no means proves the sincerity of his own Christianity. For what enraged him was not so much their rejection of Christianity as their alternative to it. They rejected it in favour of a sentimental, optimistic Deism. It was the folly of this alternative to Christianity that he could not brook. He disliked the Deists because they rejected, or at least overlooked, original sin. Original sin is the only one of the Christian doctrines in which it is not possible for a man, if he understands it, to disbelieve. For it is self-evident. But it is possible for men to overlook it, and, if, like the perfectionists, they do so they do so greatly to the peril of themselves and their neighbours.

Christianity, whether true or false, at least recognized the existence of the evils of life. You will not get rid of those evils by rejecting Christianity. The evils remained—Man with his incorrigible folly and wickedness adrift in an unfriendly universe. A high proportion of Man's quarrels may have been quarrels about theology—the meaningless controversies of Big Endians and Little Endians—but it is a superficial view that you will therefore get rid of quarrels by getting rid of theology. For Man quarrels, not because he is a theologian, but because he is a quarreller. 'Are party and faction rooted in men's hearts no deeper than phrases borrowed from religion, or founded on no firmer principles?' he asks in the *Argument*. ' . . . What for instance is easier than to vary the form of speech and, instead of the word Church, make it a question in politics Whether the Monument is in danger?' If they are not allowed to quarrel about theology they will be quarrelling about something else. How desperately true this has proved! 'For as death is a tax laid upon us, I think the sooner it is paid the better; for what is there in this world worth living for? There's nothing new but misfortunes, and even the happiest man is not exempt from 'em.' To be itself was evil, and of all men the most miserable were those wretched Struldbrugs who had forced upon them in such a world as this the awful gift of immortality.

The belief in a possibility of improvement depends on a belief that Man has some capacity for wisdom, and similarly, since there clearly is no absolute justice here, the belief in a future life where injustice is remedied clearly derives itself only from the premiss that God is good and His universe moral. If he doubted the morality of the universe Swift must logically have doubted the future rewards and punishments by which morality will be vindicated. Swift found no difficulty in believing in original sin—in believing that the human race was corrupt. His difficulty was the opposite difficulty—the difficulty of believing that there was any health or anything lovable in Man—that human nature had dignity—that, to quote the words which Chesterton puts into the mouth of Johnson in his play, *The Judgment of Dr. Johnson*, 'These are they for whom their Omnipotent Creator did not disdain to die.' 'Who that sees a little pasty mortal, droning and dreaming and drivelling to a multitude,' he writes in *The Tale of a Tub*, 'can think it agreeable to common good sense that either Heaven or Hell can be put to the trouble of influence or inspection upon what he is about?'

Swift's criticism of the human race was so fundamental as to make a little futile arguments whether he should more properly be called a reactionary or a progressive, a Tory or an anarchist. For after all political creeds depend upon a primary assumption that somehow and in some way human affairs and human beings are capable of improvement. That assumption Swift refused to make. But what is interesting is that, in his essay, written immediately after the war and immediately after *Animal Farm*, Orwell criticizes this fundamental pessimism. He writes :

The explanation must be that Swift's world-view is felt to be not altogether false—or, it would probably be more accurate to say, not false all the time. Swift is a diseased writer. He remains permanently in a depressed mood which in most people is only intermittent, rather as though some one suffering from jaundice or the after-effects of influenza should have the energy to write books. But we all know that mood and something in us responds to the expression of it.

But also, as we have already quoted, 'of course no honest person claims that happiness is *now* a normal condition among adult human beings; but perhaps it *could* be made normal, and it is upon this question that all serious political controversy really turns.' But by the time that he wrote *1984* Orwell had himself fallen almost completely a victim to Swift's mood. He set out to refute Swift, but in the end it was Swift that conquered him, and in his last testament he left us a record of a world in which, as completely as in any world of Swift, 'there is none that doeth good, no, not one'.

Another author—an author of a very different standing from Swift —whose influence on *Animal Farm* is evident is Mr. James Burnham, and again it is not surprising to find among Orwell's post-war literary essays an essay on 'Second Thoughts on James Burnham'. Mr. Burnham's theses are sufficiently well known not to need repetition in detail —the more so since Orwell gives a very competent summary of them. His arguments fall, to be brief, into two classes. First, there is the general argument that there never has been and there never can be in the nature of things equality, democracy or any large amount of freedom in a continuing state. Society always has been, and always must be, ruled by a small group of men. From time to time the leaders of the exploited—to use Marxian phraseology—rise up and extrude the exploiters. In order to do so, they use of course rhetoric about freedom and equality but, having won their victory, they do not establish a classless society but establish themselves as a new governing class. This is what Marx thought to have happened in the past, and Mr. Burnham sees no reason to doubt that it also is happening now and will happen in the future. The capitalist system, he argues, has broken down in some countries and will certainly break down in all countries, but there is not the least reason to think that Socialism either has taken its place or will take its place. On the contrary, with every day that passes the capitalists have less and less say in all capitalist countries and the Socialists have less and less say in all socialist countries, and out of the conflict between capitalist and Socialist what is manifestly emerging is the rule of a new governing class whom he calls 'the managers' —a somewhat undefined body, including managers in the ordinary sense, civil servants, officials of governmental boards and those many other persons who in the modern world have great influence without being compelled in any regular way to answer for their exercise of it.

On top of that general argument Mr. Burnham has from time to time piled a series of prophecies. The society which he envisages will, he argues, neither embrace the world in one unit nor will it tolerate the continuance of small national states. The world will be divided into a few large units, each capable of making itself self-sufficient economically. But as to which nations will survive into this final round Mr. Burnham's prophecies vary. At the time when he wrote the *Managerial Revolution*—in the middle of the last war—he prophesied that Germany would certainly defeat Russia, that Russia would split into two, the Western part falling to Germany and the Eastern to Japan. Later, after the war, he had obviously to revise this prophecy and he then in *Lenin's Heir* prophesies in its place the predominance of Russia. It would indeed be asking too much of Mr. Burnham's critics not to expect them to make gentle mock of his mistakes in prophecy and Orwell is clearly right in his contention that Mr. Burnham's great defect as a prophet is that he is a short-term determinist—that he takes whatever happens to be winning at the moment and prophesies that it will go on winning. But at the same time Orwell is equally clearly right in saying that the accuracy of Mr. Burnham's short-term prophecies has little bearing on the value of his analysis. A man might well have said in mediaeval England, 'If the monarchical power declines, then England will be delivered over to an internecine war between rival robber barons. In that the Earl of X, the Earl of Y and the Earl of Z will come out on top.' He might have been wrong in his particular prophecy of victory, but at the same time right in his general prophecy of war and anarchy.

Now it is clear enough—and Orwell frankly admits it—that Orwell in *Animal Farm* substantially agreed with Mr. Burnham that movements that called themselves Socialist were in fact moving, not towards an egalitarian society, but towards a new sort of tyranny. 'As an interpretation of what is happening,' he writes, 'Burnham's theory is extremely plausible to put it at the lowest. The events of, at any rate, the last fifteen years in the U.S.S.R. can be far more easily explained by this theory than by any other.' But, he argues, it need not always happen in this way. Class divisions were inevitable in the past because productive capacity was not sufficient for it to be possible for everybody to be cultured. The great majority could only hope to live on a subsistence level, and the only choice was whether a few should be allowed to be cultured or none should be allowed to be cultured. It was better that a few should be cultured, and therefore society was wise to tolerate within limits the love of power, because that love then served a social purpose. But now, he argues, with increased productive capacity inequality is no longer necessary. We need no longer tolerate the maniacs of power and therefore there is good hope that we shall before long be able to eliminate what has now become a wholly anti-social instinct.

Democracies, Orwell also argues, have even certain pragmatic advantages over totalitarian régimes. 'Fortunately the "Managers" are not as invincible as Burnham believes', writes Orwell. '...Within only five years this young, rising social order has smashed itself to pieces and become, in Burnham's usage of the word, "decadent". And this had happened quite largely because of the "managerial" (i.e. un-democratic) structure which Burnham admires. The immediate cause of the German defeat was the unheard-of folly of attacking the U.S.S.R. while Britain was still undefeated and America was manifestly getting ready to fight. Mistakes of this magnitude can only be made, or at any rate they are most likely to be made, in countries where public opinion has no power.'

This is doubtless true. Doubtless it is true that in the long run a totalitarian régime destroys itself by acts of folly. But in the short run it has great advantages over a democratic régime, as Orwell showed in 'England, Your England', because the democratic régime is so much less ready to prepare for war. But—what is more important—it is at least arguable that each particular totalitarian régime indeed before long smashes itself through its own folly. But it only smashes itself in an act of war—which is no great comfort for the rest of us. 'It is too early to say in just what way the Russian régime will destroy itself,' writes Orwell. 'If I had to make a prophecy I should say that a continuation of the Russian policies of the last fifteen years—and internal and external policy, of course, are merely two facets of the same thing—can only lead to a war conducted with atomic bombs, which will make Hitler's invasion look like a tea-party.' Also, it only smashes itself in order to give place to another totalitarian régime prepared in its turn to threaten the world. 'So careful of the type she seems, so careless of the single life.' So the amendment of Burnham, if amendment it be, is not one that makes things particularly better. And it was to the expectation of a future of this sort that Orwell had come by the time that he wrote *1984*.

XIV

Nationalism

SOME of the most amusing passages in *Animal Farm* are those in which Orwell describes how the pigs amend the original commandments of the Farm to suit their changing convenience—how, where the other animals had believed that their title-deed was 'All animals are equal', they now discover that the commandment reads 'All animals are equal but some animals are more equal than others', and similarly with other commandments. There is of course a most serious purpose behind this excellent fooling. As readers of *Homage to Catalonia* will remember, Orwell had been convinced by his Spanish experience that the modern totalitarians, alike on the Left and the Right, had both the power and the will totally to rewrite history to suit their convenience. They had the power and the will to destroy every record in history of events which it was inconvenient to them that their subjects should remember and to create a situation in which no record of the past was available to those subjects except that which suited their masters' purposes. Once again this notion adumbrated in *Homage to Catalonia*, developed in light-hearted satire in *Animal Farm*, was to be carried to bitter and terrifying conclusion in *1984*. Orwell's intermediate essay, the 'Prevention of Literature', written shortly after the war—between *Animal Farm* and *1984*—was to show how seriously he took this threat. Literature, he argued—and in particular prose—could only exist in conditions of freedom—in conditions under which the writer was free to proclaim the truth as he saw it. Where no such freedom existed, literature must inevitably perish.

It evidently followed that on such a formula literature must inevitably perish in totalitarian countries. The fact that it had in the past in a measure survived, whether in health or not, under tyrannical governments was neither here nor there. For the tyrannies of the past were quite different from modern totalitarianisms. Whatever they might have wished, those tyrants had not the mechanical means of controlling every detail of their subjects' lives in the modern fashion. So far this argument will create no great surprise and probably will arouse no great opposition. But Orwell carried it further than that. He always vigorously rejected the sophism that, because things in the democracies were far from perfect, therefore they were no better than in the totalitarian states. Half a loaf, he always angrily claimed, was a great deal better than no bread. Nevertheless the situation in the democracies was extremely unhealthy—so unhealthy that, as he argued in *1984*, the writer's freedom was unlikely to survive for long in the countries that were now called democratic.

The usual villains of the piece—'the press lords, the film magnates and the bureaucrats', the advertisers and the masters of the party machines—had all their share of blame for this sad state of affairs but the main blame rested with the writers themselves who had supinely accepted this evil discipline. 'Truth is the highest thing a man can hold.' It may be the duty of civil servants or politicians in the name of 'respectability' to conceal inconvenient truths, but the writer is guilty of the lie in the soul if he surrenders to such pressure.

This, Orwell would have argued, was always so, and both literature and society had been the losers through the acceptance by writers of the discipline of ecclesiastical and secular tyrannies in past ages. He disliked all 'the smelly orthodoxies', as he was pleased to call them. But at least the discipline of past tyrannies—of the Catholic Church, for instance, in the Middle Ages—was consistent. The Church taught the same doctrines from generation to generation. One surrendered one's freedom indeed—and that was an evil—but at least one surrendered it to a body of doctrine which had tradition behind it and was more than the passing whim of one tyrant. The party line of the totalitarians changed from day to day, constantly changing, as constantly demanding unconditionally absolute obedience. 'What is new in totalitarianism', he wrote, 'is that its doctrines are not only unchallengeable but also unstable. They have to be accepted on pain of damnation, but on the other hand they always have to be altered at a moment's notice.' In illustration he takes us through the familiar catalogue of the different attitudes that an obedient Communist had taken up towards Nazism in the years immediately before the war and in the years of the war. It was possible for an honest man to accept Catholic doctrine—although, as of course Orwell would have argued, it would have been a mistake for him to do so. But it was not possible for an honest man to accept all the twists and turns of the Communist party line.

But it is not merely corruption and plutocracy which has been responsible for what Orwell called 'the drying up of the inventive faculties' in our lifetime. The process has been less crude than that. There has been over the last quarter of a century the growth of a general ambient feeling that it is unsafe to let any work be produced by one man—that all work should be as far as possible the work of a committee. Thus Orwell was always very ready to complain of the development during our lifetime in the relations between publisher and author. There has, he complained, been a remarkable change in twenty-five years in the extent to which publishers will try by suggestion to rewrite the author's manuscript in the publisher's office and the extent to which the author accepts such suggestions. If there has been such a change—and my own observation from both sides of that table would incline to make me agree with Orwell that there has— it is certainly not because publishers are among the great tycoons of the modern world, worthy to be classed with press lords and film magnates. Whatever they do, they do in obedience to a general spirit of the age and not out of a positive passion for tyranny. Yet, even though all the suggestions are certainly meant in good part, it is arguable that the cumulative effect of them has been to make books increasingly like one another. The step that has been taken in the direction of the total elimination of the author, which is in Orwell's fancy to have taken place by 1984, has certainly, if there has been any step at all, been as yet a small one. But it is arguable that there has been a step and the author today is of less importance to the book than he used to be in the past.

The fundamental fault in Orwell's view lay with the writers and not with their masters. The evil of the *trahison des clercs* in democratic societies was crying. Modern democratic society, he argued, though far better than totalitarian society, was yet so corrupted that it was likely to collapse into totalitarianism. The corruption by which writers were willing to sell their souls and write to the order of press lords was clear enough. There was a yet deeper corruption in the Parliamentary system as it had developed. The point of Parliament— and a very great point it was—was to provide a forum in which free men could criticize the executive and thus prevent the corruption, otherwise inevitable, of absolute power. It was reasonable that there should be, as indeed there always had been, a degree of party discipline within which such criticism could organize itself. But, when party discipline becomes inordinate, when it is accepted that the main business of more than half of the Members of Parliament is not to criticize the Government but to keep it in power, a totally new situation is created. The man of culture, integrity and independence on the back benches, with no ambition for office—an Acton or a Lecky—who provided the main traditional argument for having a Parliament now finds his occupation gone. The pressure on him, direct and indirect— and much of it, granted the system, inevitable—to sacrifice his integrity rather than earn a reputation for irresponsibility is irresistible, and in such a society Orwell may well have been right in arguing that every man should make a definite choice whether to be a writer or a politician and that writers should not remain Members of Parliament. There is valuable work to be done in a modern Parliament for a man whose vocation is for committee work, but it is no longer the place for one who must live by the expression of ideas. There may be an exaggerated defiance in Mr. Graham Greene's assertion of 'an artist's duty of disloyalty to his group', but Orwell is surely right to maintain in 'Writers and Leviathan' that 'acceptance of any party political discipline seems to be incompatible with literary integrity'.

Such abnegation may be to Parliament's loss but it would not in itself be necessarily fatal to a free society. For a rigid two-party system with rigid discipline necessarily implies that Parliament can no longer be the place where the fundamental criticisms of authority can be uttered. Its criticisms must necessarily confine themselves to the superficial and the incidental, and the writer must resume his freedom, break with party ties and criticize society from a standpoint of independence. There is no reason why he should not, like any other citizen, make an occasional party speech at an election or occasionally canvass a voter. But, says Orwell, 'whatever else he does in the service of his party he should never write for it'. He cannot preserve his integrity if he accepts regular service with a political party.

Nor, what is almost more important, can he preserve his style. The necessity to find a general formula which all can accept is bound to lead to jargon and periphrasis and to be ruinous to style. Party political language is not, and cannot be of its nature, concerned with truth. At the best party political language can only be concerned with trying to make the half truth appear as whole truth—with boxing the facts to make it seem that all virtue is on one side and all vice on the other, and, being of that nature, it must inevitably corrupt style. 'Political language', wrote Orwell, 'is designed to make lies sound like truth and murder respectable and to give an appearance of solidity to pure wind.' It need not be as bad as that, but the politician, in so far as he has to work in a team, and to achieve ends, must inevitably be content to express a Highest Common Factor of opinion rather than his own opinion. The writer demands a freedom to which the politician cannot aspire.

'Group loyalties', Orwell wrote again, 'are necessary; yet they are poisonous to literature. As soon as they are allowed to have any influence, even a negative one, on creative writing, the result is not only falsification but often the actual drying up of the inventive faculties.' And Orwell certainly bravely asserted for himself the freedom to hit out impartially all round the wicket, letting his drives travel where they might. 'It is not at the centre, not from within the organization,' writes Mr. Aldous Huxley, 'that the saint can cure our regimented schizophrenia, it is only from without at the periphery.' Orwell, less confident about saints, was content to say the same about writers.

But he was reluctant to face the argument—he does not face it at all in this essay and only faces it in a single sentence in 'Raffles and Miss Blandish'—whether there was not an inevitable incompatibility between his two ideals of liberty and equality—whether it was reasonable to expect that independent criticism which he rightly thought so necessary save from a Parliament and a society which preserved some traces of an aristocratic structure. Orwell never fully understood how much he owed to his Etonian training. In literature there have been in the past authors who lived by their sales—and that is a perfectly honourable thing to do—but there have also been authors who lived by their patrons and authors who lived on their independent incomes, and a considerable proportion of the most important books in the world have been books which, as an immediate publishing proposition, were not worth publishing. It is by no means certain whether literature can survive in a world where there are no independent incomes. It is by no means certain whether political liberty can survive.

It would not greatly matter if the writers, having broken with party, were prepared equally to reject other claimants to their integrity. It was, to Orwell's mind, the tragedy of the modern world that through greed and timidity they had with such rare exceptions failed to do so. Some surrendered corruptly to other masters, and others, rejecting the regular discipline of the political parties, yet found it their duty, not simply to tell the truth as they saw it, but to label themselves left or right, even when they refused to call themselves Socialist or Conservative, and then to say everything good that they could about their own side and everything bad that they could about the other, irrespective of its truth. It was, to Orwell's mind, in that sense more than in any other that the Spanish War was a prelude to catastrophe. It murdered truth. 'There were only two things that you were allowed to say and both of them were palpable lies,' he wrote of that war.

He took up the point in his 'Notes on Nationalism'. One of the great evils of the day, he argues, was what he called Nationalism. By Nationalism he meant not a reasonable patriotism, of which he strongly approved, but that attitude which sets loyalty to a group above loyalty to truth. This exaggerated group loyalty was indeed found in nationalists—as a rule in those who betrayed truth for the sake of their own nation—sometimes, with some twisted intellects, in persons who betrayed truth for the sake of some nation that was not their own. But this exaggeration of loyalty was also paid to other groups than the nation and was equally evil when it was so paid.

Among the groups which demanded this evil excess of loyalty, second only to the Communists in extravagance, was, Orwell thought, the Catholic Church and he marshals in the 'Prevention of Literature' his catalogue of the ill consequences which, as he alleges, have followed from this exorbitant and dishonourable demand. Some of his illustrations seem to me to be of little weight. It would seem to be an oddly parochial argument that 'Orthodox Catholicism, again, seems to have a crushing effect upon certain literary forms, especially the novel. During a period of three hundred years, how many people have been at once good novelists and good Catholics?' If we go back into history there is no lack of good story-tellers who have been good Catholics. If you do not care to call Chaucer or Boccaccio or Cervantes novelists, it can only be through a precision of words and definition, and, if you care to say that the novel came in with Fielding, then the novel happened to come in with a totally Protestant society and it is only in that society—if we except the non-Catholic Russians —that it has flourished. France was indeed not a Protestant country but the record of the French novel does not especially support Orwell's generalization. Indeed there is evidence that Orwell did not himself take his generalization too seriously and only made it partly to annoy, for he himself wrote elsewhere that 'a fairly large proportion of the distinguished novels of the last decade have been written by Catholics and have even been describable as Catholic novels'. The generalization says very little more than that we do not commonly find snow on the

equator. Is that the fault of the snow or the fault of the equator?
Novel-writing is a respectable enough occupation but has it the right
to be erected into the test of a society's literary health or its general
well-being?

'Prose literature', Orwell again writes, 'almost disappeared during
the only age of faith that Europe has ever enjoyed.' To tell the truth,
I do not think that Orwell knew very much about mediaeval literature
and the generalization is clearly quite untrue. But, even if it had been
true, it would only have been of great importance if it had been
possible to say that all literature had tended to disappear. Manifestly
all that we can reasonably say is that in the Middle Ages people tended
to write more in verse and less in prose than they do today—and that
for the obvious reason that in an age before printing it was more
difficult to keep work in circulation than it is today and verse is more
easily memorable than prose.

Orwell compared the Catholic and the Communist.

> The Catholic and the Communist [he writes] are alike in assuming
> that an opponent cannot be both honest and intelligent. Each of
> them tacitly claims that 'the truth' has already been revealed and
> that the heretic, if he is not simply a fool, is secretly aware of 'the
> truth' and merely resists it out of selfish motives.

If we consider this as an assertion of Catholic doctrine, it is obviously
not only not true but almost exactly the opposite of the truth. It is
Catholic doctrine that there is a supernatural gift of faith which God
in His mysterious purposes grants to some and withholds from others,
and Catholics have a long line of teachers, stretching from St. Augustine, indeed from the Founder of Christianity, down to the present
Pope, to forbid them from saying what Orwell alleges that they must
say.

Yet Orwell made no claims to technical learning and there would
be little to be gained from criticizing him on that ground. He did not
pretend to know anything about Catholic theology. All that he knew
of Catholicism he knew only from personal experience. The Catholicism which he had met was the Catholicism which he had seen across
the Spanish lines in Catalonia and, to some extent, the Catholicism of
certain Catholic journalists, writing during the excitement of that war
in favour of General Franco. He is not altogether to be blamed if from
that experience he did not derive any especial impression that Catholics

had always an ambition to ascribe motives as high as possible to those who did not accept their faith. Indeed the most obedient of Catholics must agree that there has grown up in modern times in certain Catholic circles a contention that it is a failure in loyalty not to champion wholly the side in every passing controversy of any one who takes the Catholic name and that no word of criticism of authority must at any time be permitted. This disease within is certainly an obstacle to the health of Catholicism as potent as any of the attacks on it from without, and Orwell was only one of many in the modern world who was prevented from a proper examination of Catholicism's claims by the conduct of Catholics.

Chesterton stood to Orwell as the symbol of this 'nationalistic' Catholicism—using 'nationalism' in his own peculiar sense. I was interested in reading Mr. Trilling's introduction to Orwell's American edition to find that the two writers to whom Mr. Trilling compares Orwell are Péguy and Chesterton. I do not myself, I confess, find the comparison with Péguy especially illuminating, but it had often struck me that, though Orwell had no especial sympathy with Chesterton, in the sense of identity of opinion, yet it was quite clear that Chesterton's argumentative manner had a certain fascination for him, and Mr. Atkins is certainly right in his speculation that Chesterton had been a hero of Orwell's youth, of whose hero-worship he afterwards grew a little ashamed. He was for ever coming back to him, if only to disagree with him. He could not let him alone.

Orwell's mature verdict on Chesterton was indeed not at all a flattering one. He was rightly shocked by Belloc's and Chesterton's continual gibes against Jews, but his great complaint against Chesterton was that he was a man who thought it more important to say what was to the advantage of his group than to admit impartial truth.

Chesterton [he wrote] was a writer of considerable talent, who chose to suppress both his sensibilities and his intellectual honesty in the cause of Roman Catholic propaganda. During the last twenty years or so of his life, his entire output was in reality an endless repetition of the same thing, under its laboured cleverness as simple and boring as 'Great is Diana of the Ephesians'. Every book that he wrote, every paragraph, every sentence, every incident in every story, every scrap of dialogue had to demonstrate beyond possibility of mistake the superiority of the Catholic over the Protestant or the pagan. But Chesterton was not content to think of this superiority as merely intellectual or spiritual, it had to be translated into terms of national prestige and military power, which entailed an ignorant idealization of the Latin countries, especially France. Chesterton had not lived long in France, and his picture of it—as a land of Catholic peasants incessantly singing the *Marseillaise* over glasses of red wine —had about as much relation to reality as *Chu Chin Chow* to everyday life in Bagdad. And with this went not only an enormous overestimation of French military power (both before and after 1914–18 he maintained that France, by itself, was stronger than Germany) but a silly and vulgar glorification of the actual process of war. Chesterton's battle poems, such as *Lepanto* or the *Ballad of Saint Barbara*, make the *Charge of the Light Brigade* read like a pacifist tract; they are perhaps the most tawdry pieces of bombast to be found in our language. The interesting thing is that had the romantic rubbish which he habitually wrote about France and the French army been written by somebody else about Britain and the British army, he would have been the first to jeer. In home politics he was a Little Englander, a true hater of jingoism and imperialism, and according to his lights a true friend of democracy. Yet when he looked outwards into the international field, he could forsake his principles without even noticing that he was doing so. Thus, his almost mystical belief in the virtues of democracy did not prevent him from admiring Mussolini. Mussolini had destroyed the representative government and the freedom of the press for which Chesterton struggled so hard at home, but Mussolini was an Italian and had made Italy strong, and that settled the matter. Nor did Chesterton ever find a word to say against imperialism and the conquest of coloured races when they were practised by Italians or Frenchmen. His hold on reality, his literary taste and even to some extent his moral sense, were dislocated as soon as his nationalistic loyalties were involved.

In this vigorous paragraph some of the judgments are clearly right but others as clearly wrong. Orwell clearly did not in the least understand Chesterton's criticism of Parliamentary Government, whether that criticism was true or false. In fact, so far from struggling so hard for representative government at home, Chesterton had always joined with his brother and Belloc in denouncing the party system as a fraud —for reasons surprisingly similar to those for which Orwell was afterwards to denounce it as a fraud. Chesterton died in 1936, a month

after the Abyssinian campaign came to an end and before the formation of the Rome-Berlin Axis. We have therefore no means of knowing what he would have thought of that alliance. But it is simply not
true that he had no word to say against Mussolini's African policy.
The last months of his life were greatly troubled with anxiety about
that policy. As for *Lepanto* it is quite true that it was the sort of poem
that was much more likely to be written by someone who had never
seen a battle than by someone who had seen one. Orwell was justified
in complaining that the lice and the filth and the blood of war are not
to be found there and in accusing Chesterton of a 'glorification' of
the 'actual process of war'. But I am not quite clear for what reason
other than the reason of an old love turned to hate he selected *Lepanto*
for this special censure. Almost all the battle poetry in literature has
been written by people who never fought in battles and most of it
has had this quality of unrealistic 'glorification'.

Yet on the other hand it is certainly true that Chesterton had not
even a suspicion of the nature of modern French society—'a land of
Catholic peasants incessantly singing the *Marseillaise* over glasses of red
wine' is not an unfair satirical description of the picture in his mind—
and the French collapse of 1940 was something the very possibility of
which could never have entered his mind. It was also certainly true—
and this is the main point for the moment—that he tended to interpret
his deep and sincere Catholic faith as an obligation to take the side of
every individual Catholic in any quarrel that might spring up, whether
that quarrel had anything to do with Catholicism or not. Orwell had
little understanding of the depth of faith in Chesterton, which carried
him far beyond the boundaries of politics and controversy and brought
him at the end to something not very far short of sanctity. But his
criticism of his controversial methods, so far as it went, was to some
extent just.

It is a curious chance that 1984 should also be the date of the opening
scenes of Chesterton's fantasy of the future, *The Napoleon of Notting
Hill*. Both to Orwell and to Chesterton the years between their own
times and 1984 have, they fancy, been years of steady decline in the
sense of liberty and responsibility.

> The people [writes Chesterton in *The Napoleon of Notting Hill*]
> had absolutely lost faith in revolution. All revolutions are doctrinal
> —such as the French one or the one that introduced Christianity.
> For it stands to common sense that you cannot upset all existing

things, customs and compromises unless you believe in something
outside them, something positive and divine. Now England during
this century lost all belief in this. It believed in a thing called Evolu-
tion. . . . And some things did change. Things that were not much
thought of dropped out of sight. Things that had not often happened
did not happen at all. Thus, for instance, the actual physical force
ruling the country, the soldiers and police, grew smaller and smaller
and at last vanished almost to a point. The people combined could
have swept the few policemen away in ten minutes; they did not
because they did not believe that it would do them the least good.
They had lost faith in revolutions. Democracy was dead; for no
one minded the governing class governing. England was now practically a despotism but not an hereditary one. Someone in the official
class was made King. No one cared how; no one cared who. He
was merely an universal secretary.

This world of boredom Auberon Quin is able to set ablaze by
preaching to it as a joke the doctrine of suburban patriotism. There
was of course a serious point in Chesterton's joke—the point that the
soul is starved if it is not given 'a thing to love'. But there was also
an absurdity in his fancy that all public spirit could decline and yet life
and human nature go on exactly as it had been before—that nothing
really mattered except as a debating point. Chesterton, it is true, wrote
his book in 1904 as against Orwell's 1949, and it was easier to believe
that things would go on anyhow in 1904 than it was to believe it in
1949. Yet such a belief, even in 1904, was sufficient to prevent a critic
from taking the book very seriously.
    Chesterton writes in the dedicatory poem of the book addressed to
Hilaire Belloc:

> This did not end by Nelson's urn
>   Where an immortal England sits,
> Nor where our tall young men in turn
>   Drank deathlike wine at Austerlitz.
> And when the pedants bade us mark
>   What cold mechanic happenings
> Must come, our souls said in the dark,
>   'Belike; but there are likelier things.'
>
> Likelier across these flats afar,
>   These sulky levels smooth and free,

The drums shall blaze a waltz of war
  And death shall dance with liberty;
Likelier the barricades shall blare,
  Slaughter beneath and smoke above,
And death and hate and hell declare
  That men have found a thing to love.

A prophecy of the revival of a strong suburban London patriotism
was so absurd as to rob the book of serious value, and Orwell disliked
intensely the glorification of war as if it was a high-spirited undergraduate rag. But Chesterton's essential case—the case that there was a
grave danger in the growth of these gigantic impersonal units—that
there was an urgent necessity, if anything was to be saved, to give
men 'a thing to love' was exactly Orwell's case. His quarrel with
Chesterton was that Chesterton did damage to his own case by
dressing it up in these pantomime trappings, preaching it but preaching
it as if it were a joke rather than a matter of urgency. It was necessary,
thought Orwell, seriously and grimly to face the ugly dangers. They
could not be blown away merely by schoolboy high spirits and by
calling them 'dull and mechanic'. What was wanted in fact was the
serious *1984* to rebuke the flippant *Napoleon of Notting Hill* but Orwell's
criticism of Chesterton was, not that he had not asked a real question,
but that he had not given a real answer.

There never has been, nor is there ever likely to be, any serious
movement for the revival of a suburban London patriotism. But the
movement of reality that most nearly corresponded to the movement
of Chesterton's fantasy was of course Irish nationalism. *The Napoleon
of Notting Hill* was, it will be remembered, the favourite book of
Michael Collins, and for that reason copies of it were distributed to
all the members of Lloyd George's cabinet at the time of the Irish
negotiations in the hope that they might get a better understanding of
Collins' mind. Orwell never had much sympathy with, or understanding of, Irish nationalism. I do not think that he ever set foot in
Ireland, and he did not fully understand that other people might have
as deep a love for their national way of life and be prepared with un-
compromising loyalty to defend it against all attacks from without, as
he himself had for the English way. Just as there was much in common
between the sort of secular society for which Chesterton worked and
that for which Orwell worked, so, with Orwell's love of small
property, with his liking for rural life and his hatred of industrialism
and big cities, the values of Irish life had up to a point a good

deal in common with the values of, say, *Coming up for Air*. But he disliked the Irish because, as he thought, they stood, not in opposition to the evils of the times, but in a merely Tibetan isolation from them, and this prejudice in him was confirmed by their neutrality in the war. It is amusing that he gives to the Inner Party tyrant of *1984* the name of O'Brien. (O'Brien in the television version of *1984* is made to be an Irish-American but there is no suggestion in Orwell's book that he is other than Irish Irish.) Orwell hardly believed that in the modern world religious faith could be genuine. It was therefore natural for him to think that, when an Irishman moved out of the artificial atmosphere of make-belief of his own country, he came in an atheist society to acknowledge his own atheism, keeping from his religious upbringing nothing but the authoritarian habits which a Catholic training had taught him. It is in the man who has had faith and then lost it that the mania for power is most easily found.

In general Orwell's complaints about group loyalty are just, and all who accept a group loyalty, whether it be to the Catholic Church or to any other group, have certainly an obligation continually to examine their consciences to make sure that they are not playing false to their overriding loyalty to truth. And yet when that has been said where does it leave us? Once again, as so often, Orwell's argument ends in a gap. 'Prose literature, as we know it,' he writes, 'is the product of nationalism, of the Protestant centuries, of the autonomous individual' —of the Protestant centuries, we may comment, in so far as they were not Protestant. For the full traditional Protestant theology was a great deal less tolerant of secular activities than the Catholic theology. It verged more towards Manichæism. 'The autonomous individual' arose, for better or for worse, as a *tertius gaudens* out of the conflict between Catholic and Protestant. Yet who is this 'autonomous individual', this detached writer, seeking only the truth? He is an abstraction. He may lack the motives of the politician for perverting truth, but, in so far as he is a writer, as it were, *in vacuo*, he has no motive for caring about truth. For the ability to write well does not in itself constitute a motive to write truthfully, any more than the ability to paint of Salvador Dali, 'an autonomous individual' if ever there was one, made him by itself a person to be admired. As Pascal has said, 'We make an idol of truth, for truth without charity is not God, but His image and idol which we must neither love nor worship.' We have only a reason to serve truth utterly if we accept God as Truth.

Of course Orwell half-understood all this. It is only fair to him to recognize that, though a proper honesty would not allow him to say that he had faith when he had not got it, yet he proclaimed clear-headedly how much is lost by the lack of it. In 1944, before *Animal Farm* and when the war was still on, he wrote, in *Tribune* on March 3 :

> There is little doubt that the modern cult of power worship is bound up with the modern man's feeling that life here and now is the only life there is. If death ends everything, it becomes much harder to believe that you can be in the right even if you are de-feated. Statesmen, nations, theories, causes are judged almost in-evitably by the test of material success. Supposing that one can separate the two phenomena, I would say that the decay of belief in personal immortality has been as important as the rise of machine civilisation. . . . I do not want the belief in life after death to return, and in any case it is not likely to return. What I do point out is that its disappearance has left a big hole and that we ought to take notice of that fact. . . . One cannot have any worth while picture of the future unless one realises how much we have lost by the decay of Christianity.

XV

Kipling, Wells, Yeats and Koestler

SHORTLY after the war, in February, 1946, Orwell published his *Critical Essays*—essays which had been written at various dates in the previous years and most of them before, at any rate, the publication of *Animal Farm*. Most of them throw considerable light on the state of mind in which he had written *Animal Farm* and in which he was six years later to write *1984*. Of some of the essays in this volume we have already spoken—of 'Charles Dickens', of 'Boys' Weeklies', of 'Salvador Dali', of 'Raffles and Miss Blandish'. The essay in 'Defence of P. G. Wodehouse' is little more than a protest of a generous man against the hysteria which clamours for a scapegoat—although characteristically he casts his protest into a form of class criticism of dubious validity. The 'Art of Donald McGill' is a good-tempered and witty protest in favour of the vulgar postcard. We each of us have within ourselves, he argues, a Sancho Panza as well as a Don Quixote—along with the serious side which rightly insists that all the problems of the world should be considered gravely an irreverent side which insists on making its protest heard against this too great seriousness, and therefore dirty jokes have their part to play in making life tolerable. A world from which such undignified relaxation was wholly banished would be a world that we could not for long endure. This is all most certainly true and very well said.

But the most important essays in this volume are those on Kipling, Wells, W. B. Yeats and Koestler. Of these four writers Koestler is clearly the one who most directly challenges comparison with Orwell. In the beginning of his essay he notes that all the various books about totalitarianism have been written by foreigners, and the reason for that, he suggests, is that foreigners alone have direct experience of totalitarianism. To Englishmen it is still a theory in the possibility of whose translation into reality we can hardly believe—a matter for a debating society or a whimsical treatise. As we have already noted, Orwell might well have contrasted his own *Animal Farm* with Koestler's *Darkness at Noon* as an exact example of the contrast that he had in mind. Yet even then Orwell had already seen his friend, Kopp, arrested by professed revolutionaries in Barcelona for being a real revolutionary and himself almost been murdered for a similar crime. But, if so, *1984* was an evidence how far he had moved on this point from an English to a Continental approach. He was influenced on this matter by his own criticisms of Koestler just as he was influenced by his own criticisms of Swift and Burnham.

The two works of Koestler which Orwell considers in most detail are *The Gladiators* and *Darkness at Noon*. Of *The Gladiators*—the story of Spartacus's servile revolt in the Roman Empire—Orwell comments truly enough, that, in contrast with Flaubert's *Salammbo*, it is not really a historical novel. Koestler certainly did not, and probably could not, recreate the past. He rather used the story of Spartacus as a vehicle for a criticism of modern politics—as a stuff for allegory. This is certainly true, just as it is certainly true that both Orwell and many other modern readers are likely to be much more interested in an allegorical commentary than in an essay of historical reconstruction.

Orwell admits this and makes no complaint of Koestler for writing an allegory. His complaint only is that the allegory is confused. Mankind has since the beginning of time been haunted by its dream of the good society where oppression shall be no more, and it is the tragedy of history that, wherever old rulers have been overthrown in the name of that good society, it has invariably proved that the new rulers who take their place are at least as tyrannical as, and usually more tyrannical than, those whom they have supplanted. There was no one who was more familiar with this theme than Orwell who used it in *Animal Farm* and *1984*, in his essay on James Burnham and in many other places. But in Koestler's book, he complains, that, while indeed the City of the Sun—the city which the revolting slaves had established to be their Utopia—proved itself to be no better than the Roman state against which they had revolted, while all the similar beastliness of torture and crucifixion had to be reintroduced, the reason for its failure is by no means clear. Spartacus is by no means the proletarian leader, avid for power and corrupted by it as soon as he tastes it. On the contrary he is a man deeply distressed by the turn that events have taken, tempted to desert his own city, only restrained from doing so by the thought of the terrible vengeance which will fall, after defeat, on those who have followed him. The experiment of the good society fails, not because of an evil tyranny, corrupted by power, but because of hedonism on the part of the subjects, because the slaves, released from their slavery are unwilling to work or to submit to the degree of discipline that is necessary for the preservation of society. The challenge of the corruption of power is then, Orwell complains, not truly posed in *The Gladiators*.

However that may be, it is certainly posed in *Darkness at Noon*. *Darkness at Noon* is the story of two men in a Bolshevik prison. One of them is a former Czarist officer whose notion of honour is the simple old-fashioned one that on no account does one capitulate or confess to crimes of which one is innocent. The other prisoner, Rubashov, a party member, is the central character of the book. He is accused of crimes of which he is innocent. He is not submitted to any great degree of physical torture to wring confessions out of him. Yet in the end he confesses everything which they ask of him. Why? Because his loyalty to the party is such that there is no life for him outside the party, that, even if the party requires of him death and dishonour, he must be prepared to offer it death and dishonour. 'Honour', he says, 'is to be useful without fuss.' The only hesitations that he has about self-denunciation come from memories of his pre-revolutionary past on the landed estate of his father—from memories of the leaves of the poplar trees there. Gletkin, the younger communist who has no pre-revolutionary memories, has none even of Rubashov's hesitations.

Orwell thinks—probably enough—that a motive of this sort rather than crude torture or drugs is the explanation of the confessions of the Old Bolsheviks in the Stalinite purges. What is more important in criticism of Orwell is that, true or not of Russia, it is of course the explanation which Orwell himself gives of the principles which animate O'Brien and the other party members in *1984*. The notion of re-writing the newspapers of the past in order to suit the party line of the present, which is to be seriously developed in *1984*, makes what is, I fancy, its first appearance in literature in this book as a jocular suggestion made by Rubashov to his secretary, Arlova.

Orwell's general complaint against Koestler is that he has been led from his observation that power has corrupted and the Russian Revolution has turned out to be evil into a generalization that all revolution is evil, into a sentimental belief indeed, based, it appears, neither on evidence nor probability in an ultimate Golden Age, a belief that 'it will all come right in the end' but into an immediate faith of complete 'short-term pessimism'.

The only escape from pessimism, if we are driven to Koestler's view of this world, is, argues Orwell, in religion—in the acceptance of a next world. The evils of this world are undeniable, but, if in the next world these evils are to be corrected and virtues, unrewarded here, are to be rewarded there, they are at the least in a manner irrelevant. 'The easy way out', writes Orwell, 'is that of the religious believer who regards this life merely as a preparation for the next.' But that way cannot be accepted. 'Few thinking people now believe in life after death', he says dogmatically. 'The real problem is how to restore the religious attitude while accepting death as final.' But it is not a problem to which Orwell has any real answer. 'Perhaps some degree of suffering', he writes, 'is ineradicable from human life, perhaps the choice before man is always a choice of evils, perhaps even the aim of Socialism is not to make the world perfect but to make it better.' But it is irrelevant as an answer to Koestler's argument, for Koestler's argument was not that the world in this totalitarian age was not becoming perfect but that it was inevitably becoming worse. By *1984* it had become also Orwell's argument.

Of the three other writers upon whom there are essays in this book— Wells, Kipling and Yeats—it is only to the superficial reader that it will be a surprise to discover that Kipling comes out best. It is on Wells' view of science and the world state that Orwell fastens. He argues that Wells had simply accepted it as an article of faith that things under the leadership of science were moving towards world unity but that in fact in the modern world it was not so. Wells shortly after the 1914 war had rebuked Sir Winston Churchill for talking of the Bolsheviks as if they were a different order of being from the men of the Western world. But, argued Orwell, Churchill was obviously right and Wells was obviously wrong. Wells did not look at the world. He simply assumed on general principles that men were all of a kind and therefore said that they were so. Churchill, whether he reached his conclusion by observation or by accident, was clearly right in saying that with the totalitarians a new order of men had come into the world. Wells again had assumed that science was a moralizing influence and that scientists were inevitably humane. Therefore, observing that the Nazis were inhumane, he pronounced that they were unscientific, proclaimed their weakness and prophesied their defeat at a moment of their greatest strength. 'Science', said Orwell, 'is fighting on the side of superstition. But it is impossible for Wells to accept this.'

Yeats, Orwell thought to be, on this political plane, an evil influence because he used his poetic gifts to dress up this process of dehumanization in false, romantic garb. Yeats thought of himself as the champion of an aristocratic society—aristocratic and scornful of the weak, Christian virtues of pity. He called for 'the exuberant acceptance of authoritarianism as the only solution. Even violence and tyranny are not necessarily evil because the people, knowing not evil and good, would become perfectly acquiescent to tyranny. . . . Everything must come from the top. Nothing can come from the masses.' He called 'for an aristocratic civilization in its most completed form, every detail of life hierarchical, every great man's door crowded by petitioners, great wealth everywhere in a few men's hands, all dependent upon a few up to the Emperor himself, who is a God dependent on a greater God, and everywhere, in Court, in the family, an inequality made law'.

What would come out of such a programme, Orwell truly argues, would not in fact be the rule of aristocrats but the rule of totalitarians. The tyrant, who defied all tradition, would easily wrest power from the tyrant who rested his title deeds on tradition. In a competition of violence uncultured violence would have every advantage over cultured violence.

No one who has really understood Orwell's ambivalent attitude towards the imperialistic experiment will be surprised to discover that he greatly preferred Kipling to either Wells or Yeats. The fact that the left-wing intellectual world had the impudence to despise Kipling of course only encouraged Orwell to admire him the more. For Kipling, in contrast with Wells and Yeats, inventing a world as their imagination would like it to be, did at least see it as, to some extent, it was— did at least face the facts, if only some of the facts. Naturally Orwell did not admire Kipling without qualification. He disliked his sadism. He disliked his class consciousness. What more horrible story has ever been written than *Mary Postgate*, where the quiet English middle-class spinster sits watching with delight a German airman die and Kipling approves of her doing so? 'But', argues Orwell, 'though one may disagree to the middle of one's bones with the political attitude implied in the *Islanders*, one cannot say that it is a frivolous attitude.' The great virtue of Kipling in Orwell's eyes was that he accepted 'responsibility'. He believed that certain things should be done and was ready to demand the means that were necessary for doing them. The left-wing intellectuals by contrast had the vices of a permanent opposition that never expected to be the government, perpetually sneering at those who were doing things, never doing and never expecting to do anything themselves.

> The nineteenth century Anglo-Indians [writes Orwell], to name the least sympathetic of his idols, were at any rate people who did things. It may be that all they did was evil, but they changed the face of the earth (it is instructive to look at a map of Asia and compare the railway system of India with that of the surrounding countries) whereas they could have achieved nothing, could not have maintained themselves in power for a single week, if the normal Anglo-Indian outlook had been that of, say, E. M. Forster.

The standard of living of the British working classes, Orwell thought, depended on the exploitation of the Oriental, and the left-wing parties never had the courage or honesty to explain this to their constituents. 'The workers', he writes in 'Writers and Leviathan', 'were won over to socialism by being told that they were exploited, whereas the brute truth was that, in world terms, they were exploiters.' 'They [the left-wing intellectuals] always allowed it to appear that we could give up our loot and yet in some way contrive to remain prosperous.' Therefore a disillusionment was inevitable when Socialism and the collapse of imperialism brought with it what must at the very best be a temporary fall in the standard of living for the workers. The Socialists had only themselves to blame if in this disillusionment the workers whom they had deceived should turn against them. By contrast the attitude of Kipling was, if barbaric, at any rate honourable and courageous.

Whether it is true, as Orwell always thought, that, if we abandon political control of the East, we shall lose our dividends, still remains to be seen. For a time after the evacuation of the Indian Empire it appeared that it might not be true. It now appears that the last years have been an intermediate and passing phase and that Europeans cannot hope to draw many more dividends from the East. But, whatever the outcome, it does not invalidate Orwell's complaint against the left-wing intellectuals—which was that they concealed from the people that there was a problem at all. By contrast Kipling did not conceal it.

XVI

1984

1984, the last of Orwell's books, is, like *Animal Farm*, so well known that a detailed description of its story is hardly necessary. By that date, we are told, the world is divided into three great Powers—Oceania, Eurasia and Eastasia. The structure and constitution of the three great Powers is essentially the same. All three are ruled by a system of oligarchical collectivism—by a Party which has abolished all private property and has taken into its own hands all power over its subjects. It is really of no moment to the masters of the three Powers who is the owner of the no-man's land between them, for all three Powers have made themselves economically self-sufficient and, far from wishing to raise the standard of living of their subjects by developing new raw materials, it is on the contrary their purpose to keep down the standard of living. They deliberately perpetuate shortages because a world of shortages is necessary in order to maintain them in power, and the war goes on unendingly between the three Powers, with a constant switching of alliances but with no desire that any one Power should conquer the other two. They neither wish for a complete victory nor think it possible. On the contrary the three Powers, as their masters fully recognize, prop one another up 'as sheaves of corn prop one another up'. Each recognizes the necessity for it of the continuance of the war and of the survival of its rivals. The war is continued, not in order that victory should be achieved, but simply in order that shortage may be perpetuated.

In order that this system may go on each of the Powers imposes upon its subjects a total cultural self-sufficiency. No one in any one of the states is allowed to learn the language of either of the others or to visit it. No subject of one state ever sees a subject of either of the others except occasionally when a few of them are driven through the streets as prisoners and subsequently hanged as a public spectacle.

The scene of the book is laid in London, the major city of Airstrip One, as England is then called, a country ruled according to the principles of what is known as Ingsoc, *1984*'s abbreviation of English

Socialism. We are given to understand that an utterly similar life would be found in any other city of the world in whichever of the three states it might lie. Oceania, of which Airstrip One is a province, is ruled by a distant figure known as Big Brother. Though Big Brother's portrait is continually being thrown upon the telescreen, no one has ever seen him and it is still quite uncertain—right up to the end of the book—whether he exists or ever did exist. He is supposed to be opposed in all his policies by a maleficent enemy, called Goldstein, although again it is equally uncertain whether Goldstein exists or ever did exist. In fact power is exercised by the Party—and in particular by the members of the Inner Party. The great majority of the population consists of 'proles' who are allowed to live at a low standard of living in a decaying London and denied all serious cultural life but at any rate permitted a degree of freedom. The Inner Party is indifferent what the proles say or think since there is no question of their having any influence on events and feeds them with spurious culture, called *proletfeed*, to keep them quiet. Between the Inner Party and the proles are the Outer Party members—the civil servants and the like. These persons, while also denied all influence, are compelled to submit to a most rigorous control of all their actions and thoughts.

Power, as O'Brien, the Inner Party leader, explains in the final torturing scene of the book, is the object of policy. There is no pretence, as there has been in the tyrannies of the past, that Power is exercised because it is necessary for the salvation of the State or for the benefit, even the eventual benefit, of its subjects. It is exercised for its own sake. It is an end in itself.

> The party seeks power entirely for its own sake [explains O'Brien]. We are not interested in the good of others; we are interested solely in power. Not wealth or luxury or long life or happiness; only power, pure power. What pure power means you will understand presently. We are different from all the oligarchies of the past, in that we know what we are doing. All the others, even those who resembled ourselves, were cowards and hypocrites. The German Nazis and the Russian Communists came very close to us in their methods, but they never had the courage to recognize their own motives. They pretended, perhaps they even believed, that they had seized power unwillingly and for a limited time, and that just round the corner there lay a paradise where human beings would be free and equal. We are not like that. We know that no

one ever seizes power with the intention of relinquishing it. Power
is not a means, it is an end. One does not establish a dictatorship in
order to safeguard a revolution; one makes the revolution in order
to establish the dictatorship. The object of persecution is persecution.
The object of torture is torture. The object of power is power.

Power [says O'Brien] is in inflicting pain and humiliation. Power
is in tearing human minds to pieces and putting them together
again in new shapes of your own choosing. Do you begin to see
then what kind of world we are creating? It is the exact opposite
of the stupid hedonistic Utopias that the old reformers imagined. A
world of fear and treachery and torment, a world of trampling and
being trampled upon, a world which will grow not less but *more*
merciless as it refines itself. Progress in our world will be progress
towards more pain. The old civilizations claimed that they were
founded on love of justice. Ours is founded upon hatred. In our
world there will be no emotions except fear, rage, triumph and self-
abasement. Everything else we shall destroy—everything. . . . There
will be no laughter, except the laugh of triumph over a defeated
enemy. There will be no art, no literature, no science. When we are
omnipotent we shall have no more need of science. There will be
no distinction between beauty and ugliness. There will be no
curiosity, no enjoyment of the process of life. All competing
pleasures will be destroyed. But always—do not forget this, Winston
—always there will be the intoxication of power, constantly in-
creasing and constantly growing subtler. Always, at every moment,
there will be the thrill of victory, the sensation of trampling on an
enemy who is helpless. If you want a picture of the future, imagine
a boot stamping on a human face—for ever.

The weapon by which the Party maintains itself in power is that of
making its subjects all 'less conscious'. All records of the past are
systematically destroyed and altered as any shift of policy may make
it desirable. The consequence of this is to make it quite impossible for
anyone to discover what the past was like and to foster, since truth is
undiscoverable, a completely cynical indifference to truth. This is also
its purpose. The possession of objects of art from the past is forbidden
because attachment to objects diverts the mind from the unrelieved
attachment to abstract ideas which is necessary for fanaticism. He who
loves anything is soft. Thus, too, all sexual activity is discouraged. Such
of it as takes place has to be as sordid and unromantic as possible, and

O'Brien tells Winston that soon the neurologists of the Party will have discovered how to abolish the orgasm altogether. So on the one hand there is an assurance that no one will have a private loyalty which will in any way challenge his total subservience to the State. On the other hand sexual starvation creates a condition of hysteria which is just what the Party needs. Every action of every subject is watched and spied upon by the telescreen. No private life of any sort is permitted.

A totalitarian society must obviously of its nature declare war on traditional doctrines of love and marriage—the most fundamental of all assertions of a realm outside the power of the State. The simplest policy is to kill romance and love and marriage by encouraging every mechanical device to disconnect as far as possible the sexual act from any suggestion of procreation and to treat the sexual appetite as a mere physical appetite to be satisfied as a man might satisfy an appetite for sausages—brutally, without hesitation and without affection. This is the rule which Mr. Aldous Huxley imagines as reigning in his *Brave New World* and its result is of course to rob the life of its subjects of all zest. But in fact Man since the beginning of time and long before the coming of the Christian era has felt his appetites to be alike potent and mysterious—has felt the need to satisfy them but to satisfy them within the framework of rules which he at least believes to be God-given and of which he is glad that he cannot from outside wholly understand the reasons, and, if romance is tolerated at all, it inevitably leads to private life and to the return of a religion, true or false. So it is natural enough that Mr. Huxley in his later, post-war work, in the Belial-worshipping world of *Apes and Essence*, imagines people's sexual lives to be controlled by rules, fantastic indeed and disgusting but at the same time very strict, and abstinence to be rigidly and savagely imposed outside the permitted conditions. For it is certainly into such customs that societies drift, once the traditional doctrines of love and marriage are abandoned, rather than into permitting habits of casual incontinence. So Orwell imagines the Party in *1984* as exercising a control far beyond anything as yet attempted in any real totalitarian state.

In the organization of *1984* no planned revolt is conceivable, and there is no serious suggestion that any overthrow of the régime is remotely possible. Yet the members of the Inner Party torture and kill—render the life of every citizen insecure—not because their self-preservation requires such a policy but because they enjoy tortures and killings. A mysterious brotherhood, which is supposed to be devoted to the destruction of the régime, is invented in order to justify the policies of repression, and every subject who has been guilty of a dangerous thought—and many who have not—is seized and submitted to hideous torture, before being finally killed, so as to compel him to deny himself and to make certain that no one is allowed the triumph of dying in defiance of the Party.

The story of *1984* is the story of 'a smallish, frail figure', a clerk in the Ministry of Truth, thirty-nine years of age and suffering from a varicose ulcer. His name is Winston Smith. In accordance with the habits of 'double think' the Ministry of Truth is the Ministry whose duty it is to propagate lies—that is to say, to alter history from time to time as may be convenient to the masters of the Party, and Winston Smith is employed in a minor capacity in this task—in rewriting, according to orders, copies of *The Times* and similar literature in order to excise mention of any persons of whom it has subsequently become desirable to consider that he 'unexists'. He is no hero and under the ceaseless pressure of his life has come very nearly himself to accept the tyranny under which he lives. But he has just sufficient memory to doubt, curiosity to wonder what the past was like and common sense to feel the nonsense of the Party's claim that there is no past save what the present sees fit to make it. His attention is attracted by a young girl, a member of the Party, called Julia. She is attractive to the eye and at first, since she brazenly disports her Sash of Chastity, Winston imagines that she is a loyal member and therefore hates her and longs to crush her in violence. But then he learns from a note which she secretly passes to him that, as she asserts, she loves him. After a complication of manoeuvres, made necessary by the Party's hostility to romantic relations, or indeed to all private life, they are able to arrange assignations—first in a secluded wood in the country, then in a disused church tower and afterwards in an upper room in an antique-shop in Clerkenwell. Winston Smith imagines that the keeper of the antique-shop, an old man called Charrington, is what he pretends to be—a survival from other days and a friend—but it turns out in fact that he is a member of the Thought Police. The upper room is a trap. Winston and Julia are allowed to enjoy themselves there for a little but, when the time comes, the authorities pounce. They are both taken off to torture. Though they had not suspected this particular trap they had both known from the start that eventual detection and destruction were inevitable. The only victory for which they could hope was the victory of courage, if, whatever words they might say, whatever the tortures to which they might be submitted, they could yet contrive still to believe that in their hearts they did not deny their love for one another. Winston says:

'If they could make me stop loving you—that would be the real betrayal.'

She thought it over. 'They can't do that,' she said finally. 'It's the one thing they can't do. They can make you say anything—*anything*—but they can't make you believe it. They can't get inside you.'

'No,' he said a little more hopefully, 'no, that's quite true. They can't get inside you.'

But that victory is denied them. Julia, it seems—though we are not given the details—denied almost at once. Winston is obstinate under the first tortures but eventually is taken to Room 101—the room in which every victim is confronted with 'the worst thing there is'—in his case rats—an echo, it seems, according to Mr. Kenneth Alsop from Orwell's own schooldays. There he denies Julia, begs that the rats be set upon her rather than on himself.

After that he is released for a time and Julia and he meet one day by chance and meet in shame and dislike.

'I betrayed you,' she said baldly.

'I betrayed you,' he said.

She gave him another quick look of dislike.

'Sometimes,' she said, 'they threaten you with something—something that you can't stand up to, can't even think about. And then you say "Don't do it to me, do it to somebody else, do it to so-and-so." And perhaps you might pretend afterwards that it was only a trick and that you just said it to make them stop and didn't really mean it. But that isn't true. At the time when it happens you do mean it. You think there's no other way of saving yourself and you're quite ready to save yourself that way. You *want* it to happen to the other person. You don't give a damn what they suffer. All you care about is yourself.'

'All you care about is yourself,' he echoed.

'And after that you don't feel the same towards the other person any longer.'

'No,' he said, 'you don't feel the same.'

There did not seem to be anything more to say. The wind plas-
tered their thin overalls against their bodies. Almost at once it
became embarrassing to sit there in silence; besides it was too cold
to keep still. She said something about catching her Tube and stood
up to go.

> Under the spreading Chestnut tree
> I sold you and you sold me.

Julia is not a heroic character. She talks against the Party line and
Ingsoc but she has no metaphysical notions of freedom, neither plan
nor hope of throwing off its yoke. She is quite unable to understand
why Winston did not take an easy opportunity that was given to him
of murdering his wife whom he disliked. The only freedom that she
values is the freedom to have a good time. Winston is merely the last
in a long line of her lovers. But even Winston himself is no hero. It
is not so much his eventual surrender which is unheroic, for obviously
any of us would probably surrender under such tortures. But even in
freedom his ambitions have nothing heroic in them. He is irritated by
the falsity of the Party, by the impossibility of discovering the final
reason why they impose these policies, by the unnecessary sordidness
of housing and feeding. But his protest against the callous brutality
which the régime had brought to life is only intermittent. He had
behaved as badly as other children to his mother and sister. He kicks
a severed arm into the gutter without a second thought. He goes to
see at the cinema the atrocities of senseless massacre in the Mediter-
ranean and records the shouts of laughter of the audience. He excuses
himself indeed from attending the public hangings but says that he
will see them on the films. He admires the 'proles'—in particular the
fat washerwoman who was happily singing outside the antique-shop.
'If there is hope it lies in the proles,' he says.

The birds sang, the proles sang, the Party did not sing. All round
the world, in London and New York, in Africa and Brazil and in
the mysterious, forbidden lands beyond the frontiers, in the streets of
Paris and Berlin, in the villages of the endless Russian plain, in the
bazaars of China and Japan—everywhere stood the same unconquer-
able figure, made monstrous by work and childbearing, toiling from
birth to death and still singing. Out of those mighty loins a race of
conscious beings must one day come. You were the dead; theirs
was the future. But you could share in that future if you kept alive

the mind as they kept alive the body, and passed on the doctrine that two plus two makes four.

But in spite of such rhetoric he has no notion of a large policy of liberation. His only act of freedom is that of living in secret with Julia, his only clear ambition to keep that liaison intact for as long as possible. Indeed his crude notions of revolt show clearly that his revolt could never have done any good even if it had succeeded. 'I hate pity. I hate goodness. I don't want any virtue to exist anywhere. I want everyone to be corrupt to the bones,' he tells Julia, and he promises O'Brien that to weaken the Party he is prepared to murder, to commit acts of sabotage, to betray, 'to cheat, to forge, to blackmail, to corrupt the minds of children, to distribute habit-forming drugs, to encourage prostitution, to disseminate venereal disease—to do anything which is likely to cause demoralization . . . to throw sulphuric acid in a child's face.' It is clear that a revolution carried out by such means, whatever its purpose, could only succeed in substituting a new and similar tyranny for the old. New Goldstein would be but old Big Brother writ large.

What more, it may be asked—granted the constitution of society—could he have done? It is in the hope of finding an answer to this that he gets in touch with the powerful O'Brien, a highly intelligent, mysterious member of the Inner Party, who tells Winston that he is really a member of the Brotherhood that is dedicated to the overthrow of the Party. Winston believes O'Brien and takes to him an oath to serve the Brotherhood in any way required of him—in any way save only the denying of his love for Julia. But it turns out of course that O'Brien's pretence of revolt is a mere subterfuge, that he is playing with Winston and acquiring evidence against him, and it is O'Brien who is to be Winston's torturer in the final chapters.

Embedded in the main story of the book is Goldstein's *Theory and Practice of Oligarchical Collectivism*, in which, in a manner reminiscent of Dostoievski, Goldstein, the real or pretended leader of the opposition, describes the purposes of party policy.

Throughout recorded time, and probably since the end of the Neolithic Age, there have been three kinds of people in the world, the High, the Middle and the Low. They have been subdivided in many ways, they have borne countless different names, and their relative numbers, as well as their attitude towards one another, have varied from age to age; but the essential structure of society has never altered. Even after enormous upheavals and seemingly irrevocable changes, the same pattern has always reasserted itself, just as a gyroscope will always return to equilibrium, however far it is pushed one way or the other. . . .

The aims of these three groups are entirely irreconcilable. The aim of the High is to remain where they are. The aim of the Middle is to change places with the High. The aim of the Low, when they have an aim—for it is an abiding characteristic of the Low that they are too much crushed by drudgery to be more than intermittently conscious of anything outside their daily lives—is to abolish all distinctions and create a society in which all men shall be equal. Thus throughout history a struggle which is the same in its main outlines recurs over and over again. For long periods the High seem to be securely in power, but sooner or later there always comes a moment when they lose either belief in themselves or their capacity to govern efficiently, or both. They are then overthrown by the Middle, who enlist the Low on their side by pretending to them that they are fighting for liberty and justice. As soon as they have reached their objective, the Middle thrust the Low back into their old position of servitude, and themselves become the High.

In the society that emerged in the 1930s and onwards

the new aristocracy was made up for the most part of bureaucrats, scientists, technicians, trade-union organisers, publicity experts, sociologists, teachers, journalists and professional politicians. These people whose origins lay in the salaried middle class and the upper grades of the working class, had been shaped and brought together by the barren world of monopoly industry and centralized government. As compared with their opposite numbers in past ages, they were less avaricious, less tempted by luxury, hungrier for pure power and, above all, more conscious of what they were doing and more intent on crushing opposition.

It is of course pure Burnhamism.

If we try to restate the fiction of *1984* in terms of political doctrine, two things must be remembered. First, *1984* is not of course definite prophecy. As Mr. Aldous Huxley has truly written of such works, 'A book about the future can interest us only if its prophecies look as though they might conceivably come true.' There is no point in such

prophecies unless the writer is prophesying that of which he thinks
that there is danger, unless he thinks that there are tendencies abroad
which are making for such a consummation, if not resisted. It is on
that test that *The Napoleon of Notting Hill* fails. But Orwell certainly
thought that there were such tendencies abroad as those of *1984*,
though it would not of course be fair to him to deduce that he therefore thought that the tendencies were irresistible. 'If there is hope it
lies in the proles', and, as far as the book goes, O'Brien is of course
allowed to have the last word and to explain that there is no chance
of a successful proletarian revolt. Even Goldstein, the leader of the
opposition, explains in his parable of the three sorts of people that the
Low never have asserted and never will assert themselves. But Orwell
cannot necessarily be committed to the opinions either of O'Brien or
of Goldstein. All that we can fairly say is that he thought that there
was no hope unless people were found ready to assert themselves
against party tyranny—against the tyranny alike of organized governments and of organized oppositions. That was doubtless his opinion
and in it he was doubtless right.

Secondly, we must note that the tyranny of *1984* has not come to
us as a result of Communist revolution or of defeat in war. In *1984*
the masters of the Party have learnt how to use and manage their wars.
Ingsoc is English Socialism. It was the deterioration of the English
Socialist party—in the name of resistance to totalitarianism taking
upon itself an increasingly totalitarian nature—which he feared. 'We
become that which we fight', to quote Mr. Roy Campbell again, and
there again experience has shown how much Orwell had to fear.

The obvious criticism of the society of *1984* is that no society can
survive unless there is in it a degree of virtue and loyalty. There must
be at least some sort of honour among thieves. Why should such a
man as O'Brien have fanatically given himself to the service of the
Party, where it was obviously only too probable that one day before
long the masters of the Party, in their insatiable sadistic appetite, would
seize him and torture him in his turn?

The only sort of honour among thieves in *1984* is the tacit agreement between the rulers of the three Powers to 'prop one another up
like sheaves of corn' and not to push their wars so far as to upset any
of the three governments. And it might well be argued that men to
whom the whole end of life was Power, would not have been capable
of the self-restraint necessary to refrain from destroying a rival. Mr.
Deutscher has recorded how at the end of the war he found Orwell

'unshakably convinced that Stalin, Churchill and Roosevelt consciously plotted to divide the world, and to divide it for good, among themselves, and to subjugate it in common. . . . "They are all power-hungry," he used to repeat.' But obviously the more power-hungry each of them was, the less likely would he be to be content with merely a third share. Among such men the argument that a full-scale use of all the weapons of destruction would destroy the whole world would be insufficient as a deterrent, for before long in the mad lust for power there would certainly arise some man of Ragnorak, some maniac to whom the total destruction of the world would be the only satisfaction of his final lust. So doubtless there will if ever we allow ourselves to accept such a society. Yet who knows how such things will work out? One might point to the example of Russia—argue that it was inconceivable that there should after Stalin's purges have been any genuine loyalty to the system, at any rate among high party members—prophesy, as so many did prophesy, its collapse at least with the coming of war—and yet it did not collapse. But whether the parallel between the Russia of reality and the Oceania of *1984* be exact or not, at any rate the point is irrelevant to a criticism of Orwell's moral challenge. For it is the essence of the moral challenge of *1984* that it would really make no difference if the rule of the Party collapsed or not. For the Party had already done its work before 1984. It had already destroyed all virtue and, even if it should be overthrown, its place must necessarily be taken, not by a good society, but by squalid anarchy. In all other books of this nature there is always, as with the Savage in *Brave New World*, one character at least, a relic of older and more human times, who stands out in protest against the dehumanizing tyranny. There is no such character in *1984*. From his own real experience of treachery and brutality in Catalonia Orwell was left, as he himself wrote, 'with not less but more belief in the decency of human beings'. But the sufferings of *1984* had no such purgative effect.

The trouble is that, if the materialist premises which Winston Smith and O'Brien share are true, if death is inevitable and the end of all things, if, whatever Winston Smith says or does, no one will ever hear of him or his protest again, then O'Brien is right. Smith is mad. There is no purpose in his integrity. O'Brien may be mad too, with his rant about 'God is Power', but there is no comfort in that, and Winston Smith is indeed but half a man, defeated before the battle is joined, because he has already been shut off from all knowledge of the past, from the knowledge what Man really is. O'Brien has been shut off, too. 'If he can make complete, utter submission, if he can escape from his identity, if he can merge himself in the Party, so that he is the Party, then he is all-powerful and immortal,' says O'Brien. But even if we accept O'Brien's rhetoric and his metaphors, what use to possess the future if you cannot possess the past? And O'Brien is yet more completely shut off from the past than is Winston himself.

But Orwell himself at the time that he wrote *1984* was shut off from the past. *1984*, as Mr. Deutscher has pointed out in his essay on *1984*—'The Mysticism of Cruelty' in *Heretics and Renegades*, owes at the least a considerable debt to Zamyatin's *We*. Zamyatin is, if no more, at least Orwell's *Holinshed*. An essay which Orwell wrote in *Tribune* on January 4, 1946, praised Zamyatin's book, claiming that Mr. Aldous Huxley's *Brave New World* 'must be partly derived' from *We*, and criticized Mr. Huxley because the masters of the Brave New World had not the motive for their tyranny of a conscious, brutal love of power. This proves Orwell's familiarity with Zamyatin's work and the parallels between *We* and *1984* are, as Mr. Deutscher truly says, striking. Zamyatin was a Russian Socialist who had been disgusted by the treachery of his Socialist colleagues to one another in the 1905 revolution, had left the Socialist movement, was imprisoned by the Bolshevists when they came to power but released and went to Paris, where he wrote *We*. He describes society, supposed to be existing in 2600 A.D., where, to quote Orwell's essay, the members

> have so completely lost their individuality as to be known only by numbers. They live in glass houses which enables the political police, known as the 'Guardians', to supervise them more easily. They all wear identical uniforms, and a human being is commonly referred to either as 'a number' or a 'unif' (uniform). . . . The Single State is ruled over by a person known as the Benefactor. . . . The guiding principle of the State is that happiness and freedom are incompatible.

Love, as in London of 1984, is a crime. The central character falls in love with a girl called 'I-330'. For this crime he, like Winston Smith, is arrested and tortured so as to cure him of 'imagination', which is the great enemy of happiness—the parallel to *1984*'s ambition to make the citizen 'less conscious'. Under torture he 'betrays his confederates to the police' and professes devotion to the Benefactor.

The parallels between *We* and *1984* are evident enough. The difference is that Orwell was an Englishman and Zamyatin a Russian. To Zamyatin this inhuman tyranny was foretold as the consequence of the acceptance of a machine civilization. Zamyatin was of a Russian tradition, which stretches back to Dostoievski and beyond, to which the West, alike with its capitalism and its communism, was the enemy of freedom and to which the Russian soul could only be saved and Russian freedom preserved if Russia kept herself uncontaminated by the complexities of Europe. Salvation to him lay in a return to primitive ways. Whatever his incidental criticisms of industrialism, made here and there, this was a gospel which was of course alien to Orwell's intensely English nature. In its extreme form he would have dismissed it as 'cranky'. If therefore—as I daresay was so—Zamyatin's *We* was consciously present to his mind as he wrote *1984*, we can then say that he reshaped Zamyatin's warnings to show their relevance to an English society and to a modern world in which totalitarian governments had appeared impartially on the right and on the left. In opposition to those who look on *1984* as an exposure of what would happen to us if we were conquered by Russia, Orwell was anxious to show that the Russian features of such a society are but incidental and that in essence it can happen here just as well as there. The tri-partite division of the world plays no part in Zamyatin's picture.

I think that it is fair to say that Zamyatin's book has at least one advantage over Orwell's. Zamyatin with his gospel of primitivism has at least an answer to the question 'What can we do to escape all this?' The answer may be to many people a silly answer, but it is at any rate an answer. Orwell gives no answer. Mr. Deutscher is justified in saying of his warning that 'the warning defeats itself because of its underlying boundless despair'.

The remedy clearly lies, whether it be for Zamyatin or for Orwell, not in a return to the accidents of the past—accidents which are irrelevant and the return to which is probably impossible—but to its essence. For the past is not the mere absence of machines nor is it men and women reciting rhymes about oranges and lemons or admiring bits of coral set in a hemisphere. These are incidental. The essential of the past—the essential belief of Man ever since he has become Man—has been his belief in God and in some form of future life where in some way the injustices of this world will be corrected. 'If after the manner of men, I have fought with beasts at Ephesus, what advantageth it me if the dead rise not?' On that faith the achievement of Man has been built. To it alone is there the *consensus universalis*. It is our existing society which is unique among societies in the small regard which it pays to religion—we do not need to go forward to 1984 for an example of that—and it is not surprising that there should be on it a certain mark of death, or that those empty souls, that have nothing else to worship, should give themselves to the mad worship of power. In the world that we know—the world of our life today—the pursuit of power is indeed the explanation of much of human conduct. But men weary in that pursuit, if from no higher motive, out of mere laziness. How much of what men do they do out of boredom and of what they neglect to do they neglect to do out of laziness! How deep the debt that we owe to the laziness of the decent half-believing *homme moyen sensuel*! But the lazy man has time to stand and stare. Who knows whether the 'stream-lined man', defiant in his awful, insane, nihilistic philosophy, would dare to relax, to stop and look at himself and find himself nothing? whether he would not continue in his frenzied energy as the only refuge from the terrible alternative of self-contemplation?

As long ago as his essay on Koestler, Orwell had seen that the religious answer offered a way out—the easiest way out—if only one could accept it. 'The easy way out', he wrote, 'is that of the religious believer who regards this life merely as the preparation for the next.' But, if that way cannot be accepted, then 'the real problem is how to restore the religious attitude while accepting death as final'. *1984* shows, whether Orwell recognized it or not, that that problem is insoluble—that in a world in which death is accepted by both sides as final the last word must inevitably be with O'Brien. It is a world that lacks hope. The last word must be with O'Brien because O'Brien in his pursuit of brutality is single-minded—Winston Smith in his protest against it is ambivalent. He, too, believes that death is the end of all and can give no clear answer to the question what purpose can be served by the preservation of freedom. He appeals to truth but cannot clearly tell what truth is. There is no court of appeal save his own feelings, and his own feelings are confused. What purpose is served in such a confusion in enduring agonizing torture in order to bear witness that there are four fingers instead of five?

XVII

Gandhi and Lear

BUT suppose that the basic premiss from which O'Brien, Winston Smith and Orwell alike had argued is false? 'God is Power', O'Brien had said. He meant of course that Power is God—that Power alone is worth pursuing. But suppose that O'Brien, in spite of himself, was right—that there was a God who mysteriously ruled the universe, that the explanation of the co-existence of so much suffering and injustice in this world with the obstinate persistence of the belief of Man that goodness was good, was that this life was not all, that there was a further existence, where somehow—we cannot say how—recompense will be paid, suppose that what Orwell had called 'the real problem' was insoluble but that on the other hand 'the easy way out' was the way out?

Of course such reasoning would not by itself compel an acceptance of the historical Christian claims. Indeed, as far as the historical Christian claims go, the sceptic could well turn against the Christian the Christian's argument against O'Brien. 'You complain against O'Brien,' he could say, 'that, appealing to general consent, he appeals to the general consent of a comparatively few generations in a small corner of the world. But the vast majority of men and women who have lived and died have got on perfectly well without ever having heard of Jesus Christ. *Securus iudicat orbis terrarum.* The Christian is all but as parochial as the atheist.' Or again the sceptic might object that the Christian has taken advantage of a metaphysical argument that this must be the general shape of things to come to slip in a detailed picture of the particular furniture of that future—claiming illegitimately historical truth for stories whose truth is at best symbolic.

Both these are serious arguments, deserving on their own merits of serious answer. To get further light on them, we must turn back to Orwell's essay, 'Reflections on Gandhi', written some years before.

There is a certain fashion these days, as Mr. Fyvell notes, of writing about Orwell as 'a saint'. The word is more often used than defined, and I can well imagine the sardonic chuckle with which Orwell's

202

excellent humour would have greeted such a suggestion about himself. That Orwell was a man of great integrity, prepared to suffer for his beliefs—that, as the undergraduate whom Mr. Trilling quotes in his introduction to Orwell's American edition said, 'he was a virtuous man'—I am the last person to dispute. He was indeed almost the exact opposite of Samuel Butler, whom he was fond of quoting. Butler was a man who had no very keen sense of honour himself and cynically imagined that others had not got it either. He thought that honour was a fraud. But to Orwell honour was native, his whole philosophy of life was built out of his unshakable belief in 'decency'. Yet such qualities do not by themselves constitute sanctity, as the word is generally used. A saint, as a matter of history, is a person of whom it is thought that God has given some overt sign that He has accepted him. Catholics and Protestants, as they have used the word, have had very different views how God gives His sign of acceptance, but they have agreed that the sign is the test. A saint is a person who has attained a special relationship with God, and it is hard to see how the word can bear any meaning to one who does not believe in God or does not believe in the possibility of personal relationship with Him.

Orwell certainly not only did not claim sanctity for himself. He did not admit sanctity to be a desirable quality. He had the instinctive scepticism, which every sane man has, before claims to sanctity. 'Saints', he wisely writes, 'should be judged guilty until they are proved innocent.' But beyond that he thought that there were saints, and he did not like them. He develops the point in his essay on Gandhi. A saint to Orwell did not in the least mean, as it meant to his admirers, a very good man. It meant a man who deliberately rejected the love of the things of this world and turned instead to the direct companionship of God. Gandhi's teachings, he explains, 'make sense only on the assumption that God exists and that the world of solid objects is an illusion to be escaped from'. Therefore Gandhi imposed upon himself a régime of rigid asceticism—no meat-eating, no alcohol, no tobacco, for himself, *bramahcharyam* or no sexual intercourse at all—for the generality only the minimum of sexual intercourse that is necessary to repopulate the world, no close friendships or exclusive loves. To Orwell Gandhi's programme appeared silly. For, whatever the deficiencies of this world, this world was to Orwell all that there was. We escaped from the shades and images, if we insisted on escaping, not into truth but into nothing, and he argued that, if we were not all saints, it was not, as the cant phrase told us, because we were unworthy and failed to achieve sanctity but because normal, sane, healthy human beings did not want to achieve it. 'Many people genuinely do not want to be saints', he wrote. '. . . One must choose between God and Man, and all "radicals" and "progressives" from the mildest Liberal to the most extreme Anarchist, have in effect chosen Man.'

This is perfectly honest, and, if the choice is put to us in the stark way in which Orwell puts it, it is certainly true that most of us, whether we believe in God or not, have chosen Man—that we have no wish to sunder ourselves from all human affections. It is certainly true also that sanctity does demand of us a considerable exercise of asceticism—does bid us always to be on our watch against the temptations of the flesh—but does it demand such an absolute renunciation as Gandhi thought necessary? The Christian tradition has never taught that it does—has never taught the necessity, or indeed even the desirability, of an absolute choice between the love of God and the love of Man. We are commanded to seek both. Orwell wrote as if the love of this world was something natural to Man with which religion then interfered by its demands of asceticism. But the whole history of asceticism outside the Christian tradition proves the opposite. It proves that the ascetical instincts are among Man's most deep natural instincts. It is as natural for him to reject as to desire. Asceticism, uncontrolled by Christian discipline, often ran to extremes, as with the priests of Attis, as with Gandhi. Christian authority did not invent asceticism. At its best it controlled it—by its rules kept it sane and human and in balance with Man's other instincts. Though Orwell never set his two arguments explicitly side by side, they can, I think, be fairly set side by side. If the logical conclusion of 1984 is that it is only by the appeal to God that O'Brien can be defeated, 'Reflections on Gandhi' proves that there is danger in that appeal if it is not made within the balancing, humanistic idiom of the Christian tradition—if, in fact, the appeal to God is not an appeal to a God who became Man.

Let us turn to one of Orwell's most interesting works—his essay on 'Lear, Tolstoy and the Fool'. This essay is a criticism of a pamphlet which Tolstoy had written in very savage denunciation of Shakespeare in general and *King Lear* in particular. I have not read Tolstoy's pamphlet, but, if Orwell's account of it is just, then his answer to Tolstoy is wholly convincing. His answer is, in brief, that the only test of greatness in art is general consent. If a writer has been as generally admired over as many generations as Shakespeare, if so many people have found greatness in him, then there must be greatness in him. To dismiss his reputation as the result of what Tolstoy calls 'epidemic suggestion' is merely to dismiss it with a foolish and question-begging phrase. As for why Tolstoy chose *King Lear* as the special target for his attack, Orwell makes the interesting suggestion that there was a certain parallel between Tolstoy and King Lear. Both made a great parade of renunciation of worldly position, and in both cases the renunciation had not been a success, because, renouncing the trappings of power, they had not wholly renounced the psychology of power. They both still expected to be treated with the deference due to the powerful. They lacked humility. Therefore Tolstoy—consciously or not—saw in the criticism a criticism of himself and resented it.

However that may be, more interesting is Orwell's contrast between the characters of Tolstoy and of Shakespeare. Tolstoy was, he argued, a would-be saint—a failed saint. He tried to renounce the world, even if he did not wholly succeed. But Shakespeare, like most of us, was not a would-be saint. He was a lover of the world, a man who disliked sanctity. 'The morality of the tragedies', Orwell thinks, 'is not religious in the ordinary sense, and certainly it is not Christian.' Indeed he thinks that 'it is doubtful whether the sense of tragedy is compatible with belief in God; at any rate it is not compatible with disbelief in human dignity and with the kind of "moral demand" which feels cheated when virtue fails to triumph'.

As for Shakespeare's own beliefs there is little to be said save that some of the plays—*Hamlet*, for instance, and *Measure for Measure*—are written on an assumption of the truth of an after-life (though the actual theology of Hamlet is inextricably confused. If Hamlet's father had got to purgatory, why was it so great an addition to his uncle's villainy that he had killed him 'unhouseled, disappointed, unaneled'?). Yet against that we have to set the many other plays in which there is no hint of spiritual consolations against suffering and the great pessimistic speeches. 'To be or not to be', 'Tomorrow and tomorrow and tomorrow', 'Ay, but to die and go we know not where'.

> As flies to wanton boys, are we to the gods.
> They plague us for their sport.

Certainly he often met the challenges of life in an irreligious mood, which gave no thought to a future life.

But it was the oddity of all Orwell's arguments about religion and a future life that he always tended to argue as if the human race was absolutely divided between those who felt that there was a future life and lived every hour in its regard and those who felt certain that there was no such life. It is surely a very small proportion of mankind that falls into either the one class or the other. So wholly unknown are the details of the future life and the way in which its recompenses will be paid that even the most pious for most of their time act on calculations of the advantages of this life. So impressive on the other hand is the persisting belief of mankind through all history that this life is not all and that virtue has its value that even the most impious are not wholly reconciled to a prospect of extinction. Nor indeed is there anything in the least wrong on Christian teaching, whatever may be true of some Oriental religions, in an interest in this world. On Christian teaching one is indeed required in a manner to 'choose between this world and the next'. But the Christian, even if he chooses the next, does not therefore stop, as Orwell expects him to stop, from 'working, breeding and dying instead of crippling his faculties in the hope of obtaining a new lease of existence elsewhere'. For even to the Christian who has chosen the next world, this world is the testing ground, the place where he makes use of his talents so as to prove himself worthy of his inheritance. This world indeed is in a manner 'offal', but Orwell writes as if this world becomes somehow more valuable if we believe that it is the end of all things. But it does not. We do not confer immortality on mortal things by refusing to believe in a future life.

> Beauty vanishes, beauty passes,
> However rare—rare it be,

alike whether there is a future life or not.

So Orwell is certainly right in saying that tragedy 'is not compatible with disbelief in human dignity and with the kind of "moral demand" which feels cheated when virtue fails to triumph'. Indeed I do not know what 'tragedy' could mean to one who did not hold those beliefs. But, when he goes on to doubt whether the sense of tragedy is compatible with a belief in God, he is guilty of a misuse of language. Suppose that every detail of the arrangement of the future life was absolutely plain and certain. Suppose that, when Lear was more sinned against than sinning, it was merely necessary to look it up in the book of the words to see how and when he would be recompensed, and how and when Regan and Goneril would be punished, then indeed it is hard to see how there could be any sense of tragedy. Life would be but a series of ready-reckoner calculations. But because it is the very teaching of revelation that so much is unrevealed, because all things go out into mystery, therefore there is required even of the believer a continual effort of imagination and faith to sustain in him a continuing, real belief that the defeat of virtue in this world is not its ultimate defeat. The manner of the defeat of virtue in this world is so evident in detail, the manner of the ultimate triumph of virtue in the next world is so wholly unknown in detail that it is not difficult for the believer at the same time to 'feel cheated' (if we may use Orwell's phrase) at the apparent defeat of virtue and also to retain his faith that ultimately God is not mocked and justice will be done. The protest of the believer derives its dignity from its venture of faith, but the protest of one who was certain in unbelief would be without meaning.

★   ★   ★

'Our age is dominated by politics,' wrote Bertrand Russell, 'as the fourth century was dominated by theology, and it is by his political writings that Orwell will be remembered.' Both judgments are certainly just, but it is a question whether an age that is dominated by politics can possibly escape its consummation in totalitarianism. Liberty is of its nature a protest of the apolitical against the inordinate claims of the political, and the lesson was implicit both in other writings of Orwell and above all in his last work, *1984*. To what extent the precise form of that work was influenced by personal circumstances it is beyond the task of a mere work of literary criticism to consider. Orwell himself wrote of *1984* that 'it wouldn't have been so gloomy if I had not been so ill'. But literary criticism must consider the work as it is. As such it is tantalizing, for it marks clearly the end of a certain road. He had come to a turning point, but whither he would have turned we can never exactly know.

Before it was done he had to leave the island of Jura to which he had retreated and the book was finished in a hospital in Gloucestershire. In that hospital and in another hospital in London the last months of his life were spent. His health was such that for the time no further work was possible, but in his last days he was planning to write on Joseph Conrad, whose study of revolutionaries in such works as *Under Western Skies* greatly interested him, and was intending to devote himself, at any rate for the immediate future, to what he called 'the study of human relationships'. Arrangements had been made for him to fly out to Switzerland to recuperate. The aeroplane had actually been chartered, but a day or two before he was to go, on January 23, 1950, he suffered a haemorrhage and died.

Whatever judgment may be passed on this or that detail of his arguments no one can challenge the final verdict on Orwell that in an age when all good things were desperately assailed by tyrants of so many sorts and when so many at one time or another belittled the dangers on the one flank in order to concentrate on the dangers of the other, he almost alone from first to last dealt out his blows impartially and defended without fear and without compromise the cause of liberty and the decencies from whatever quarter they might be assailed.

Index

Abyssinia, 104, 135
Adelphi, 39, 41, 57
Alsop, Kenneth, 193
America, 107, 116, 122, 133, 139, 167
Anarchists, in Spain, 95, 96, 100, 102, 103
Animals, love of, 148, 154
Antinomianism at Eton, 16–18
Aquinas, St. Thomas, 159
Aragon, 92, 93, 103
Arnold, Dr., 19
Asceticism, 203–4
Atkins, John, 119, 175
Atrocities in Spanish Civil War, 106
Auden, W. H., 124
Augustine, St., 66, 67, 174
Australia, 69
Austria, 138

Baldwin, Stanley (later Earl), 132
Barcelona, 92, 95, 96, 100, 101, 102, 104–5
B.B.C., 138
Beggars and begging, 52–3
Belloc, Hilaire, 90, 157, 175, 176, 178
Bengal, 1
Birth-control, 74, 82
Bismarck, 11
Blair, Eric—Orwell's real name, his reasons
    for disliking it, 44; reasons for adopt-
    ing 'George Orwell', 45
Blakiston, Noel, 15
Blougram, Bishop, 43
Brander, Laurence, 17, 20, 38, 45, 49, 98,
    138, 152
British Pamphleteers, 81
Brutus and Brutus Junius, 161
Buddhist priests, 38–9
Burma, 20, 22, 26 ff., 41, 55, 78
Burnham, James, 165–7, 183
    Managerial Revolution, 166
    Lenin's Heir, 166
Butler, Samuel, 43, 208
    The Way of all Flesh, 16

Cambridge University, 26
Campbell, Roy, 136, 199
Camrose, Lord, 24
Capital punishment, 39–40
Capitalism, 115, 165
Catalonia, 93, 99–100, 101, 103, 105, 151,
    174, 198

Catholic Church, Catholicism, 41–2,
    89–91, 93–4, 150, 169, 173 ff., 203
Cato, 161
Chamberlain, Joseph, 115
Chamberlain, Neville, 130
Chase, James Hadley, *He won't Need it
    Now*, 15
Chaucer, 148, 154, 173
Chesterton, G. K., 90, 120, 164, 175
    Ballad of Saint Barbara, 176
    The Judgment of Dr. Johnson, 164
    Lepanto, 176, 177
    The Napoleon of Notting Hill, 177, 197
China, 135
Christianity—*see* Religion
Christie, John, 16, 26
Churchill, Sir Winston, 46, 185, 198
Class distinction, 2, 19, 21–2, 25, 77, 79,
    81 ff., 102, 186
Collins, Michael, 179
Communism, Communists, 90, 100, 101,
    103, 105, 106, 124, 127, 137, 145, 150,
    151, 153, 169, 174
Connolly, Cyril, 3–4, 8, 11, 16, 17, 18, 19,
    62, 133
    Enemies of Promise, 3, 11, 18
Conrad, Joseph, 207
Conservatism, 114–15, 152–3
Cornwall, 2
Corporal punishment, 3–4, 5, 9, 13–14,
    15–16, 18, 27
'Cranks', 82
'Crossgates', Orwell's prep school, 1–10,
    12, 15, 22, 24, 63

Daily Worker, 90, 100
Dali, Salvador, 103, 125, 180
Deism, 163
Deutscher, Isaac, 197–8, 199, 200
Dickens, Charles, 72, **119–23**, 152
    Barnaby Rudge, 121, 125
    David Copperfield, 121
    Tale of Two Cities, 121
Dostoievski, 195, 200
Dryden, 154

East Anglia, 80
Education, 87–8, 134; classical, 24
Eliot, T. S., 43, 124
    Four Quartets, 43

England and the English, 129 ff.
Epaminondas, 161
Essex, 77
Eton, 2, 3, 6, 7, 8, 9, 11–25, 122

Fascism, Fascists, 98–9, 104, 105, 135, 151, 153
Fishing, 112–13
Forster, E. M., 187
France, 173, 176
Franco, General, 94, 99, 103, 104, 106–7, 127, 151, 174
Fyfell, T. R., 7, 17, 24, 46, 122, 131, 202

Galsworthy, John, 16
Gandhi, 128–9, 202–4
Gaudi, 102–3
Gem, The, 24
Germany, 135, 136, 137, 138, 166, 167
Glasgow University, 101
Gloucestershire, 207
Gollancz, Victor, 78, 79, 81, 83, 84
Gow, A. S. F., 16, 26
Greene, Graham, 171
Guinea Pig, 7

Halifax, Lord, 134
Heppenstall, Rayner, 150
Hertfordshire, 108
History, falsification of, 106
Hitler, 99, 104, 115, 127, 129, 130, 132, 133, 134, 137, 167
Home Guard, 17, 126, 132
Honour, man's, 67, 203
Hopkinson, Tom, 57, 77
Horizon, 115
Housman, Laurence, 124
Huesca, 98
Huxley, Aldous, 18, 155, 160, 172, 191, 196
Apes and Essence, 160, 191
Brave New World, 160, 191, 198, 199

Imperialism, 28, 39, 81, 108–9
Income, limitation of, 134
India, 129, 135, 187
Indian Imperial Police, Orwell as officer in, 26, 27, 28, 39, 55
Industrial Revolution, 157
Industrialism, 84 ff., 114
International Brigade, 95, 100
Ireland and the Irish, 179–80

Jackson, T. A., 120
Japan, 104, 166
Jews, The, 108, 128–9, 175
Joyce, James, 124, 125
Jura, 207

Kipling, Rudyard, 27–8, 182, 185, 186–7
The Islanders, 186
Mary Postgate, 186
Knox, Mgr. Ronald, 16, 90, 159, 162
God and the Atom, 159
Koestler, Arthur, 182–5, 201
Darkness at Noon, 182, 183, 184
The Gladiators, 183–4
Kopp, Orwell's friend in Spain, 96, 97–8, 101, 106, 183

Lancashire, 89, 90
Laski, Professor, 78
Leeds Grammar School, 5, 7, 21
Left Book Club, 78
Lehmann, John, 23
Lenin, 16, 17, 145
Letchworth, 80
Literary criticism, 119 ff.
Literature, 186 ff., 174, 180
London, passim 41–56, 57, 207
Longden, Robert, 23
Lunn, Arnold, 90

Madrid, 93
Magnet, The, 24
Malaya, 138
Manchuria, 104
Marx, 130, 165
Maugham, Somerset, 22
Meredith, George, Lucifer in Starlight, 159
Miller, Henry, 124, 125, 126
Black Spring, 124
Tropic of Cancer, 124, 125
Milton, 27
More, Sir Thomas, 161
Morocco, 101, 108
Muggeridge, Malcolm, 28, 35
Murray, Professor Gilbert, 55
Mussolini, 99, 104, 151, 176, 177

Nationalism, 173 ff.
Nationalization, 83, 134, 136, 152
Nazi-Soviet Pact, 103, 127, 139
Nazism, Nazis, 136, 145, 151, 169
New English Weekly, 131
New Statesman, 104
New Writing, 109
News Chronicle, 104
Novel, The, 173–4

Observer, 18, 138
Oman, Sir Charles, Memories of Victorian Oxford, 11
ORWELL, GEORGE (Eric Blair)— early years, 1; prep school days, 2–10; at Eton, 11–26; in Indian Imperial Police in Burma, 26 ff.; returns to England and begins writing, 41; first articles and poems published, 41; adopts

ORWELL, GEORGE (Eric Blair)—*cont.*
'George Orwell' as his name, 44–5;
experiences poverty in London and
Paris, 45 ff.; successively a dish-washer,
private tutor and teacher in cheap
private schools, 57; part-time assistant
in London book-shop and part-time
journalist, 57; first books published,
57; marries and takes on village store
in Essex, 77; undertakes documentary
work on conditions among the unemployed in north of England, 78;
goes to Spain shortly after outbreak of
Civil War and joins the P.O.U.M.
militia, 92 ff.; is wounded at Aragonese front, 97; on the run to avoid
arrest in Communist reign of terror in
Barcelona, 97; escapes into France, 98;
settles in cottage in Hertfordshire and
continues writing, 108; visits Morocco
for health reasons, 108; joins Home
Guard, 132; war-time propaganda,
132 ff.; temporary work with B.B.C.
Far Eastern service, 138; becomes
correspondent for *Observer* in France,
Germany and Austria after his wife's
death, 138; has more time for creative
writing, 139 ff.; ill-health forces him
to leave isle of Jura, 207; last months
and death, 207–8

Books by:
Animal Farm, 10, 84, 98, 136, **139–53**,
154, 160, 164, 166, 168, 181, 182, 183,
188
Betrayal of the Left, 139
Burmese Days, 10, 28, **29–39**, 57
A Clergyman's Daughter, **57–68**, 74, 112,
156
Coming up for Air, **108–18**, 124, 136, 180
Critical Essays, 115, 119, 182 ff.
Down and Out in Paris and London, **41–56**,
57
England, Your England, see under Essays
Homage to Catalonia, 81, **92–107**, 168
Inside the Whale, 19, 124, 131
Keep the Aspidistra Flying, 1, 21, 27, 35,
44, 57, **69–76**, 77, 82, 109, 110, 112
The Lion and the Unicorn, 107, 129, 132
1984, 84, 99, 108, 138, 160, 165, 167,
168, 169, 179, 180, 182, 184, 185,
188–201, 204, 207
Notebooks, 126, 127, 131, 137
The Road to Wigan Pier, 2, 21, 22, 24,
27, 28, 34, 35, 38, 45, 47, 54, 55, 56,
62, **77–91**, 100, 114, 136
Shooting an Elephant, 1, 27, 28, **38–9**, 73
Such, Such were the Joys, 2, 3, 8, 10, 12,
22, 148
War Diary of 1940, 109

Essays and articles by:
'Art of Donald McGill', 182
'Boys' Weeklies', 24
'Salvador Dali', 103, 125, 180, 182
'Decline of English Murder', 116
'Defence of P. G. Wodehouse', 182
'Charles Dickens', 119–23
'England, Your England', 35, 83, 129,
130–1, 152, 167
'The English Revolution', 129, 133 ff.
'For ever Eton', 18
'A Hanging', 28, **39**, 41
'How the Poor Die', 46
'Rudyard Kipling', 182, 185, 186–7
'Arthur Koestler', 154, **182–5**, 201
'Lear, Tolstoy and the Fool', 128, 204
'Limit to Pessimism', 131
'Looking Back on the Spanish War',
43, 103, 106, 107
'Marrakesch', 108
'Notes on Nationalism', 154, 173 ff.
'Pleasure Spots', 86
'Politics v. Literature', 154, **156–65**
'Prevention of Literature', 154, 168, 173
'Raffles and Miss Blandish', 115, 122,
137, 172
'Reflections on Gandhi', 128, **202–4**
'Riding Down from Bangor', 116
'Second Thoughts on James Burnham',
154, **165–7**
'Shopkeepers at War', 129, **133**
'The Spike', 41
'H. G. Wells', 182, 185, 186
'Why I Write', 8
'Writers and Leviathan', 171, 187
'W. B. Yeats', 182, 185–6
Orwell, River, 41, 45
O'Shaughnessy, Eileen (wife of Orwell),
77, 96, 97, 98, 131
Oxford University, 26

Pacifism, 126, 127–8
Paris, 7, 8, 45 ff., 125; hotels and restau-
rants in, 48–52
Parliament and Party discipline, 170 ff., 176
Partisan Review, 137
Pascal, 180
Patterson, Keith, 103
Péguy, Charles, 175
Poetry Quarterly, 87
Polemic, 154
P.O.U.M. militia, 92, 95, 97, 98
Public-school system, 24
Publisher and author, relations between,
170

Quinton, Edward, 22

Rabelais, 125–6
Rangoon, 26, 27, 28

Read, Herbert, *Coat of Many Colours*, 87
Rees, Sir Richard, 19, 57, 62, 73
Religion, 42–4, 58, 66–7, 88 ff., 92 ff.,
  161 ff., 181, 185, 201, 203–4, 205–6;
  see also Catholic Church
Roosevelt, Franklin D., 198
Russell, Bertrand, 162, 207
Russia, 137, 138, 139, 140, 166, 167, 184,
  196, 200

Saints, sanctity, 203 ff.
Science and scientists, 157, 185
Schools, private, 62–3; public, 24
Scotland, 44
Sex, 155, 191
Shakespeare, 105, 119, 204
  Hamlet, 205
  King Lear, 204, 205
  Measure for Measure, 205
Shaw, George Bernard, 16, 83
  Androcles and the Lion, 16
Smell, sense of, Orwell's preoccupation
  with, 22–3, 79, 155
Smillie, Orwell's friend, 97, 101, 106
Snobbery, 3, 5, 19, 21, 77, 81, 116
Socialism, Socialists, 78 ff., 132, 134, 136,
  137, 151–2, 165, 185
Socrates, 161
Spain, 43, 78, 92–107
Spanish Civil War, 91, **92–107**, 173
Spender, Stephen, 20, 124
Stalin, 127, 145, 198
Strachey, John, 78
Suffolk, 41
Summer Fields (prep school), 4–5

Swift, Jonathan, 119, **154–65**
  *Argument to Prove that the Abolishing of
  Christianity will be Attended with some
  Inconveniences*, 162 ff.
  Gulliver's Travels, 156, 158, 162
  Tale of a Tub, 161–2, 164
Switzerland, 207

Totalitarianism, 23, 167, 168 ff., 182
Tolstoy, 204–5
Tramps, 53
Tribune, 15, 86, 116, 132, 181, 199
Trilling, Lionel, 37–8, 203
Trotzky, 145
Trotzkyites in Spain, 92, 95, 100

'Ugliness' of Orwell as a schoolboy, 8–9,
  22
Universe, Catholic newspaper, 42

Valentia, 97, 102

War, First World, 8; Second World, 109,
  127–38
Warburg, Frederick, 132
Webb, Mr. and Mrs. Sidney, 83
Wells, H. G., 16, 182, 185, 186
Whitman, Walt, 122, 127
Wigan, 78
Williams, Dr., of Summer Fields, 4, 5, 7, 8
Wilson, Woodrow, 16
Wodehouse, P. G., 182
World Review, 46

Yeats, W. B., 107, 182, 185–6

Zamyatin, 199–200
  We, 199